MISTER MIRACLE

The Great esCape

written by
VARIAN JOHNSON

illustrated by
DANIEL ISLES

lettered by
ANDWORLD DESIGN

MISTER MIRACLE

The Great escape

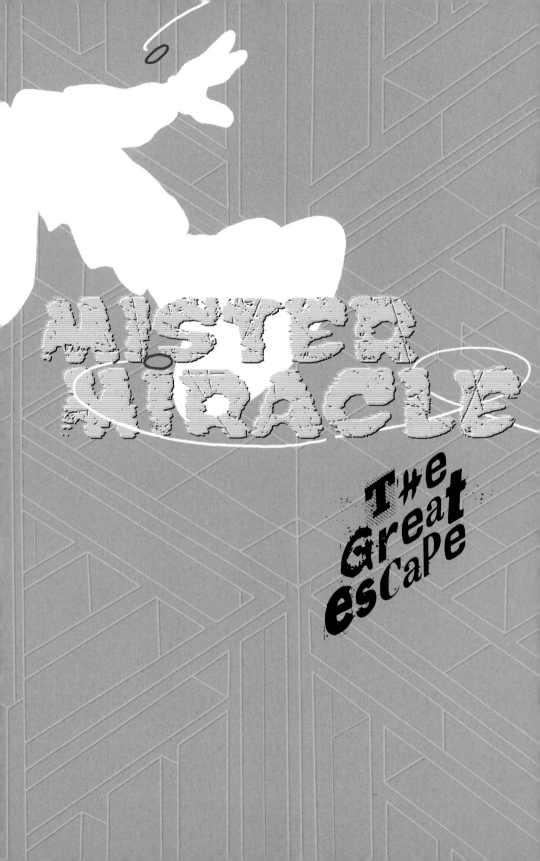

SARA MILLER Editor
DIEGO LOPEZ Associate Editor
STEVE COOK Design Director - Books
AMIE BROCKWAY-METCALF Publication Design
TIFFANY HUANG Publication Production

MARIE JAVINS Editor-in-Chief, DC Comics

DANIEL CHERRY III Senior VP - General Manager
JIM LEE Publisher & Chief Creative Officer
JOEN CHOE VP - Global Brand & Creative Services
DON FALLETTI VP - Manufacturing Operations & Workflow Management
LAWRENCE GANEM VP - Talent Services
ALISON GILL Senior VP - Manufacturing & Operations
NICK J. NAPOLITANO VP - Manufacturing Administration & Design
NANCY SPEARS VP - Revenue

CONTENT NOTES: The following story includes depictions of PTSD and discussions about suicide. To anyone impacted by these issues, we encourage you to use our list of resources at the end of the book for support.

MISTER MIRACLE: THE GREAT ESCAPE

DC Comics, 2900 West Alameda Ave., Burbank, CA 91505
Printed by Worzalla, Stevens Point, WI, USA. 12/10/21.
First Printing.
ISBN: 978-1-77950-125-7

Library of Congress Cataloging-in-Publication Data

Names: Johnson, Varian, writer. | Isles, Daniel, illustrator. | Bennett, Deron, letterer.
Title: Mister Miracle : the great escape / written by Varian Johnson ; illustrated by Daniel Isles ; lettered by Deron Bennett.
Description: Burbank, CA : DC Comics, [2022] | Audience: Ages 13-17 | Audience: Grades 10-12 | Summary: Scott Free, a student at the Goodness Academy on the planet Apokolips, wants to escape to Earth but falls in love with the head of the Female Furies--the one person tasked with ensuring he never escapes.
Identifiers: LCCN 2021029099 | ISBN 9781779501257 (trade paperback)
Subjects: CYAC: Graphic novels. | Self-realization--Fiction. | Coming of age--Fiction. | Love--Fiction. | LCGFT: Superhero comics. | Graphic novels.
Classification: LCC PZ7.7.J644 Mi 2022 | DDC 741.5/973--dc23
LC record available at https://lccn.loc.gov/2021029099

MIX
Paper from responsible sources
FSC® C002589
FSC www.fsc.org

For Kevin and Liston
—*Varian*

For K.A.I.
—*Daniel*

CHAPTER ONE

It's Gonna Take a Miracle

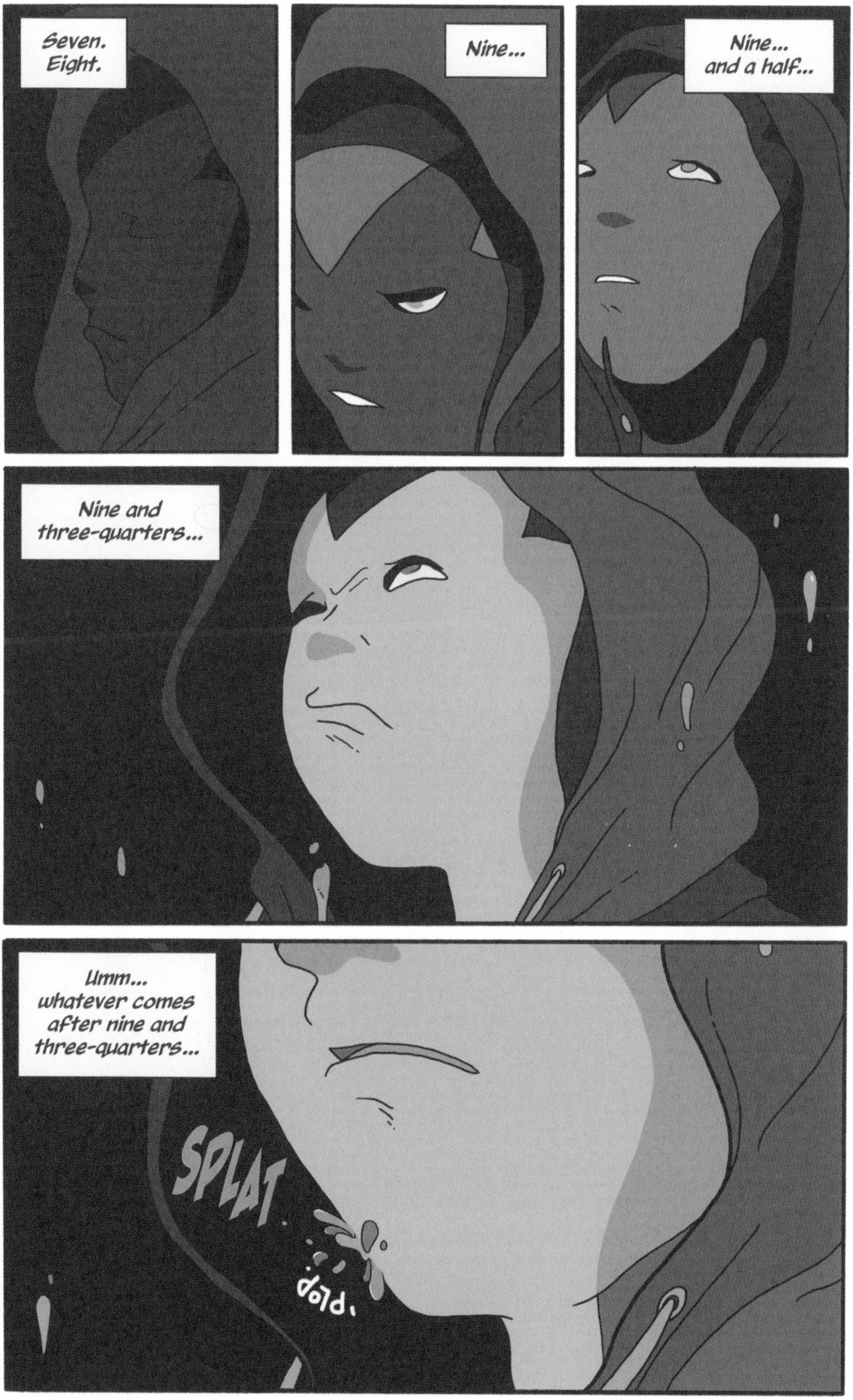
Seven.
Eight.
Nine...
Nine...
and a half...
Nine and
three-quarters...
Umm...
whatever comes
after nine and
three-quarters...
SPLAT
plop

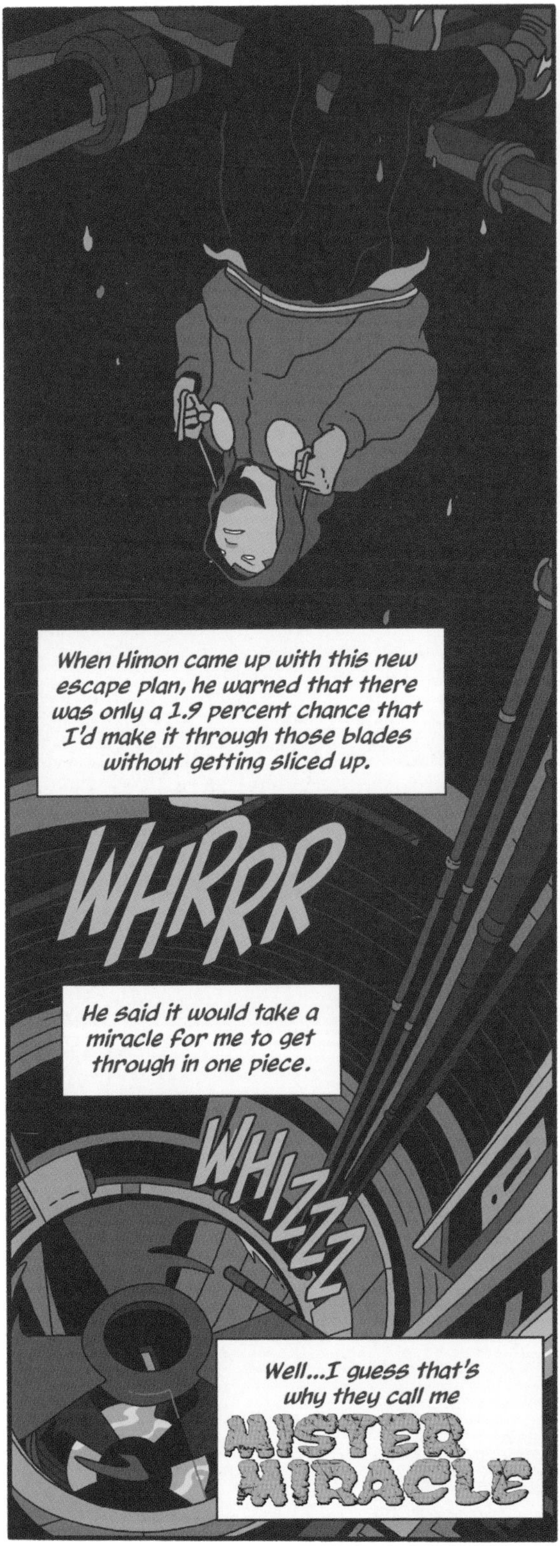
When Himon came up with this new escape plan, he warned that there was only a 1.9 percent chance that I'd make it through those blades without getting sliced up.
WHRRR
He said it would take a miracle for me to get through in one piece.
WHIZZZ
Well...I guess that's why they call me
MISTER MIRACLE
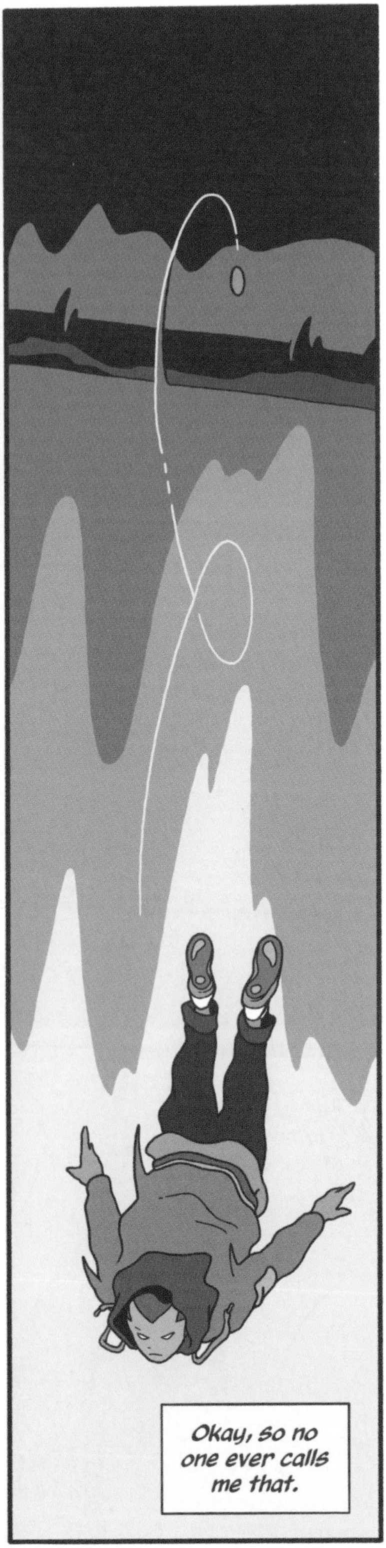
Okay, so no one ever calls me that.

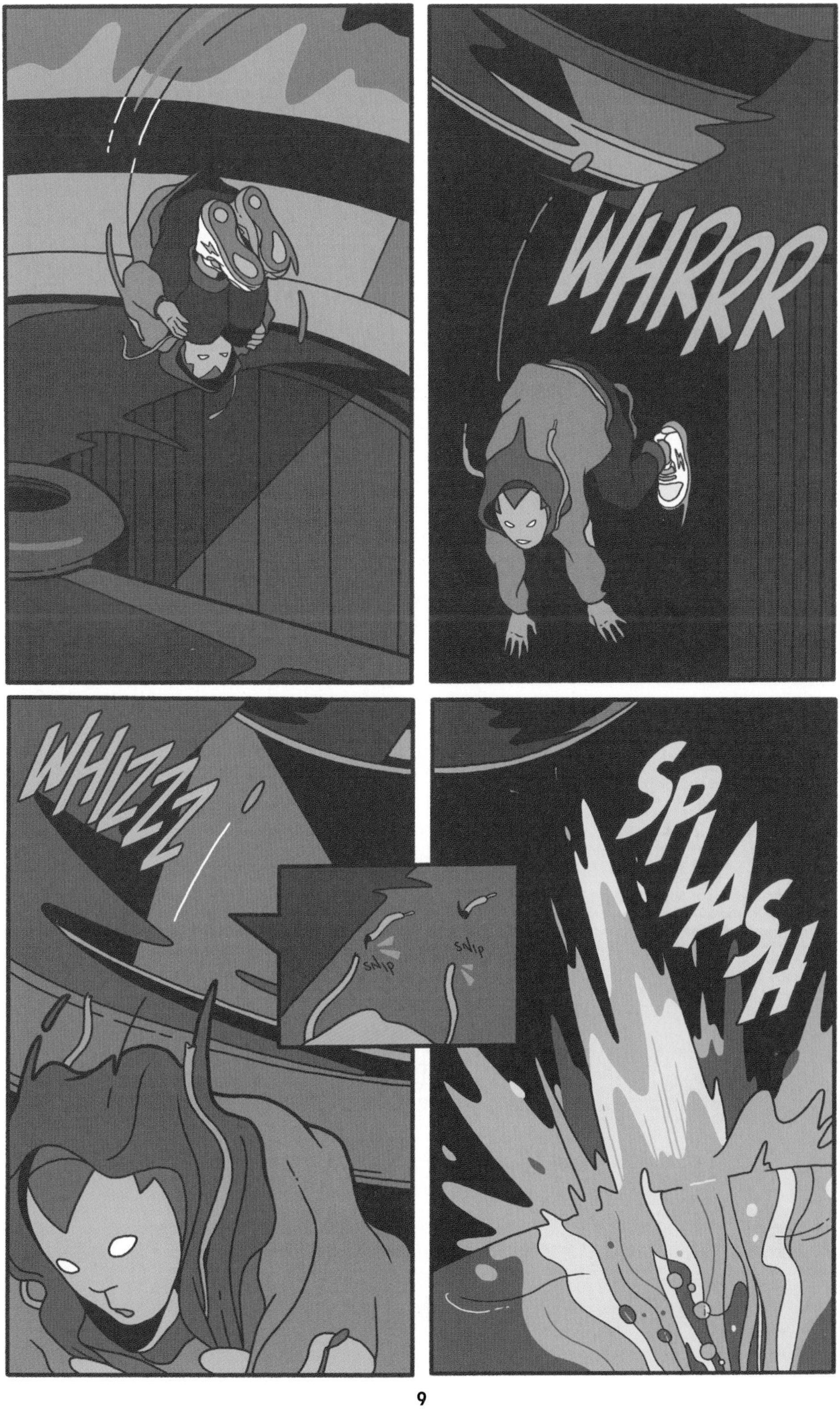
WHRRR
WHIZZZ
SNIP
SNIP
SPLASH

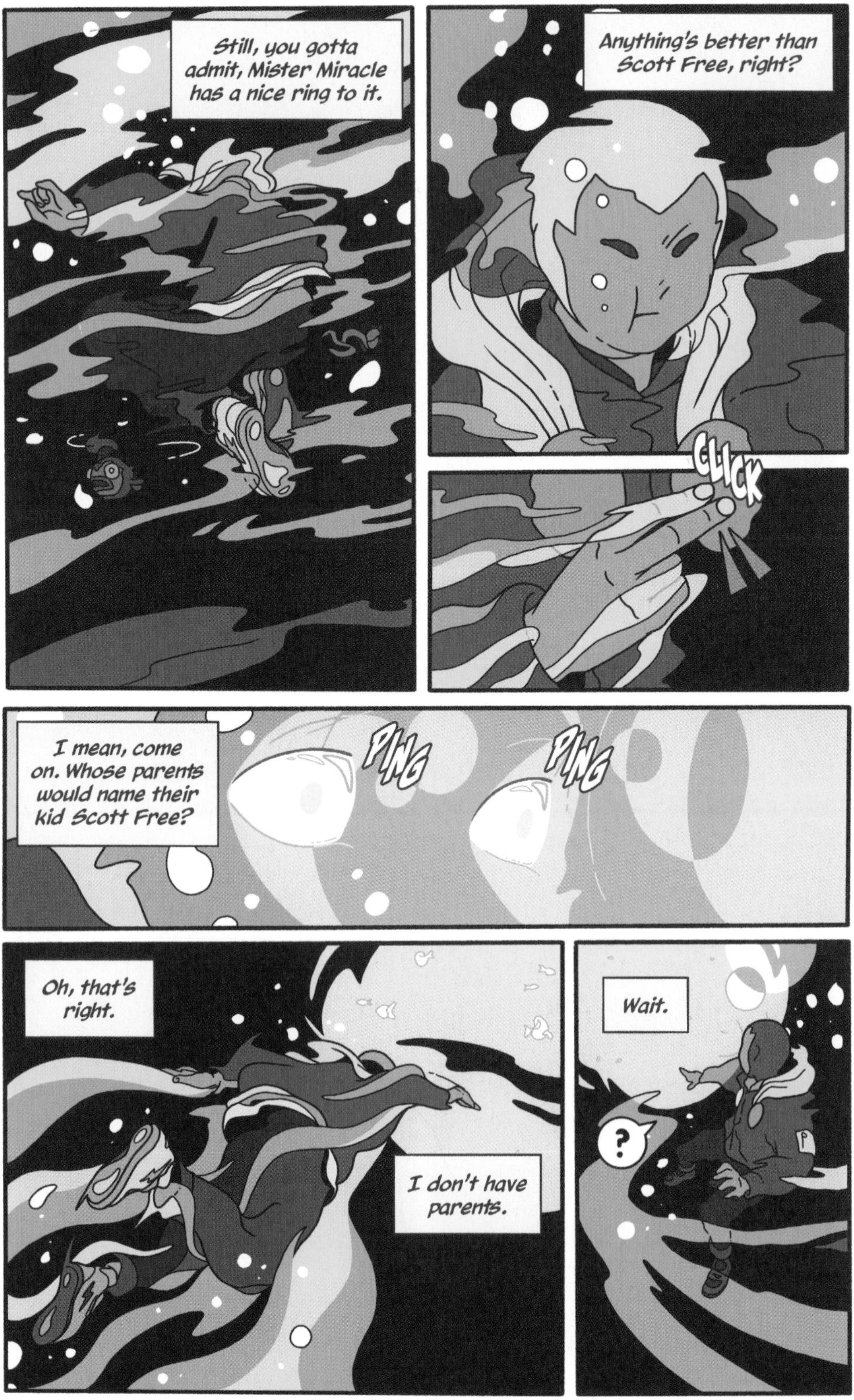
Still, you gotta admit, Mister Miracle has a nice ring to it.
Anything's better than Scott Free, right?
CLICK
I mean, come on. Whose parents would name their kid Scott Free?
PING
PING
Oh, that's right.
I don't have parents.
Wait.
?

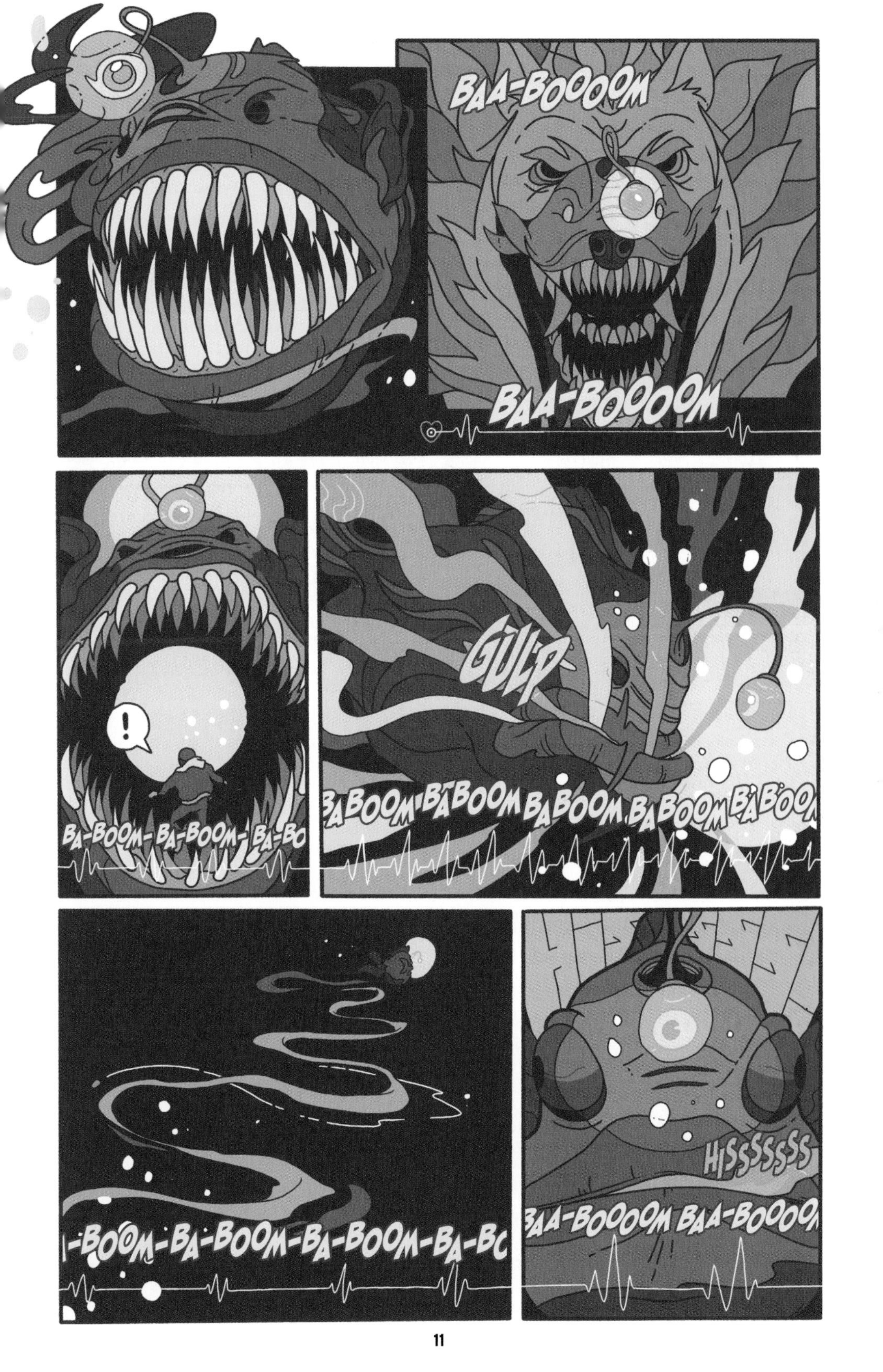
BAA-BOOOOM
BAA-BOOOOM
!
BA-BOOM-BA-BOOM-BA-BO
GULP
BABOOM-BABOOM BABOOM BABOOM BABOO
-BOOM-BA-BOOM-BA-BOOM-BA-BO
HISSSSSSS
BAA-BOOOM BAA-BOOOM

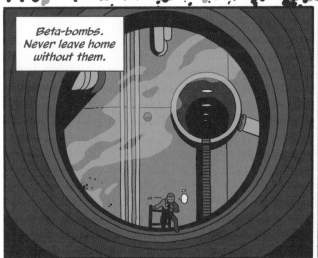

Beta-bombs. Never leave home without them.

Pant Pant

For a woman who loves order, you'd think Granny Goodness would get around to cleaning up this place every once in a while.

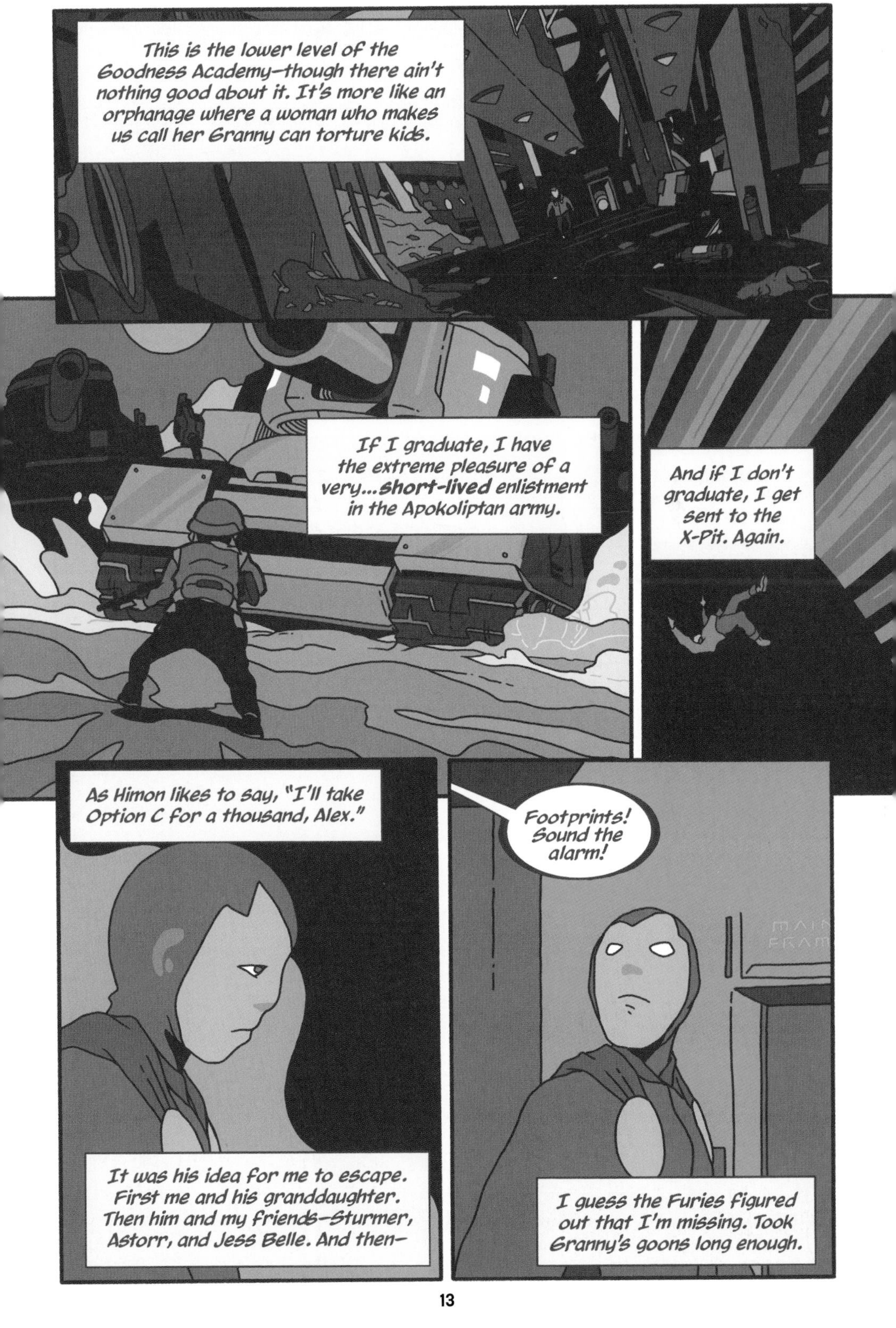
This is the lower level of the Goodness Academy—though there ain't nothing good about it. It's more like an orphanage where a woman who makes us call her Granny can torture kids.
If I graduate, I have the extreme pleasure of a very...**short-lived** enlistment in the Apokoliptan army.
And if I don't graduate, I get sent to the X-Pit. Again.
As Himon likes to say, "I'll take Option C for a thousand, Alex."
It was his idea for me to escape. First me and his granddaughter. Then him and my friends—Sturmer, Astorr, and Jess Belle. And then—
Footprints! Sound the alarm!
I guess the Furies figured out that I'm missing. Took Granny's goons long enough.

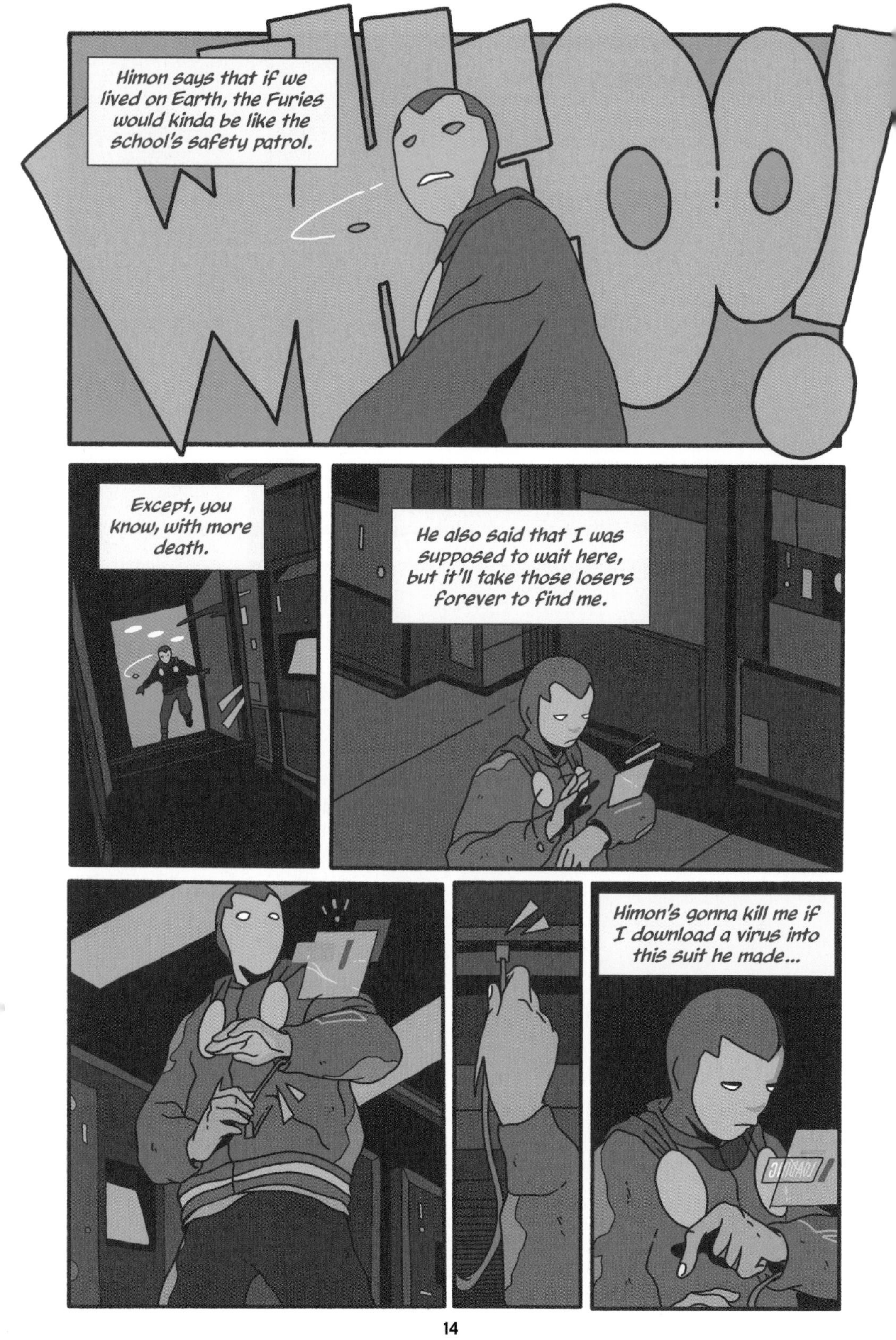
Himon says that if we lived on Earth, the Furies would kinda be like the school's safety patrol.
Except, you know, with more death.
He also said that I was supposed to wait here, but it'll take those losers forever to find me.
Himon's gonna kill me if I download a virus into this suit he made...

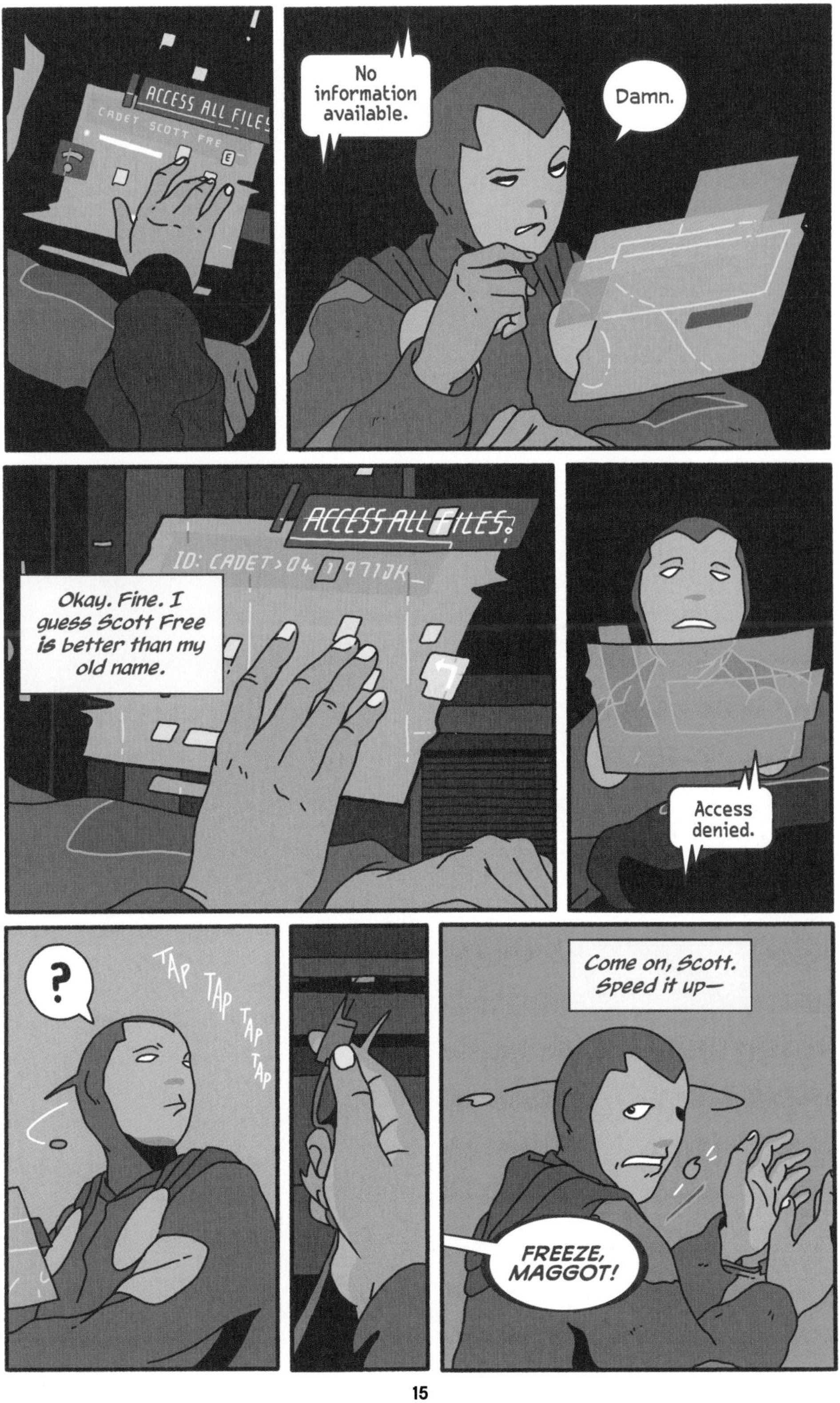
ACCESS ALL FILES
CADET SCOTT FREE
No information available.
Damn.
ACCESS ALL FILES?
ID: CADET>04 971JK_
Okay. Fine. I guess Scott Free is better than my old name.
Access denied.
?
TAP TAP TAP TAP
Come on, Scott. Speed it up—
FREEZE, MAGGOT!

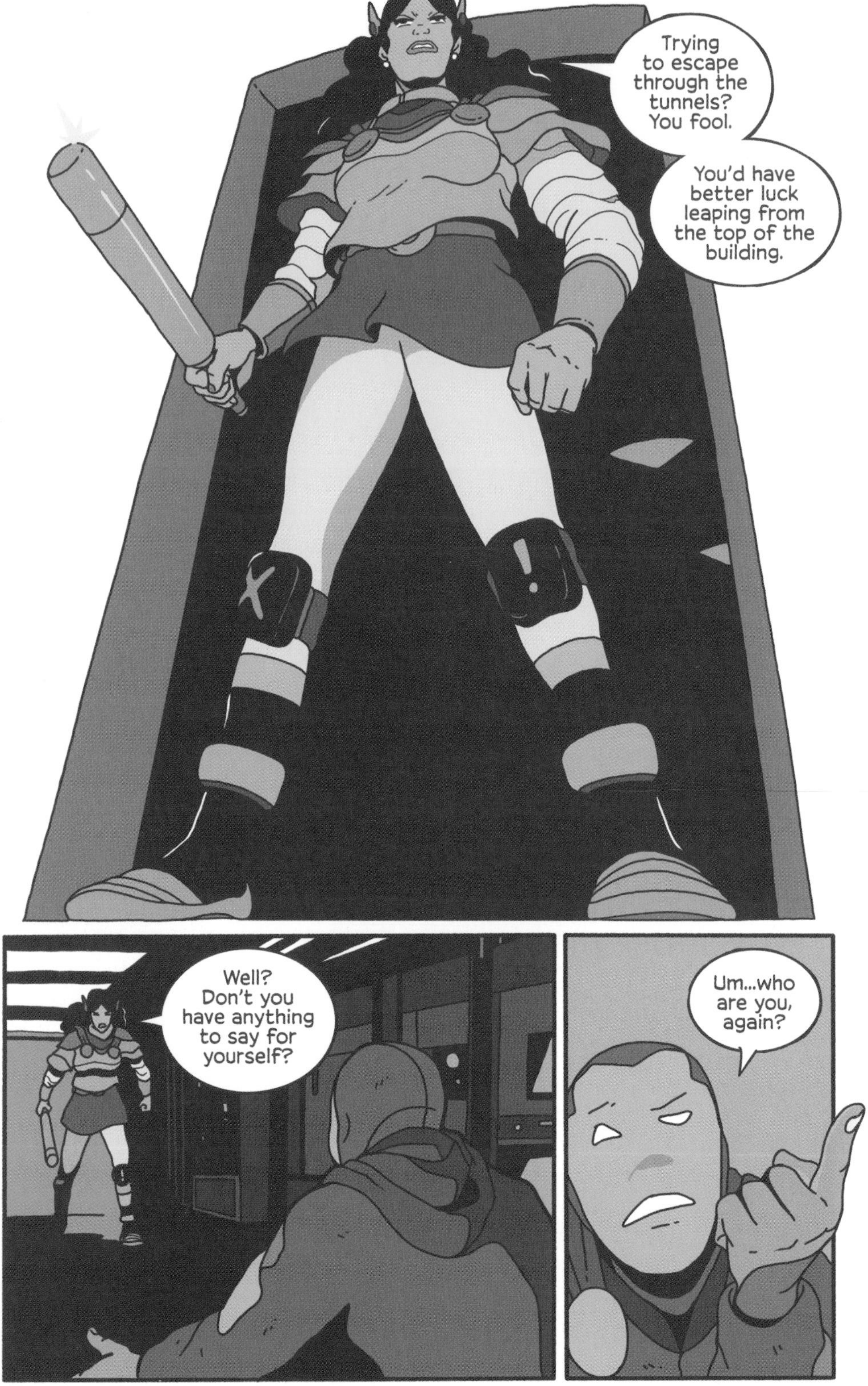
Trying to escape through the tunnels? You fool.
You'd have better luck leaping from the top of the building.
Well? Don't you have anything to say for yourself?
Um...who are you, again?

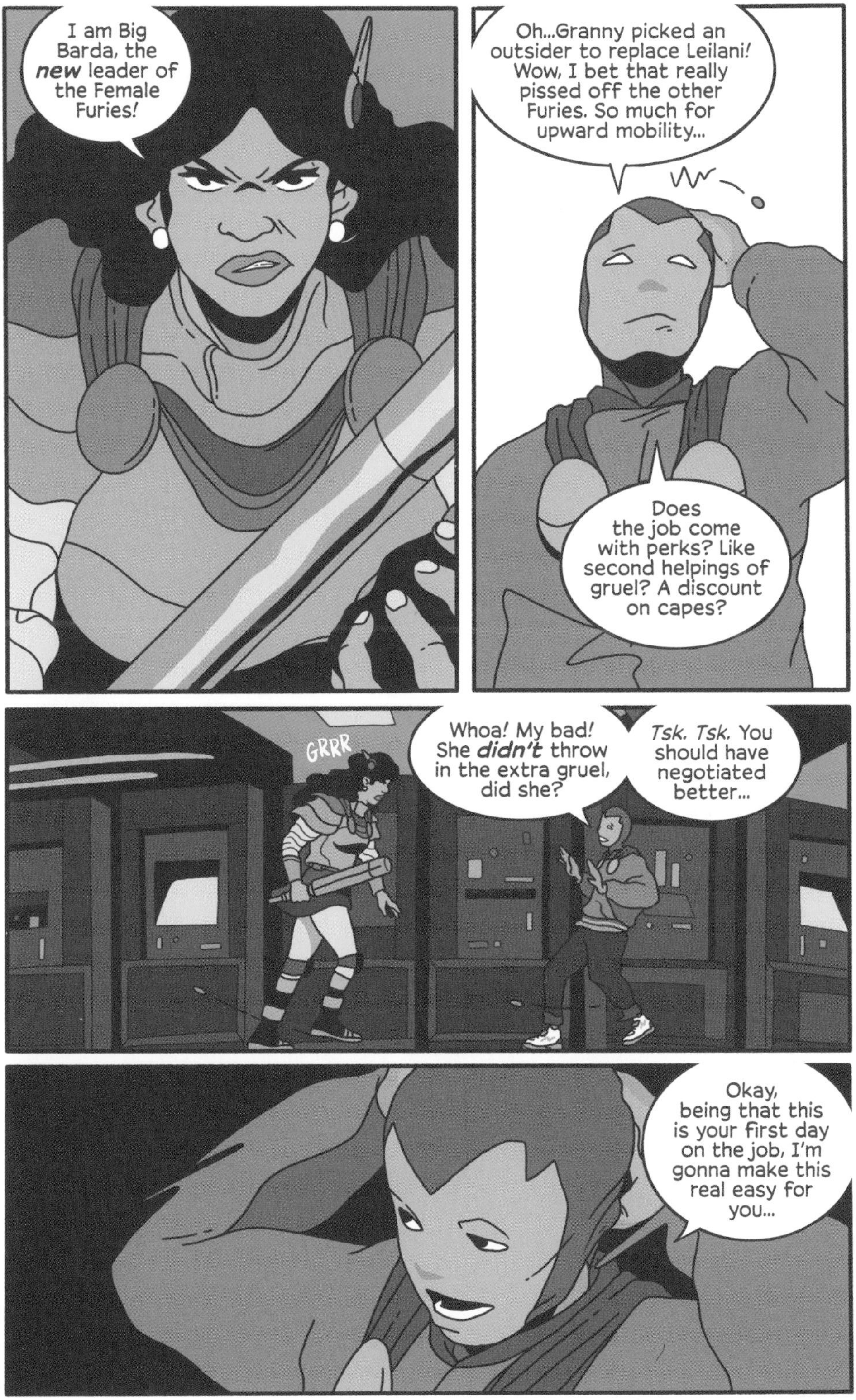
I am Big Barda, the **new** leader of the Female Furies!
Oh...Granny picked an outsider to replace Leilani! Wow, I bet that really pissed off the other Furies. So much for upward mobility...
Does the job come with perks? Like second helpings of gruel? A discount on capes?
GRRR
Whoa! My bad! She ***didn't*** throw in the extra gruel, did she?
Tsk. Tsk. You should have negotiated better...
Okay, being that this is your first day on the job, I'm gonna make this real easy for you...

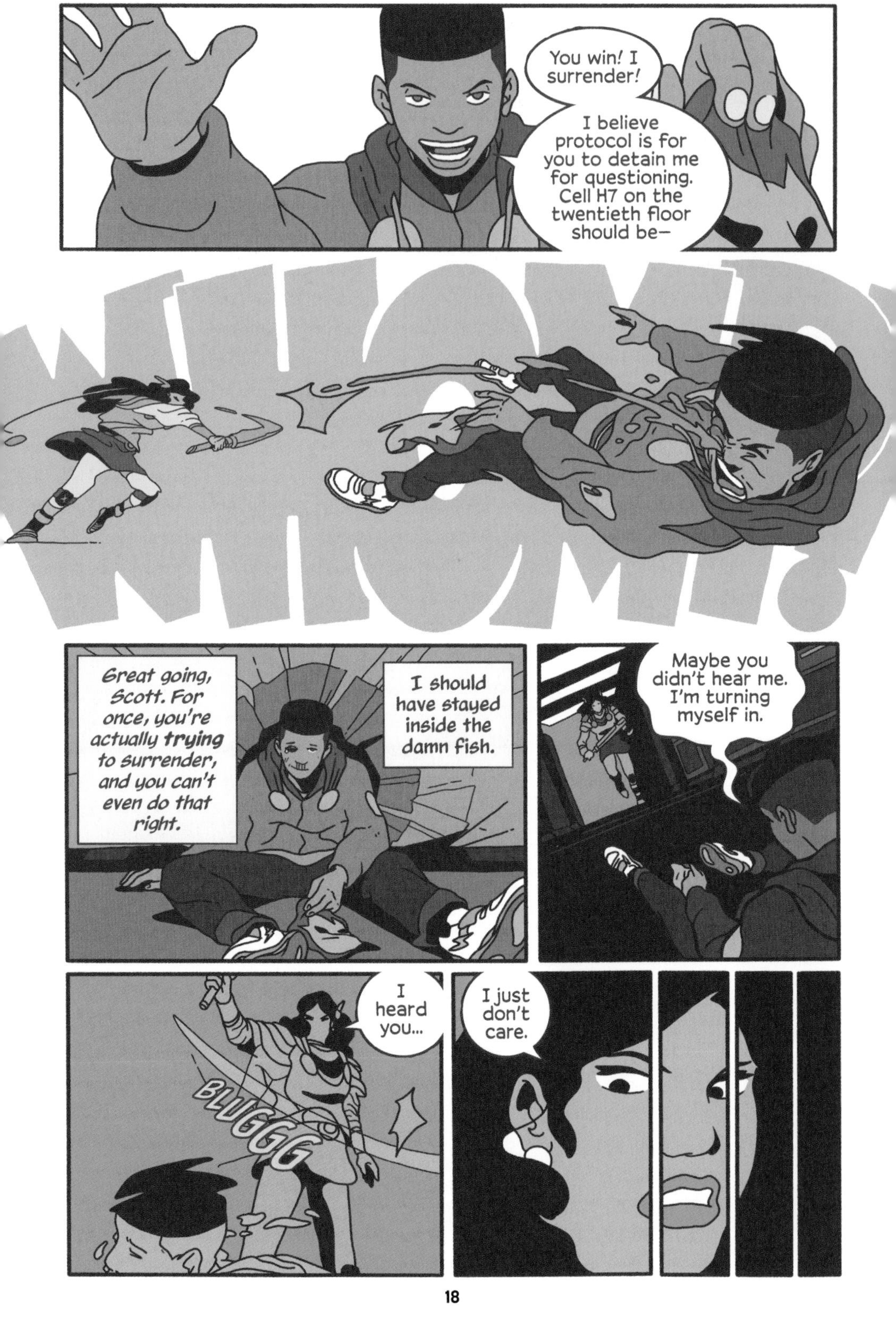
You win! I surrender!
I believe protocol is for you to detain me for questioning. Cell H7 on the twentieth floor should be—
WHOMP!
Great going, Scott. For once, you're actually trying to surrender, and you can't even do that right.
I should have stayed inside the damn fish.
Maybe you didn't hear me. I'm turning myself in.
I heard you...
BLUGGG
I just don't care.

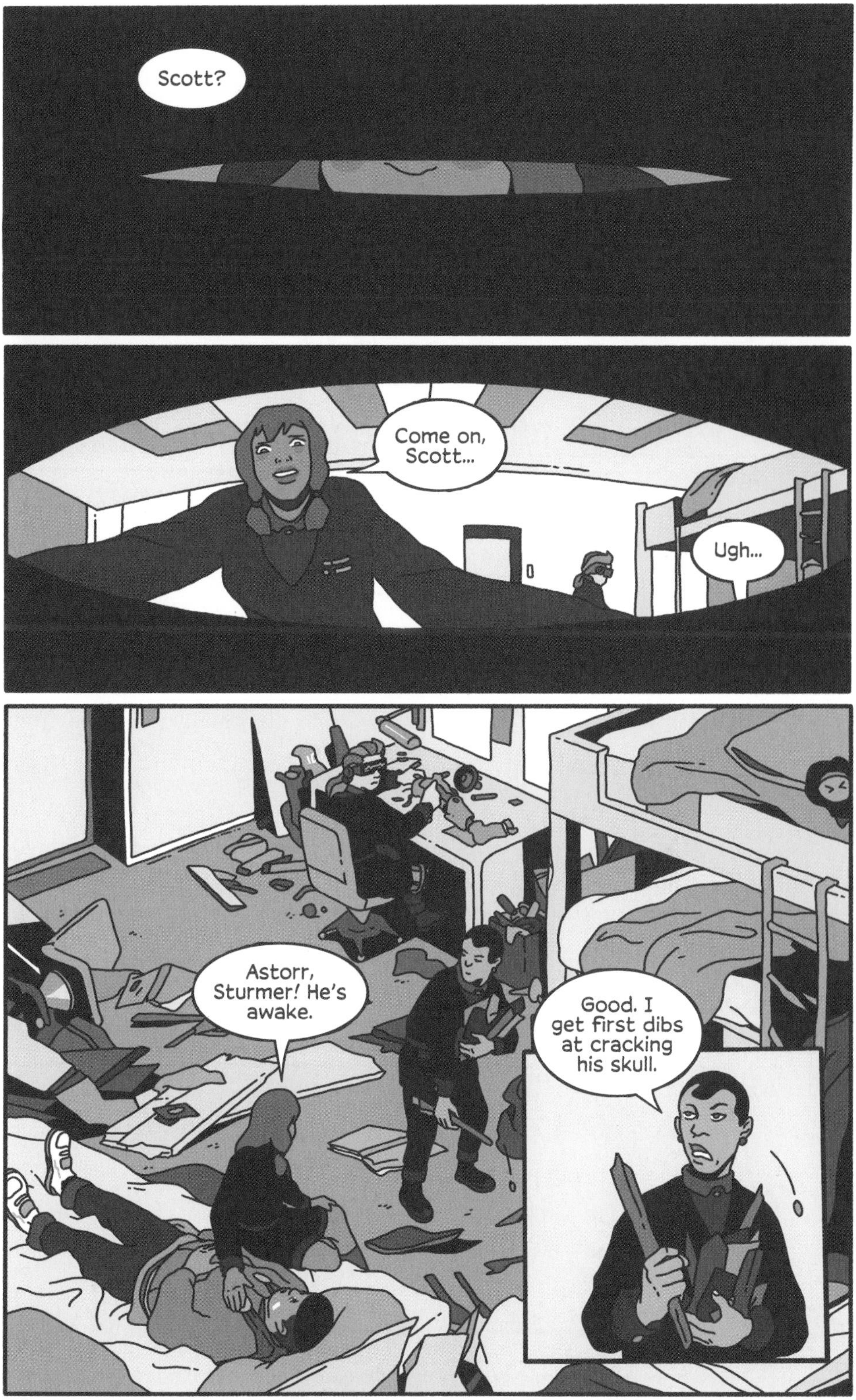
Scott?
Come on, Scott...
Ugh...
Astorr, Sturmer! He's awake.
Good. I get first dibs at cracking his skull.

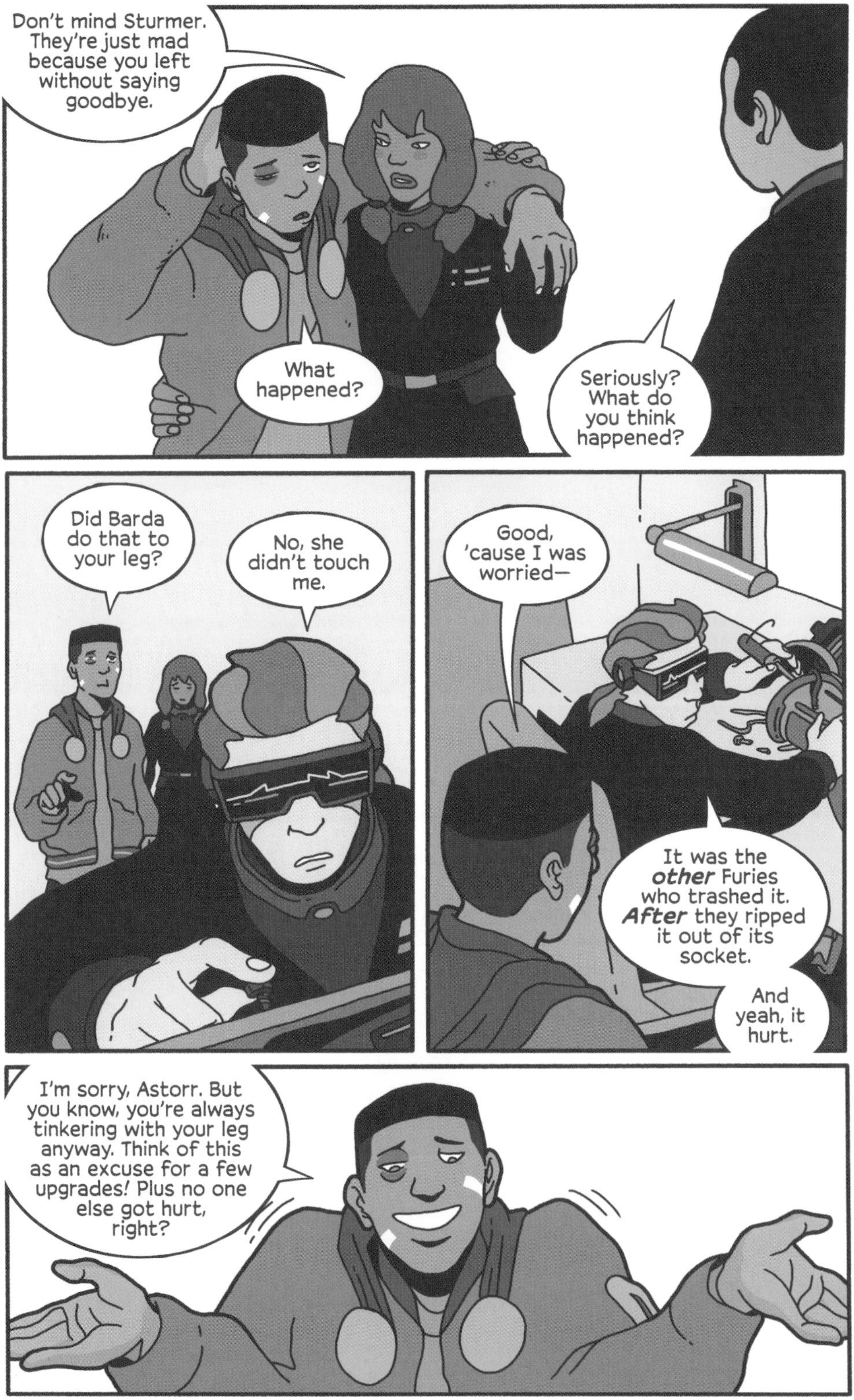
Don't mind Sturmer. They're just mad because you left without saying goodbye.
What happened?
Seriously? What do you think happened?
Did Barda do that to your leg?
No, she didn't touch me.
Good, 'cause I was worried—
It was the *other* Furies who trashed it. *After* they ripped it out of its socket.
And yeah, it hurt.
I'm sorry, Astorr. But you know, you're always tinkering with your leg anyway. Think of this as an excuse for a few upgrades! Plus no one else got hurt, right?

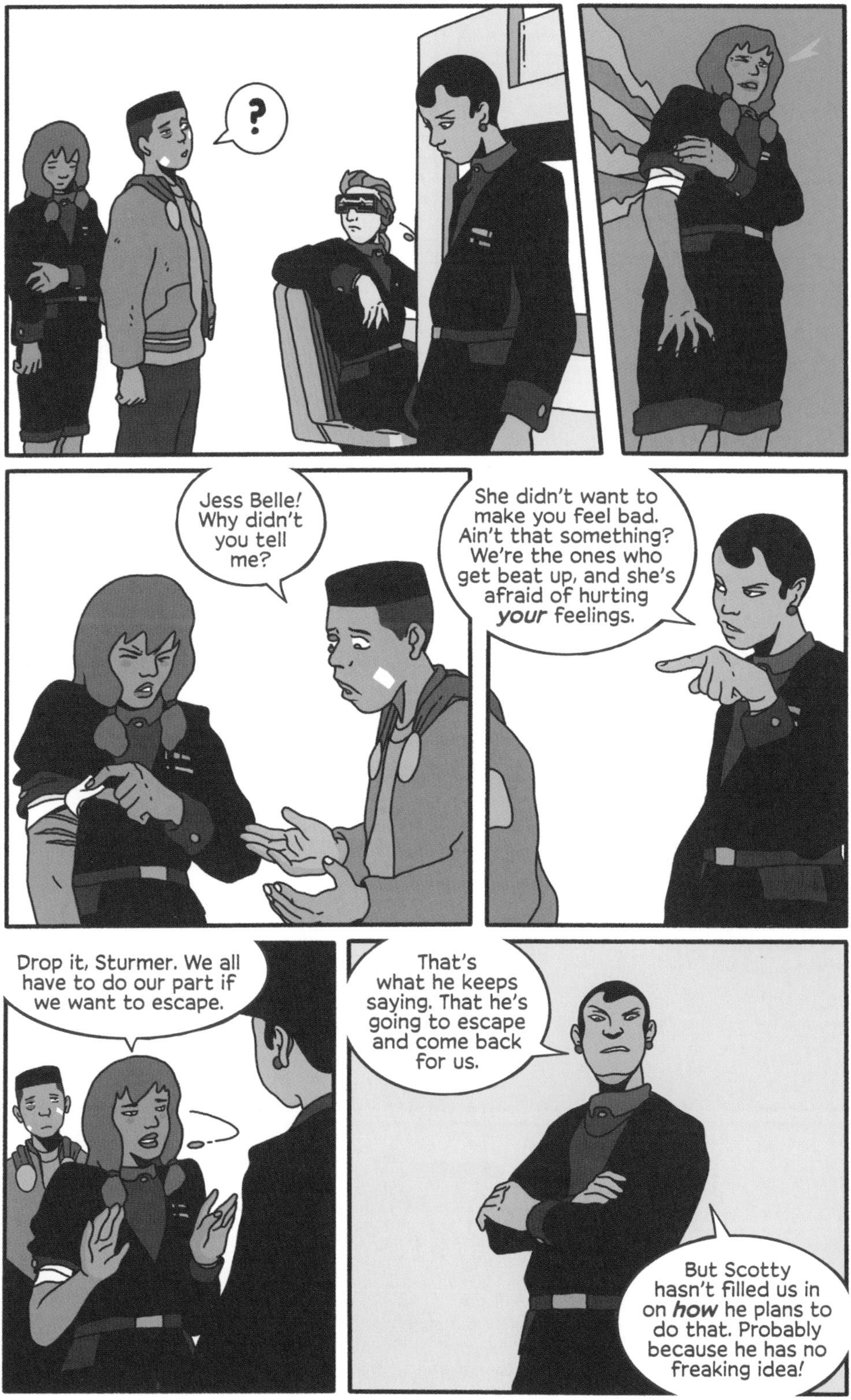
?
Jess Belle! Why didn't you tell me?
She didn't want to make you feel bad. Ain't that something? We're the ones who get beat up, and she's afraid of hurting *your* feelings.
Drop it, Sturmer. We all have to do our part if we want to escape.
That's what he keeps saying. That he's going to escape and come back for us.
But Scotty hasn't filled us in on *how* he plans to do that. Probably because he has no freaking idea!

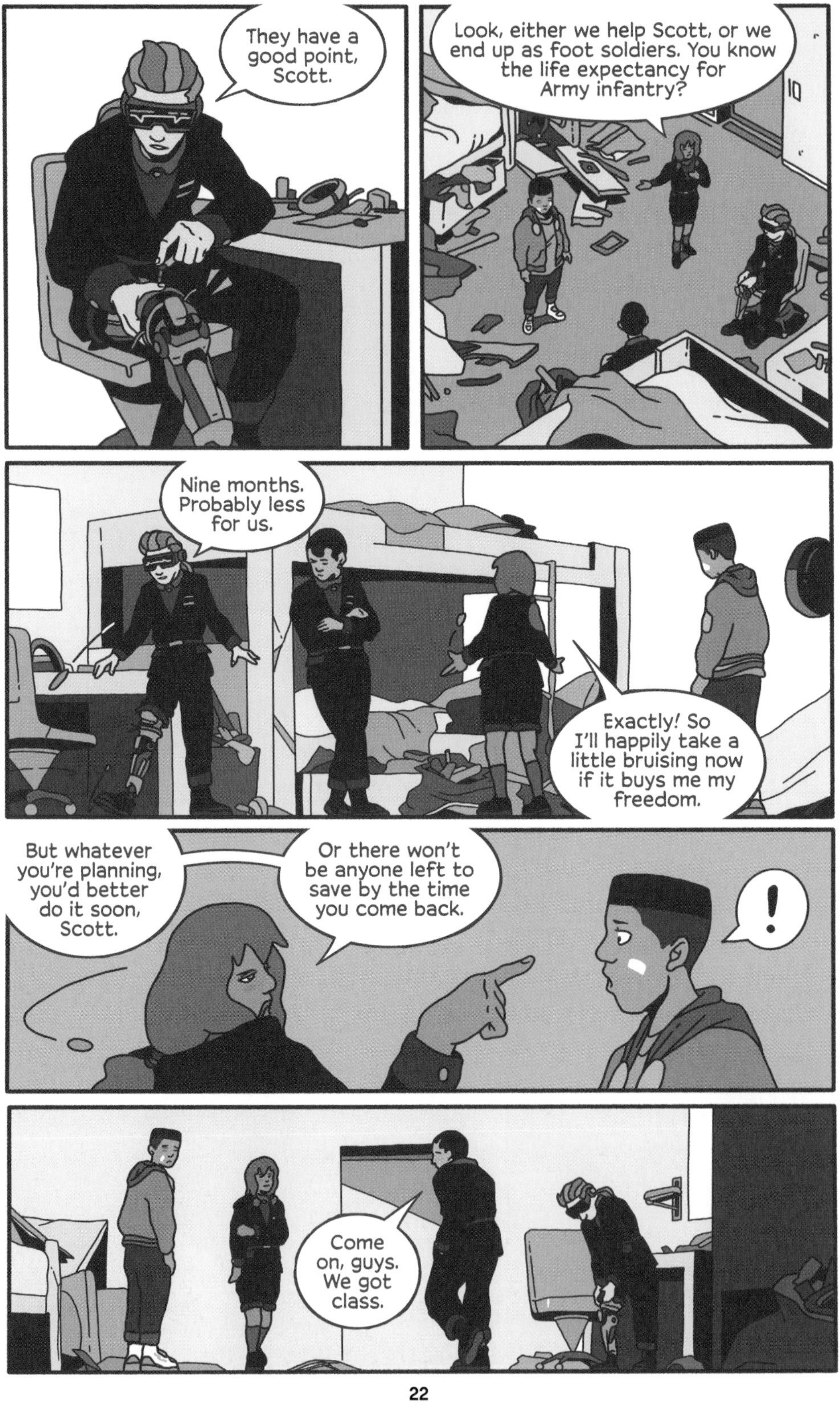
They have a good point, Scott.
Look, either we help Scott, or we end up as foot soldiers. You know the life expectancy for Army infantry?
10
Nine months. Probably less for us.
Exactly! So I'll happily take a little bruising now if it buys me my freedom.
But whatever you're planning, you'd better do it soon, Scott.
Or there won't be anyone left to save by the time you come back.
!
Come on, guys. We got class.

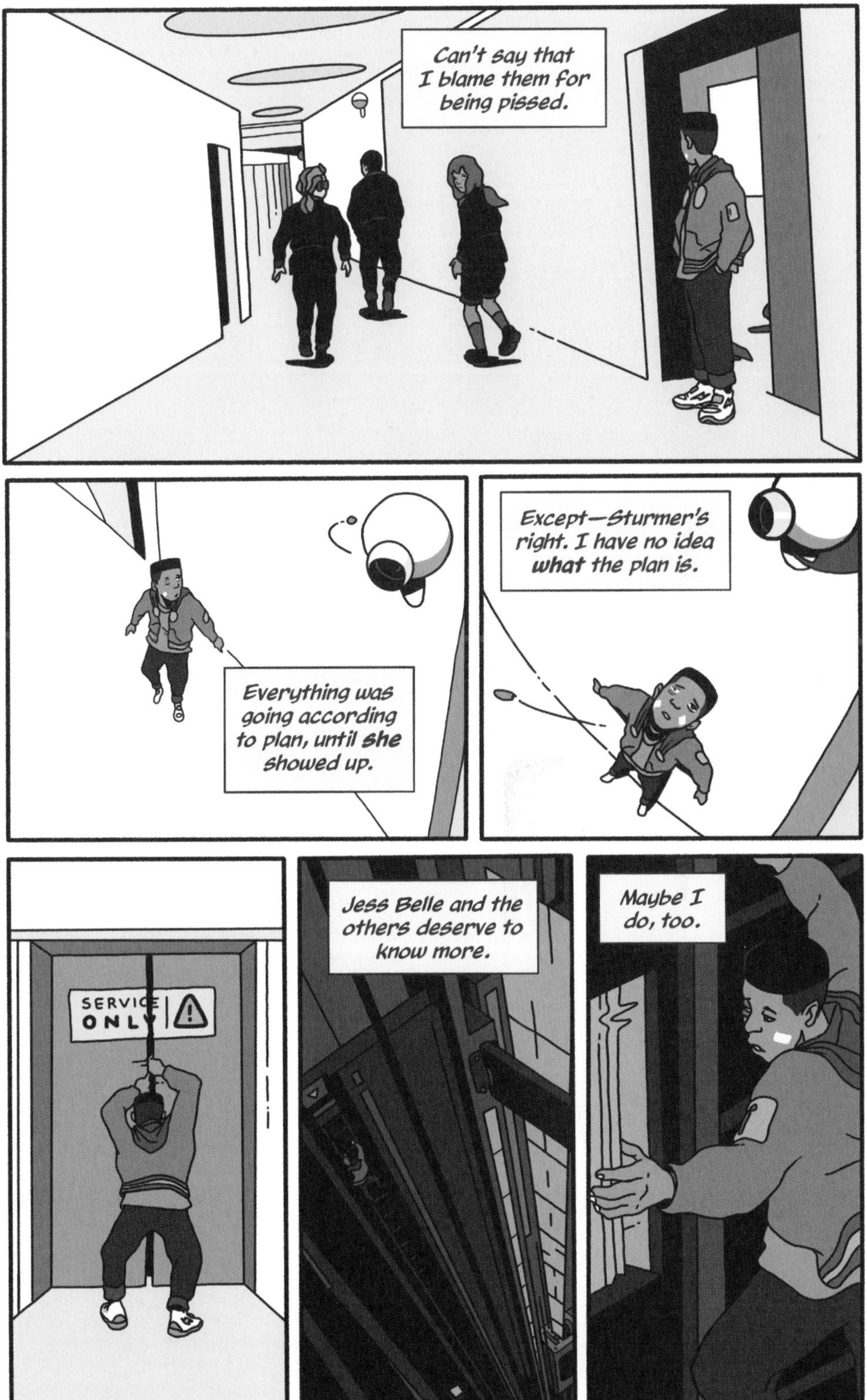
Can't say that I blame them for being pissed.
Everything was going according to plan, until she showed up.
Except—Sturmer's right. I have no idea what the plan is.
SERVICE ONLY
Jess Belle and the others deserve to know more.
Maybe I do, too.

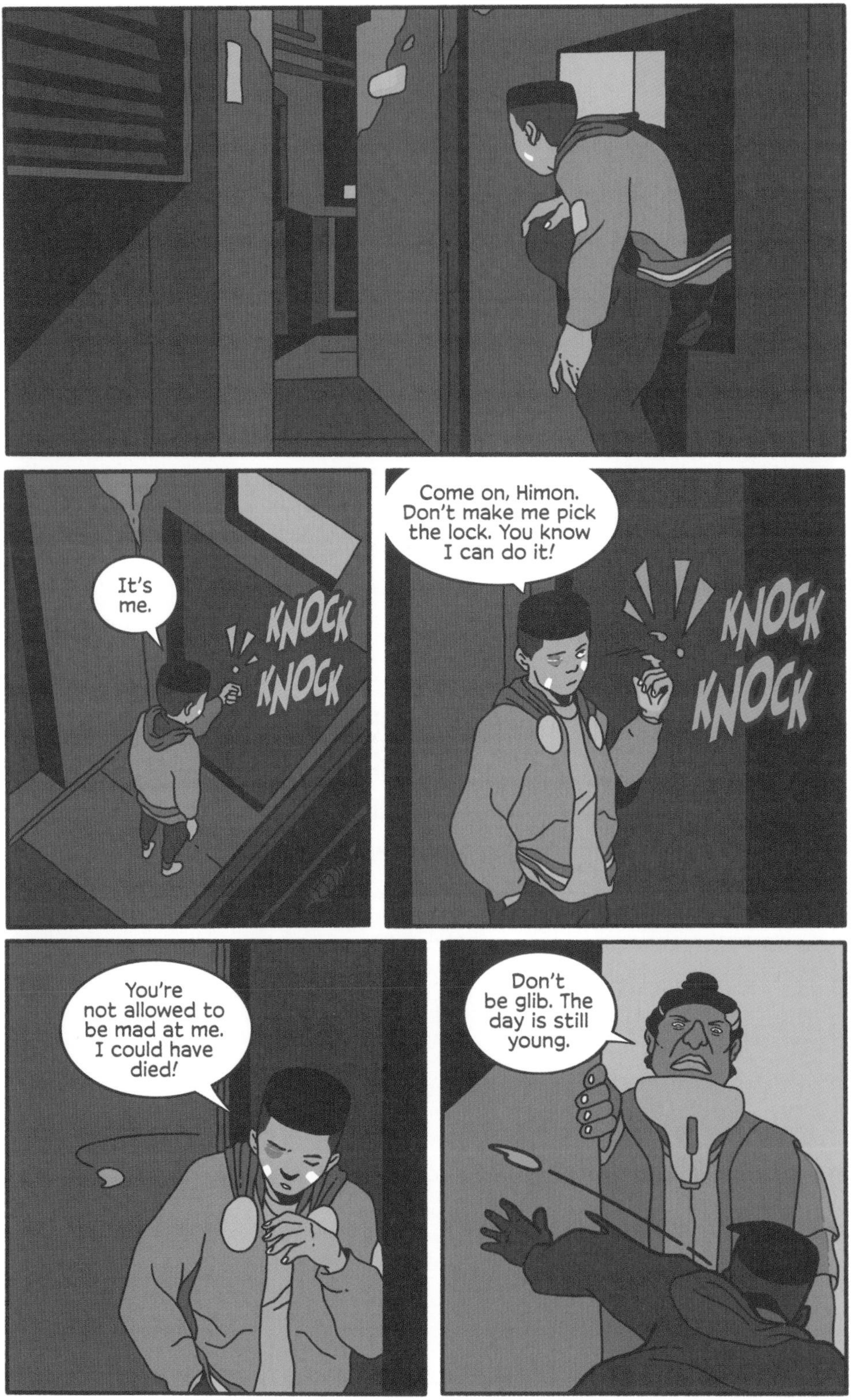
It's me.
KNOCK KNOCK
Come on, Himon. Don't make me pick the lock. You know I can do it!
KNOCK KNOCK
You're not allowed to be mad at me. I could have died!
Don't be glib. The day is still young.

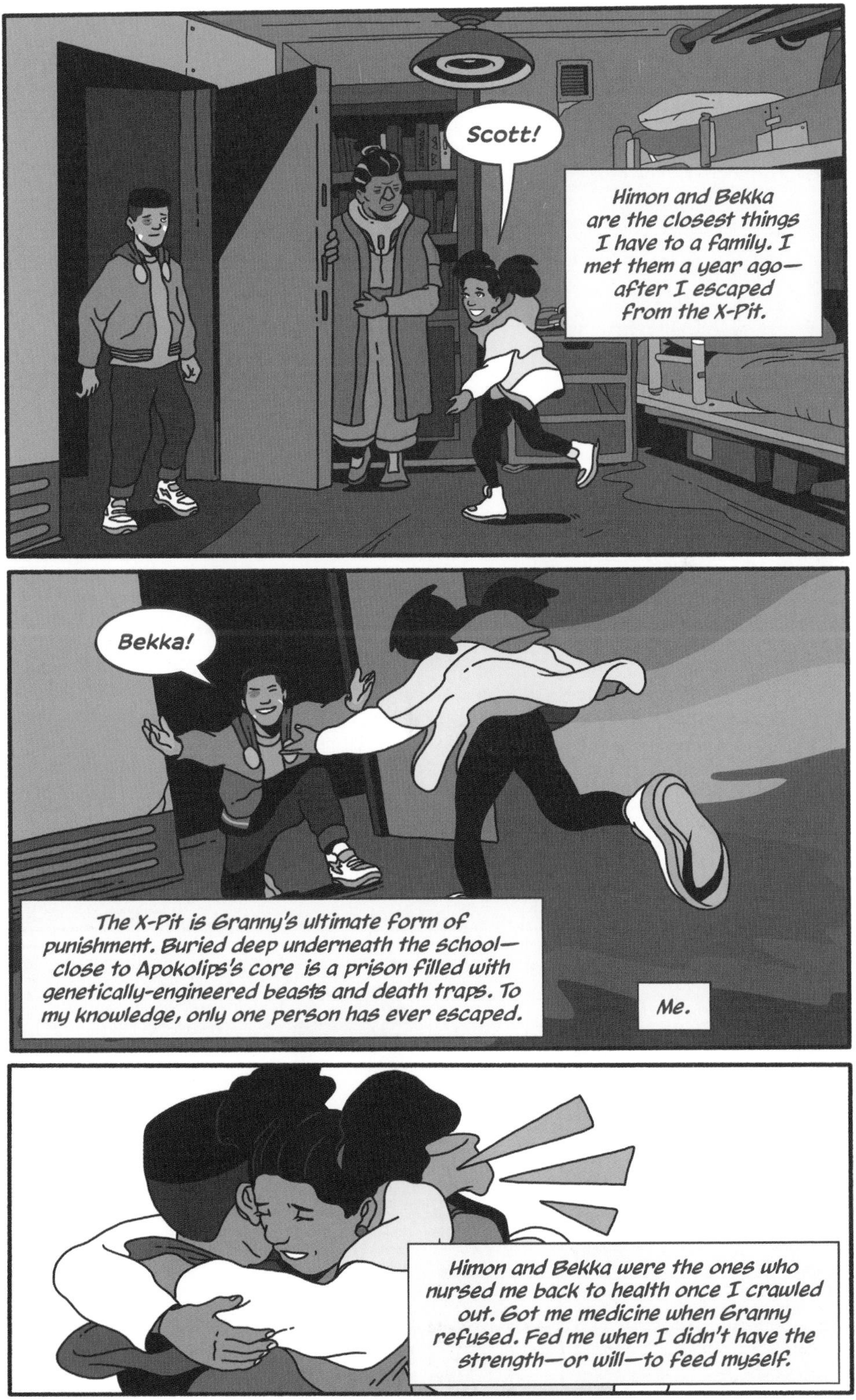
Scott!
Himon and Bekka are the closest things I have to a family. I met them a year ago—after I escaped from the X-Pit.
Bekka!
The X-Pit is Granny's ultimate form of punishment. Buried deep underneath the school—close to Apokolips's core is a prison filled with genetically-engineered beasts and death traps. To my knowledge, only one person has ever escaped.
Me.
Himon and Bekka were the ones who nursed me back to health once I crawled out. Got me medicine when Granny refused. Fed me when I didn't have the strength—or will—to feed myself.

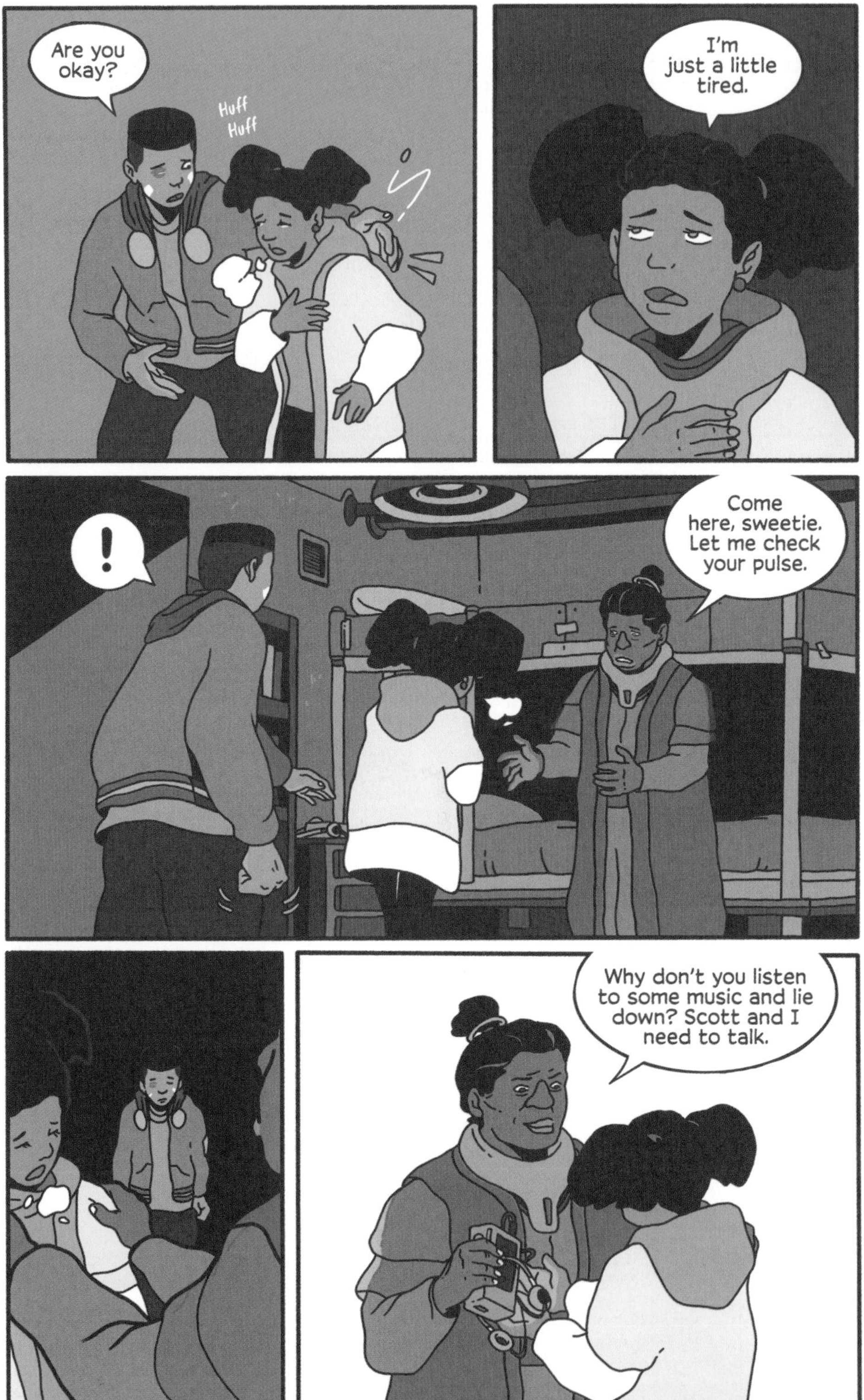
Are you okay?
Huff Huff
I'm just a little tired.
!
Come here, sweetie. Let me check your pulse.
Why don't you listen to some music and lie down? Scott and I need to talk.

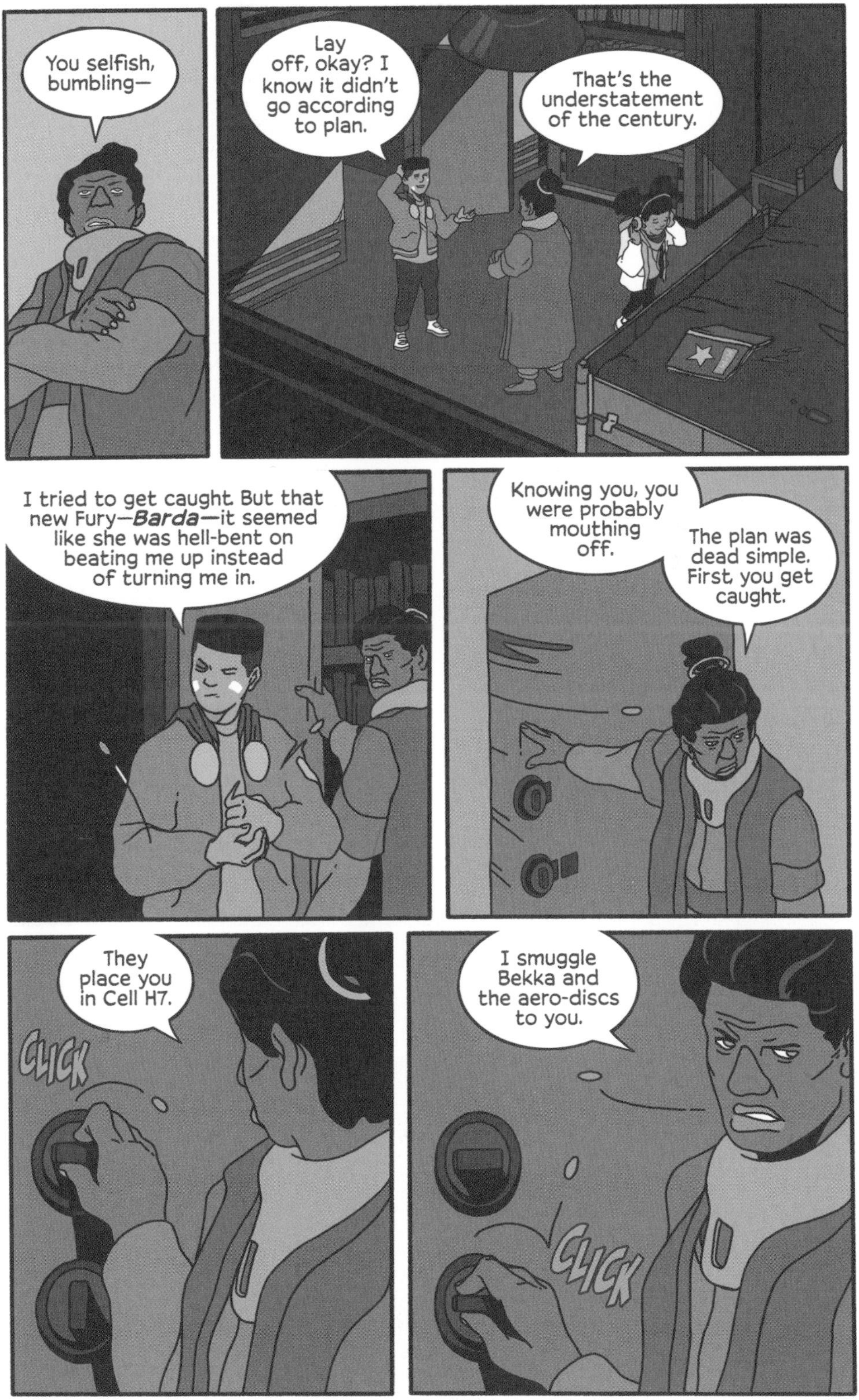
You selfish, bumbling—
Lay off, okay? I know it didn't go according to plan.
That's the understatement of the century.
I tried to get caught. But that new Fury—*Barda*—it seemed like she was hell-bent on beating me up instead of turning me in.
Knowing you, you were probably mouthing off.
The plan was dead simple. First, you get caught.
They place you in Cell H7.
CLICK
I smuggle Bekka and the aero-discs to you.
CLICK

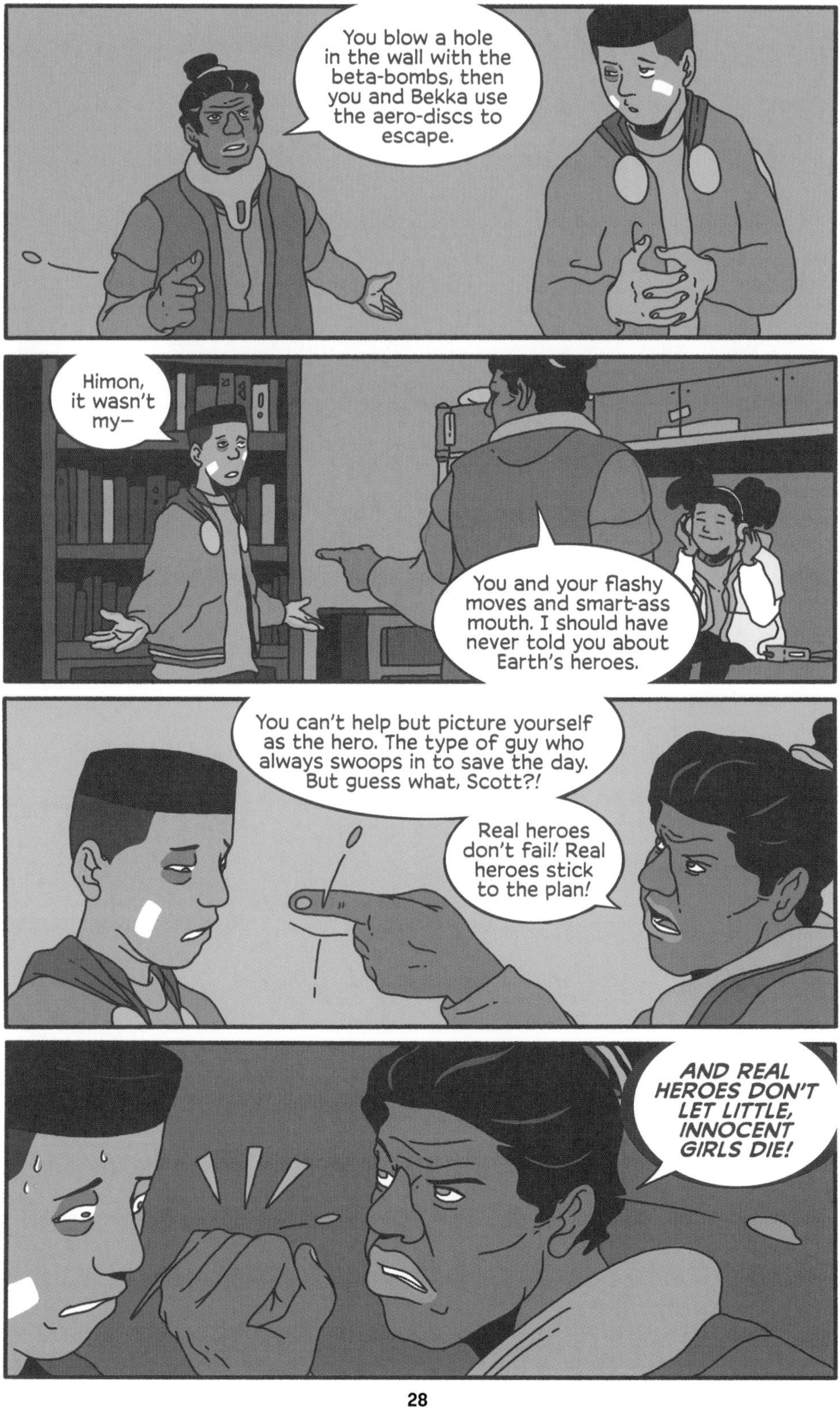
You blow a hole in the wall with the beta-bombs, then you and Bekka use the aero-discs to escape.
Himon, it wasn't my—
You and your flashy moves and smart-ass mouth. I should have never told you about Earth's heroes.
You can't help but picture yourself as the hero. The type of guy who always swoops in to save the day. But guess what, Scott?!
Real heroes don't fail! Real heroes stick to the plan!
AND REAL HEROES DON'T LET LITTLE, INNOCENT GIRLS DIE!

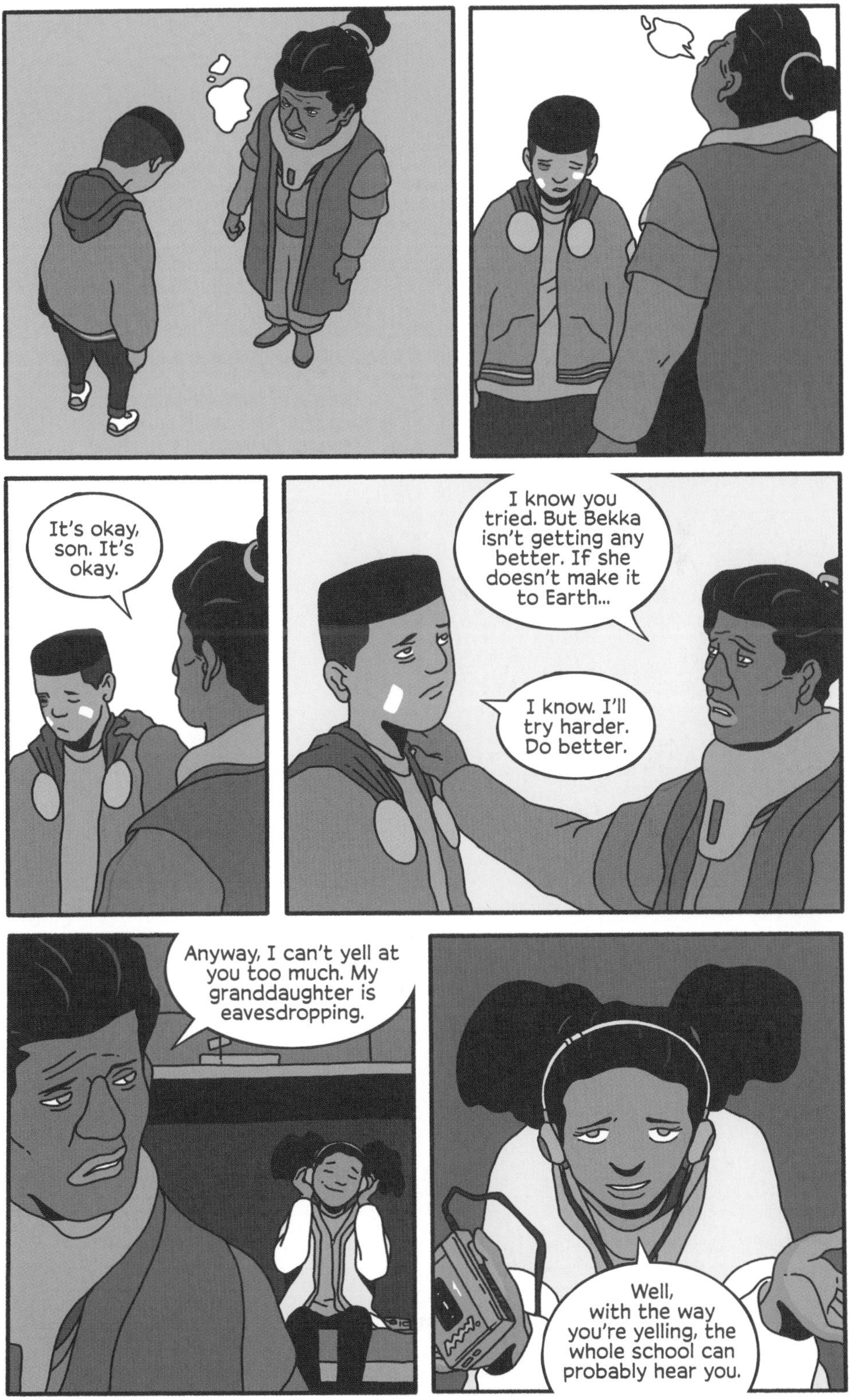
It's okay, son. It's okay.
I know you tried. But Bekka isn't getting any better. If she doesn't make it to Earth...
I know. I'll try harder. Do better.
Anyway, I can't yell at you too much. My granddaughter is eavesdropping.
Well, with the way you're yelling, the whole school can probably hear you.

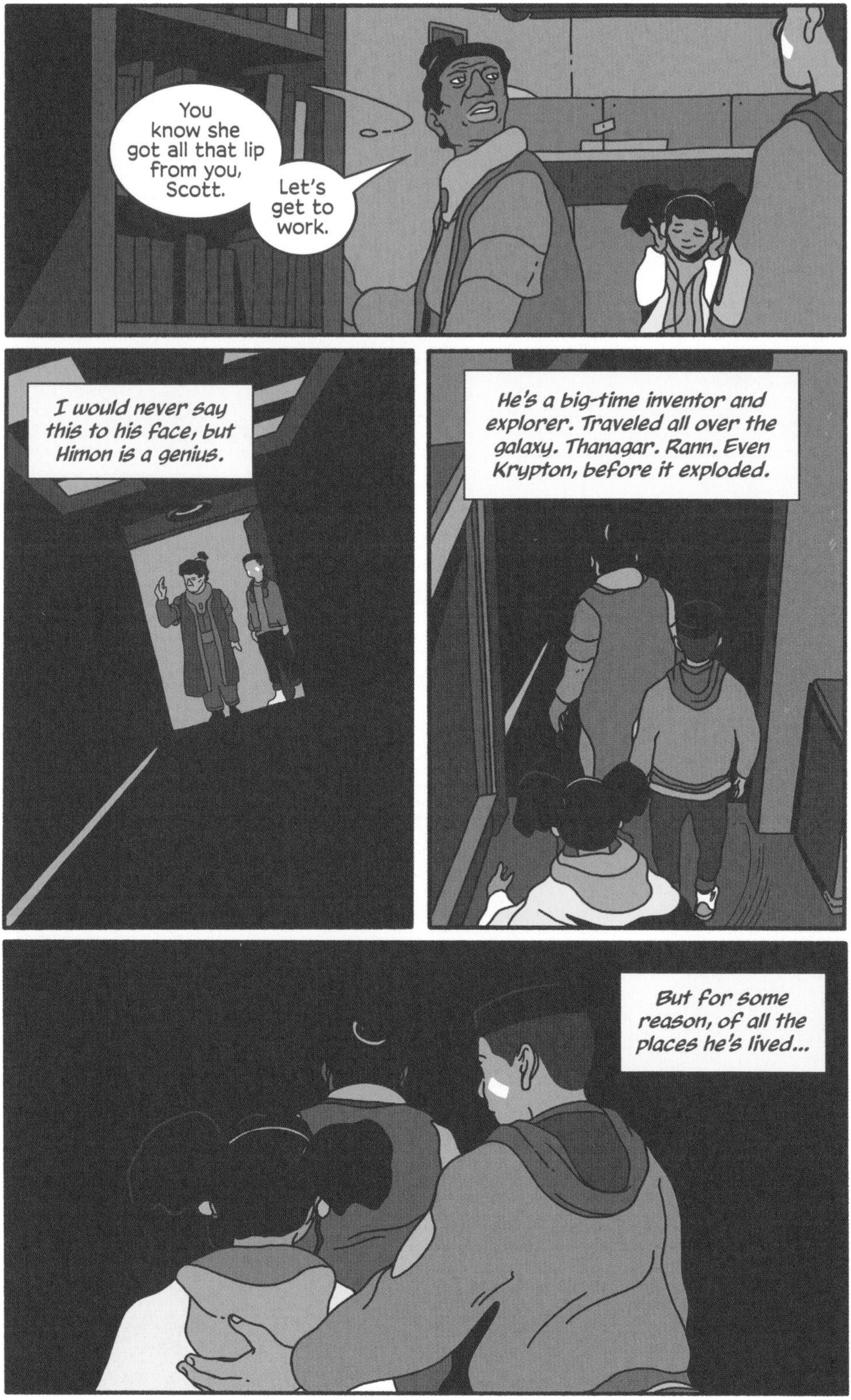
You know she got all that lip from you, Scott.
Let's get to work.
I would never say this to his face, but Himon is a genius.
He's a big-time inventor and explorer. Traveled all over the galaxy. Thanagar. Rann. Even Krypton, before it exploded.
But for some reason, of all the places he's lived...

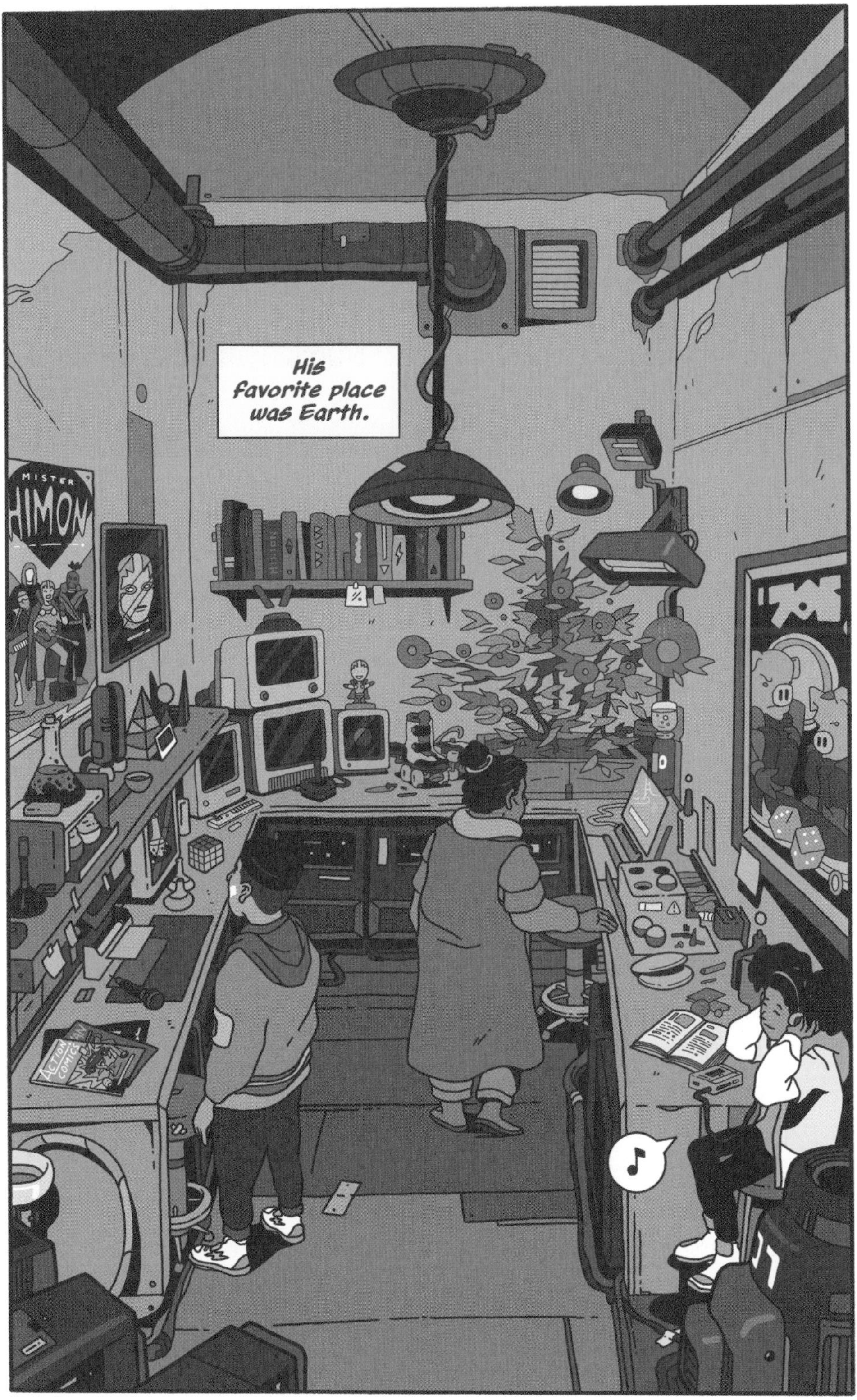
His favorite place was Earth.
MISTER
HIMON
ACTION COMICS

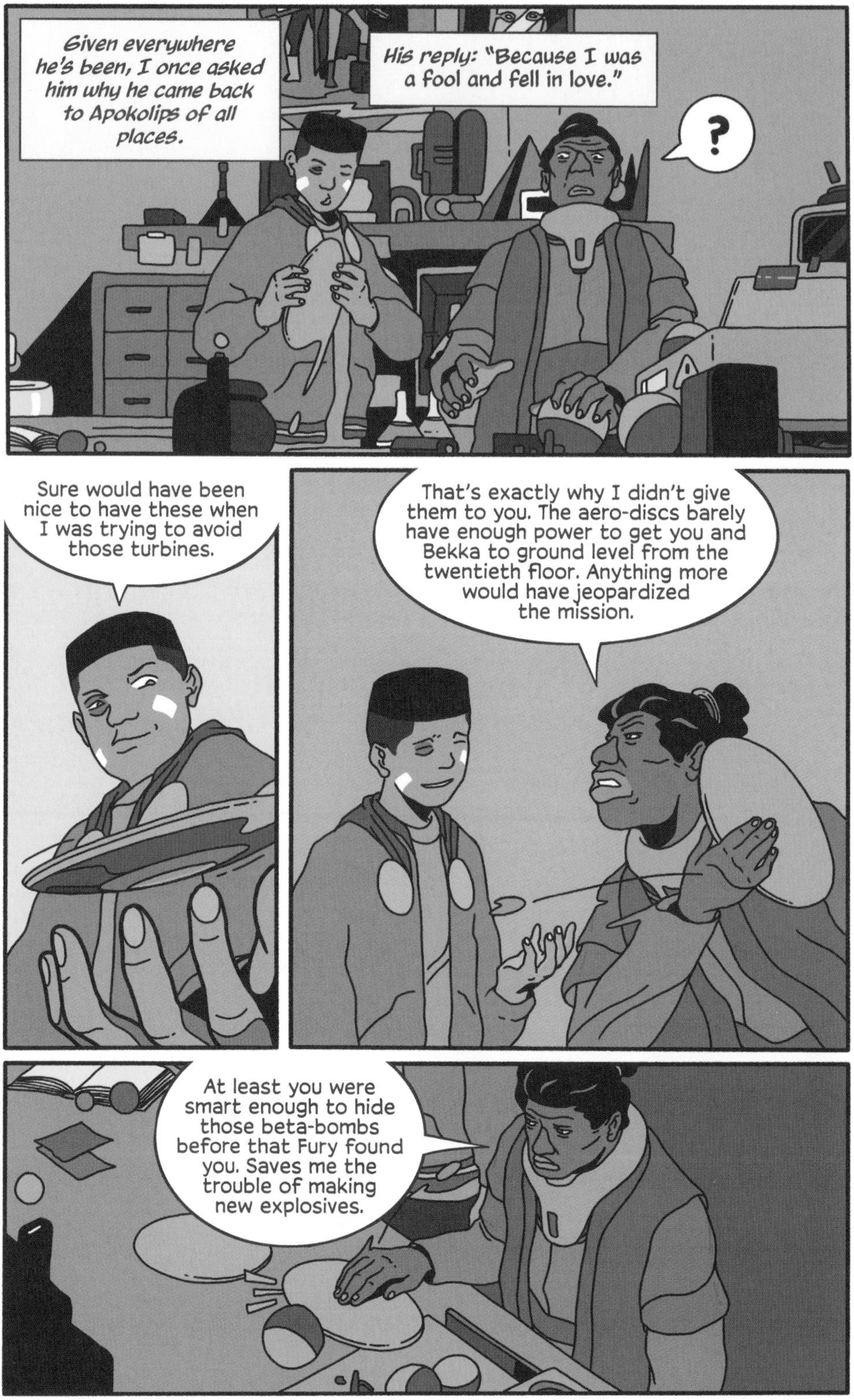
Given everywhere he's been, I once asked him why he came back to Apokolips of all places.
His reply: "Because I was a fool and fell in love."
?
Sure would have been nice to have these when I was trying to avoid those turbines.
That's exactly why I didn't give them to you. The aero-discs barely have enough power to get you and Bekka to ground level from the twentieth floor. Anything more would have jeopardized the mission.
At least you were smart enough to hide those beta-bombs before that Fury found you. Saves me the trouble of making new explosives.

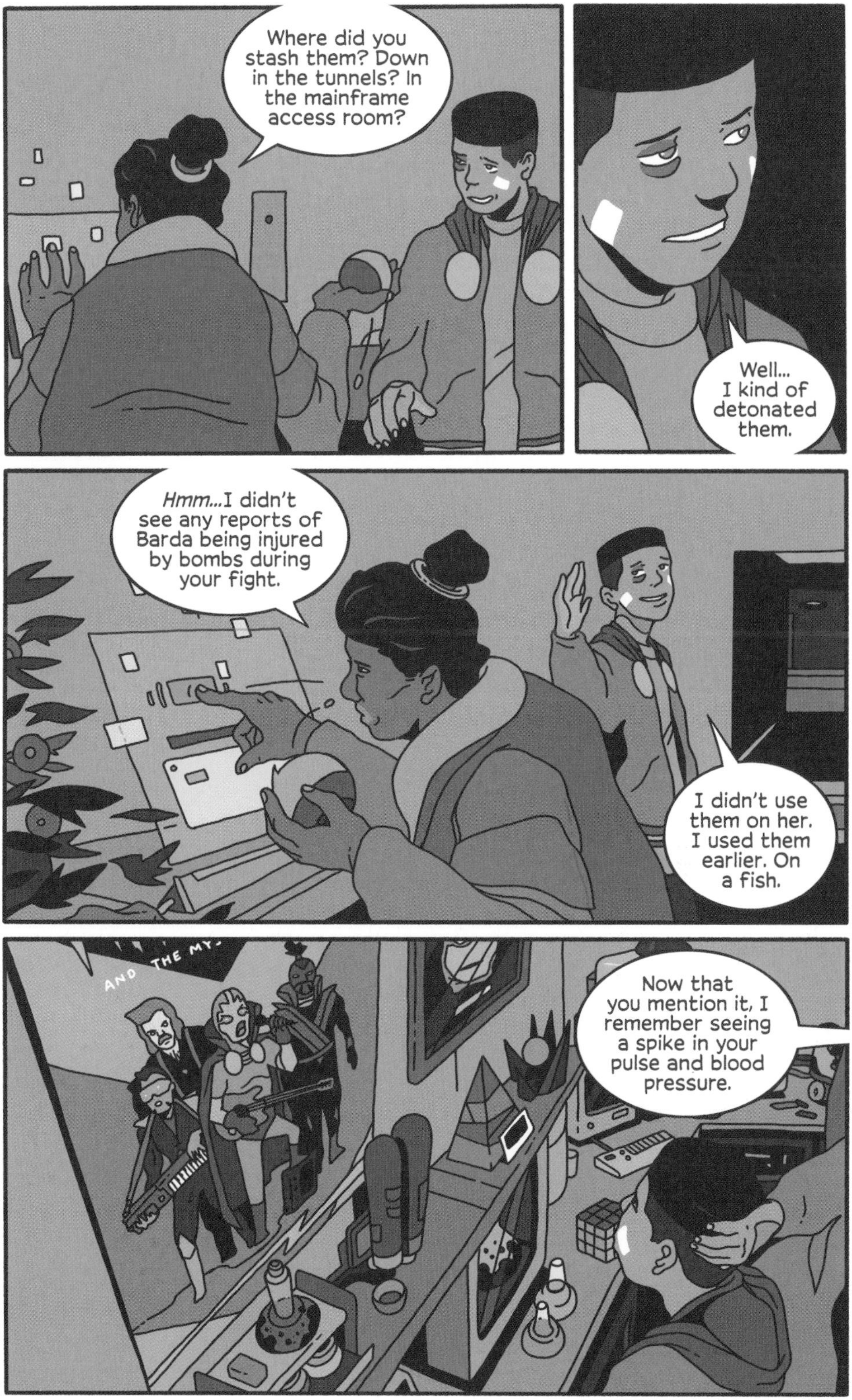
Where did you stash them? Down in the tunnels? In the mainframe access room?
Well... I kind of detonated them.
Hmm... I didn't see any reports of Barda being injured by bombs during your fight.
I didn't use them on her. I used them earlier. On a fish.
Now that you mention it, I remember seeing a spike in your pulse and blood pressure.

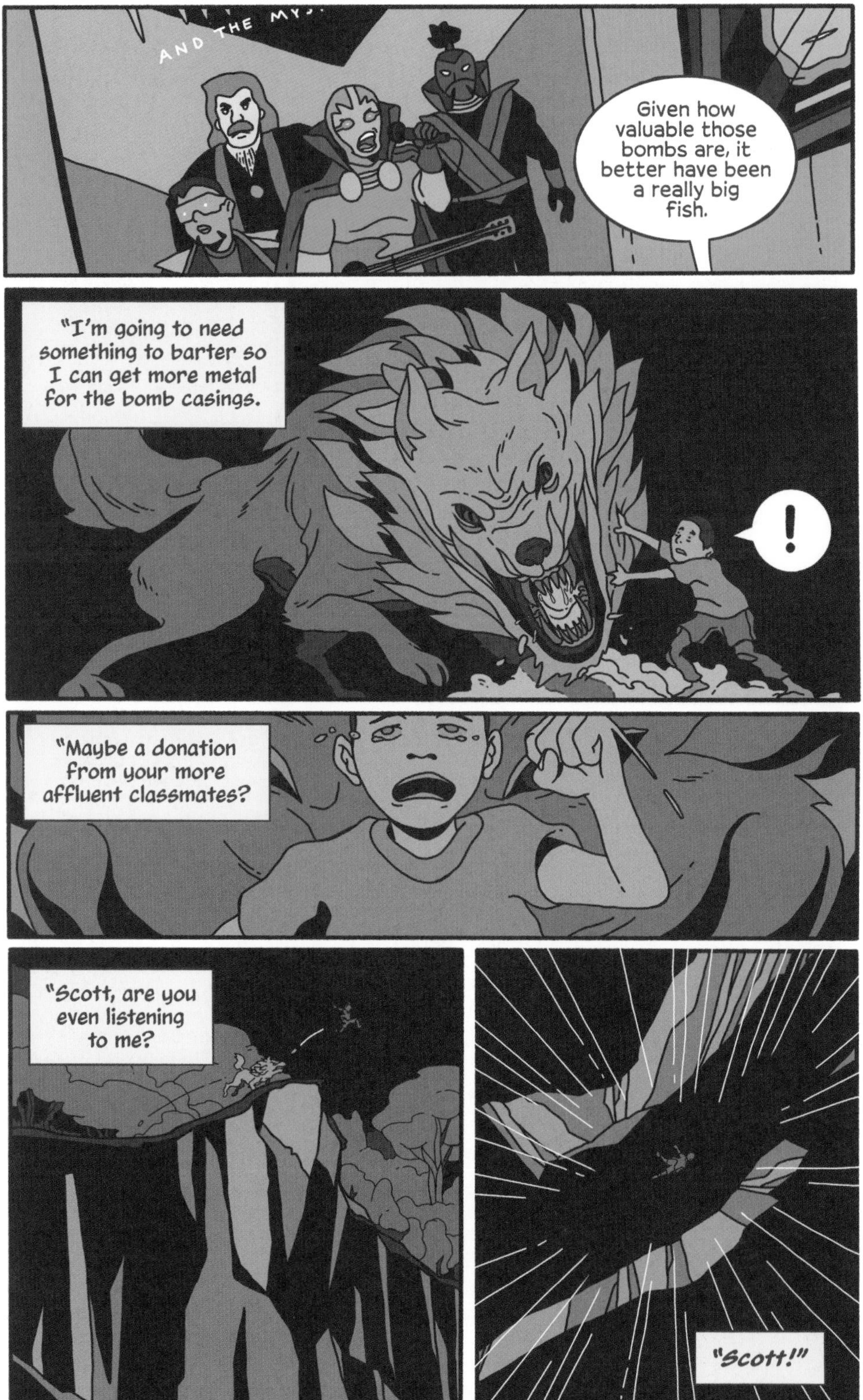
AND THE MYS
Given how valuable those bombs are, it better have been a really big fish.
"I'm going to need something to barter so I can get more metal for the bomb casings.
!
"Maybe a donation from your more affluent classmates?
"Scott, are you even listening to me?
"Scott!"

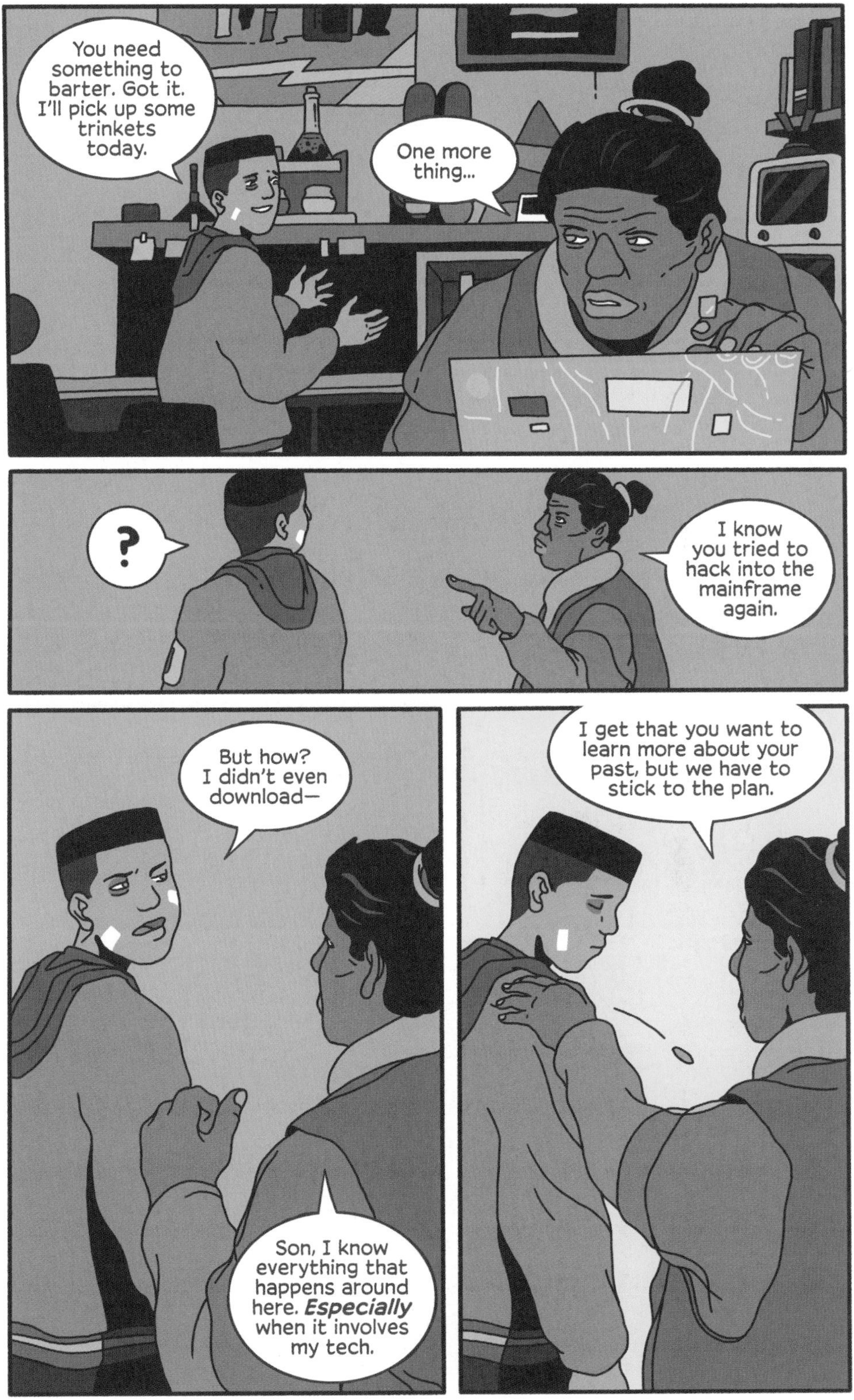
You need something to barter. Got it. I'll pick up some trinkets today.
One more thing...
?
I know you tried to hack into the mainframe again.
But how? I didn't even download—
Son, I know everything that happens around here. *Especially* when it involves my tech.
I get that you want to learn more about your past, but we have to stick to the plan.

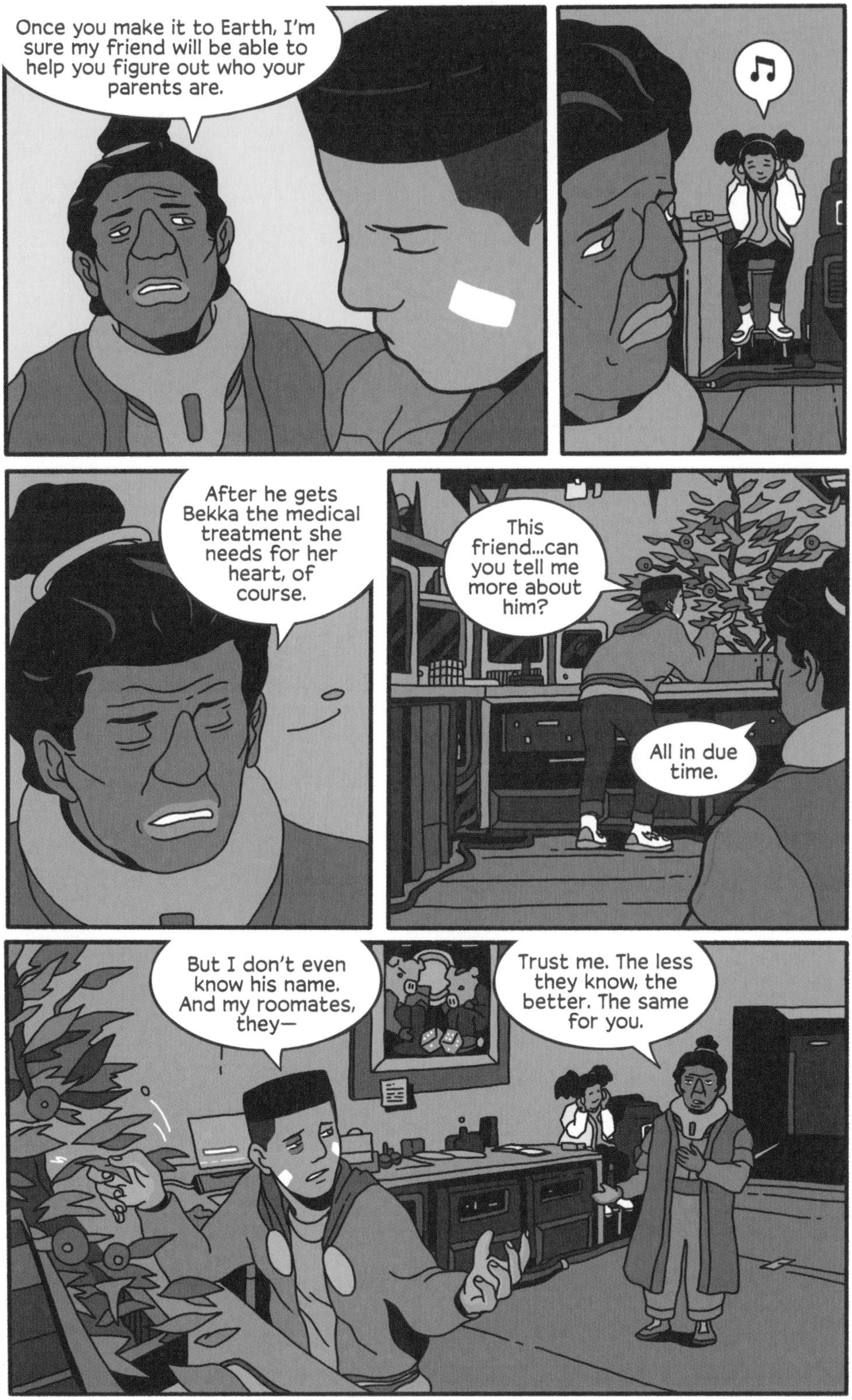
Once you make it to Earth, I'm sure my friend will be able to help you figure out who your parents are.
♫
After he gets Bekka the medical treatment she needs for her heart, of course.
This friend...can you tell me more about him?
All in due time.
But I don't even know his name. And my roomates, they—
Trust me. The less they know, the better. The same for you.

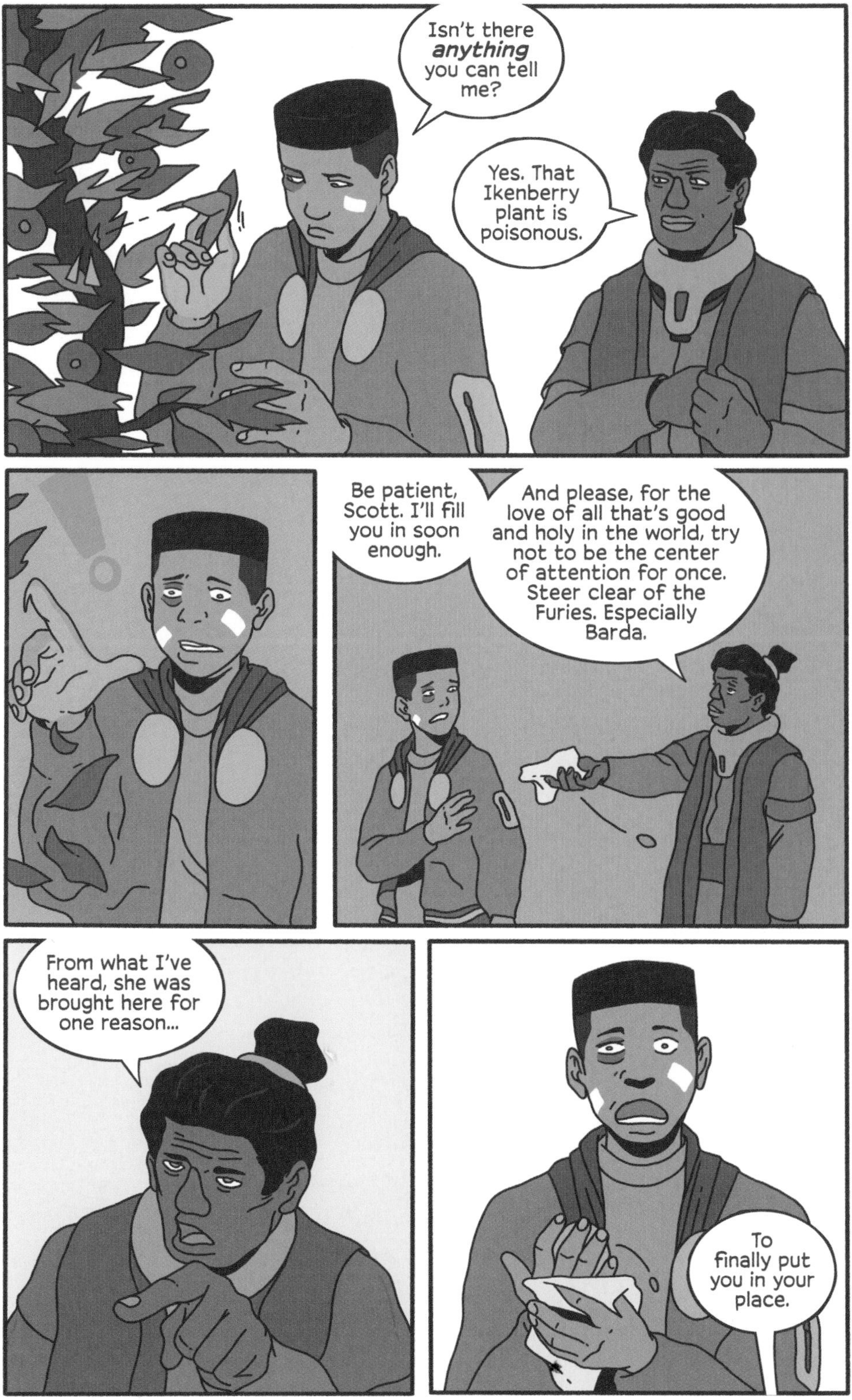
Isn't there *anything* you can tell me?
Yes. That Ikenberry plant is poisonous.
Be patient, Scott. I'll fill you in soon enough.
And please, for the love of all that's good and holy in the world, try not to be the center of attention for once. Steer clear of the Furies. Especially Barda.
From what I've heard, she was brought here for one reason...
To finally put you in your place.

CHAPTER TWO

Stubborn Kind of Fella

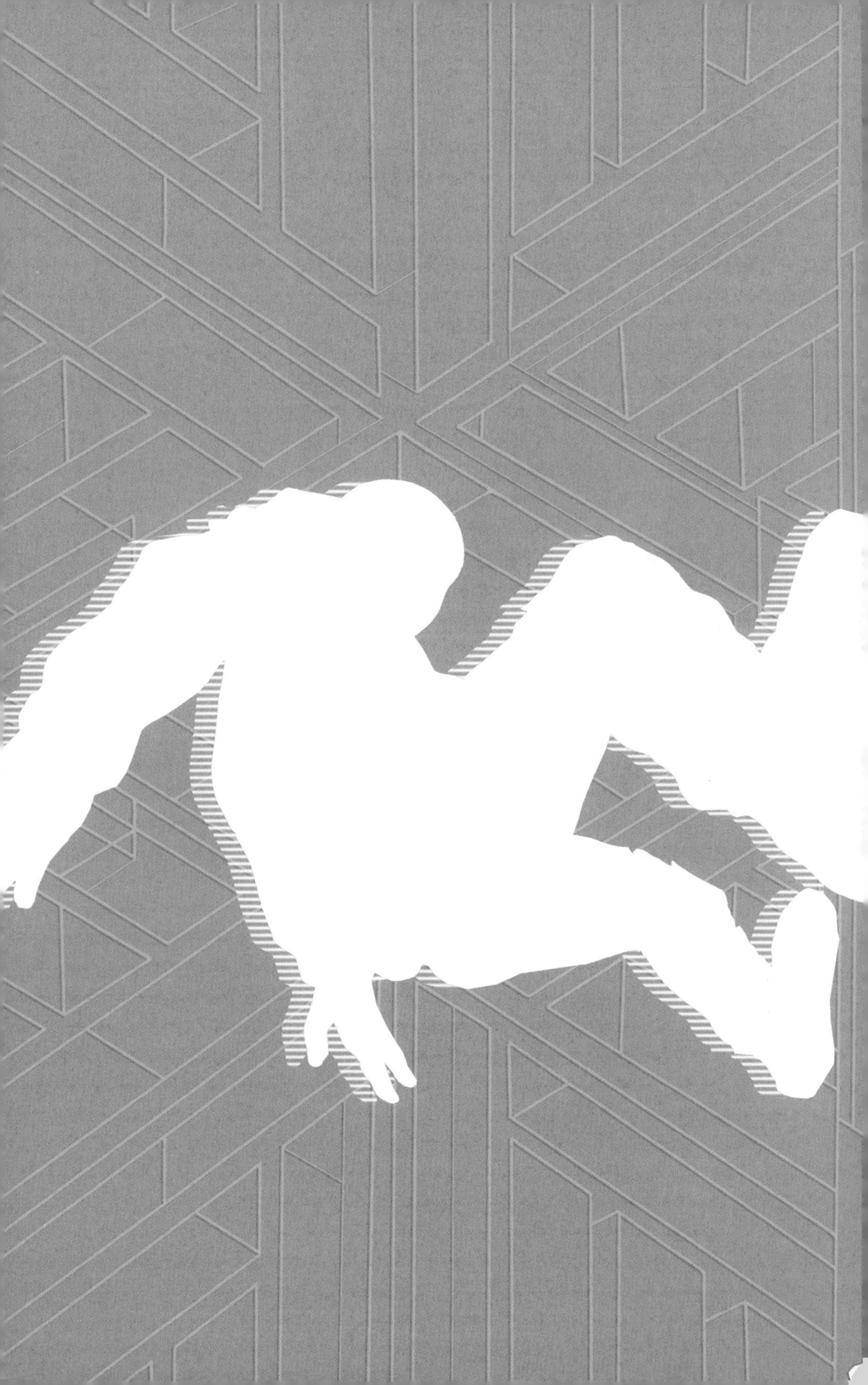

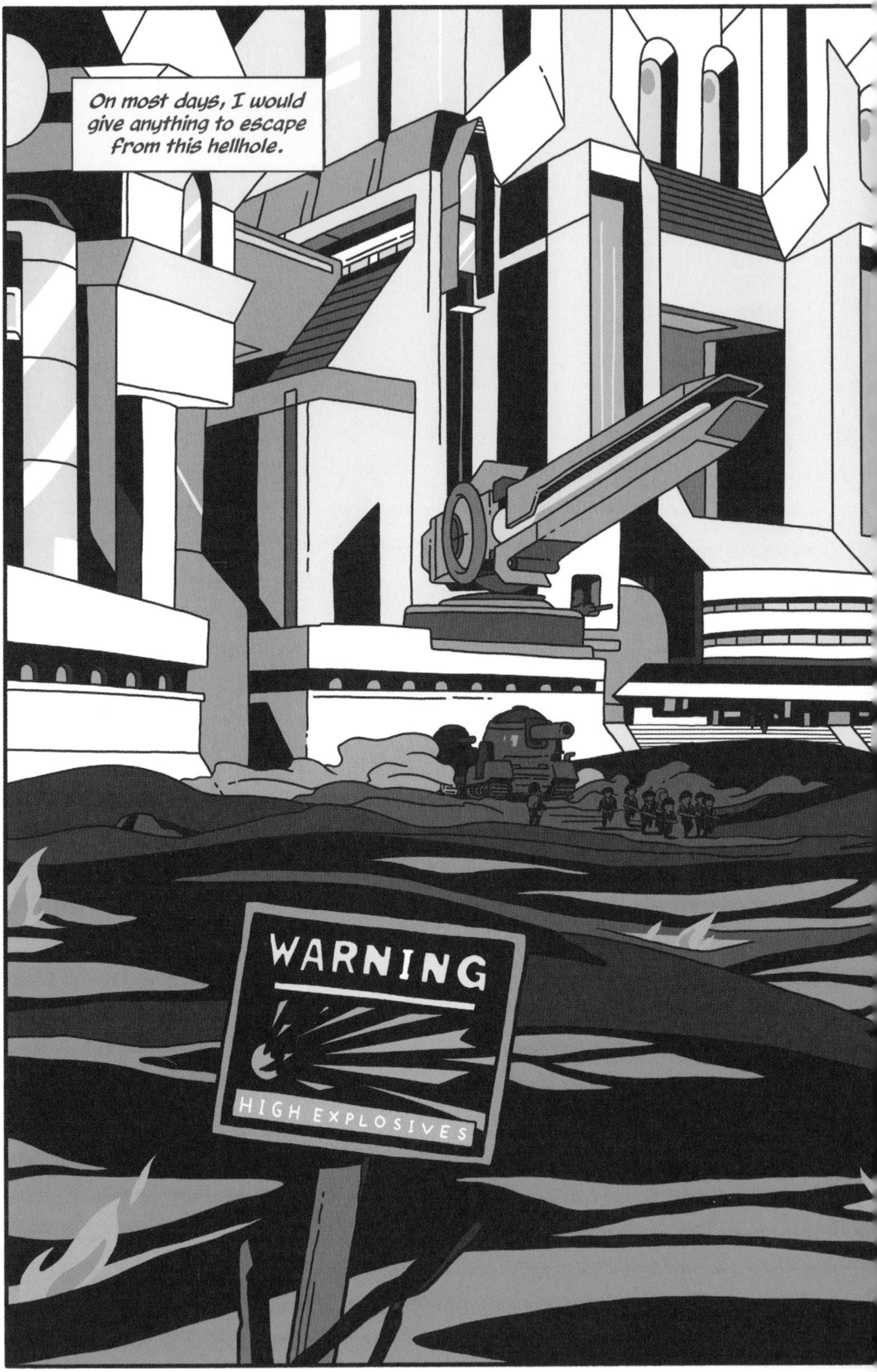
On most days, I would give anything to escape from this hellhole.
WARNING
HIGH EXPLOSIVES

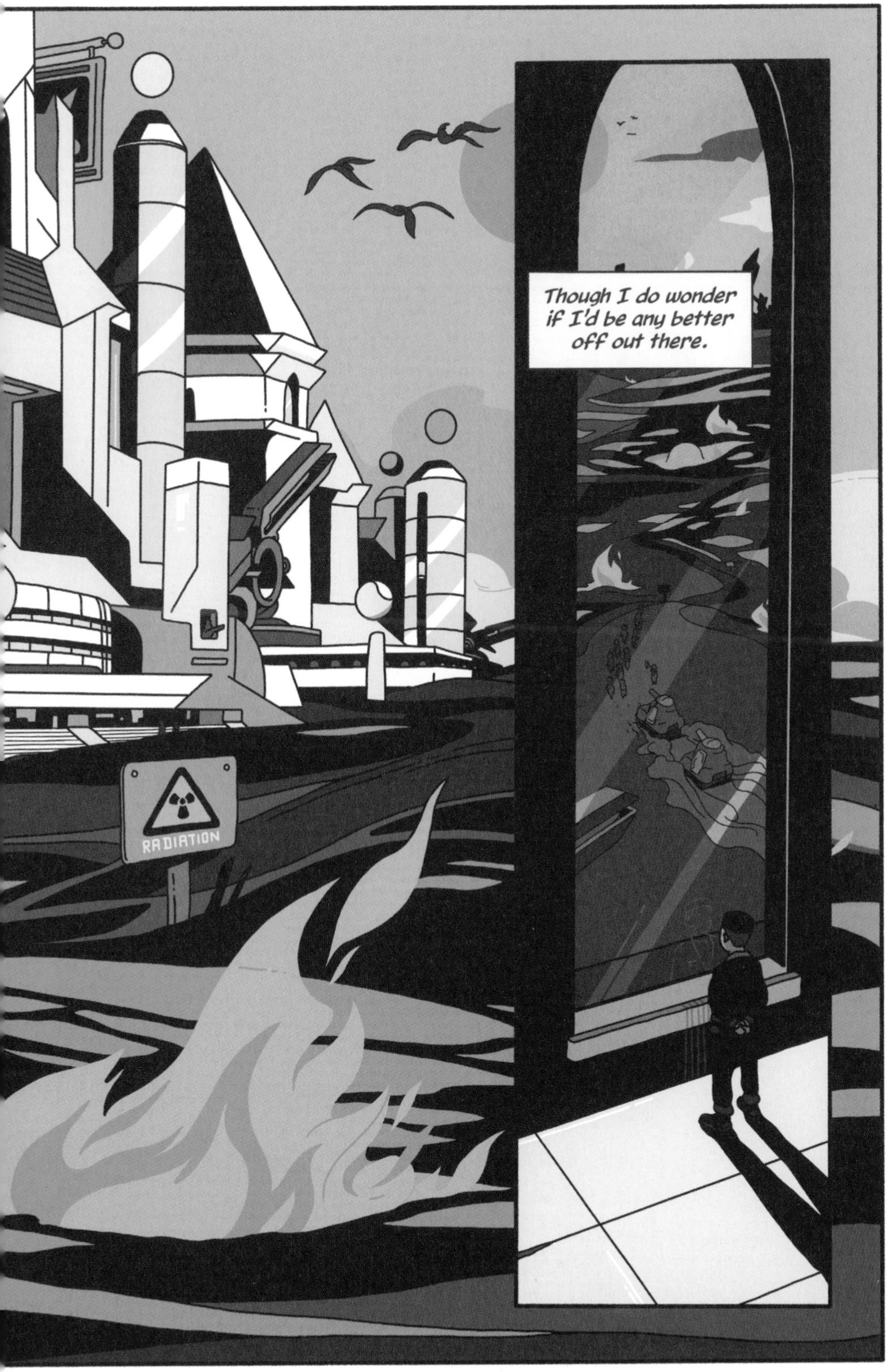
Though I do wonder if I'd be any better off out there.
RADIATION

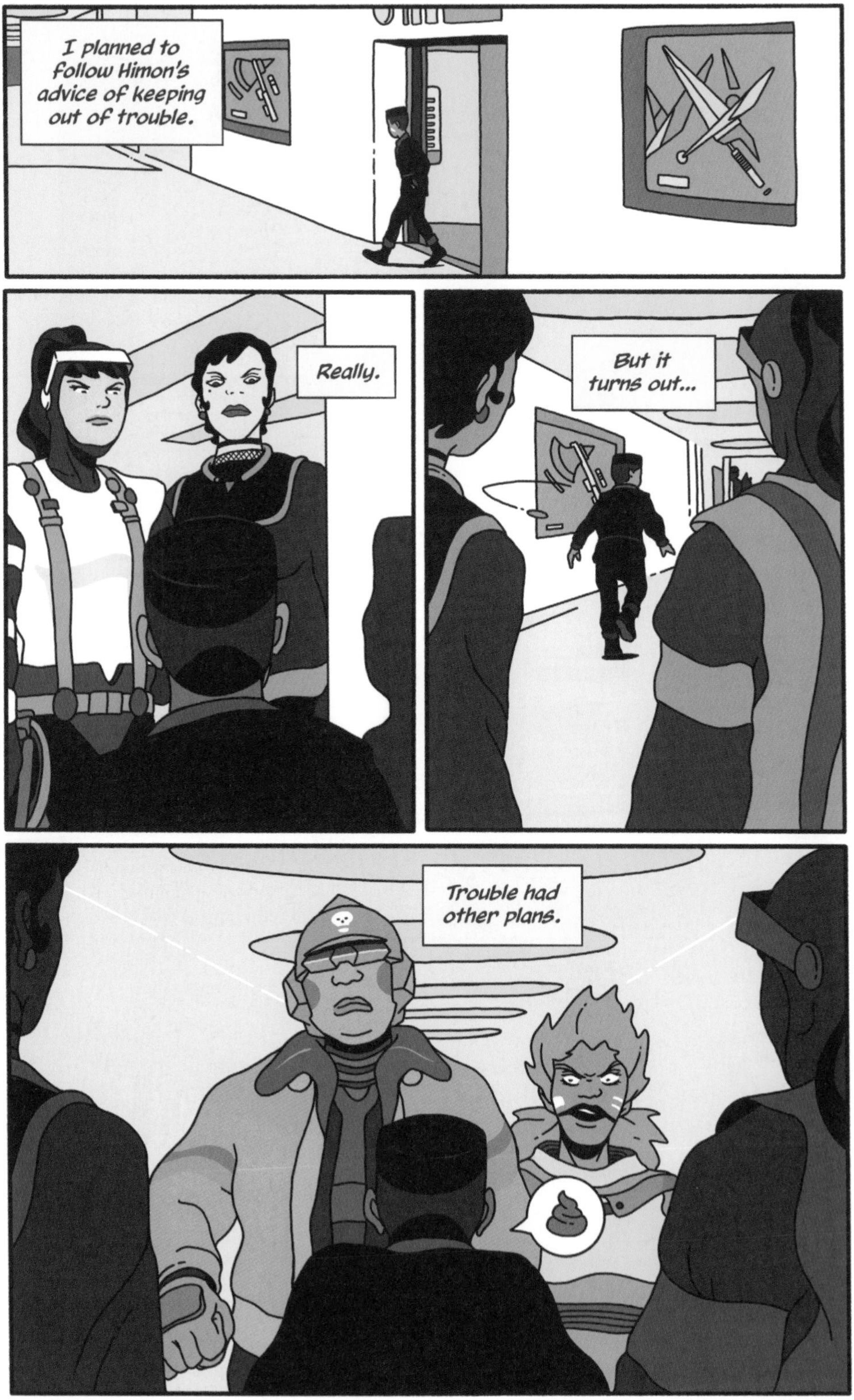
I planned to follow Himon's advice of keeping out of trouble.
Really.
But it turns out...
Trouble had other plans.

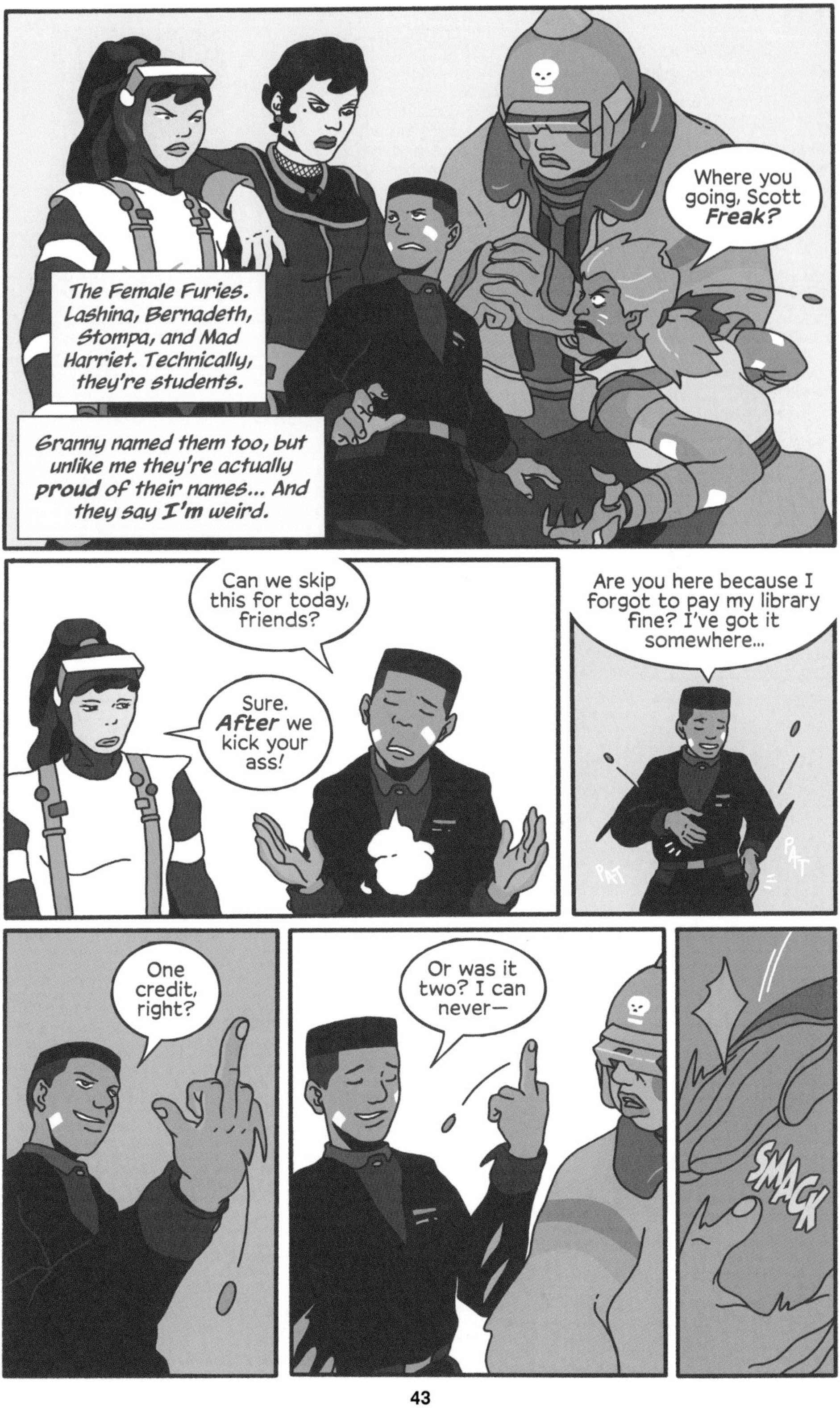
The Female Furies. Lashina, Bernadeth, Stompa, and Mad Harriet. Technically, they're students.
Granny named them too, but unlike me they're actually **proud** of their names... And they say **I'm** weird.
Where you going, Scott **Freak?**
Can we skip this for today, friends?
Sure. **After** we kick your ass!
Are you here because I forgot to pay my library fine? I've got it somewhere...
PAT
PAT
One credit, right?
Or was it two? I can never—
SMACK

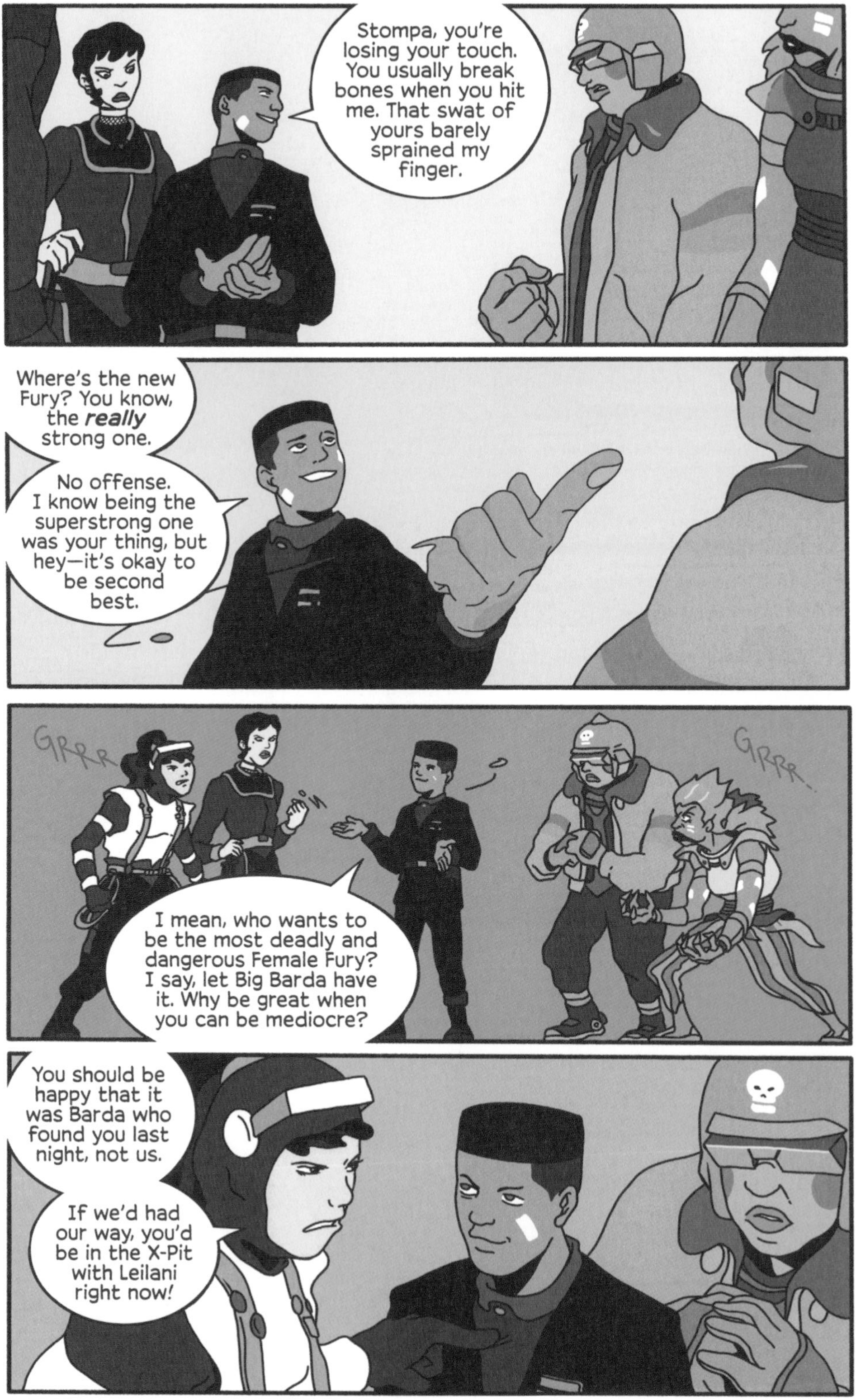
Stompa, you're losing your touch. You usually break bones when you hit me. That swat of yours barely sprained my finger.
Where's the new Fury? You know, the ***really*** strong one.
No offense. I know being the superstrong one was your thing, but hey—it's okay to be second best.
GRRR
GRRR
I mean, who wants to be the most deadly and dangerous Female Fury? I say, let Big Barda have it. Why be great when you can be mediocre?
You should be happy that it was Barda who found you last night, not us.
If we'd had our way, you'd be in the X-Pit with Leilani right now!

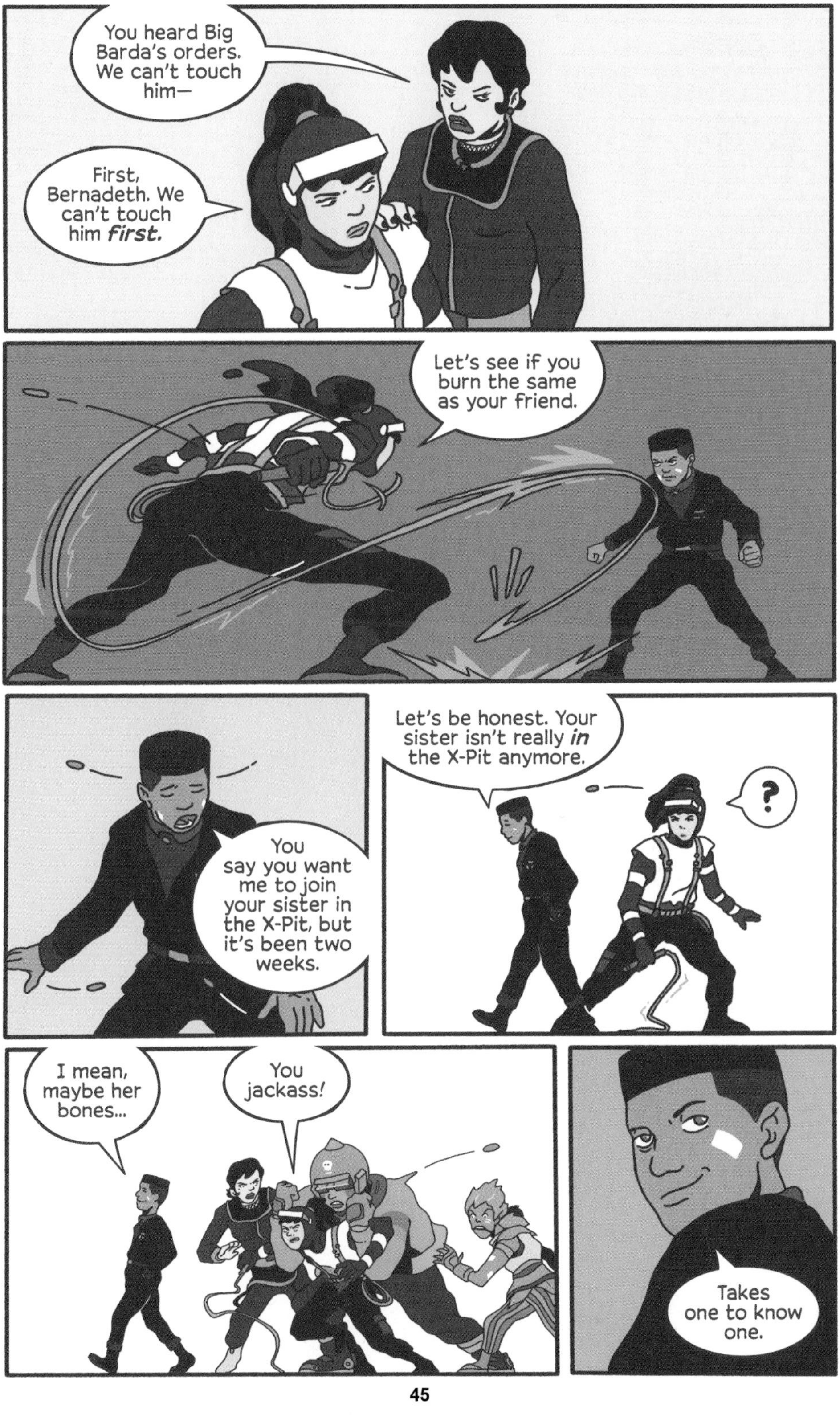
You heard Big Barda's orders. We can't touch him—
First, Bernadeth. We can't touch him *first.*
Let's see if you burn the same as your friend.
You say you want me to join your sister in the X-Pit, but it's been two weeks.
Let's be honest. Your sister isn't really *in* the X-Pit anymore.
?
I mean, maybe her bones...
You jackass!
Takes one to know one.

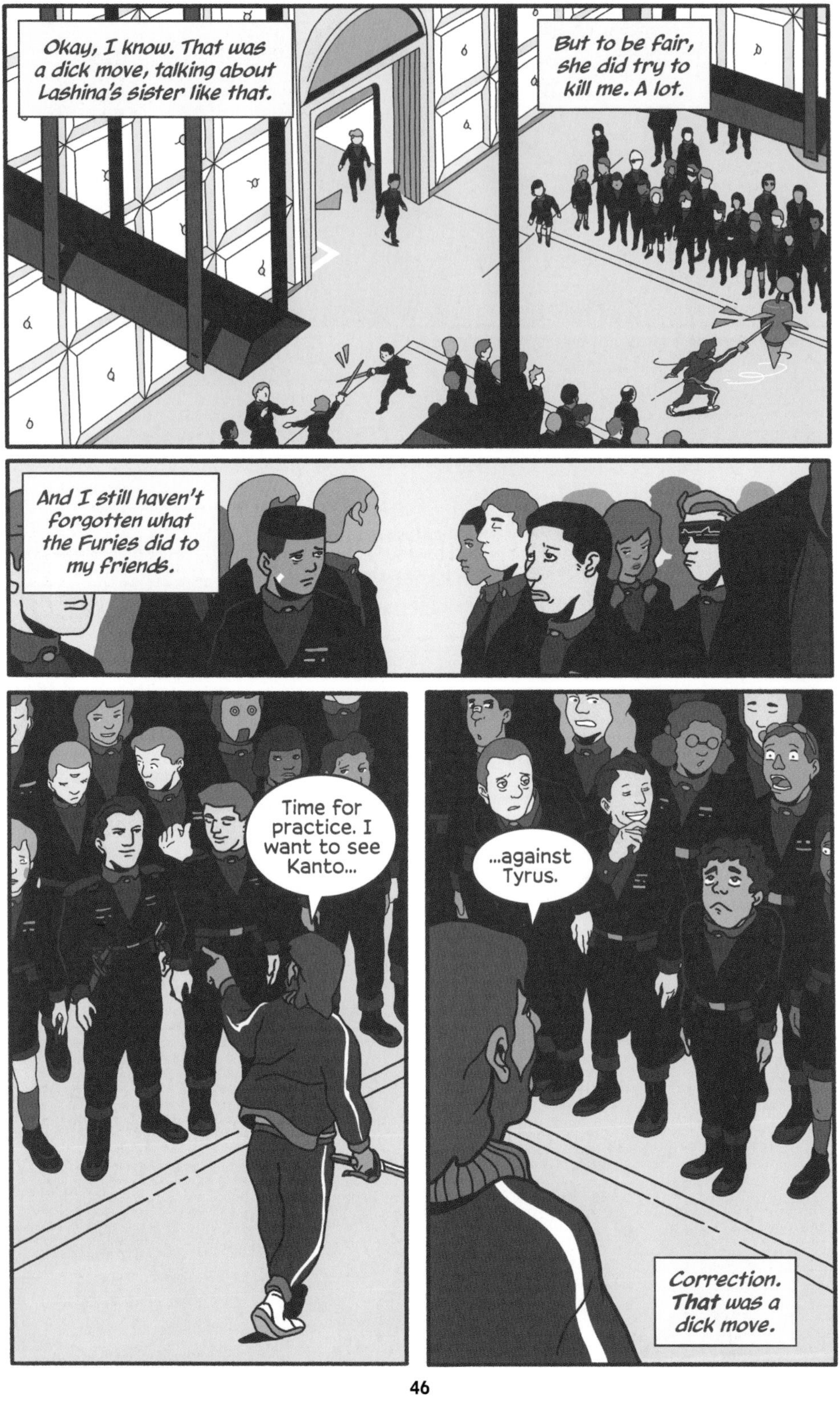
Okay, I know. That was a dick move, talking about Lashina's sister like that.
But to be fair, she did try to kill me. A lot.
And I still haven't forgotten what the Furies did to my friends.
Time for practice. I want to see Kanto...
...against Tyrus.
Correction. That was a dick move.

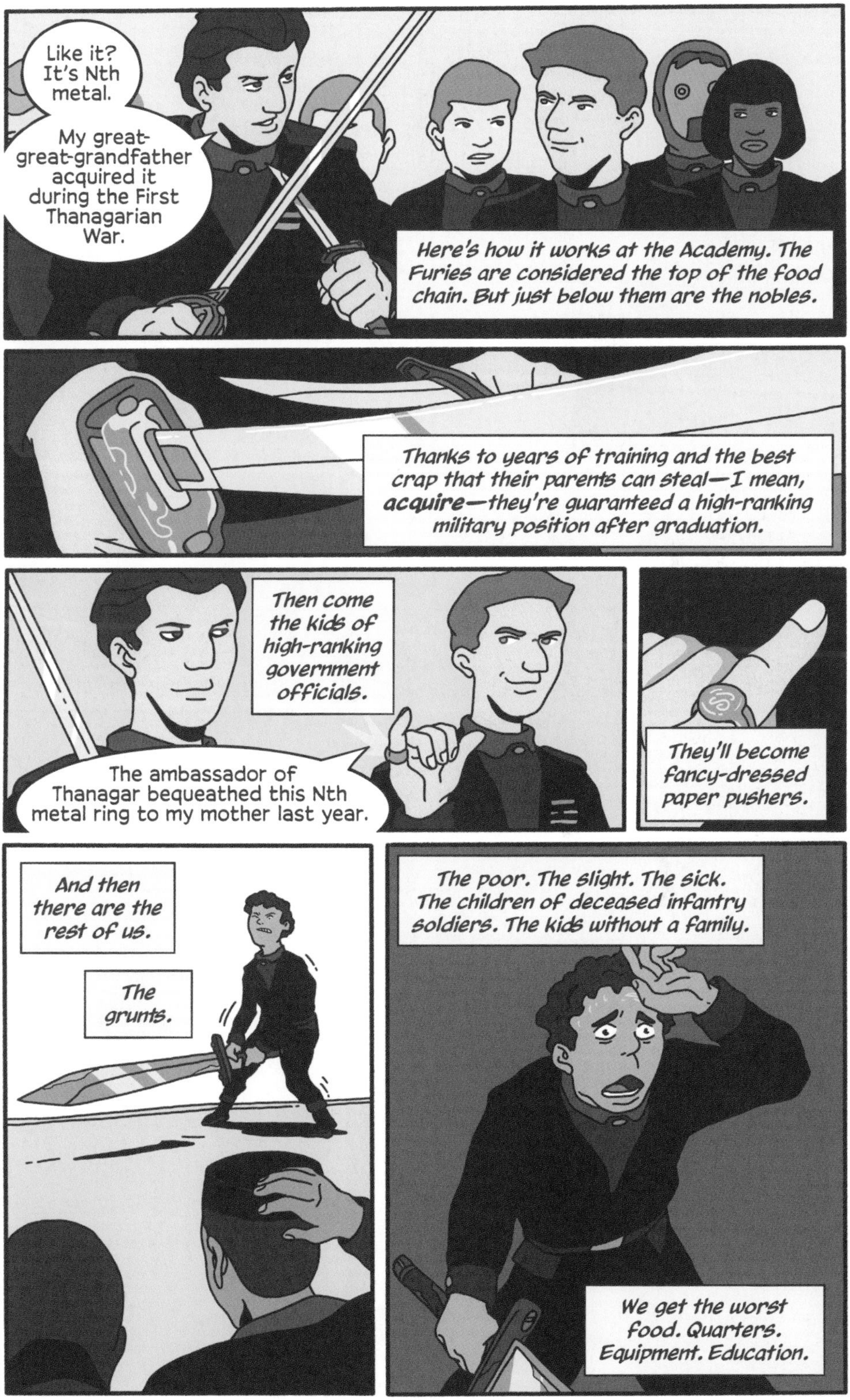
Like it? It's Nth metal.
My great-great-grandfather acquired it during the First Thanagarian War.
Here's how it works at the Academy. The Furies are considered the top of the food chain. But just below them are the nobles.
Thanks to years of training and the best crap that their parents can steal—I mean, acquire—they're guaranteed a high-ranking military position after graduation.
Then come the kids of high-ranking government officials.
The ambassador of Thanagar bequeathed this Nth metal ring to my mother last year.
They'll become fancy-dressed paper pushers.
And then there are the rest of us.
The grunts.
The poor. The slight. The sick. The children of deceased infantry soldiers. The kids without a family.
We get the worst food. Quarters. Equipment. Education.

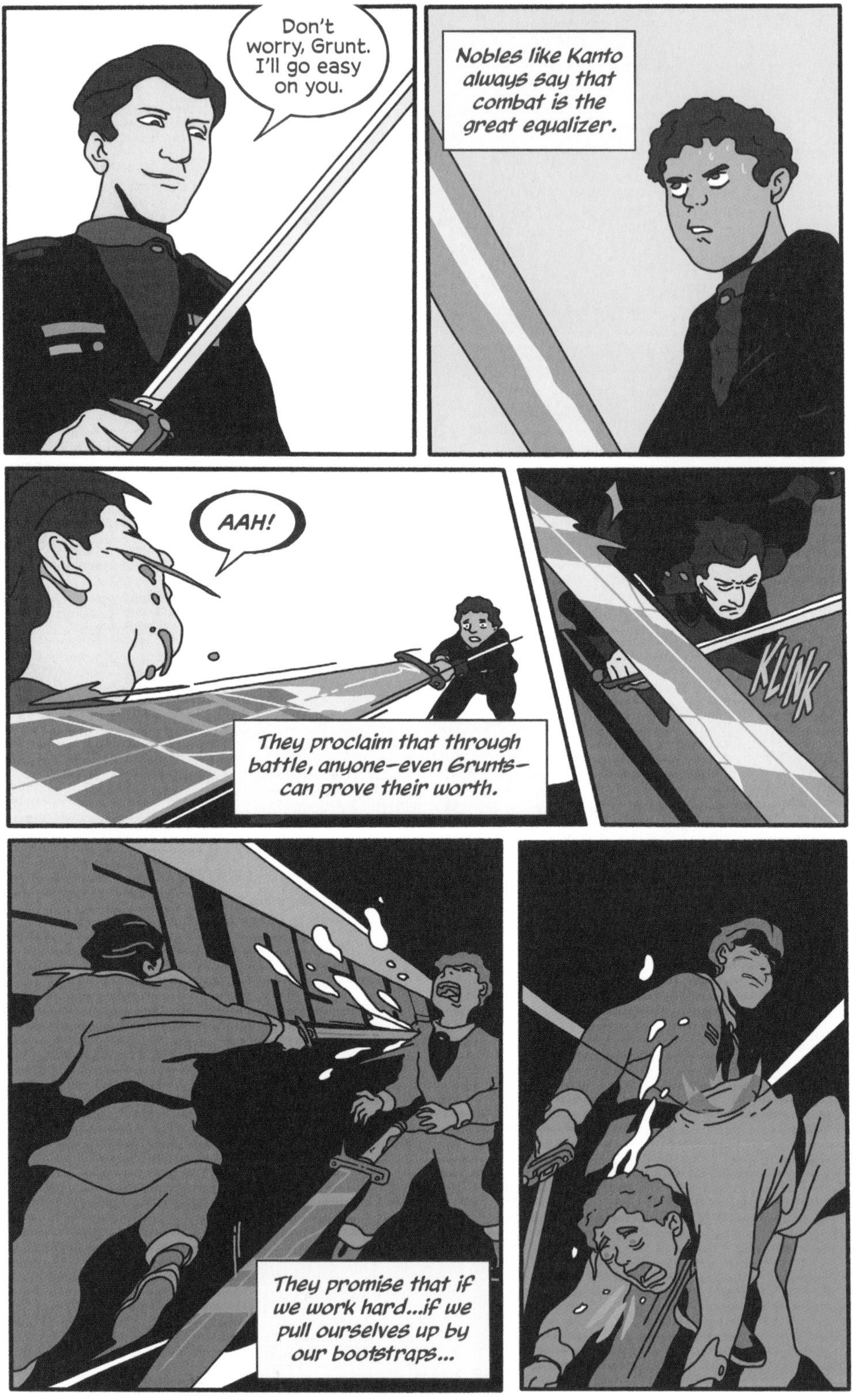
Don't worry, Grunt. I'll go easy on you.
Nobles like Kanto always say that combat is the great equalizer.
AAH!
They proclaim that through battle, anyone—even Grunts—can prove their worth.
KLINK
They promise that if we work hard...if we pull ourselves up by our bootstraps...

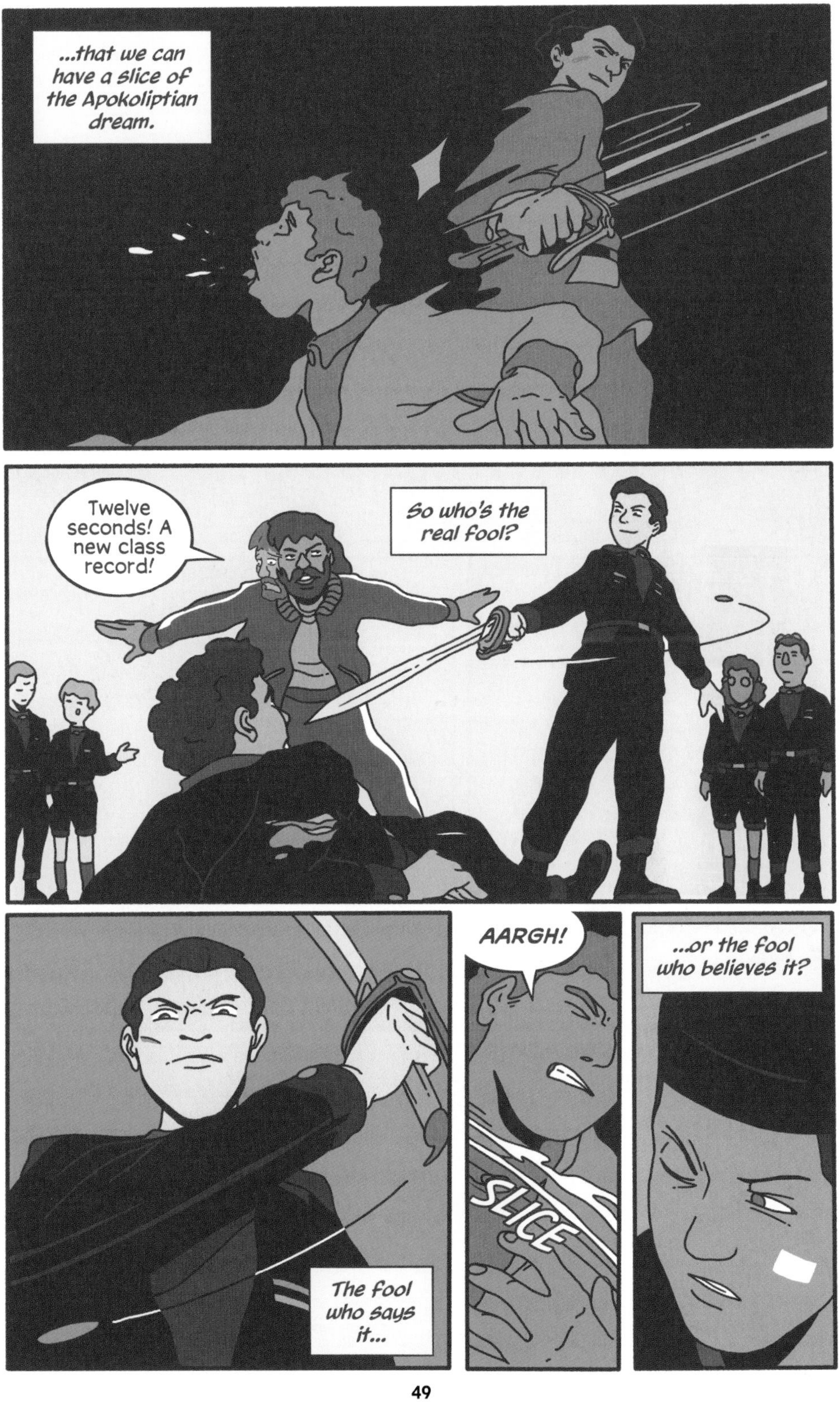
...that we can have a slice of the Apokoliptian dream.
Twelve seconds! A new class record!
So who's the real fool?
The fool who says it...
AARGH!
SLICE
...or the fool who believes it?

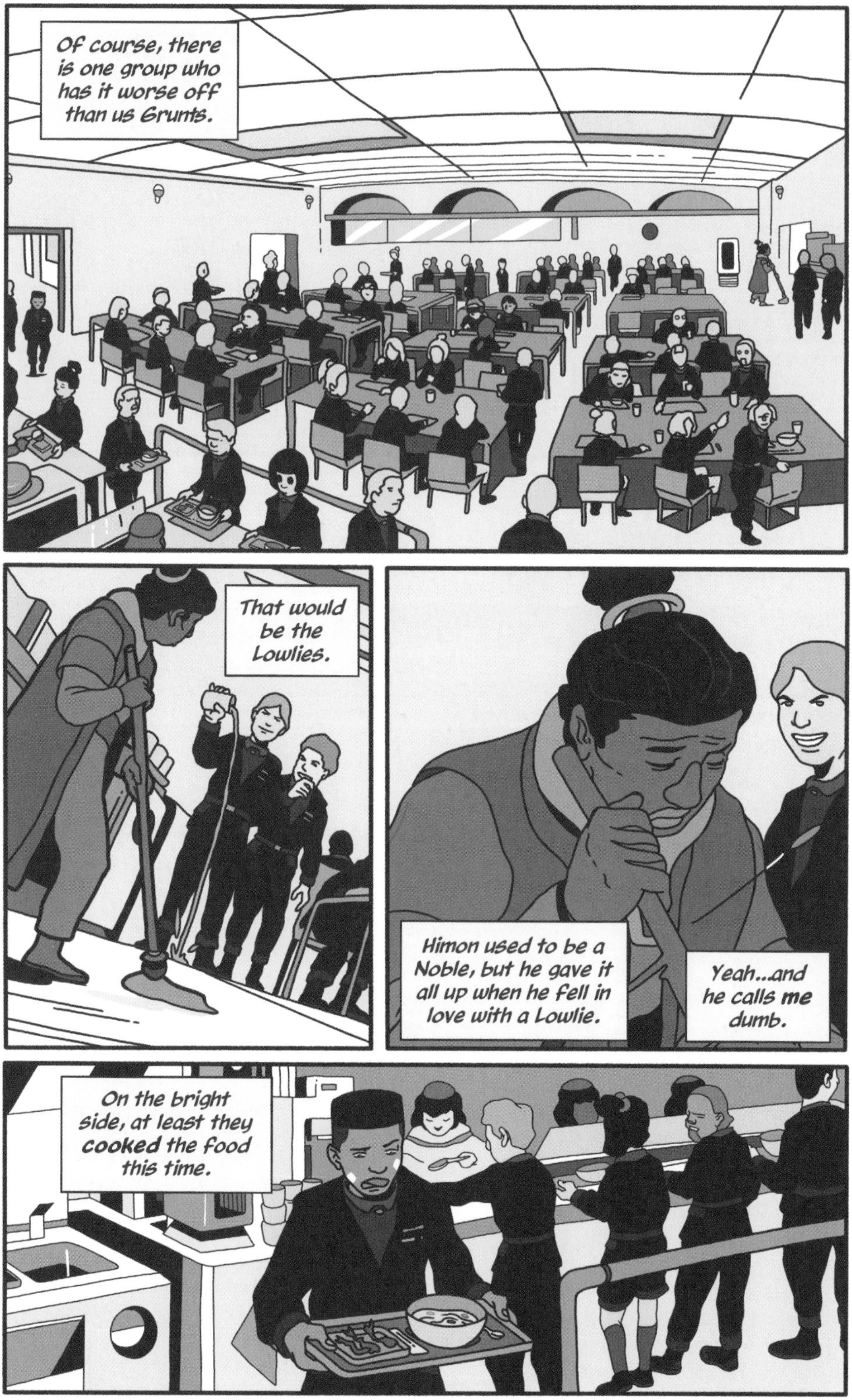
Of course, there is one group who has it worse off than us Grunts.
That would be the Lowlies.
Himon used to be a Noble, but he gave it all up when he fell in love with a Lowlie.
Yeah...and he calls **me** dumb.
On the bright side, at least they **cooked** the food this time.

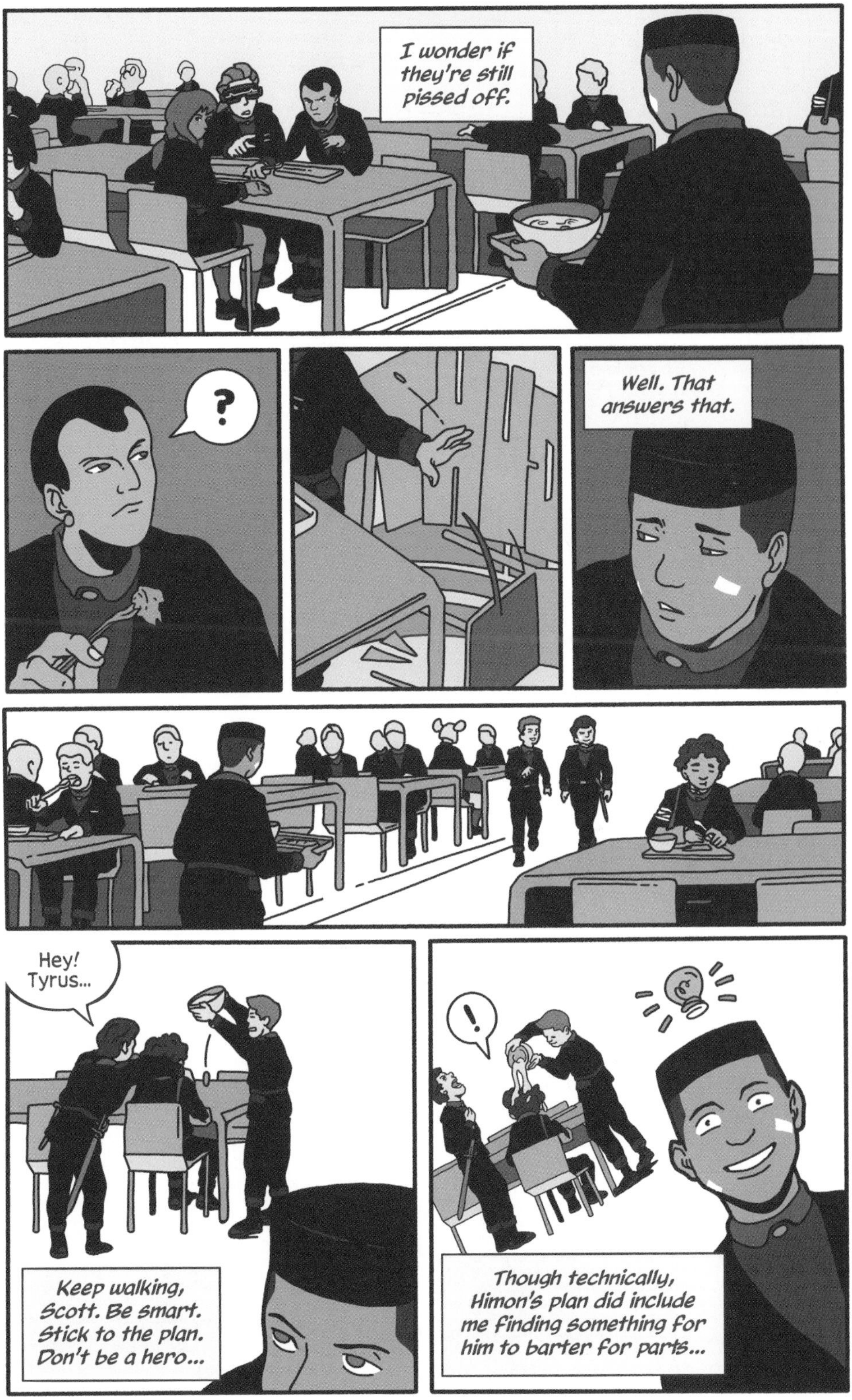
I wonder if they're still pissed off.
?
Well. That answers that.
Hey! Tyrus...
Keep walking, Scott. Be smart. Stick to the plan. Don't be a hero...
!
Though technically, Himon's plan did include me finding something for him to barter for parts...

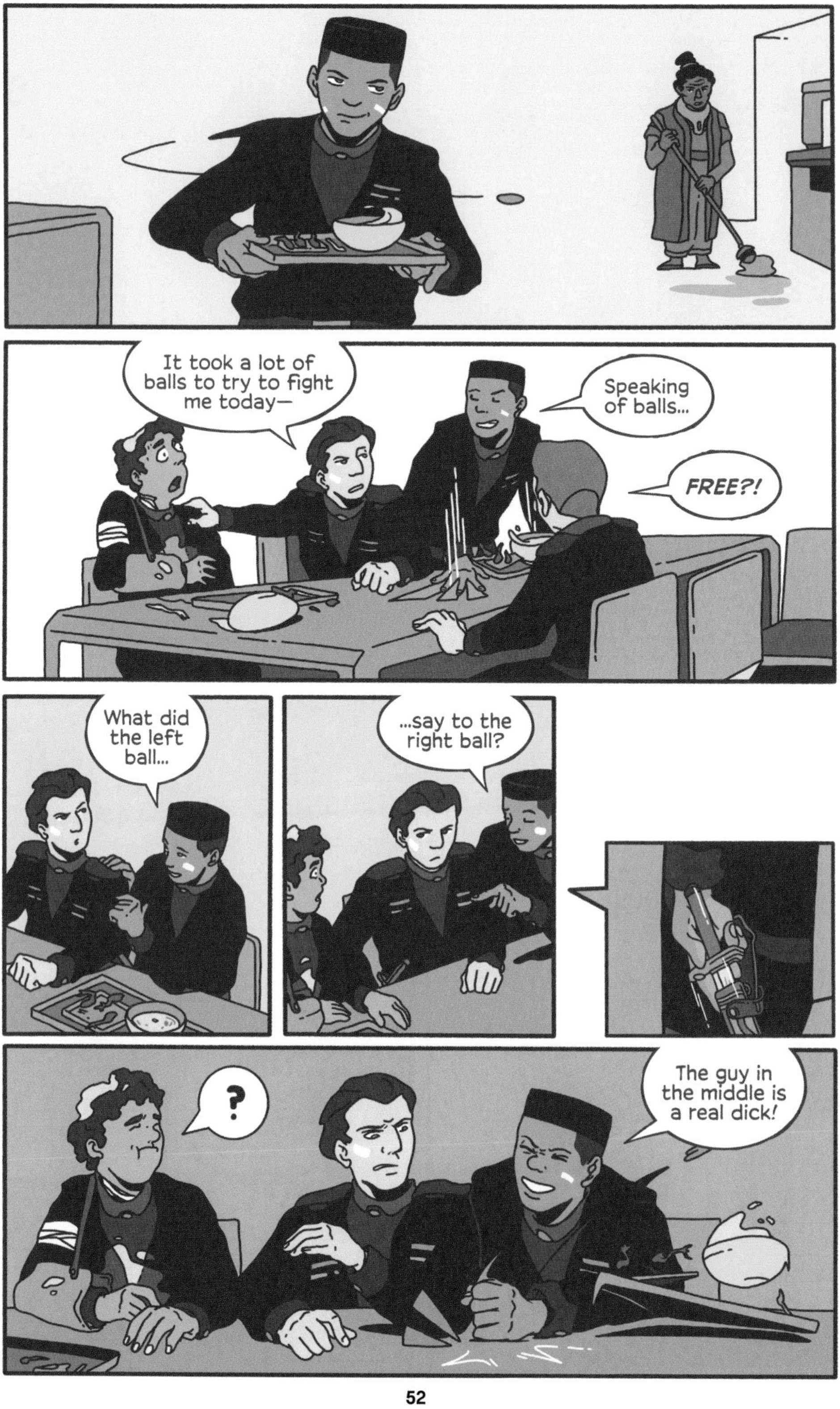
It took a lot of balls to try to fight me today—
Speaking of balls...
FREE?!
What did the left ball...
...say to the right ball?
?
The guy in the middle is a real dick!

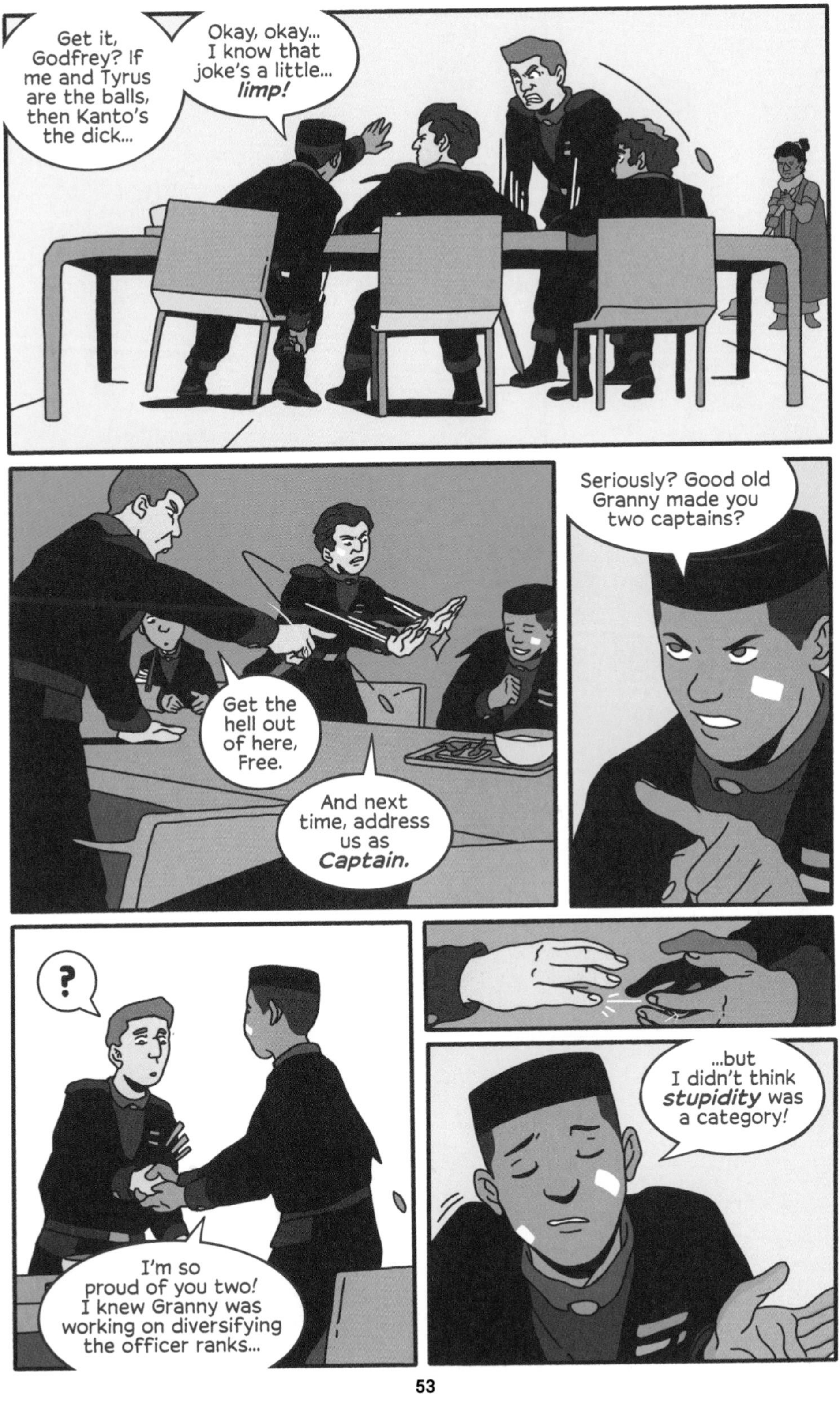
Get it, Godfrey? If me and Tyrus are the balls, then Kanto's the dick...
Okay, okay... I know that joke's a little... *limp!*
Get the hell out of here, Free.
And next time, address us as *Captain.*
Seriously? Good old Granny made you two captains?
?
I'm so proud of you two! I knew Granny was working on diversifying the officer ranks...
...but I didn't think *stupidity* was a category!

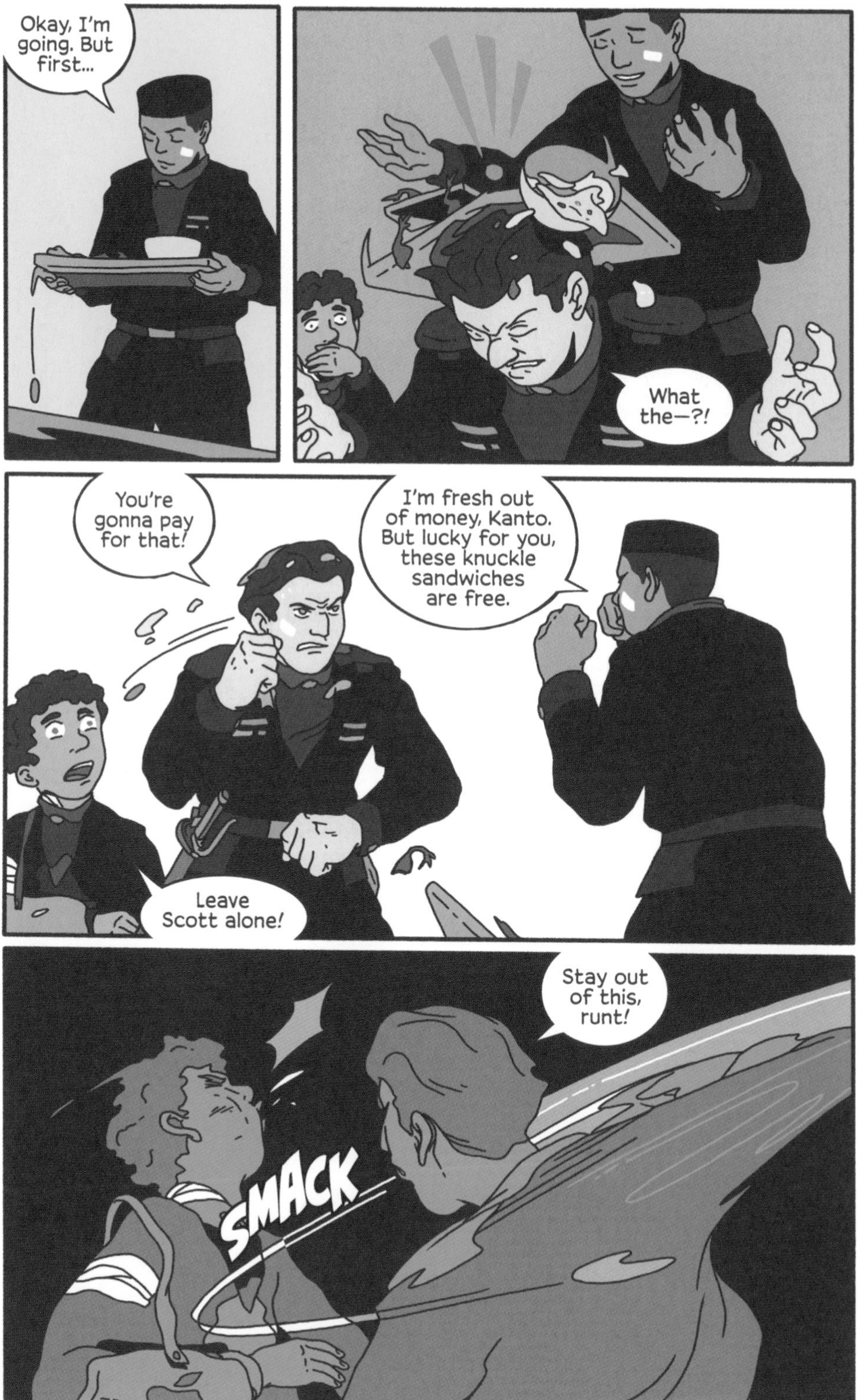
Okay, I'm going. But first...
What the—?!
You're gonna pay for that!
I'm fresh out of money, Kanto. But lucky for you, these knuckle sandwiches are free.
Leave Scott alone!
Stay out of this, runt!
SMACK

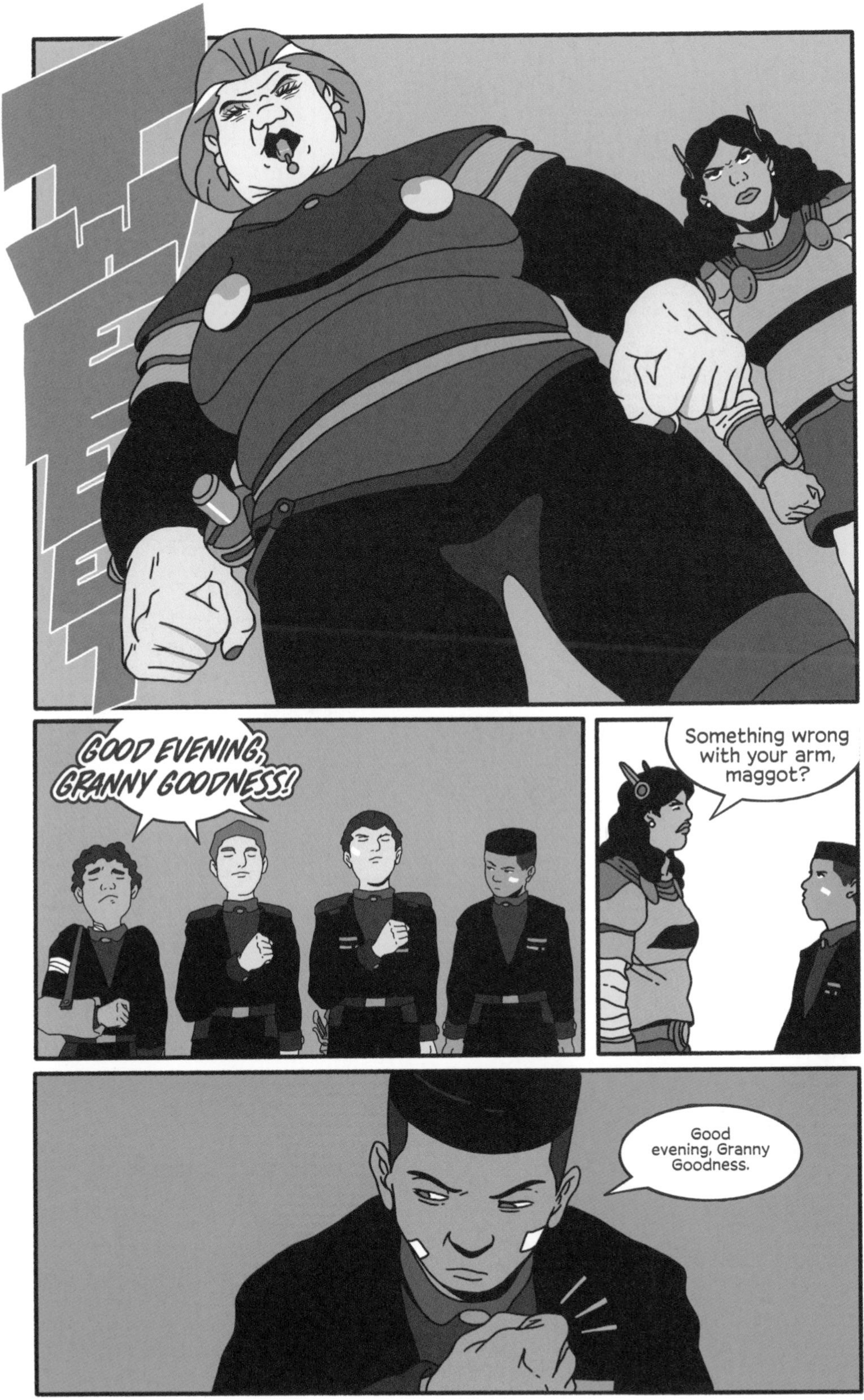
GOOD EVENING, GRANNY GOODNESS!
Something wrong with your arm, maggot?
Good evening, Granny Goodness.

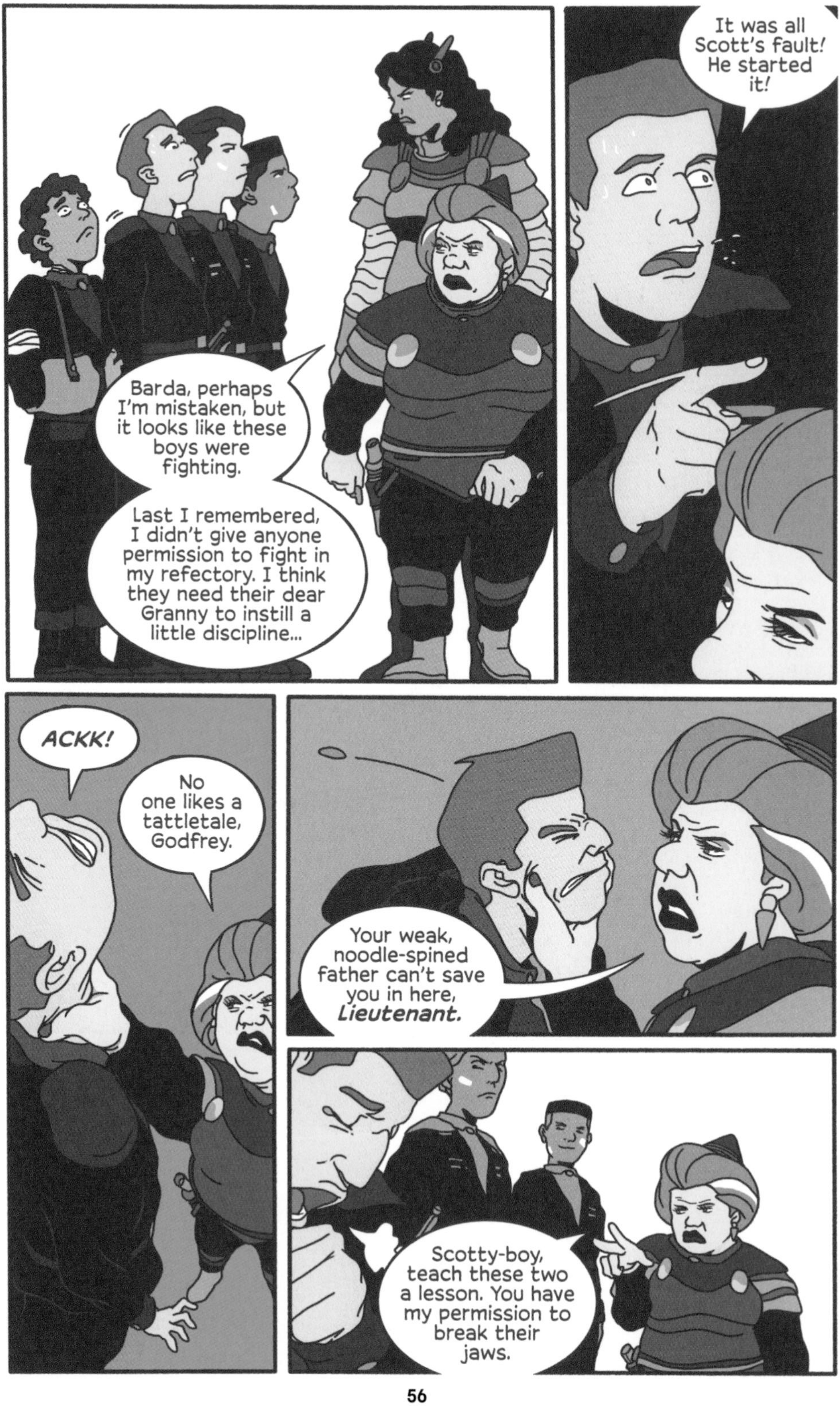

Barda, perhaps I'm mistaken, but it looks like these boys were fighting.
Last I remembered, I didn't give anyone permission to fight in my refectory. I think they need their dear Granny to instill a little discipline...
It was all Scott's fault! He started it!
ACKK!
No one likes a tattletale, Godfrey.
Your weak, noodle-spined father can't save you in here, *Lieutenant.*
Scotty-boy, teach these two a lesson. You have my permission to break their jaws.

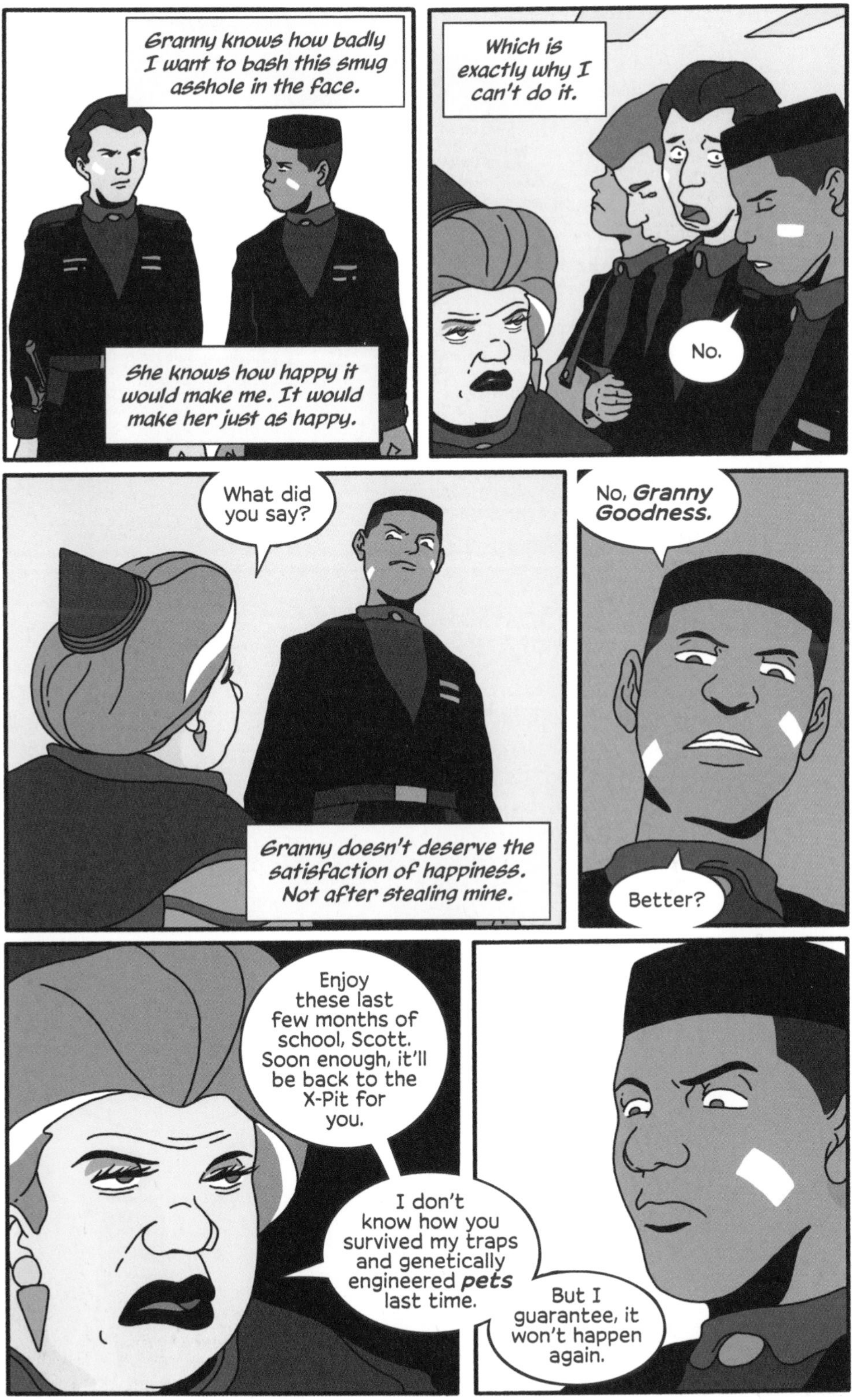
Granny knows how badly I want to bash this smug asshole in the face.
She knows how happy it would make me. It would make her just as happy.
Which is exactly why I can't do it.
No.
What did you say?
Granny doesn't deserve the satisfaction of happiness. Not after stealing mine.
No, Granny Goodness.
Better?
Enjoy these last few months of school, Scott. Soon enough, it'll be back to the X-Pit for you.
I don't know how you survived my traps and genetically engineered pets last time.
But I guarantee, it won't happen again.

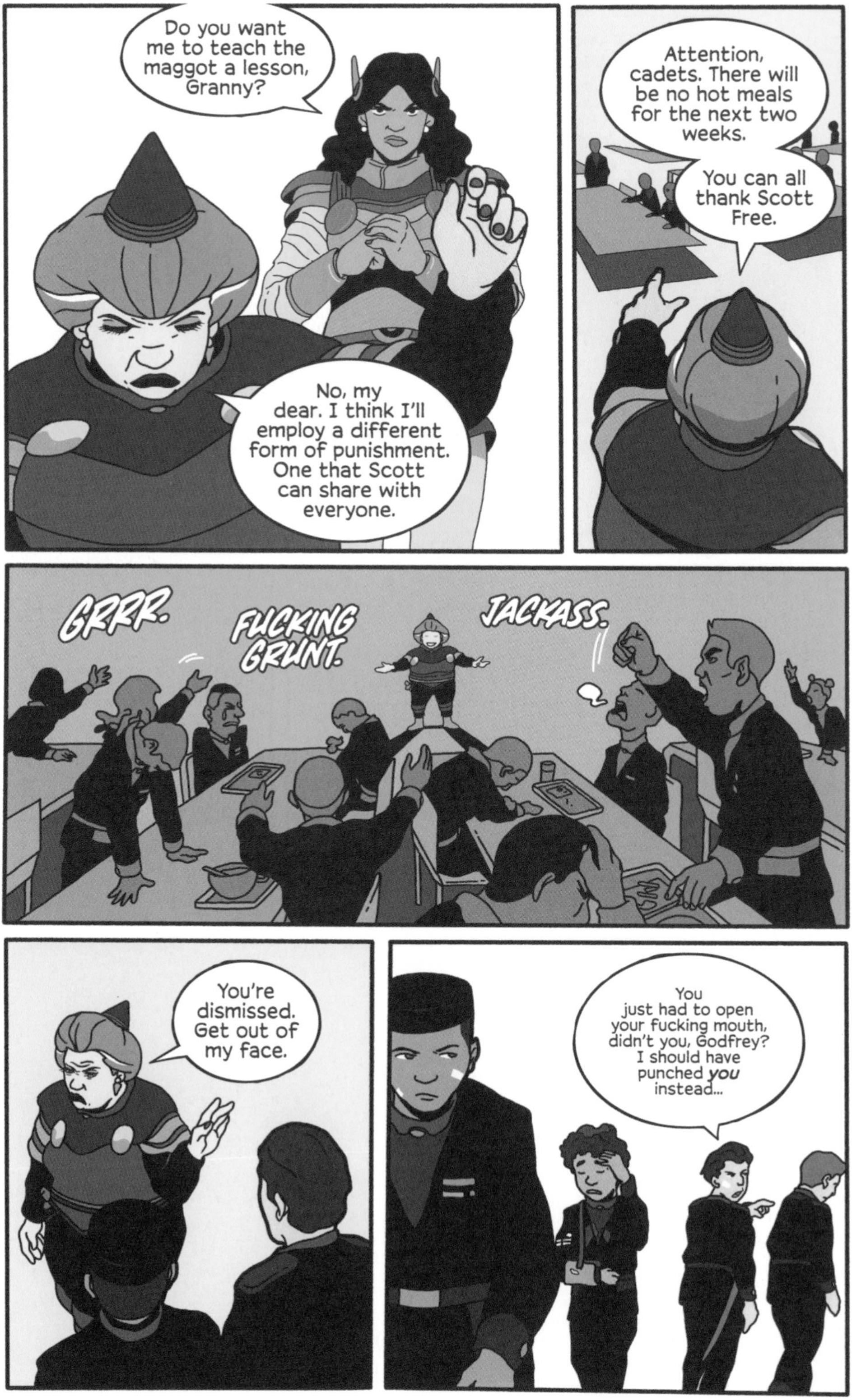

Do you want me to teach the maggot a lesson, Granny?
No, my dear. I think I'll employ a different form of punishment. One that Scott can share with everyone.
Attention, cadets. There will be no hot meals for the next two weeks.
You can all thank Scott Free.
GRRR.
FUCKING GRUNT.
JACKASS.
You're dismissed. Get out of my face.
You just had to open your fucking mouth, didn't you, Godfrey? I should have punched *you* instead...

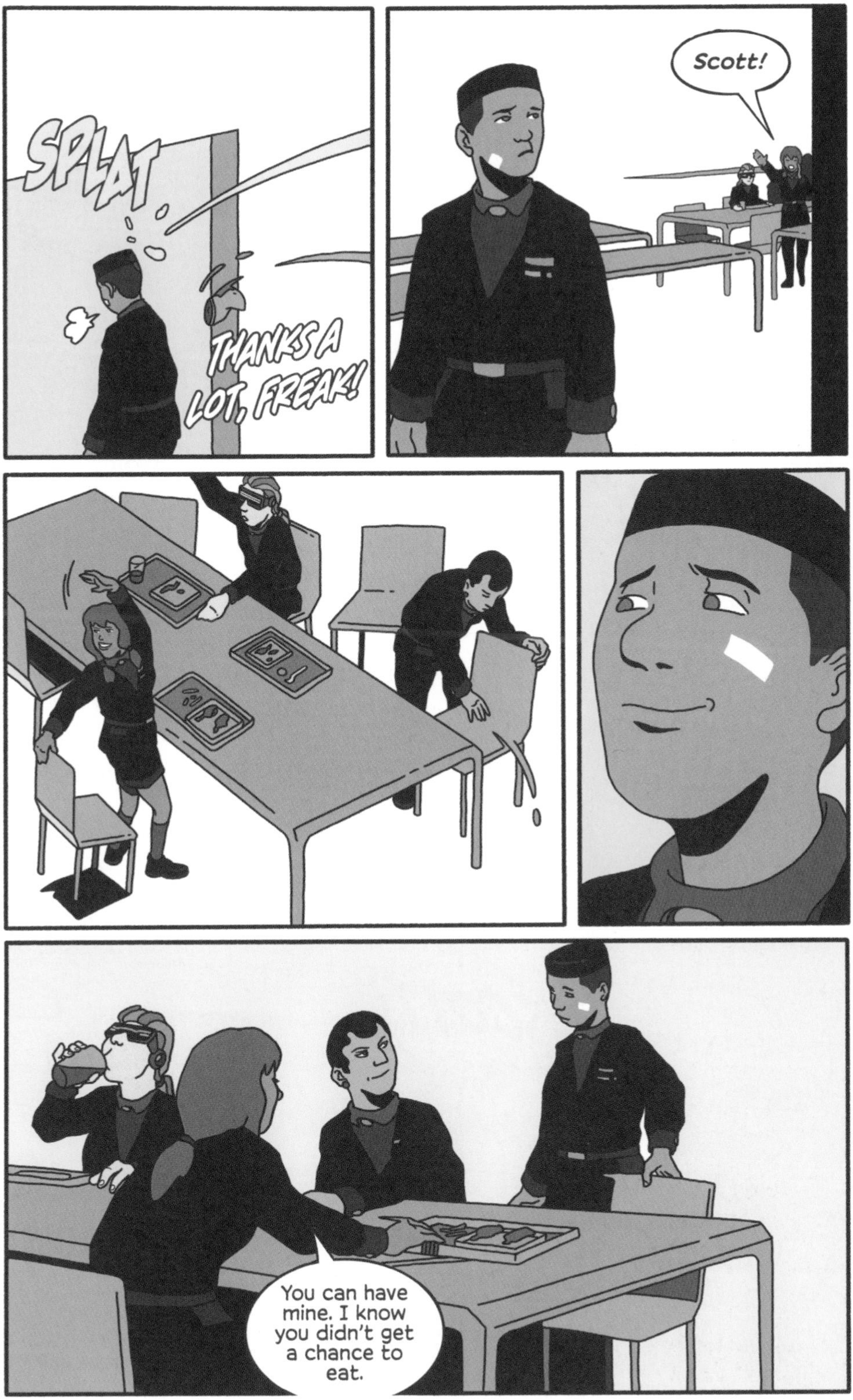
SPLAT
THANKS A LOT, FREAK!
Scott!
You can have mine. I know you didn't get a chance to eat.

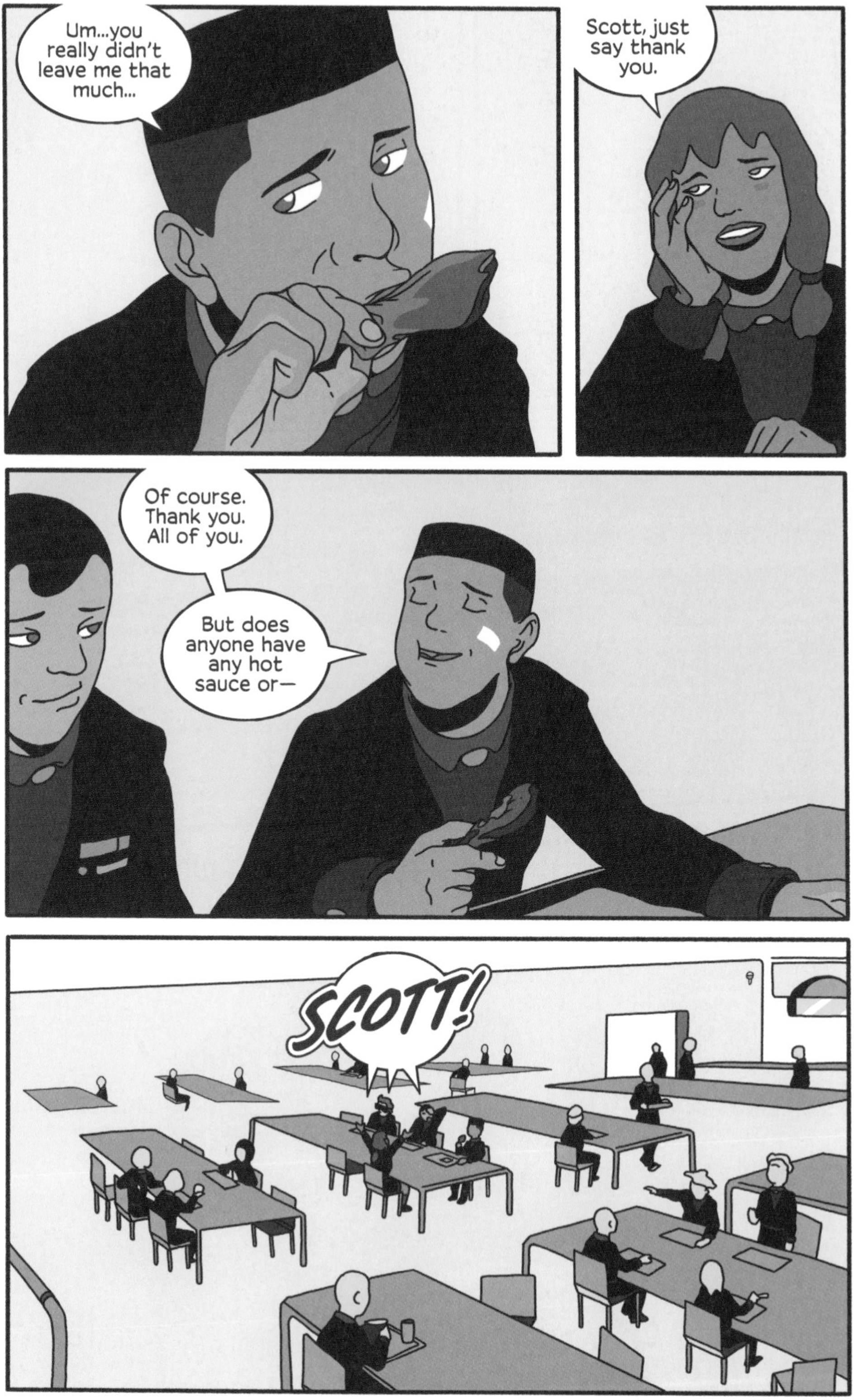
Um...you really didn't leave me that much...
Scott, just say thank you.
Of course. Thank you. All of you.
But does anyone have any hot sauce or—
SCOTT!

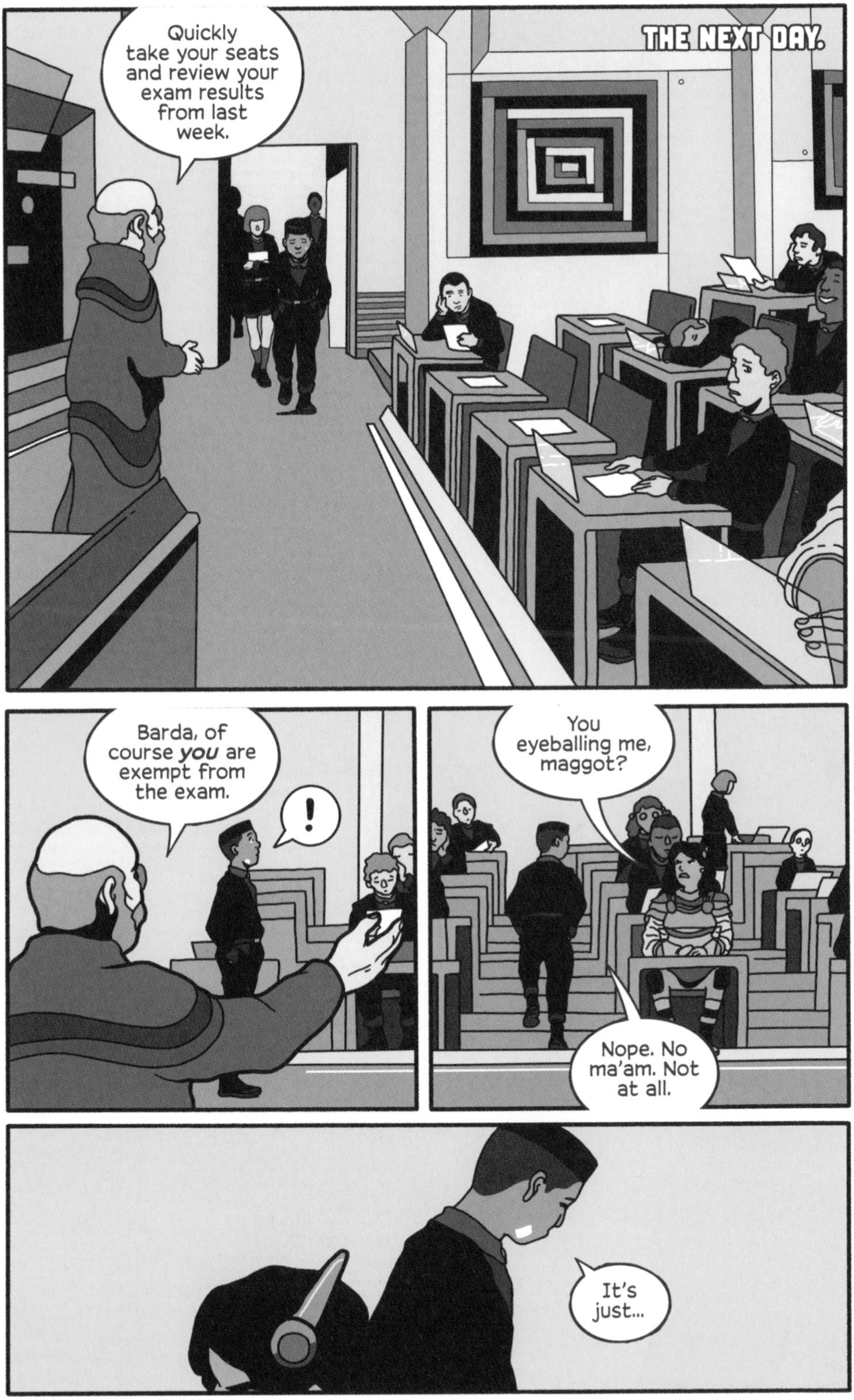
THE NEXT DAY.
Quickly take your seats and review your exam results from last week.
Barda, of course *you* are exempt from the exam.
!
You eyeballing me, maggot?
Nope. No ma'am. Not at all.
It's just...

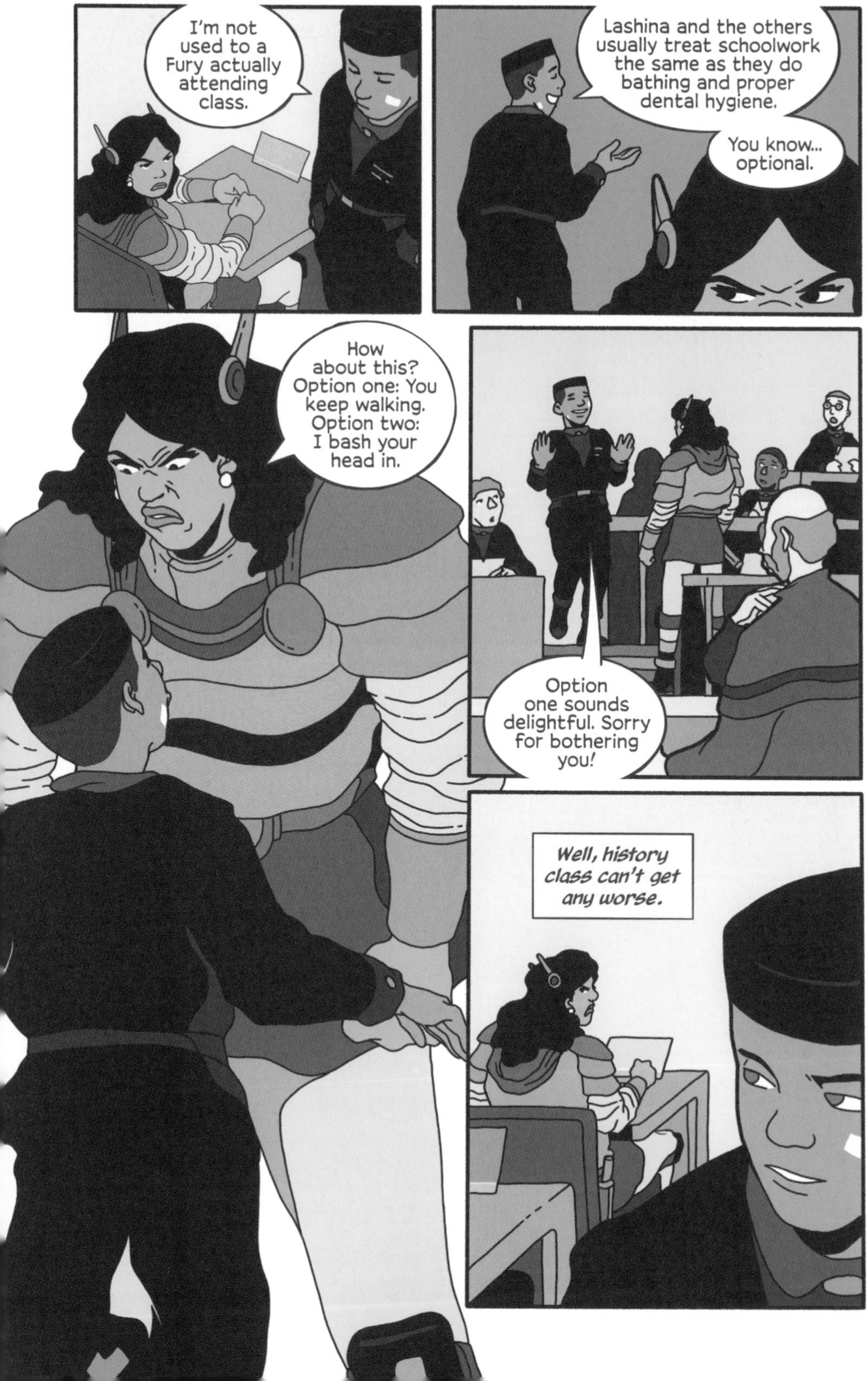
I'm not used to a Fury actually attending class.
Lashina and the others usually treat schoolwork the same as they do bathing and proper dental hygiene.
You know... optional.
How about this? Option one: You keep walking. Option two: I bash your head in.
Option one sounds delightful. Sorry for bothering you!
Well, history class can't get any worse.

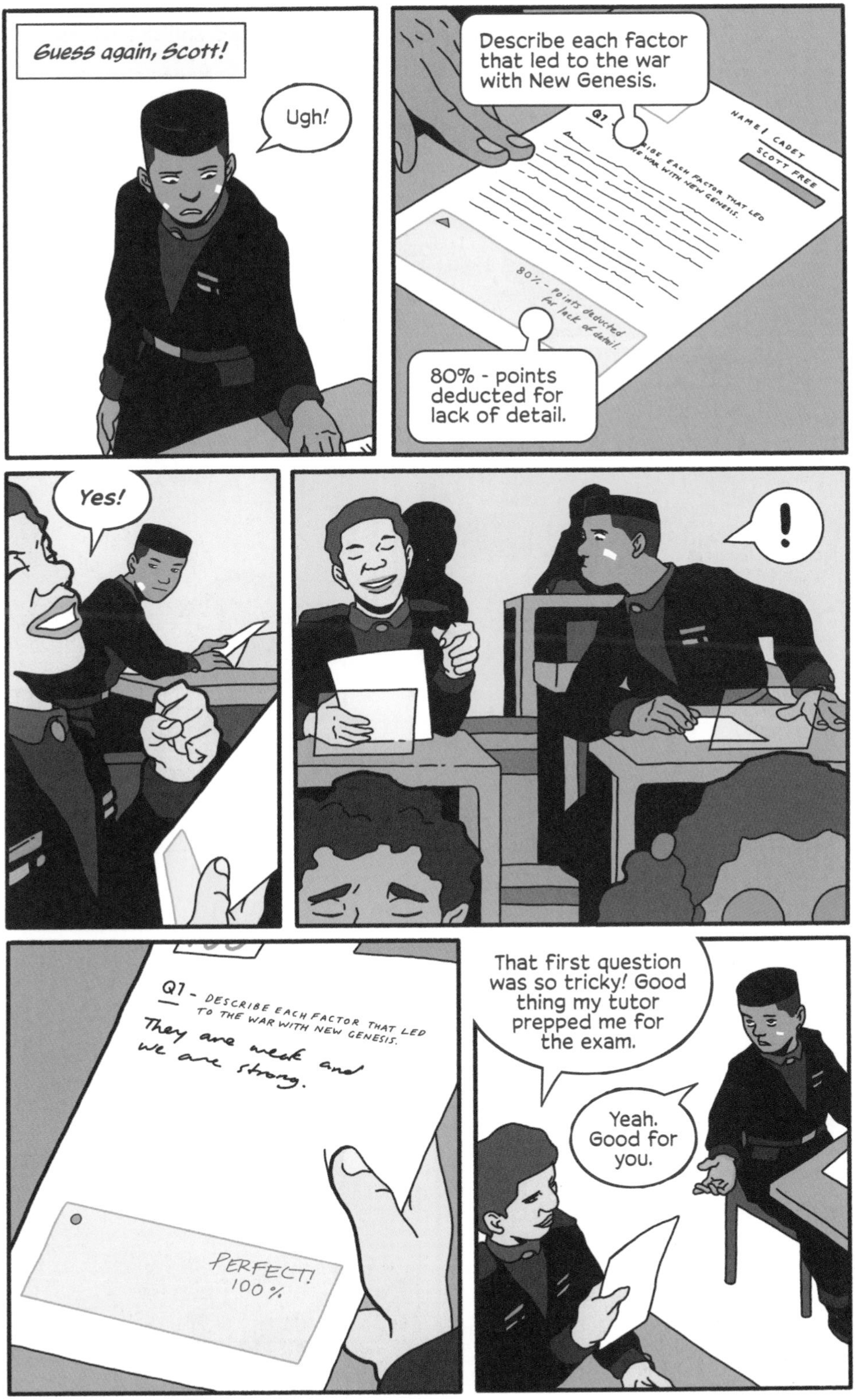
Guess again, Scott!
Ugh!
Describe each factor that led to the war with New Genesis.
NAME / CADET
SCOTT FREE
80% - points deducted for lack of detail.
80% - points deducted for lack of detail.
Yes!
!
Q1 - DESCRIBE EACH FACTOR THAT LED TO THE WAR WITH NEW GENESIS.
They are weak and we are strong.
PERFECT! 100%
That first question was so tricky! Good thing my tutor prepped me for the exam.
Yeah. Good for you.

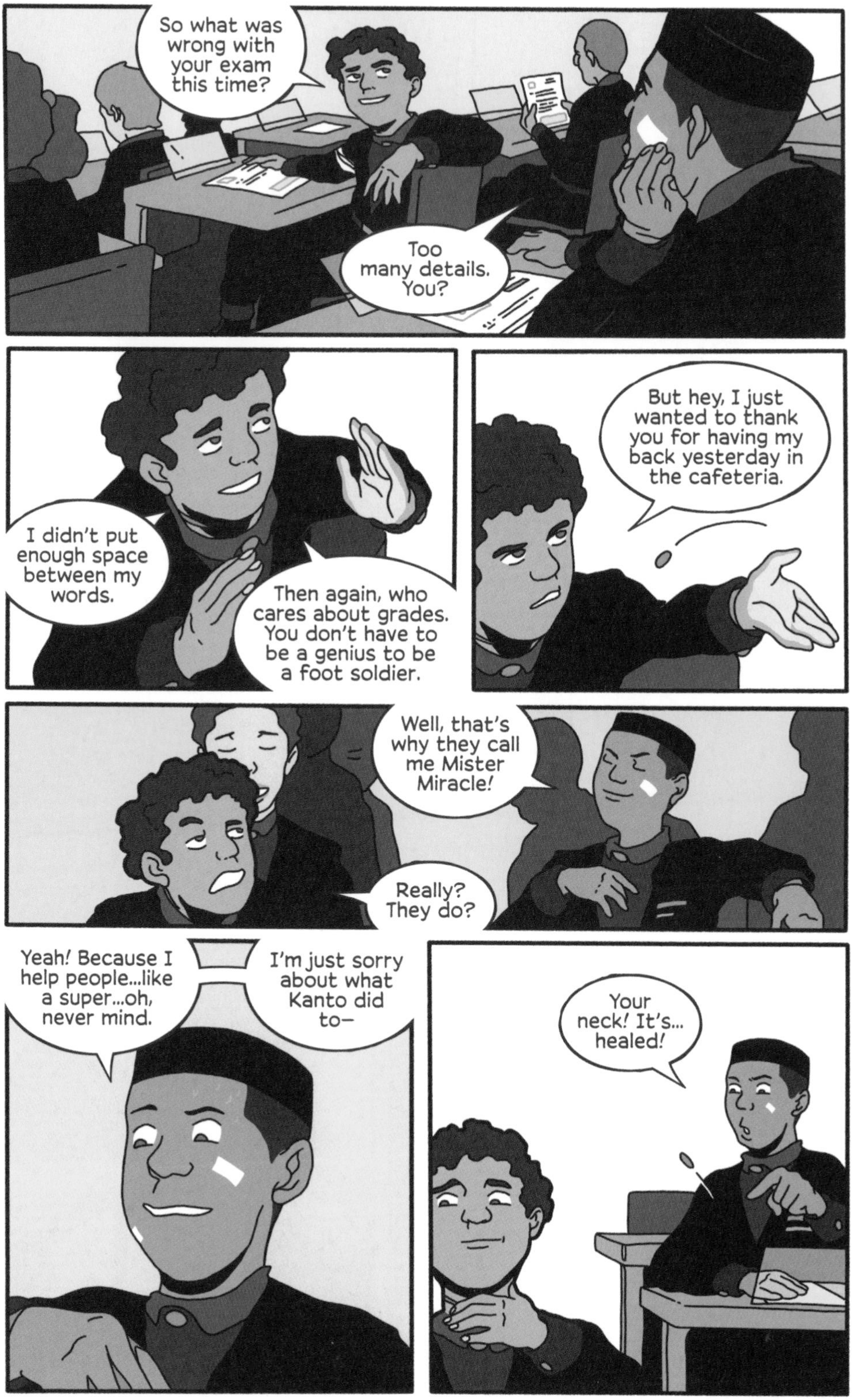
So what was wrong with your exam this time?
Too many details. You?
I didn't put enough space between my words.
Then again, who cares about grades. You don't have to be a genius to be a foot soldier.
But hey, I just wanted to thank you for having my back yesterday in the cafeteria.
Well, that's why they call me Mister Miracle!
Really? They do?
Yeah! Because I help people...like a super...oh, never mind.
I'm just sorry about what Kanto did to—
Your neck! It's... healed!

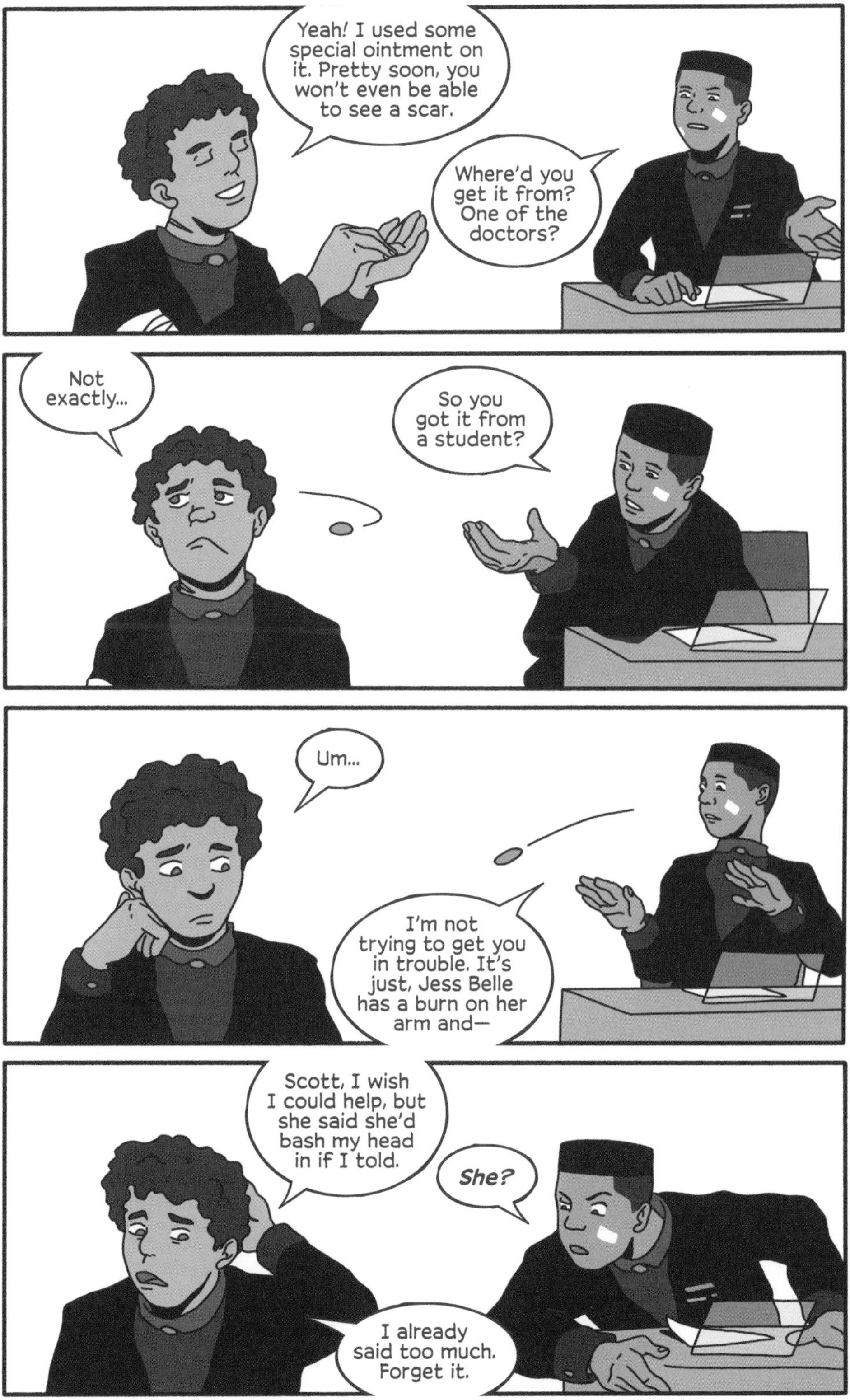
Yeah! I used some special ointment on it. Pretty soon, you won't even be able to see a scar.
Where'd you get it from? One of the doctors?
Not exactly...
So you got it from a student?
Um...
I'm not trying to get you in trouble. It's just, Jess Belle has a burn on her arm and—
Scott, I wish I could help, but she said she'd bash my head in if I told.
She?
I already said too much. Forget it.

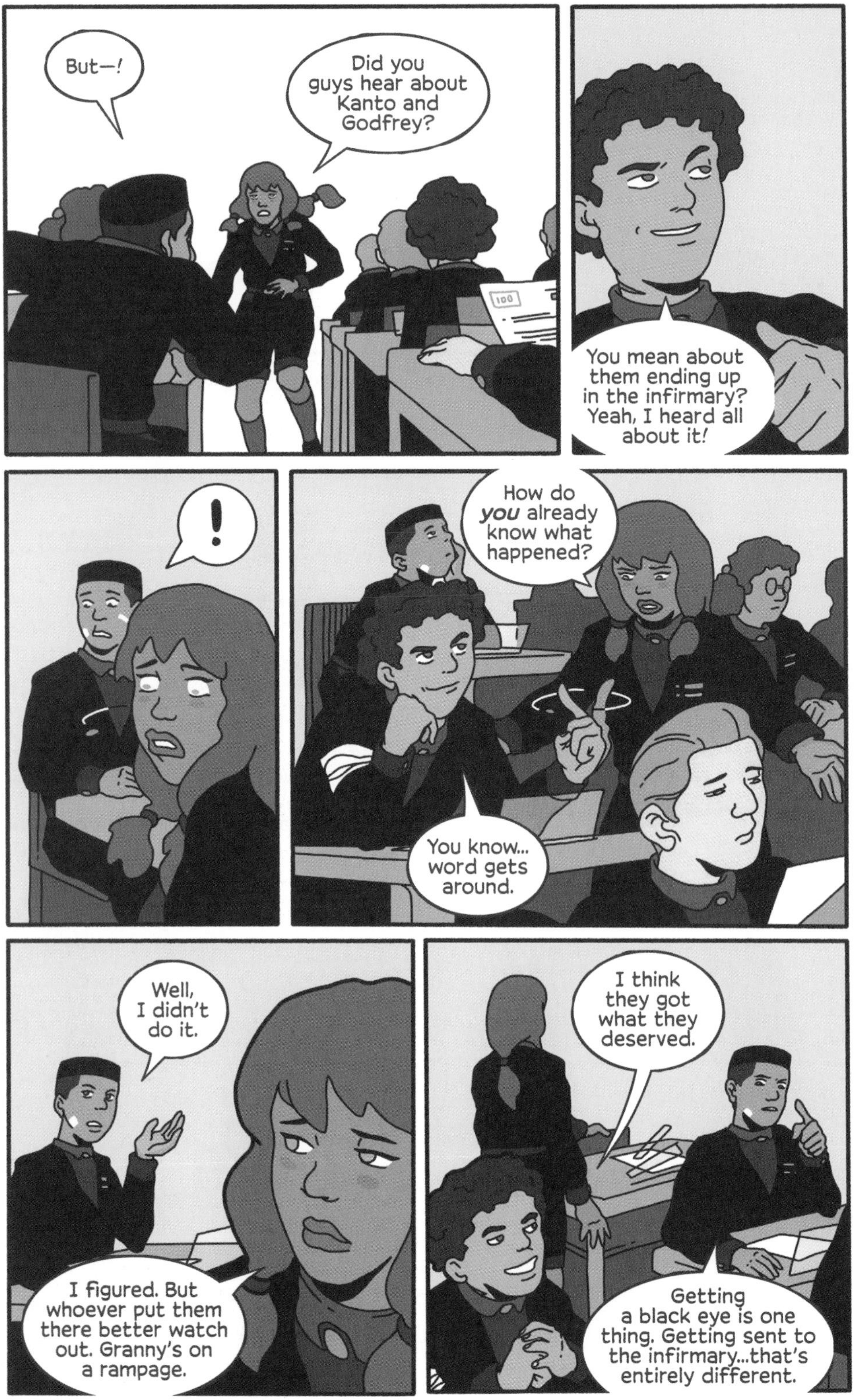
But—!
Did you guys hear about Kanto and Godfrey?
100
You mean about them ending up in the infirmary? Yeah, I heard all about it!
!
How do *you* already know what happened?
You know... word gets around.
Well, I didn't do it.
I figured. But whoever put them there better watch out. Granny's on a rampage.
I think they got what they deserved.
Getting a black eye is one thing. Getting sent to the infirmary...that's entirely different.

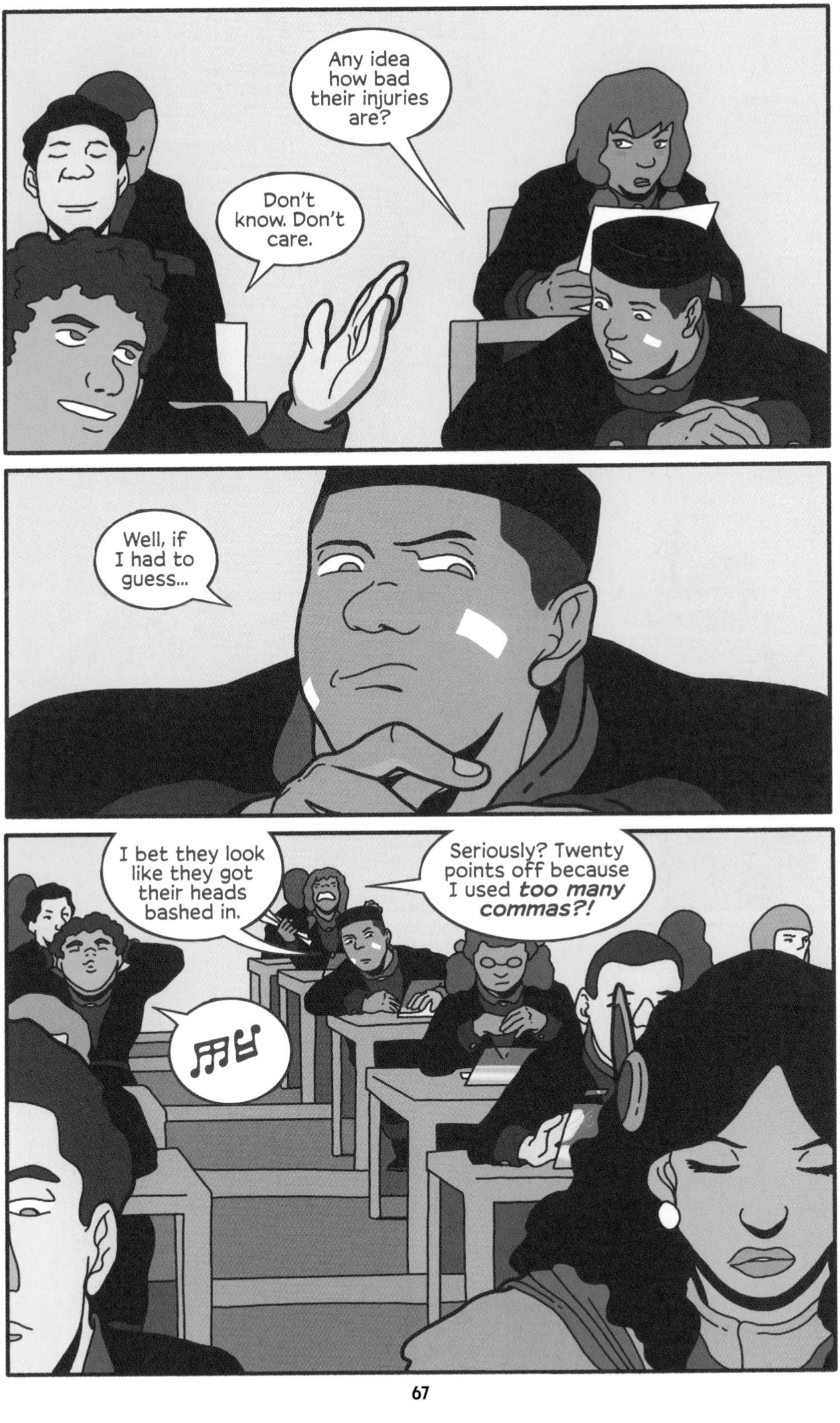
Any idea how bad their injuries are?
Don't know. Don't care.
Well, if I had to guess...
I bet they look like they got their heads bashed in.
Seriously? Twenty points off because I used *too many commas?!*

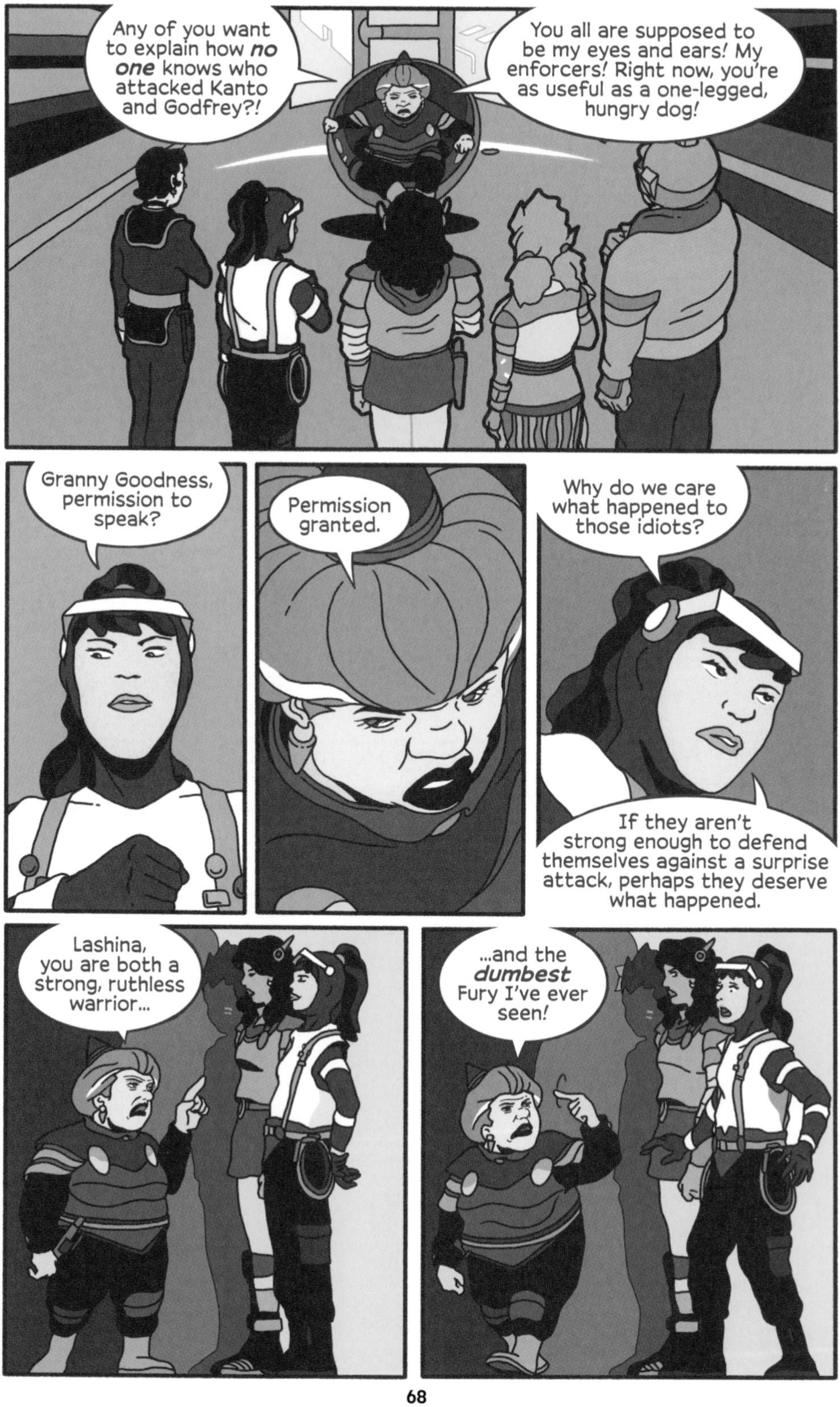
Any of you want to explain how **no one** knows who attacked Kanto and Godfrey?!
You all are supposed to be my eyes and ears! My enforcers! Right now, you're as useful as a one-legged, hungry dog!
Granny Goodness, permission to speak?
Permission granted.
Why do we care what happened to those idiots?
If they aren't strong enough to defend themselves against a surprise attack, perhaps they deserve what happened.
Lashina, you are both a strong, ruthless warrior...
...and the **dumbest** Fury I've ever seen!

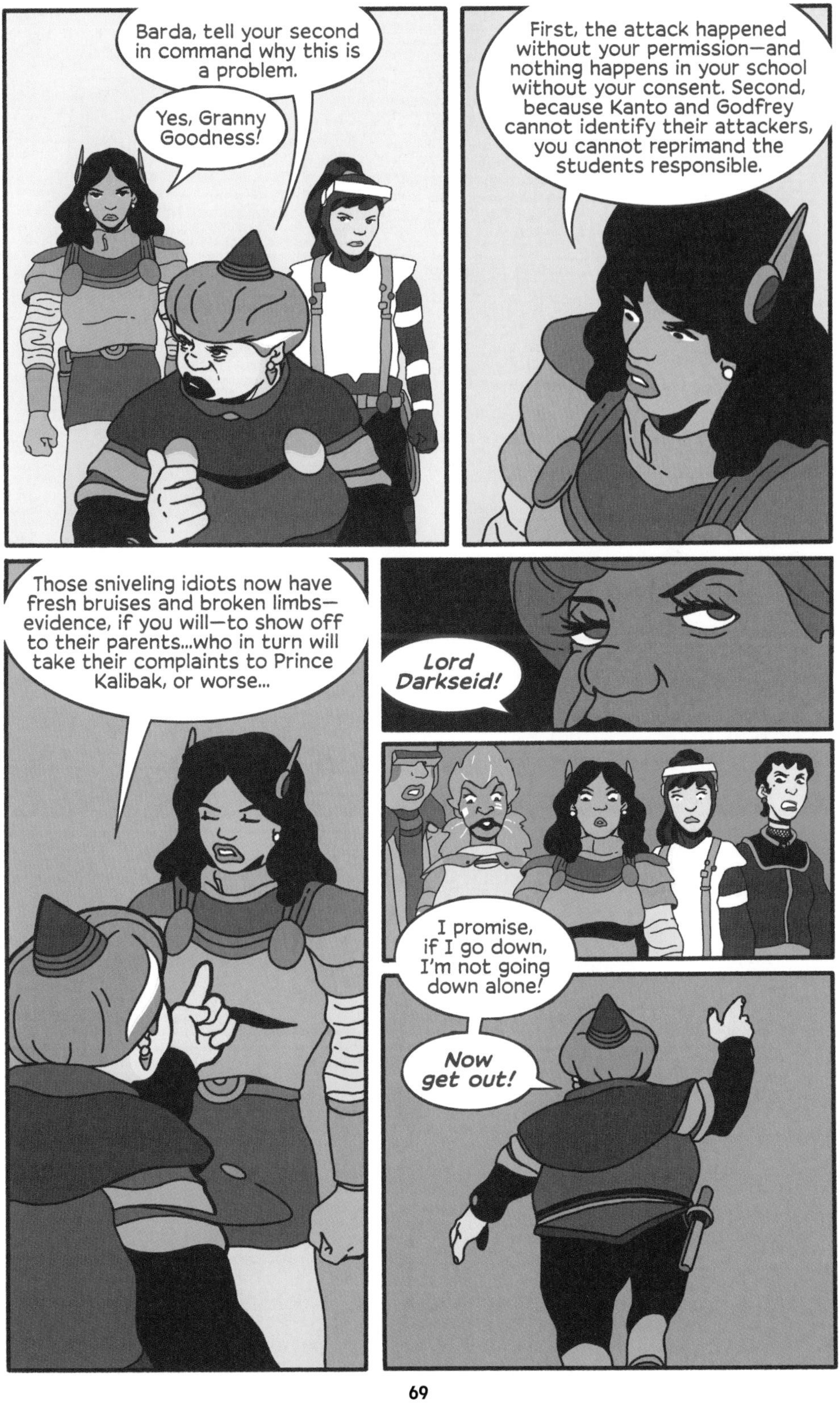
Barda, tell your second in command why this is a problem.
Yes, Granny Goodness!
First, the attack happened without your permission—and nothing happens in your school without your consent. Second, because Kanto and Godfrey cannot identify their attackers, you cannot reprimand the students responsible.
Those sniveling idiots now have fresh bruises and broken limbs—evidence, if you will—to show off to their parents...who in turn will take their complaints to Prince Kalibak, or worse...
Lord Darkseid!
I promise, if I go down, I'm not going down alone!
Now get out!

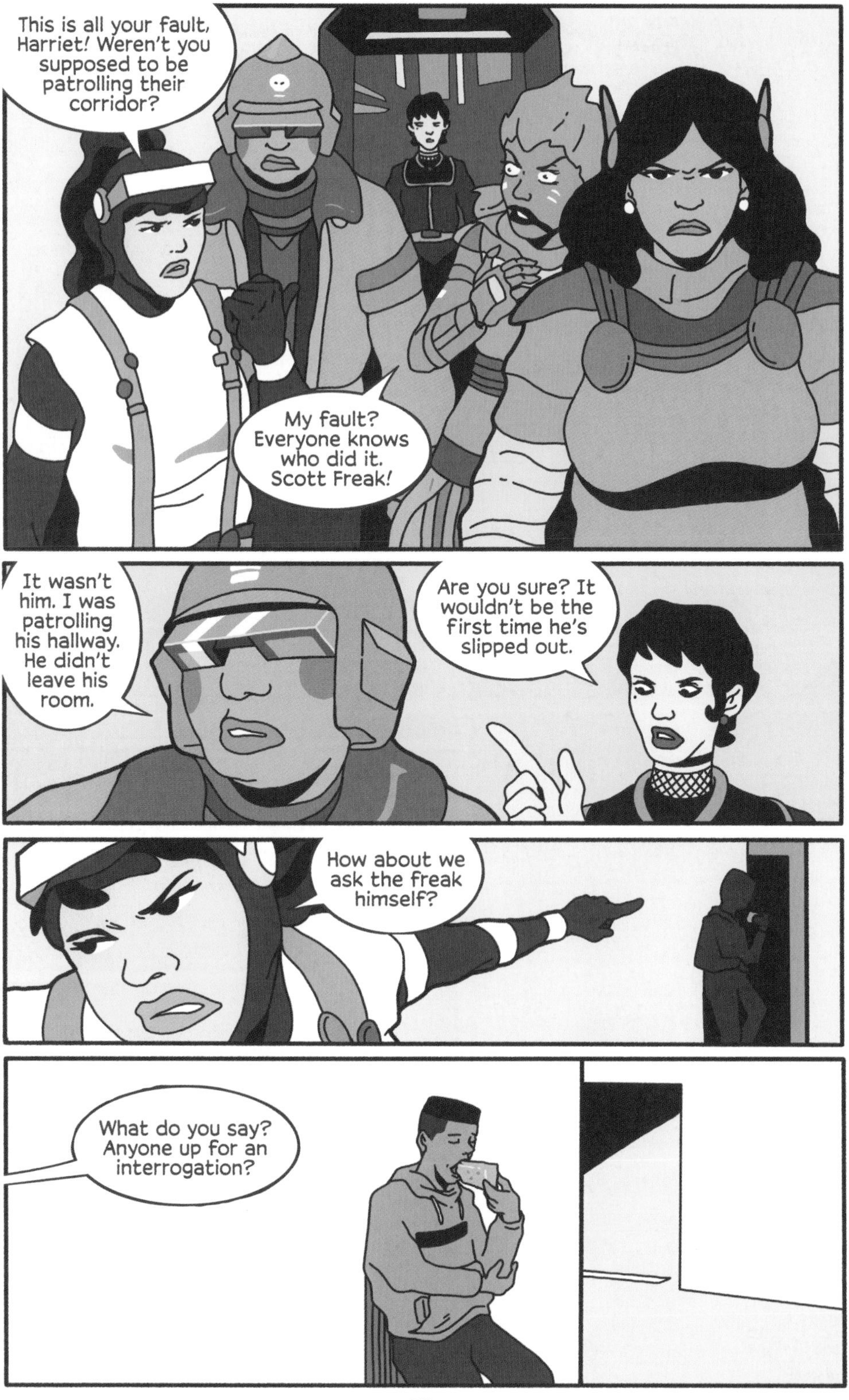
This is all your fault, Harriet! Weren't you supposed to be patrolling their corridor?
My fault? Everyone knows who did it. Scott Freak!
It wasn't him. I was patrolling his hallway. He didn't leave his room.
Are you sure? It wouldn't be the first time he's slipped out.
How about we ask the freak himself?
What do you say? Anyone up for an interrogation?

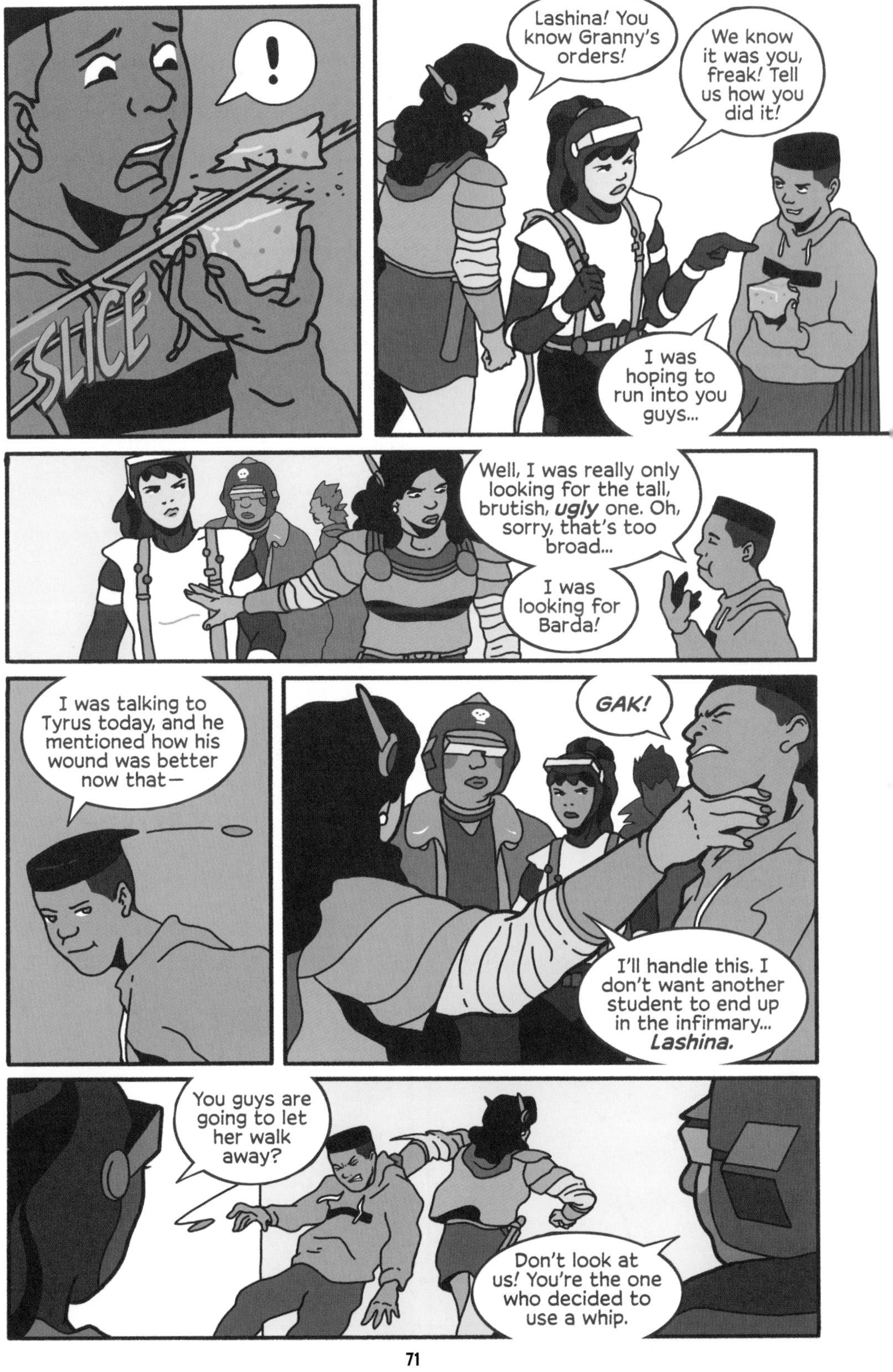
!
SLICE
Lashina! You know Granny's orders!
We know it was you, freak! Tell us how you did it!
I was hoping to run into you guys...
Well, I was really only looking for the tall, brutish, *ugly* one. Oh, sorry, that's too broad...
I was looking for Barda!
I was talking to Tyrus today, and he mentioned how his wound was better now that—
GAK!
I'll handle this. I don't want another student to end up in the infirmary... *Lashina.*
You guys are going to let her walk away?
Don't look at us! You're the one who decided to use a whip.

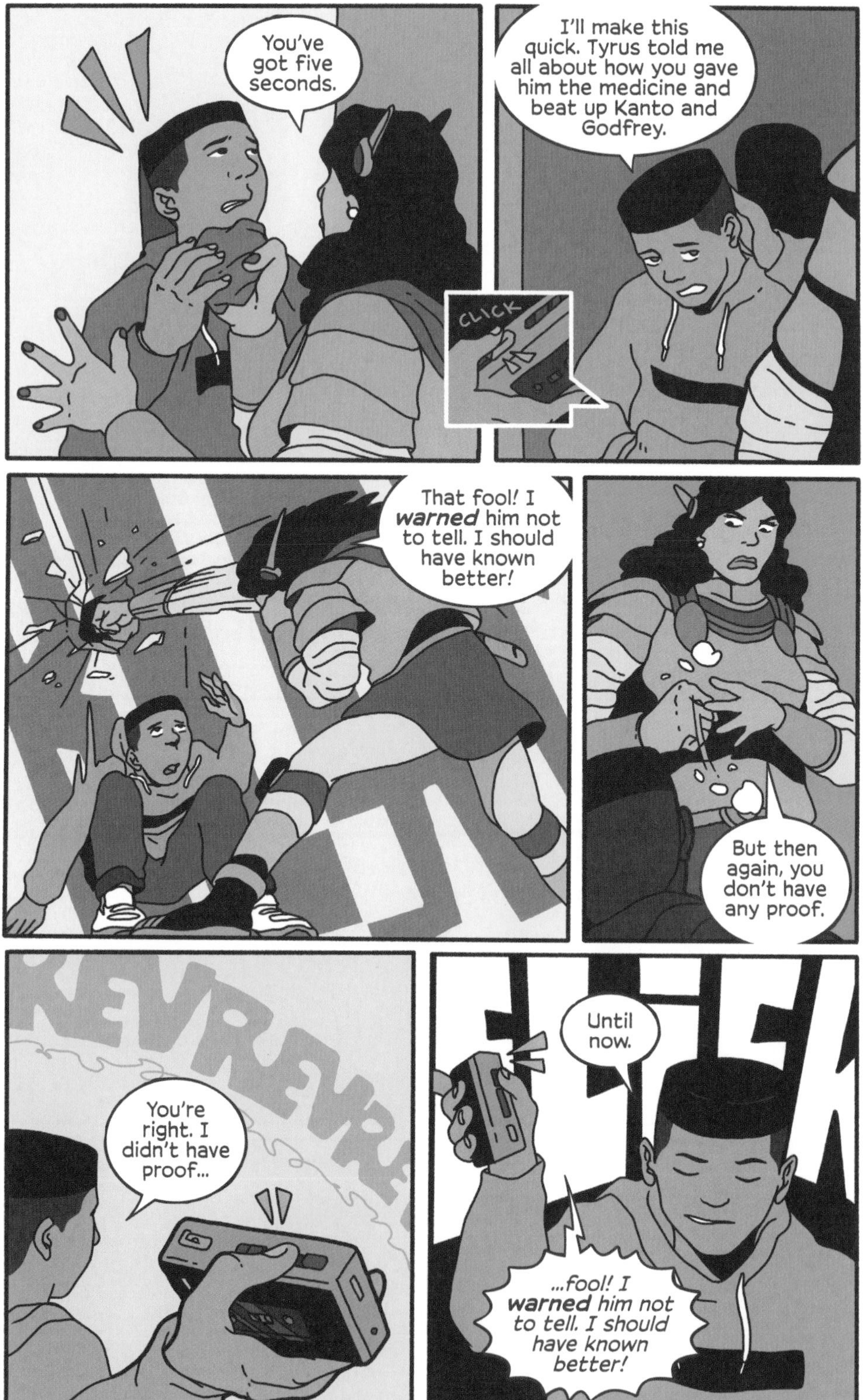
You've got five seconds.
I'll make this quick. Tyrus told me all about how you gave him the medicine and beat up Kanto and Godfrey.
CLICK
That fool! I *warned* him not to tell. I should have known better!
But then again, you don't have any proof.
REVREVREV
You're right. I didn't have proof...
Until now.
...fool! I *warned* him not to tell. I should have known better!

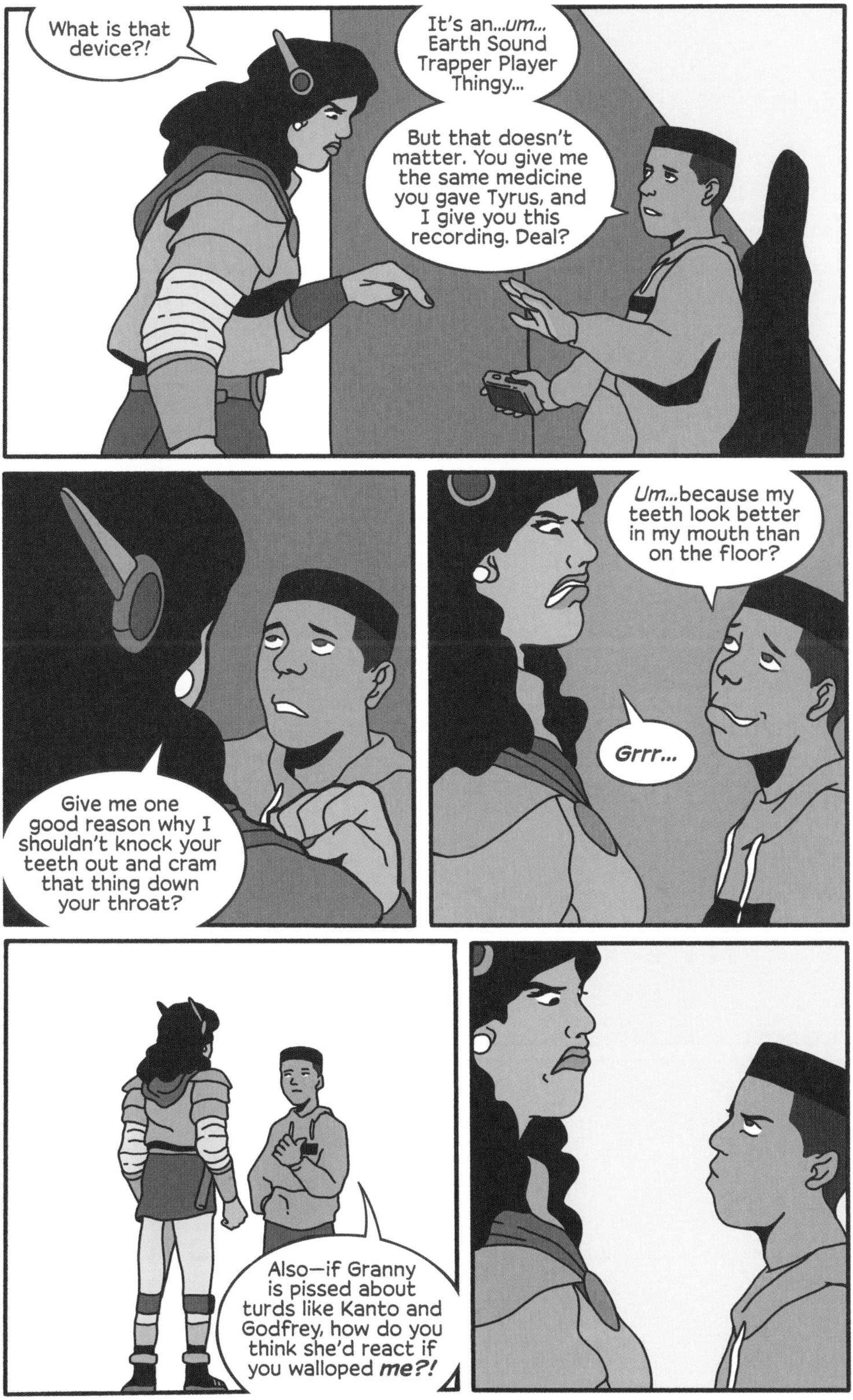
What is that device?!
It's an...*um*... Earth Sound Trapper Player Thingy...
But that doesn't matter. You give me the same medicine you gave Tyrus, and I give you this recording. Deal?
Give me one good reason why I shouldn't knock your teeth out and cram that thing down your throat?
Um...because my teeth look better in my mouth than on the floor?
Grrr...
Also—if Granny is pissed about turds like Kanto and Godfrey, how do you think she'd react if you walloped ***me?!***

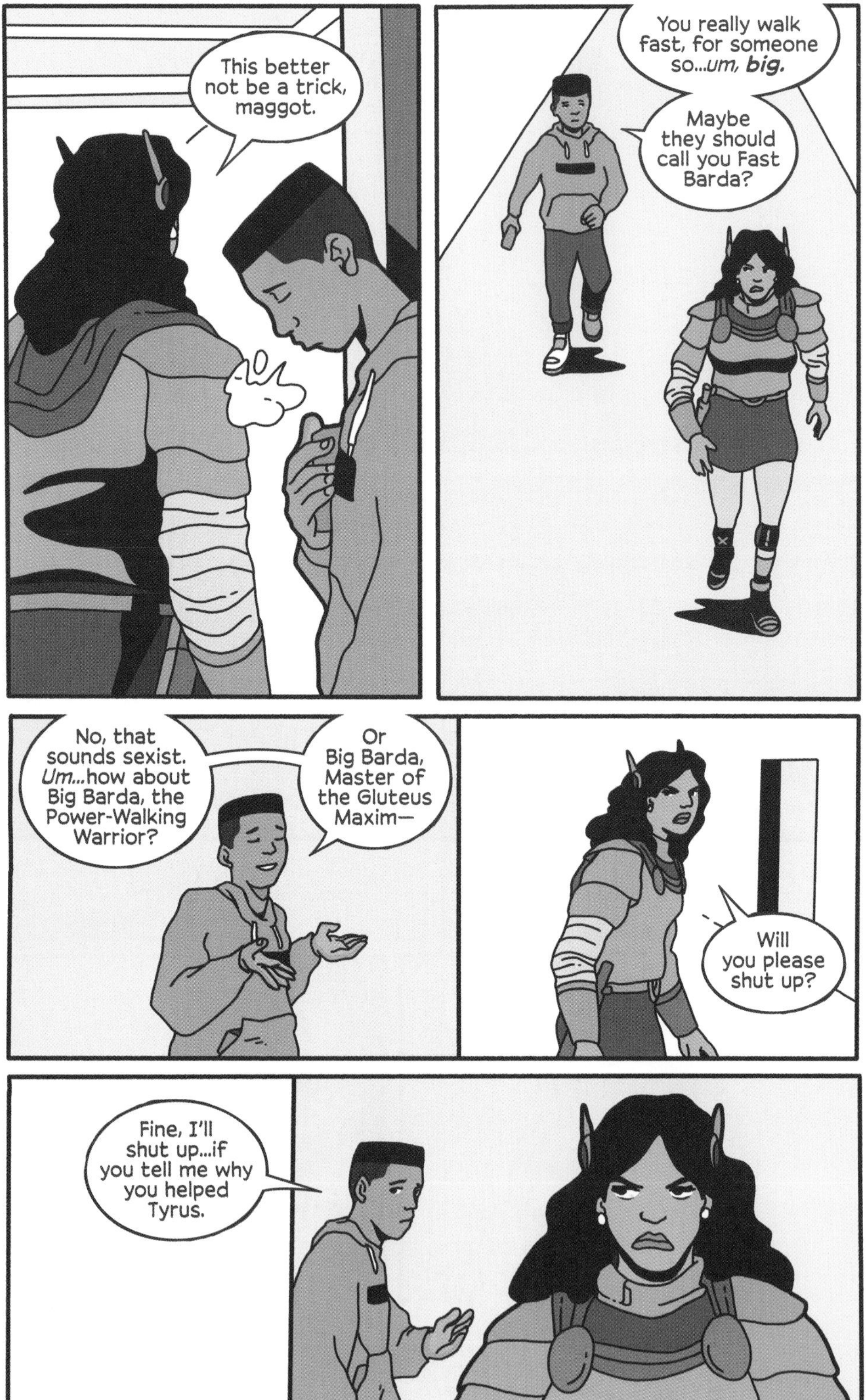
This better not be a trick, maggot.
You really walk fast, for someone so...*um,* ***big.***
Maybe they should call you Fast Barda?
No, that sounds sexist. *Um*...how about Big Barda, the Power-Walking Warrior?
Or Big Barda, Master of the Gluteus Maxim—
Will you please shut up?
Fine, I'll shut up...if you tell me why you helped Tyrus.

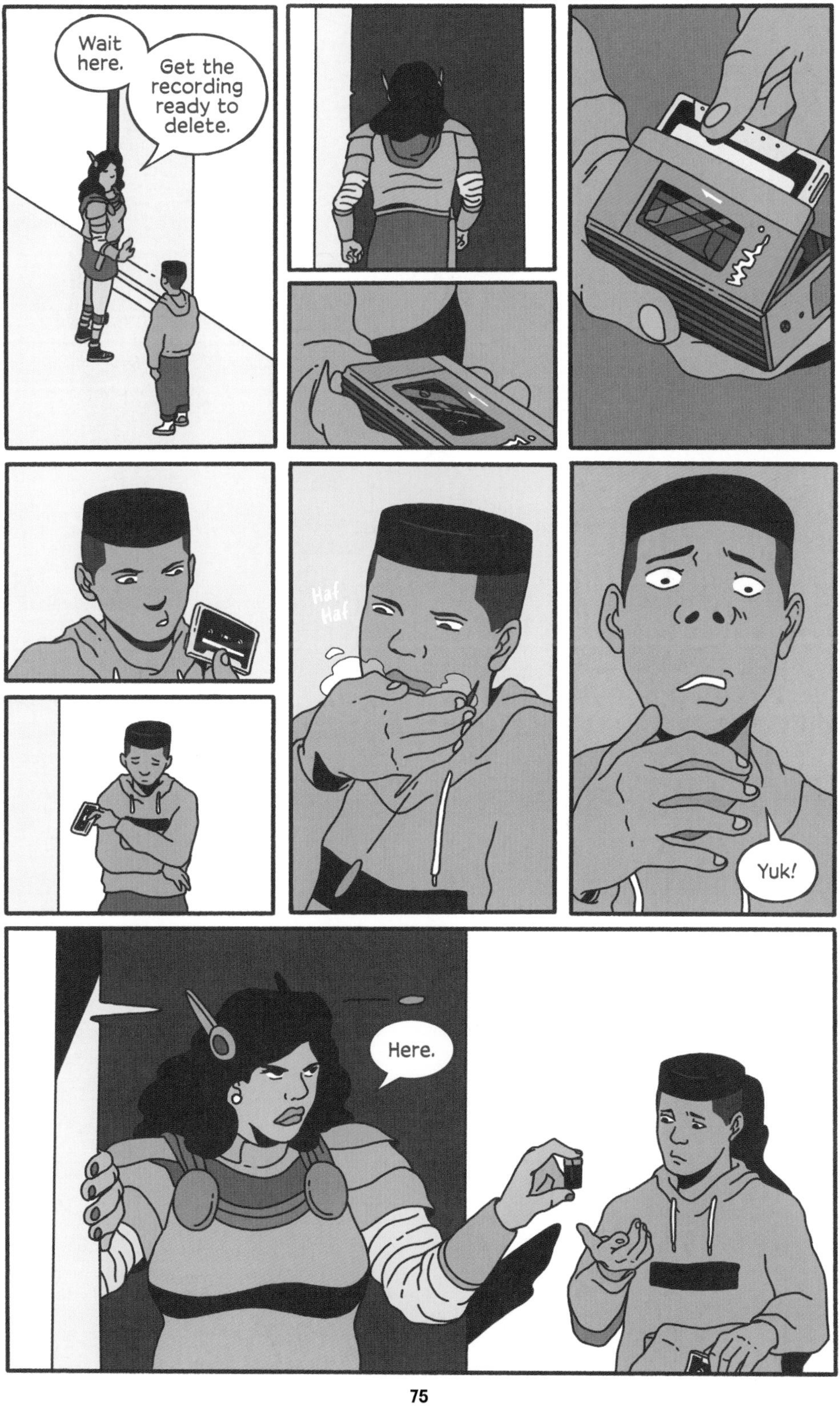
Wait here.
Get the recording ready to delete.
Haf Haf
Yuk!
Here.

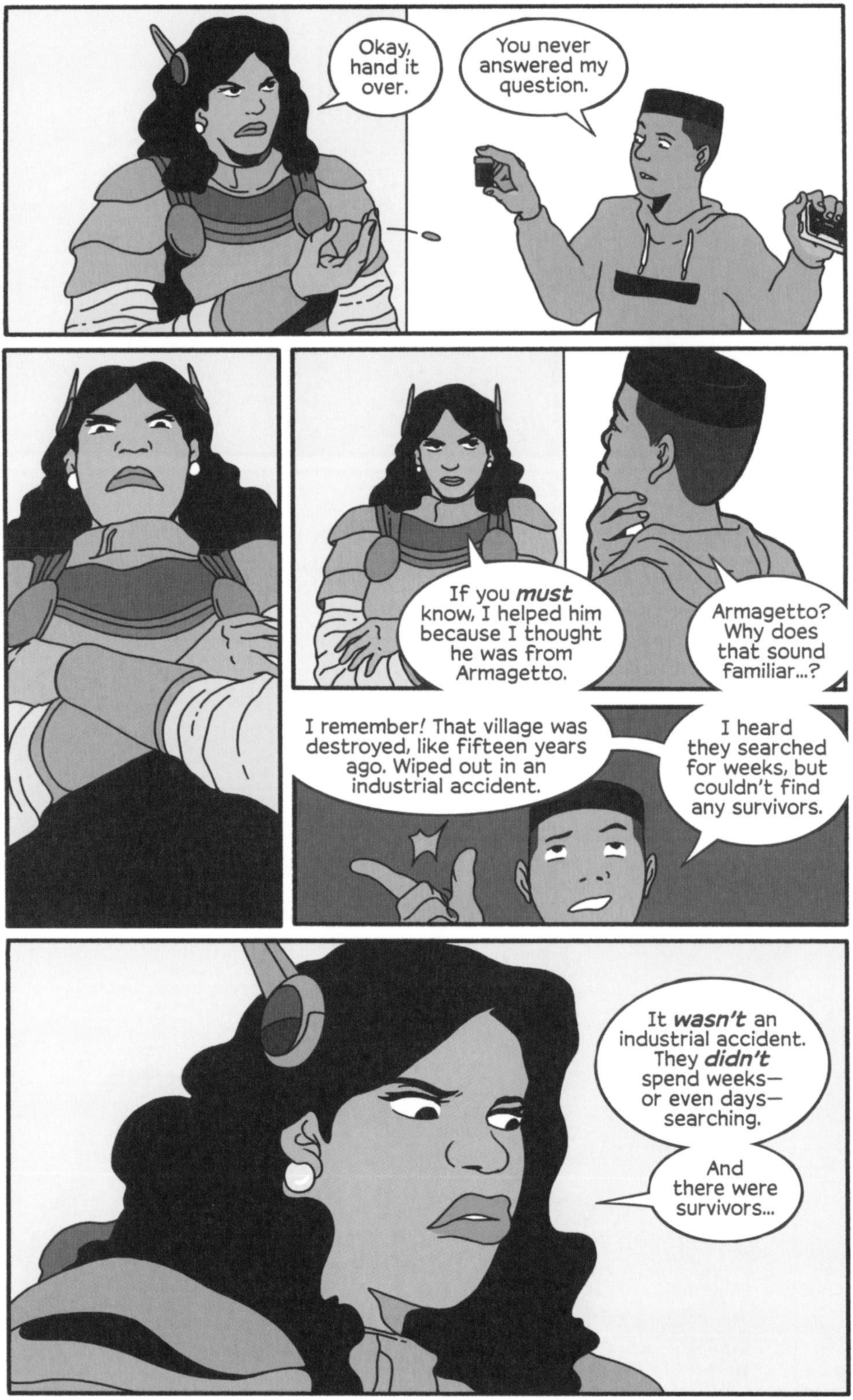
Okay, hand it over.
You never answered my question.
If you *must* know, I helped him because I thought he was from Armagetto.
Armagetto? Why does that sound familiar...?
I remember! That village was destroyed, like fifteen years ago. Wiped out in an industrial accident.
I heard they searched for weeks, but couldn't find any survivors.
It *wasn't* an industrial accident. They *didn't* spend weeks—or even days—searching.
And there were survivors...

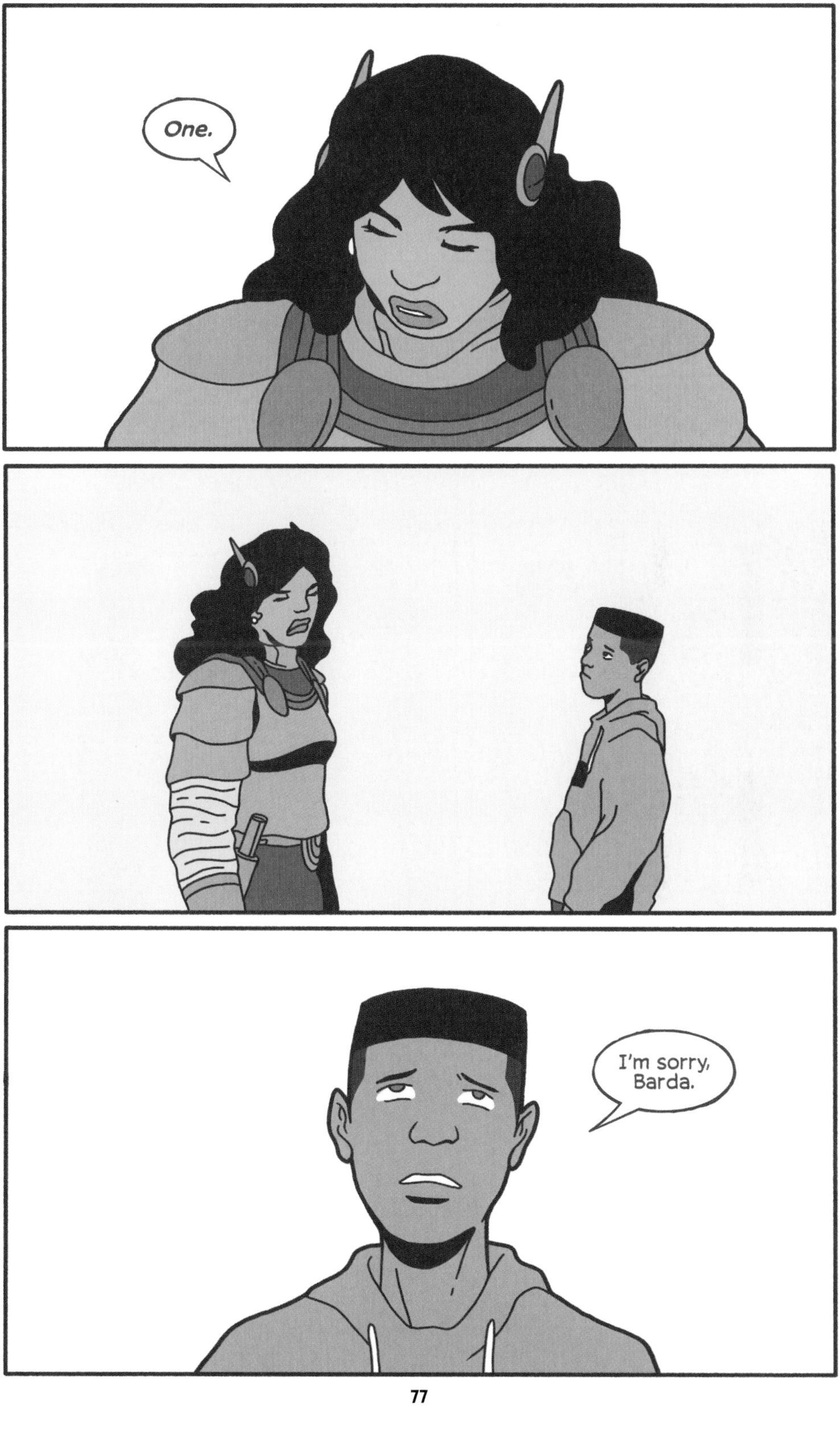
One.
I'm sorry, Barda.

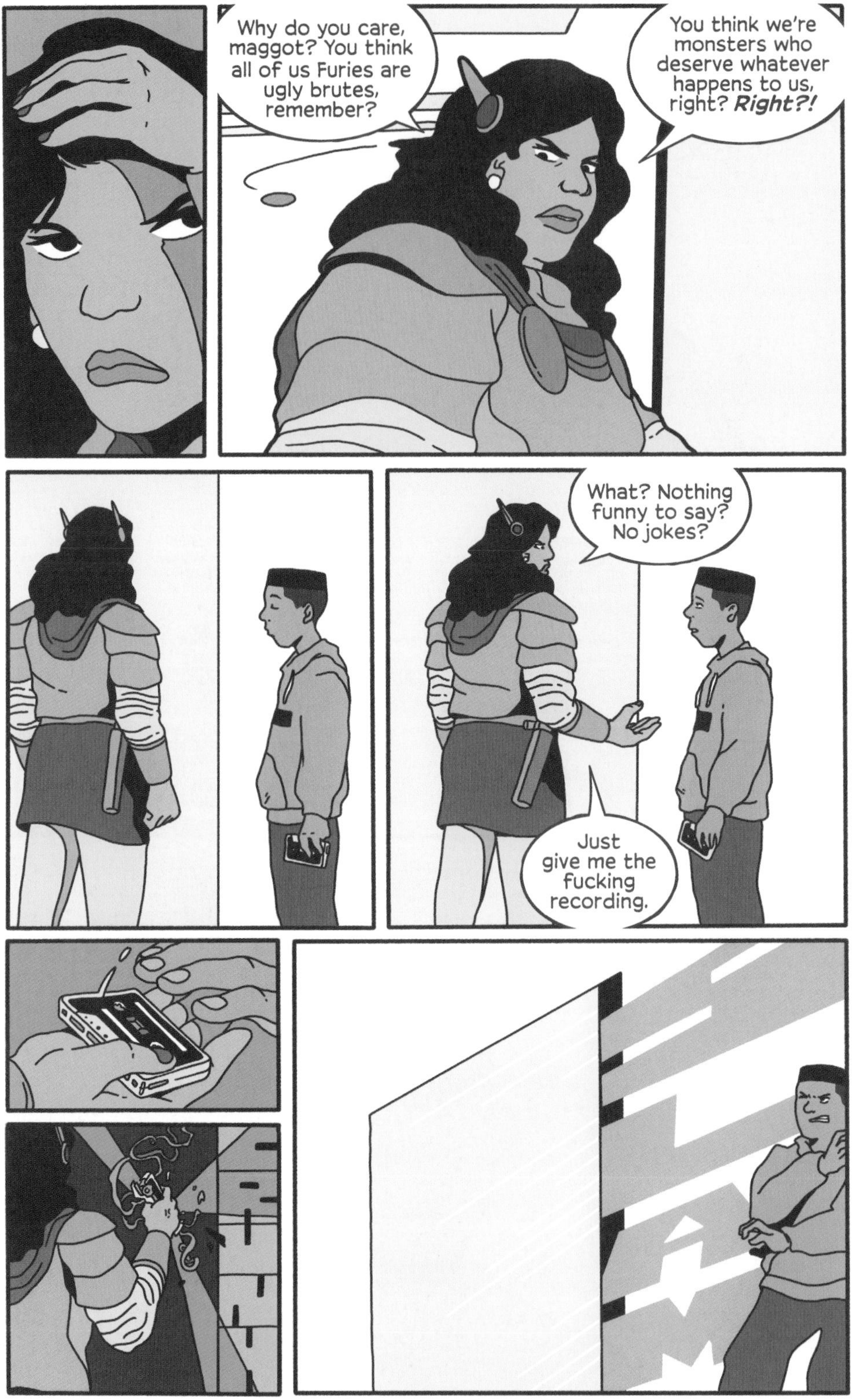
Why do you care, maggot? You think all of us Furies are ugly brutes, remember?
You think we're monsters who deserve whatever happens to us, right? ***Right?!***
What? Nothing funny to say? No jokes?
Just give me the fucking recording.

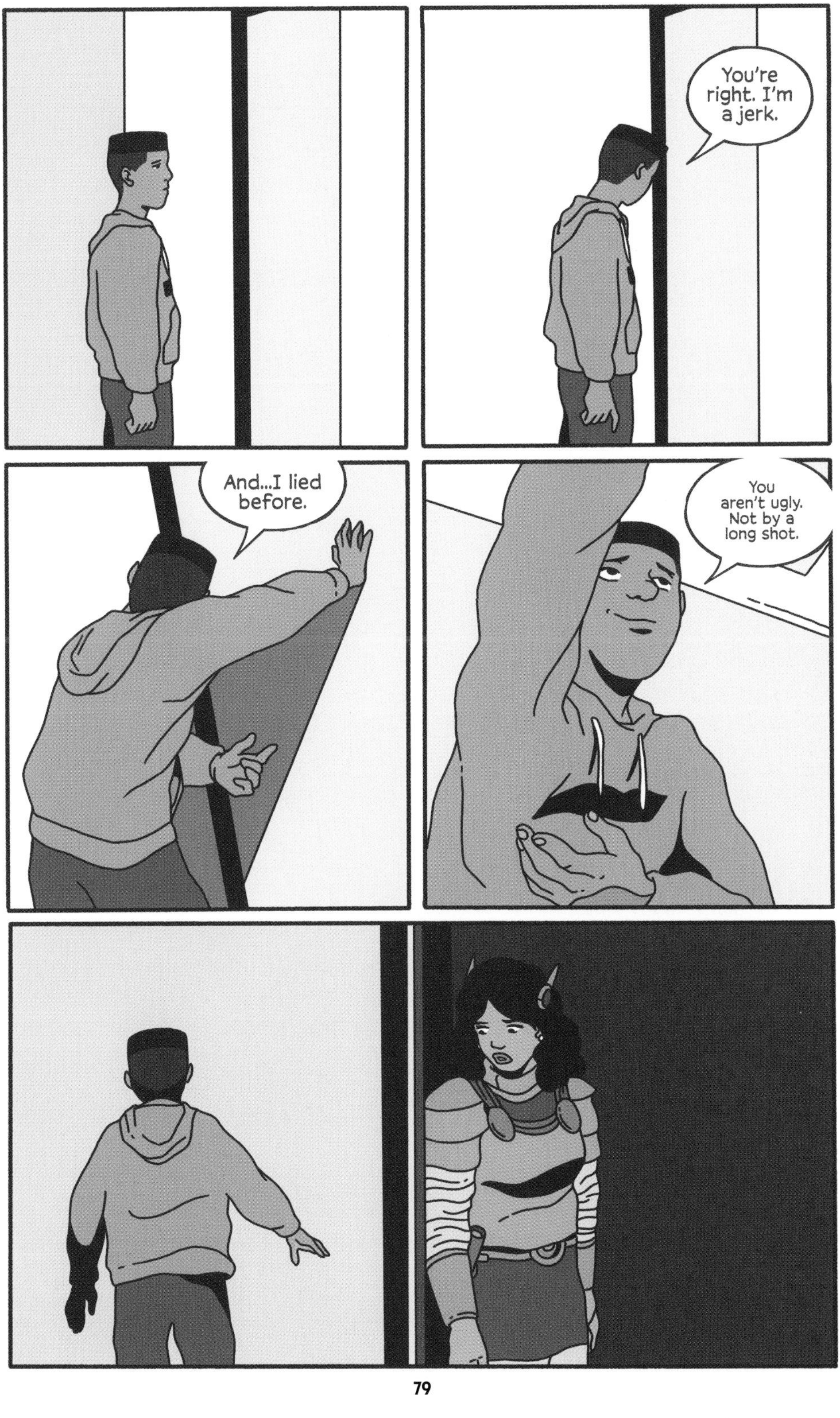
You're right. I'm a jerk.
And...I lied before.
You aren't ugly. Not by a long shot.

CHAPTER THREE

Float On

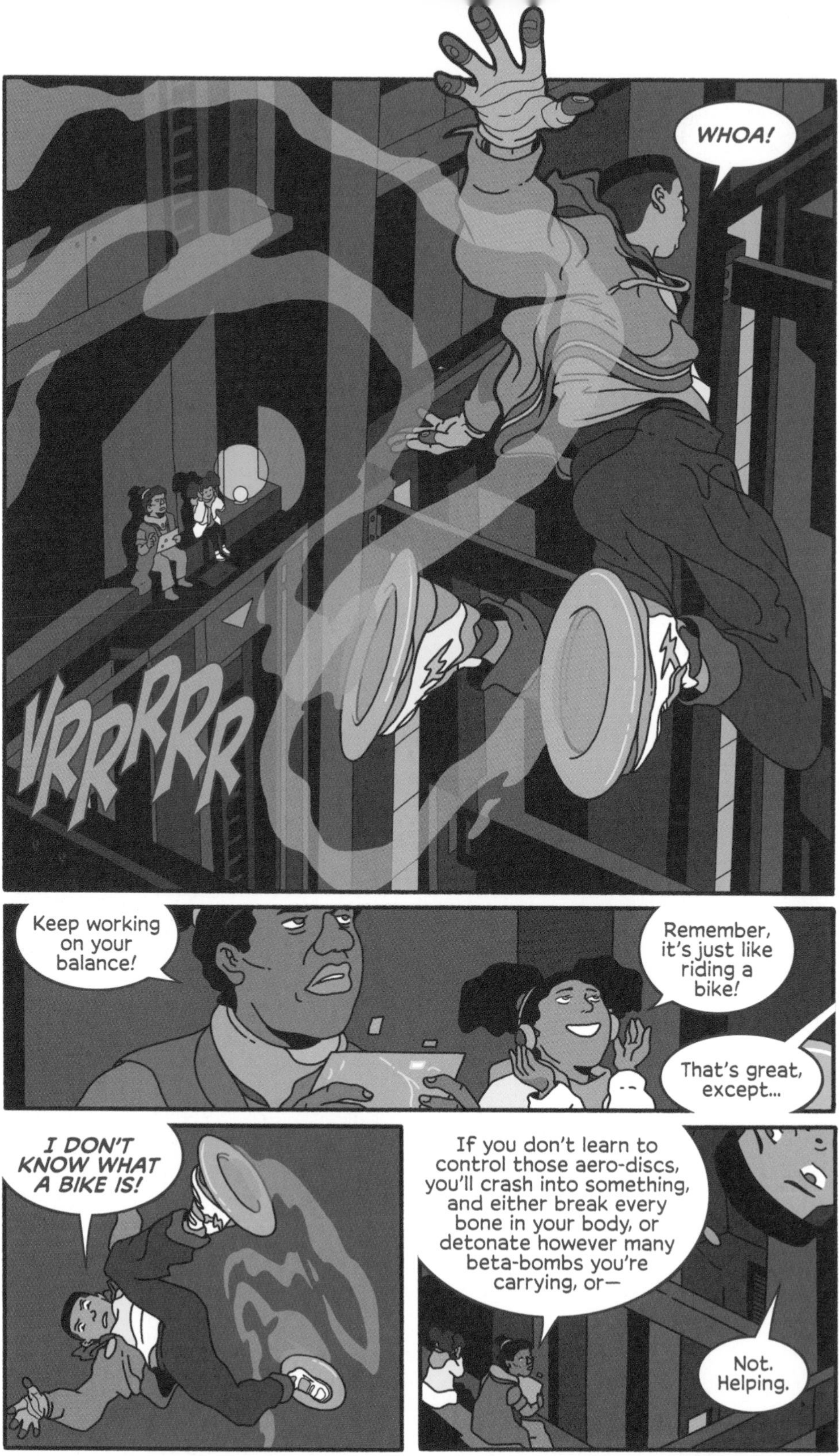
WHOA!
VRRRRR
Keep working on your balance!
Remember, it's just like riding a bike!
That's great, except...
I DON'T KNOW WHAT A BIKE IS!
If you don't learn to control those aero-discs, you'll crash into something, and either break every bone in your body, or detonate however many beta-bombs you're carrying, or—
Not. Helping.

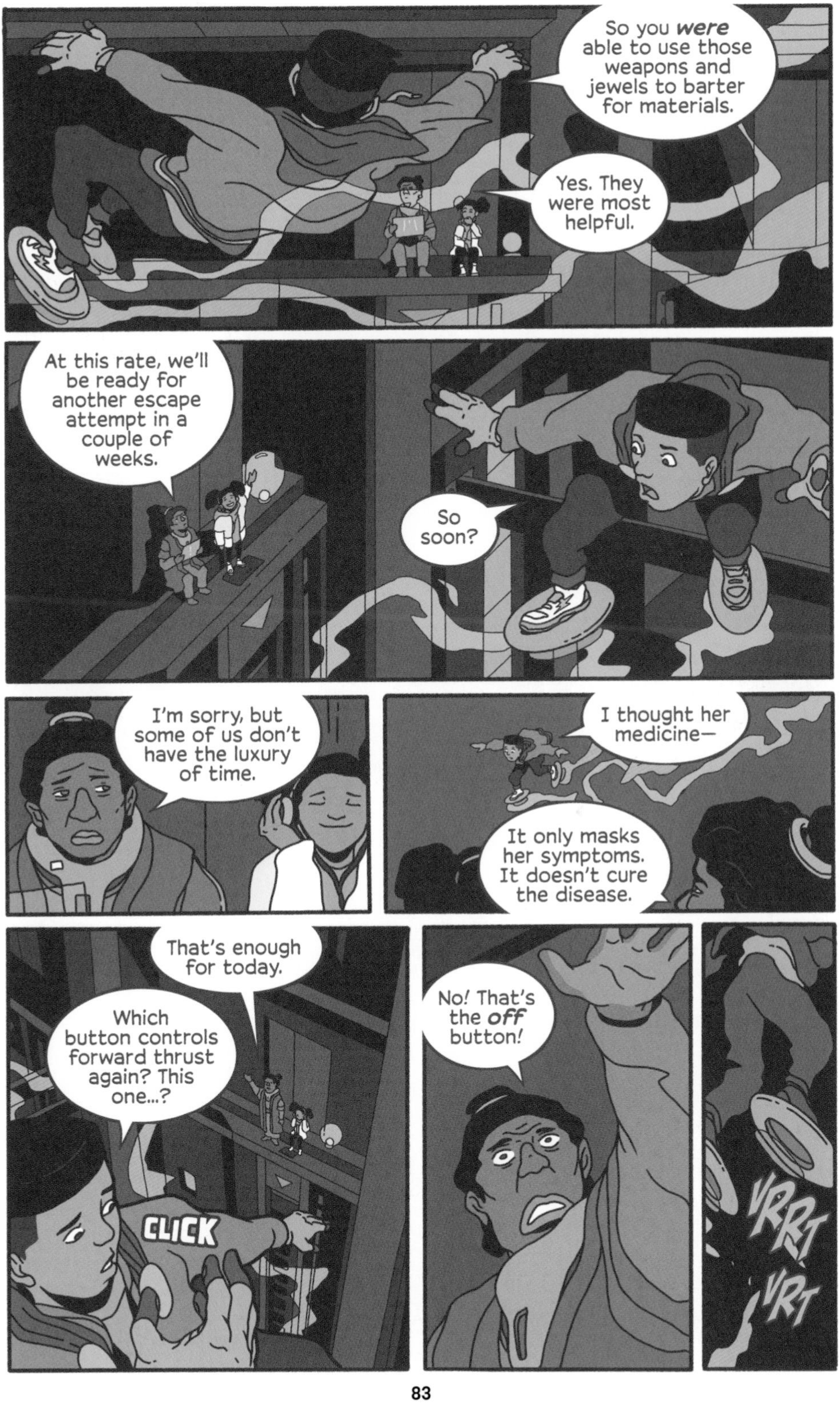

So you *were* able to use those weapons and jewels to barter for materials.
Yes. They were most helpful.
At this rate, we'll be ready for another escape attempt in a couple of weeks.
So soon?
I'm sorry, but some of us don't have the luxury of time.
I thought her medicine—
It only masks her symptoms. It doesn't cure the disease.
That's enough for today.
Which button controls forward thrust again? This one...?
CLICK
No! That's the *off* button!
VRRT
VRT

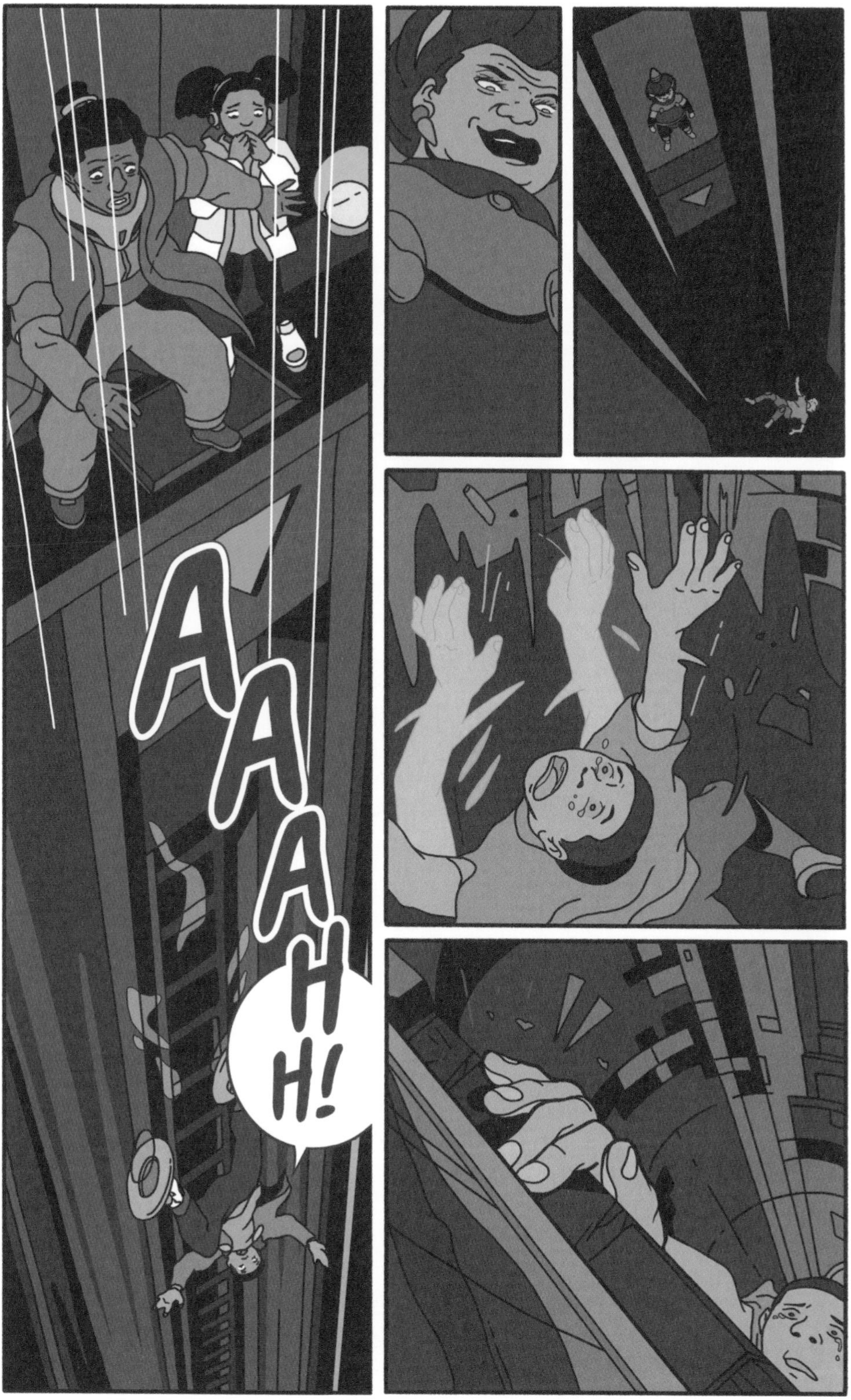
AAAAHH!

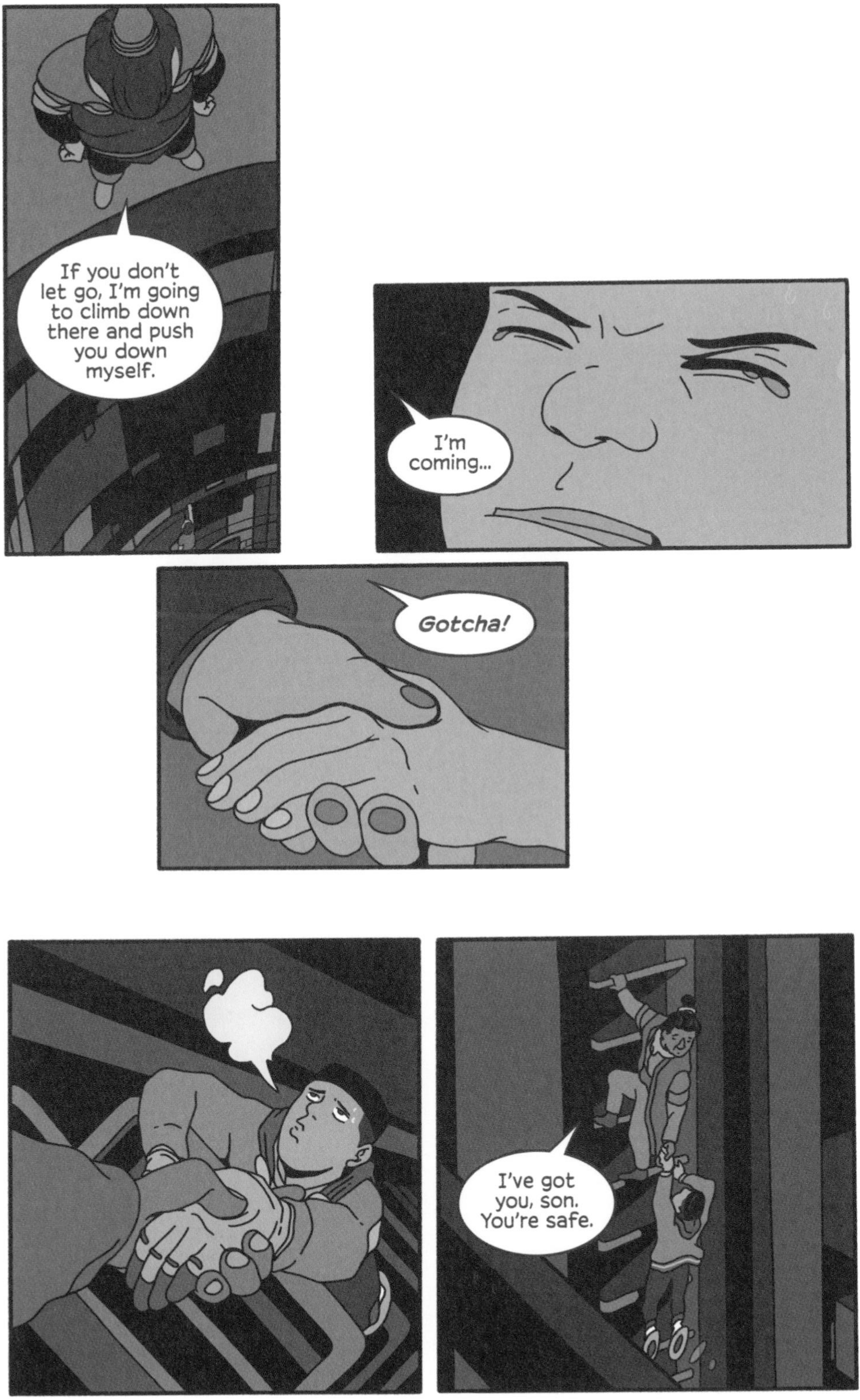
If you don't let go, I'm going to climb down there and push you down myself.
I'm coming...
Gotcha!
I've got you, son. You're safe.

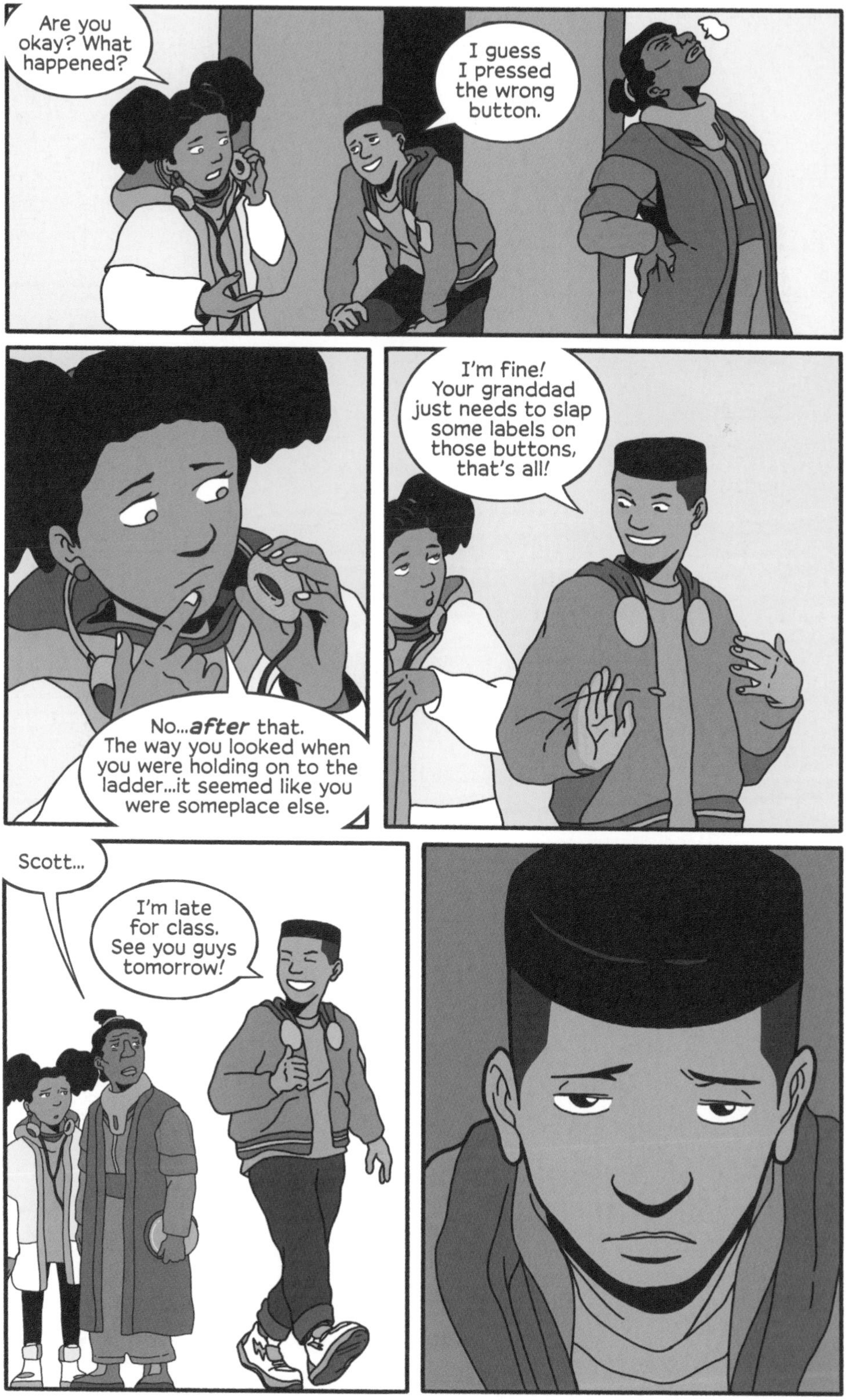
Are you okay? What happened?
I guess I pressed the wrong button.
I'm fine! Your granddad just needs to slap some labels on those buttons, that's all!
No...**after** that. The way you looked when you were holding on to the ladder...it seemed like you were someplace else.
Scott...
I'm late for class. See you guys tomorrow!

THAT NIGHT.

PLOP.

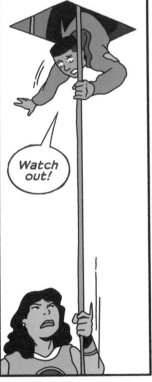

Watch out!

CRASH

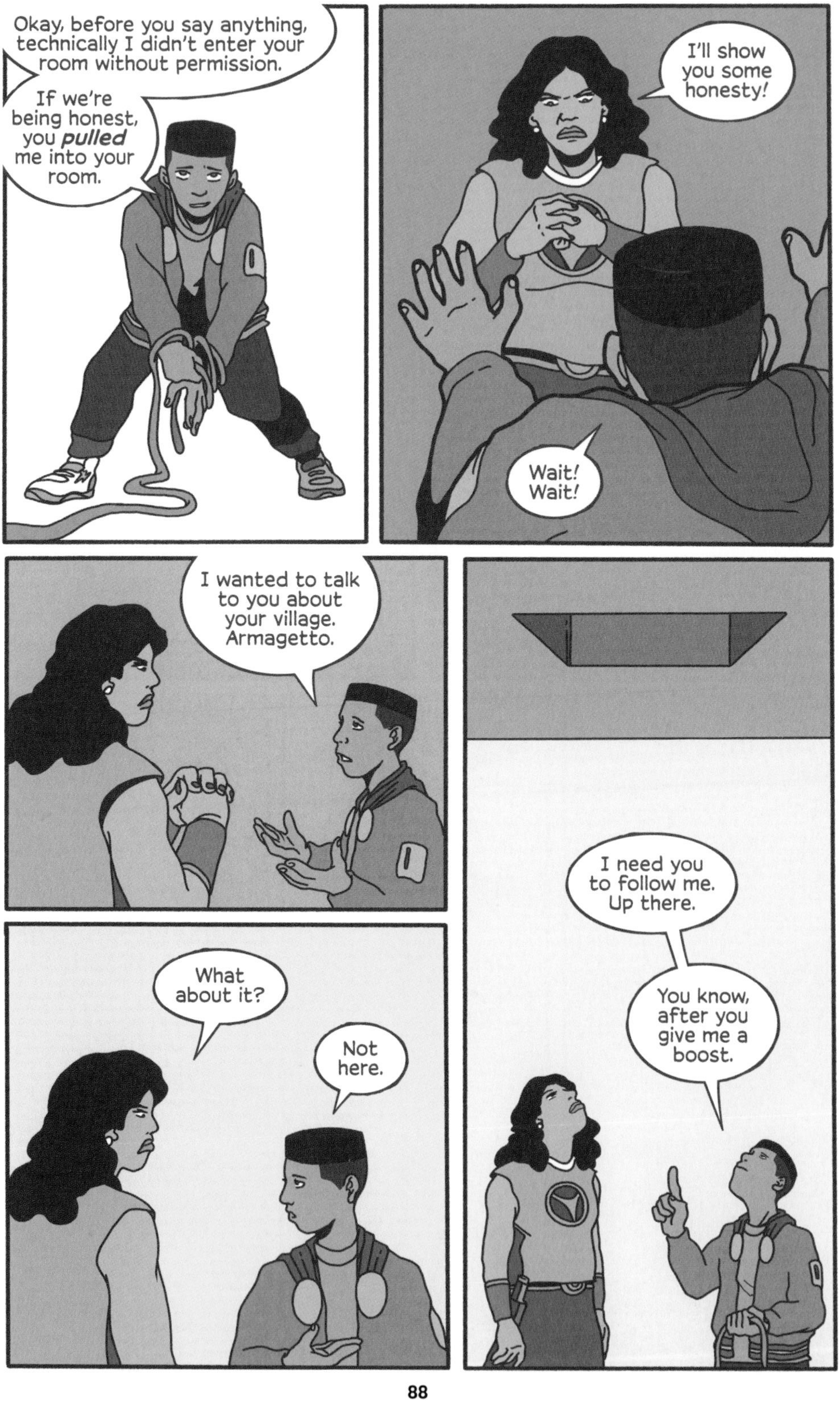
Okay, before you say anything, technically I didn't enter your room without permission.
If we're being honest, you *pulled* me into your room.
I'll show you some honesty!
Wait! Wait!
I wanted to talk to you about your village. Armagetto.
What about it?
Not here.
I need you to follow me. Up there.
You know, after you give me a boost.

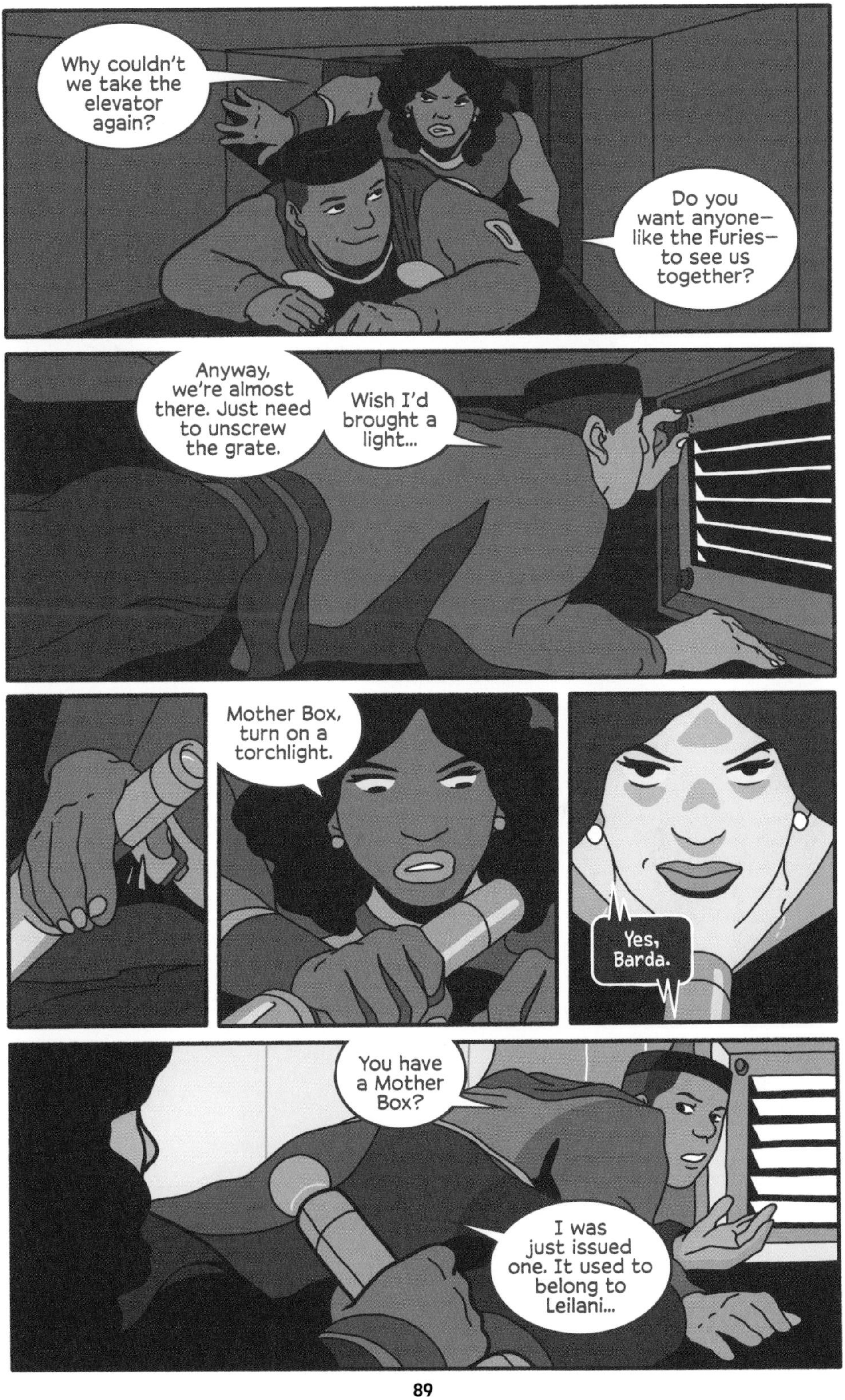

Why couldn't we take the elevator again?
Do you want anyone— like the Furies— to see us together?
Anyway, we're almost there. Just need to unscrew the grate.
Wish I'd brought a light...
Mother Box, turn on a torchlight.
Yes, Barda.
You have a Mother Box?
I was just issued one. It used to belong to Leilani...

Can I see it? I've never seen a Mother Box before.

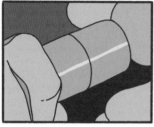

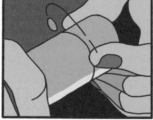

Granny Goodness integrated it into my Mega Rod.

But it's a stripped-down version. I can access the central database, but I can't create boom tubes.

Oh, that's too bad.

I mean, it seems like you'd want the ability to go... booming.

You know... through a tube.

You have no idea what a boom tube is, do you?

90

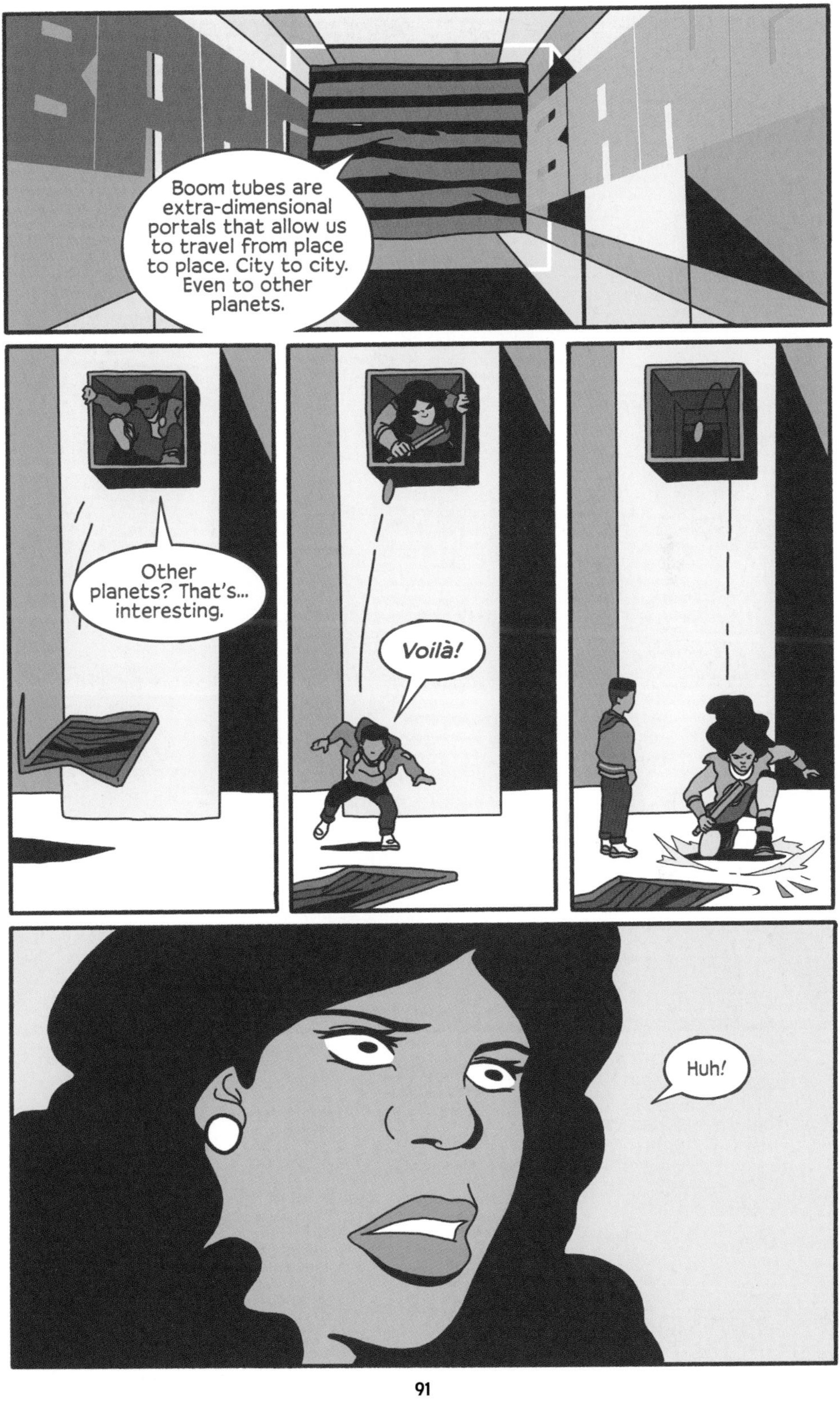
Boom tubes are extra-dimensional portals that allow us to travel from place to place. City to city. Even to other planets.
Other planets? That's... interesting.
Voilà!
Huh!

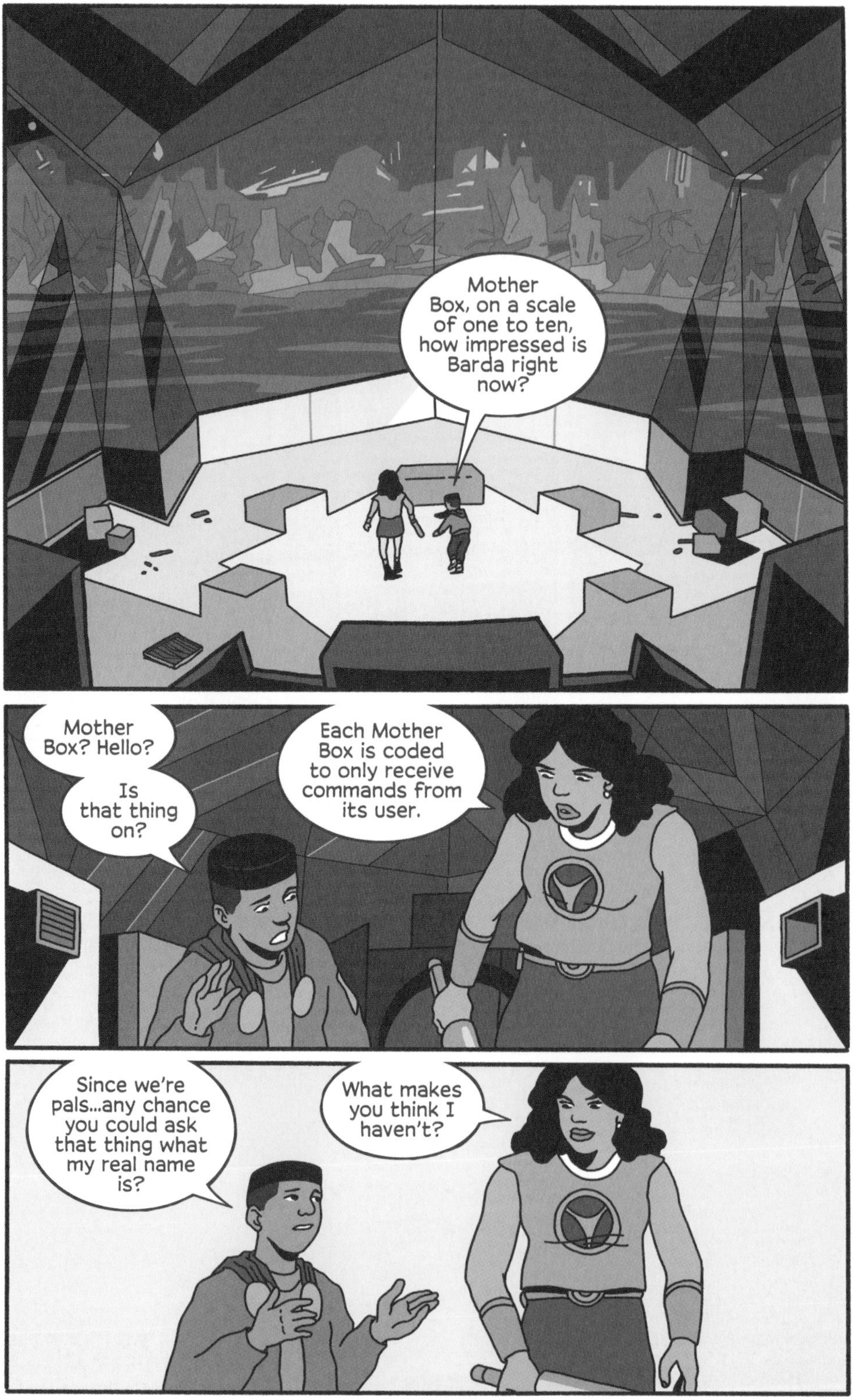
Mother Box, on a scale of one to ten, how impressed is Barda right now?
Mother Box? Hello?
Is that thing on?
Each Mother Box is coded to only receive commands from its user.
Since we're pals...any chance you could ask that thing what my real name is?
What makes you think I haven't?

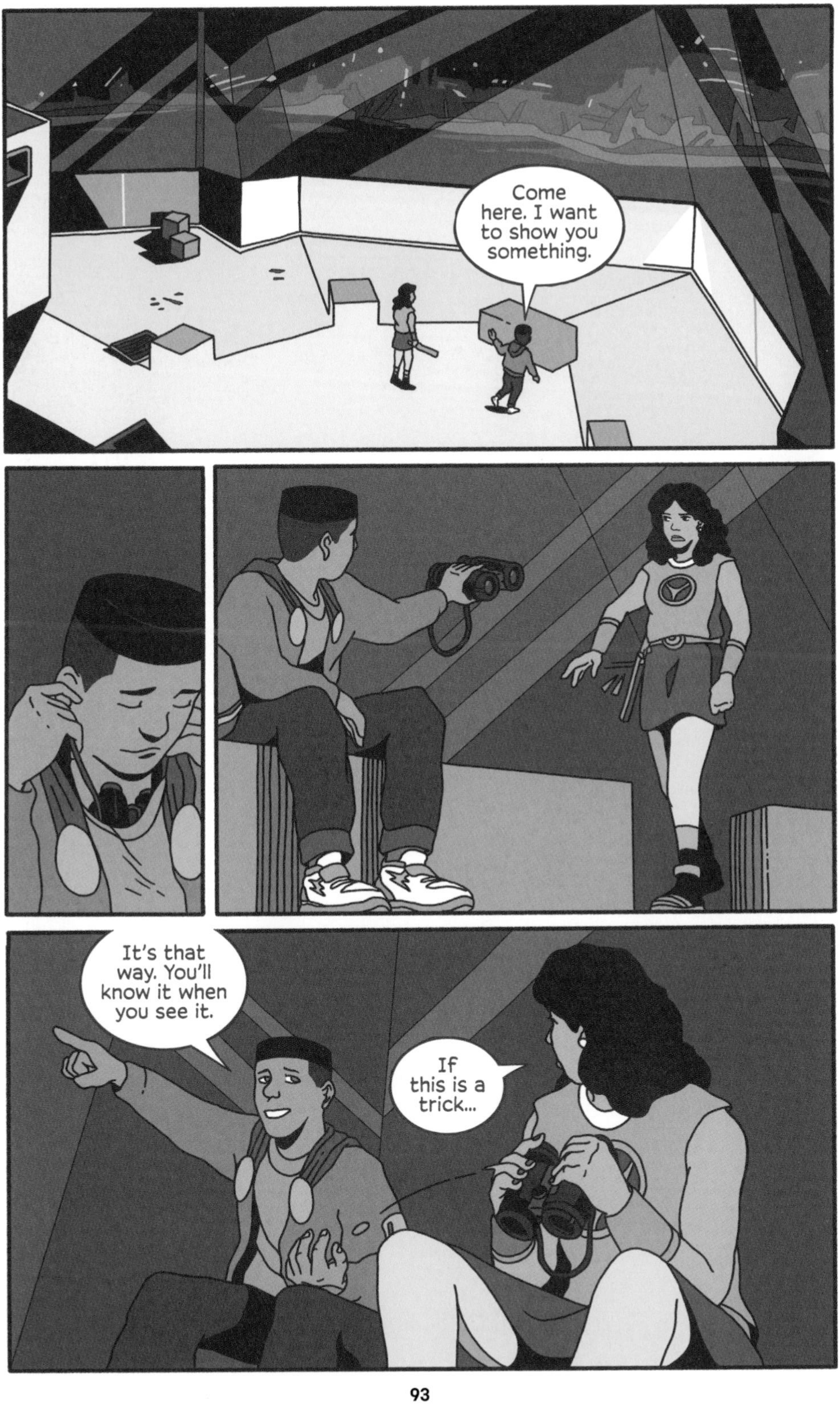
Come here. I want to show you something.
It's that way. You'll know it when you see it.
If this is a trick...

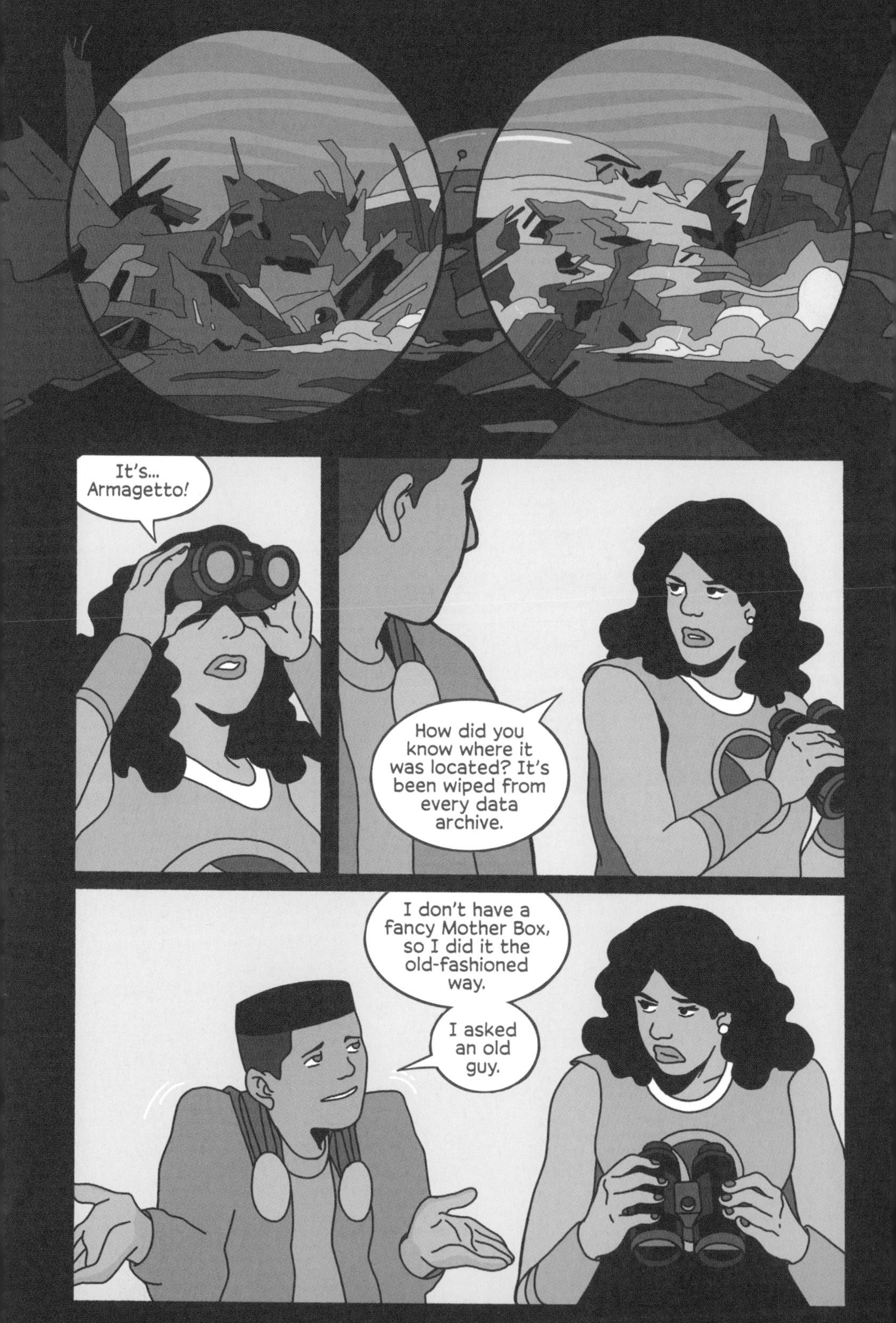
It's... Armagetto!
How did you know where it was located? It's been wiped from every data archive.
I don't have a fancy Mother Box, so I did it the old-fashioned way.
I asked an old guy.

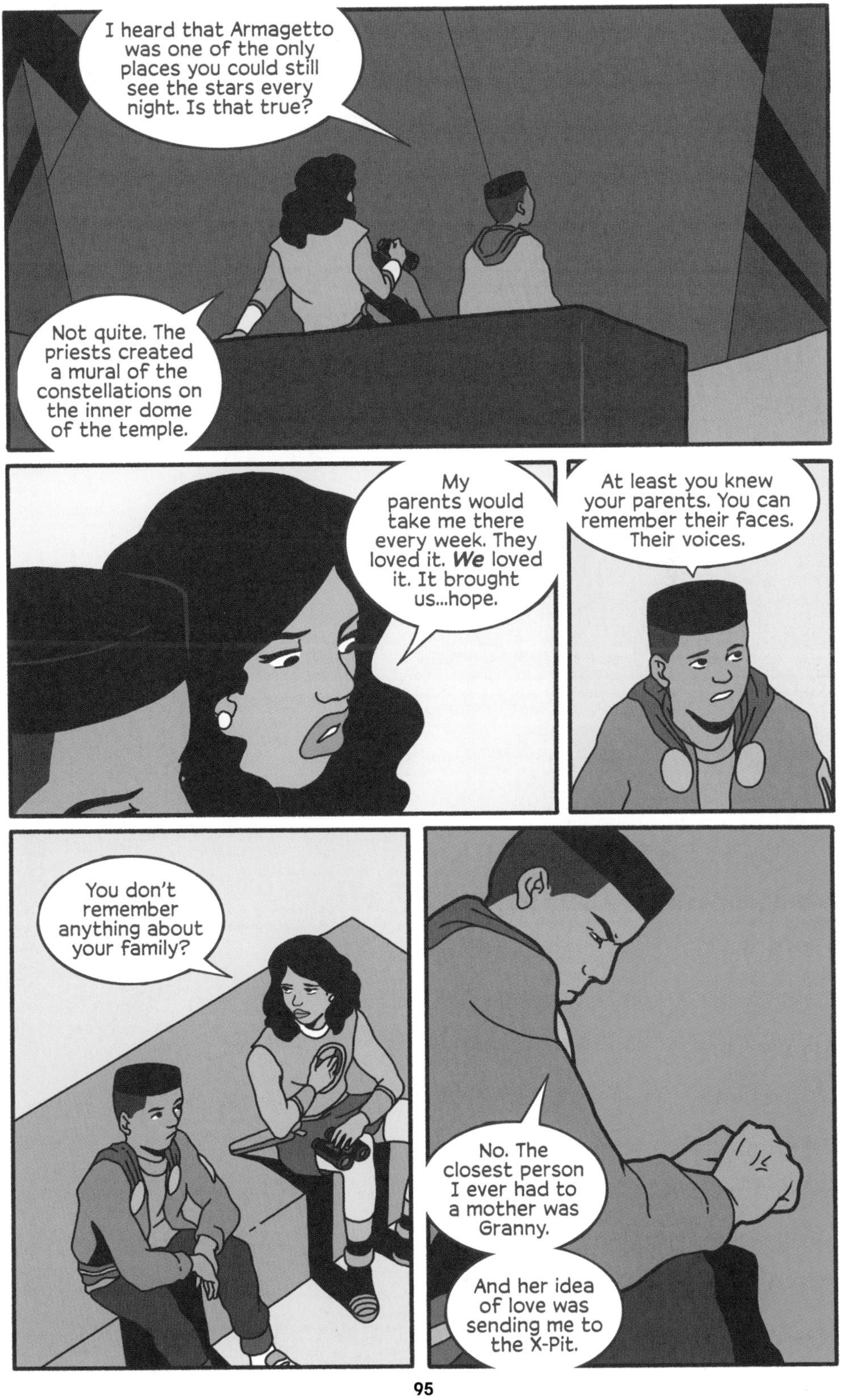
I heard that Armagetto was one of the only places you could still see the stars every night. Is that true?
Not quite. The priests created a mural of the constellations on the inner dome of the temple.
My parents would take me there every week. They loved it. *We* loved it. It brought us...hope.
At least you knew your parents. You can remember their faces. Their voices.
You don't remember anything about your family?
No. The closest person I ever had to a mother was Granny.
And her idea of love was sending me to the X-Pit.

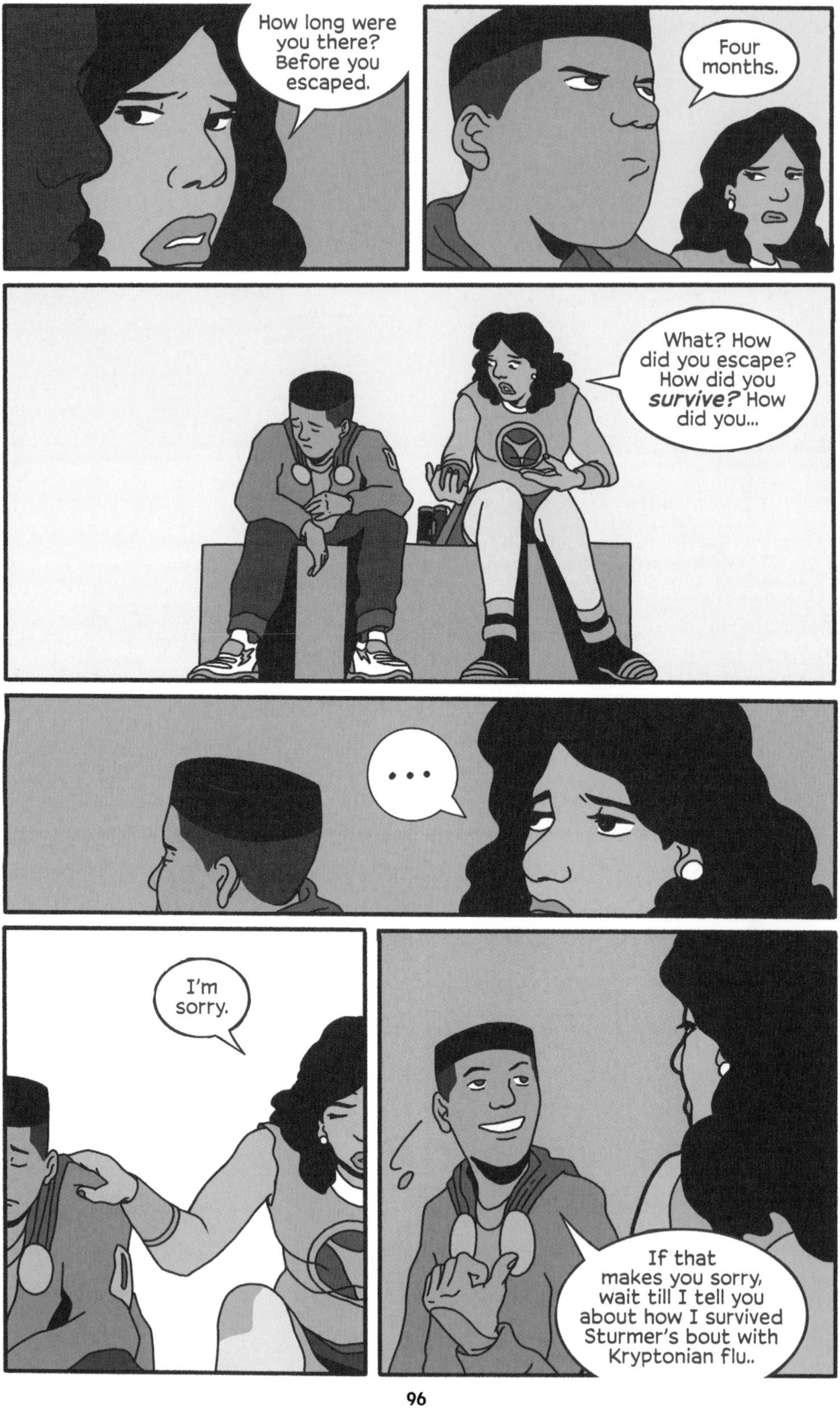
How long were you there? Before you escaped.
Four months.
What? How did you escape? How did you *survive?* How did you...
...
I'm sorry.
If that makes you sorry, wait till I tell you about how I survived Sturmer's bout with Kryptonian flu..

Can't you take anything seriously? I should go—

Don't go! It's almost time!

Every night, this section of Apokolips— well, everything besides the Academy— powers down for sixty seconds.

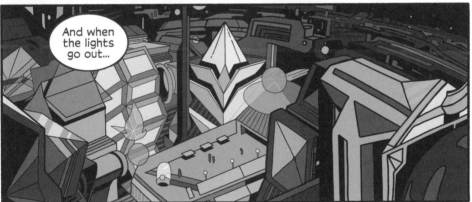

And when the lights go out...

...there's nothing stopping you...

...from seeing...

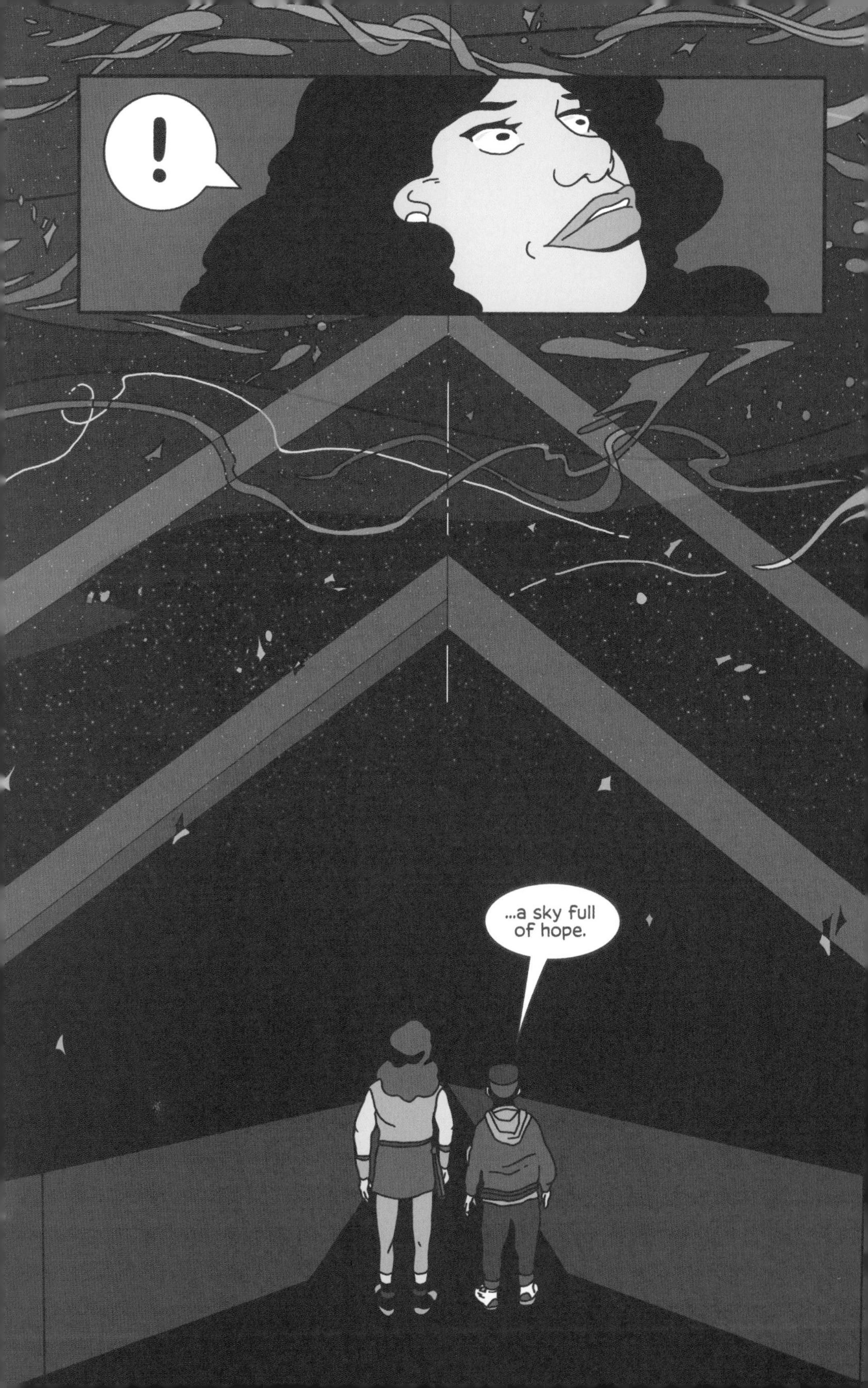
!
...a sky full of hope.

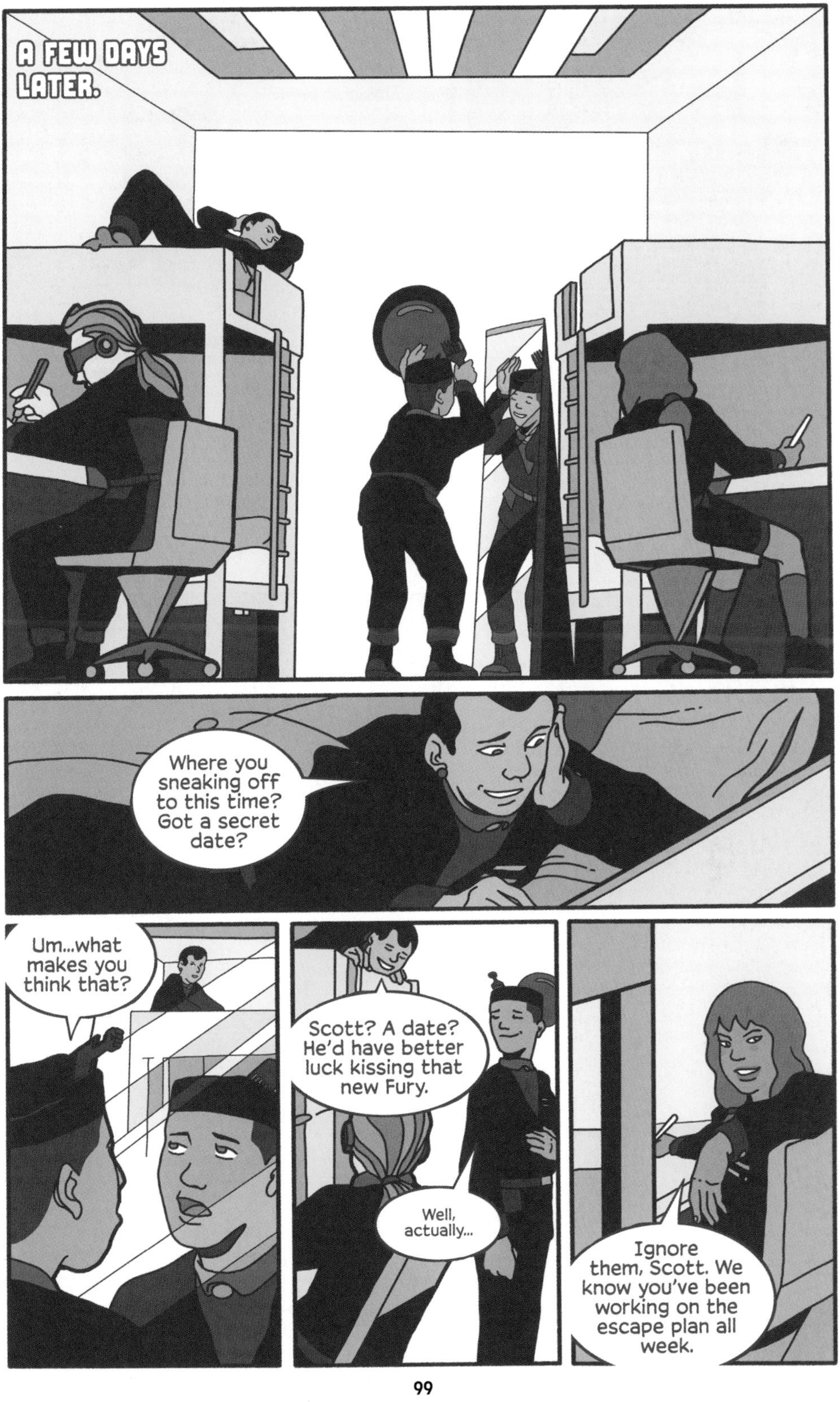
A FEW DAYS LATER.
Where you sneaking off to this time? Got a secret date?
Um...what makes you think that?
Scott? A date? He'd have better luck kissing that new Fury.
Well, actually...
Ignore them, Scott. We know you've been working on the escape plan all week.

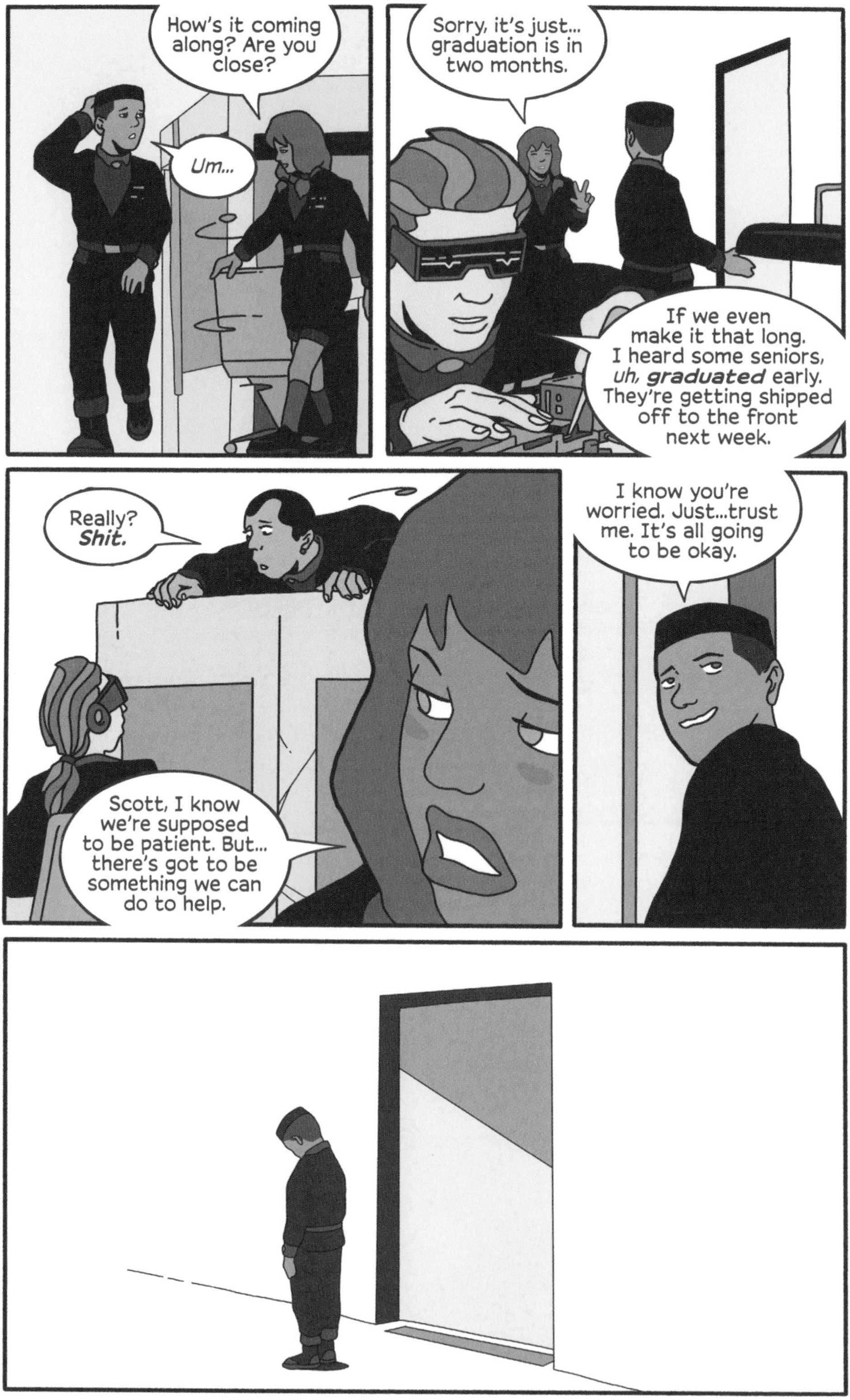
How's it coming along? Are you close?
Um...
Sorry, it's just... graduation is in two months.
If we even make it that long. I heard some seniors, *uh,* ***graduated*** early. They're getting shipped off to the front next week.
Really? ***Shit.***
Scott, I know we're supposed to be patient. But... there's got to be something we can do to help.
I know you're worried. Just...trust me. It's all going to be okay.

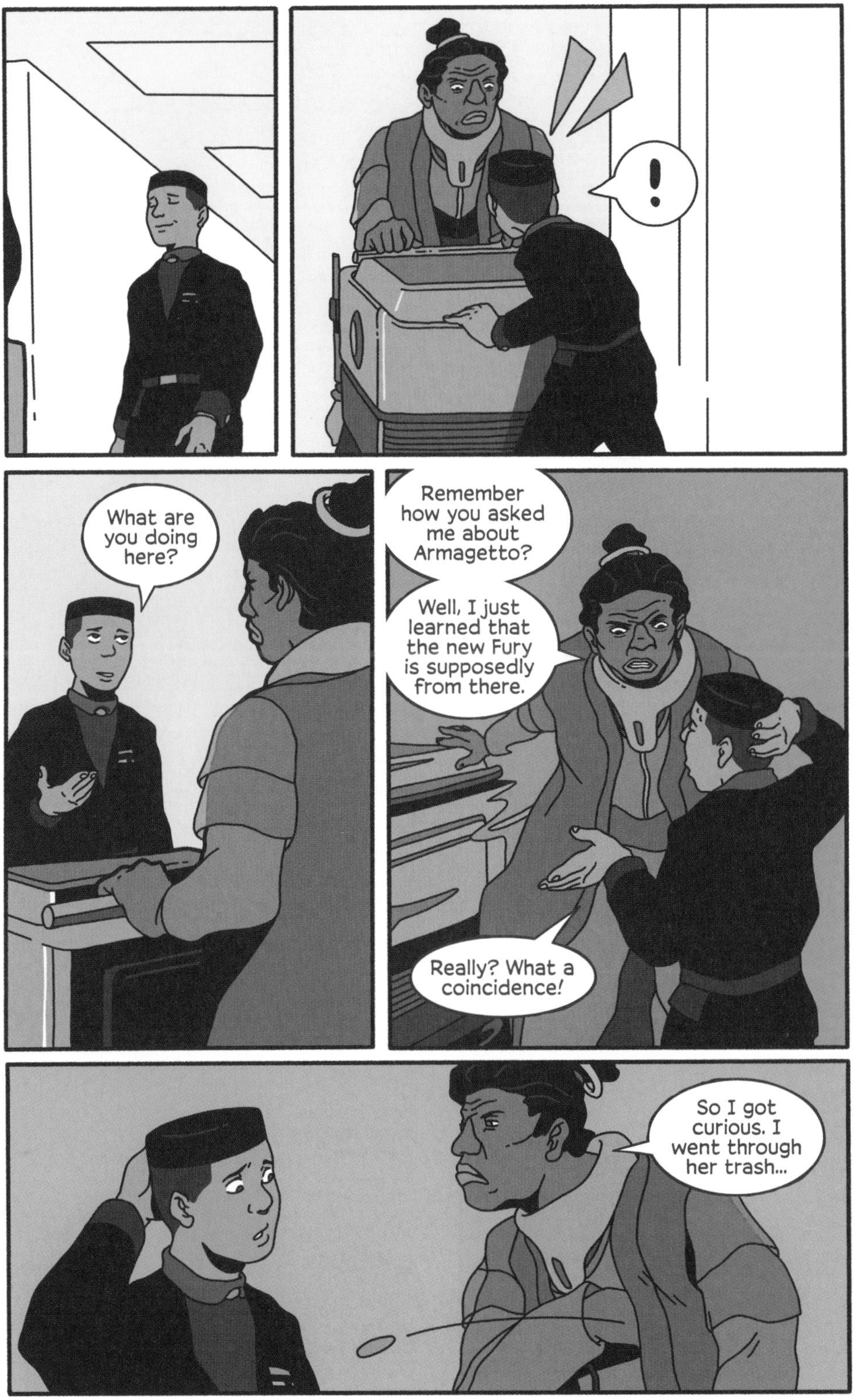
!
What are you doing here?
Remember how you asked me about Armagetto?
Well, I just learned that the new Fury is supposedly from there.
Really? What a coincidence!
So I got curious. I went through her trash...

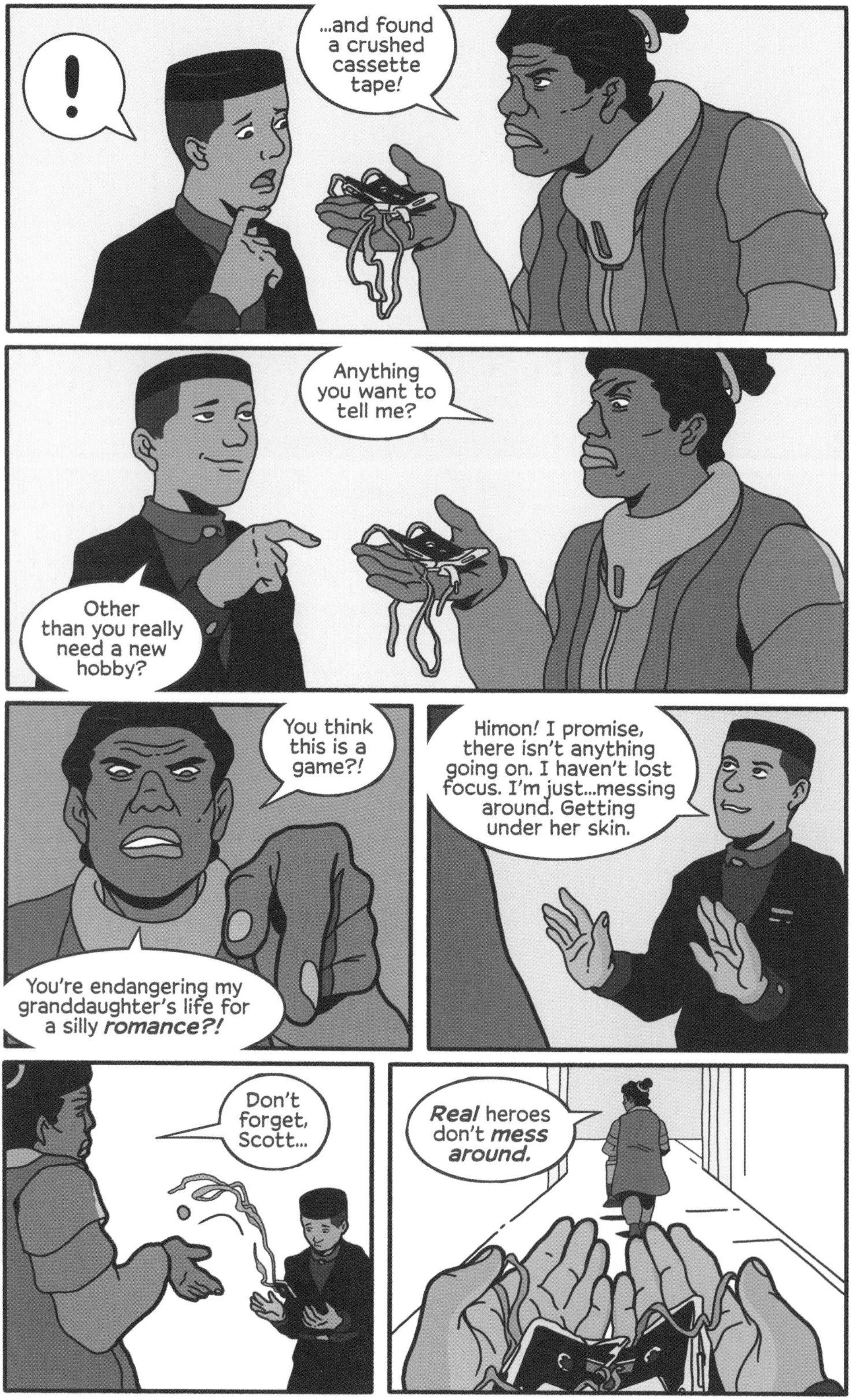
!
...and found a crushed cassette tape!
Anything you want to tell me?
Other than you really need a new hobby?
You think this is a game?!
You're endangering my granddaughter's life for a silly *romance?!*
Himon! I promise, there isn't anything going on. I haven't lost focus. I'm just...messing around. Getting under her skin.
Don't forget, Scott...
Real** heroes don't **mess around.

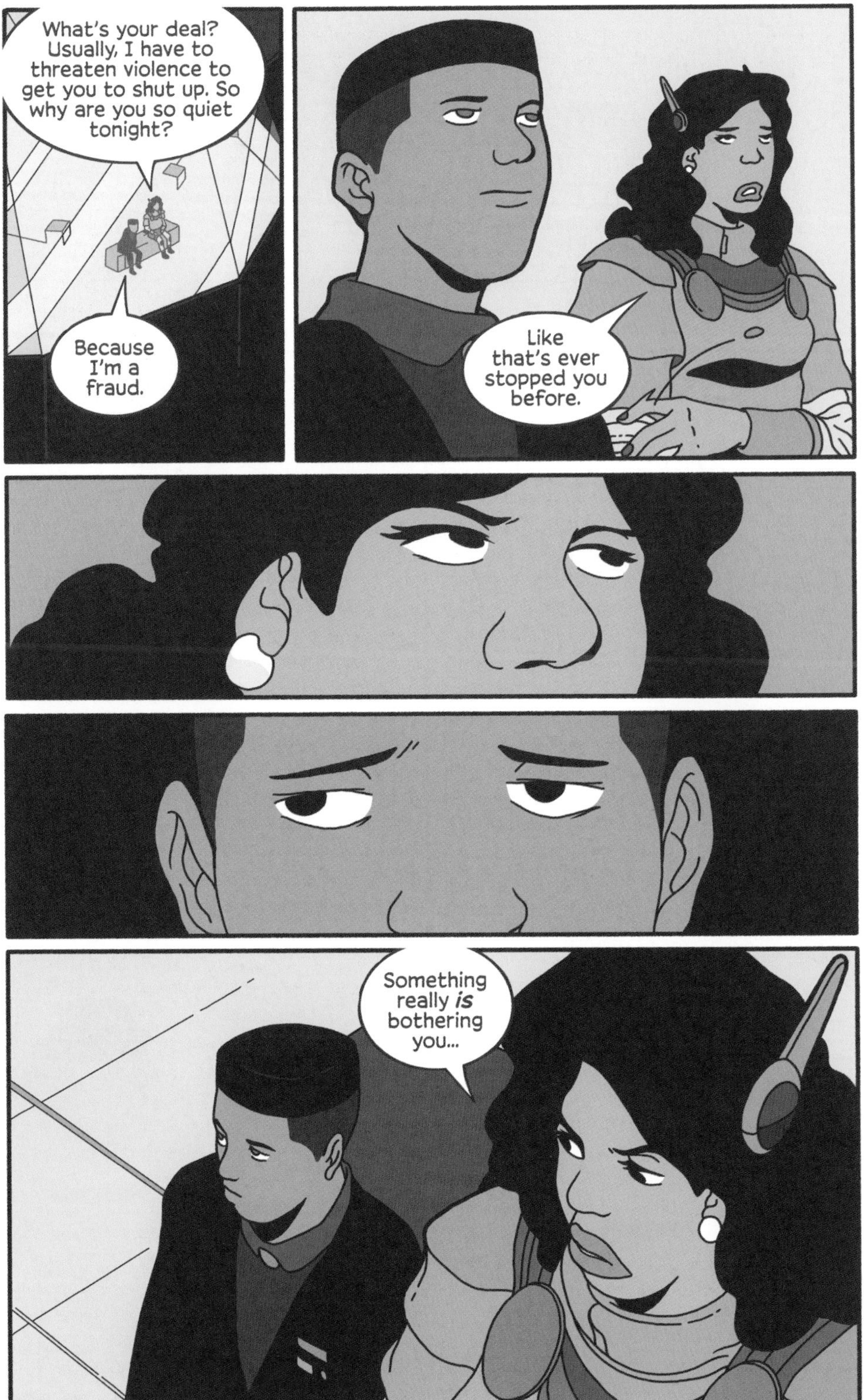
What's your deal? Usually, I have to threaten violence to get you to shut up. So why are you so quiet tonight?
Because I'm a fraud.
Like that's ever stopped you before.
Something really *is* bothering you...

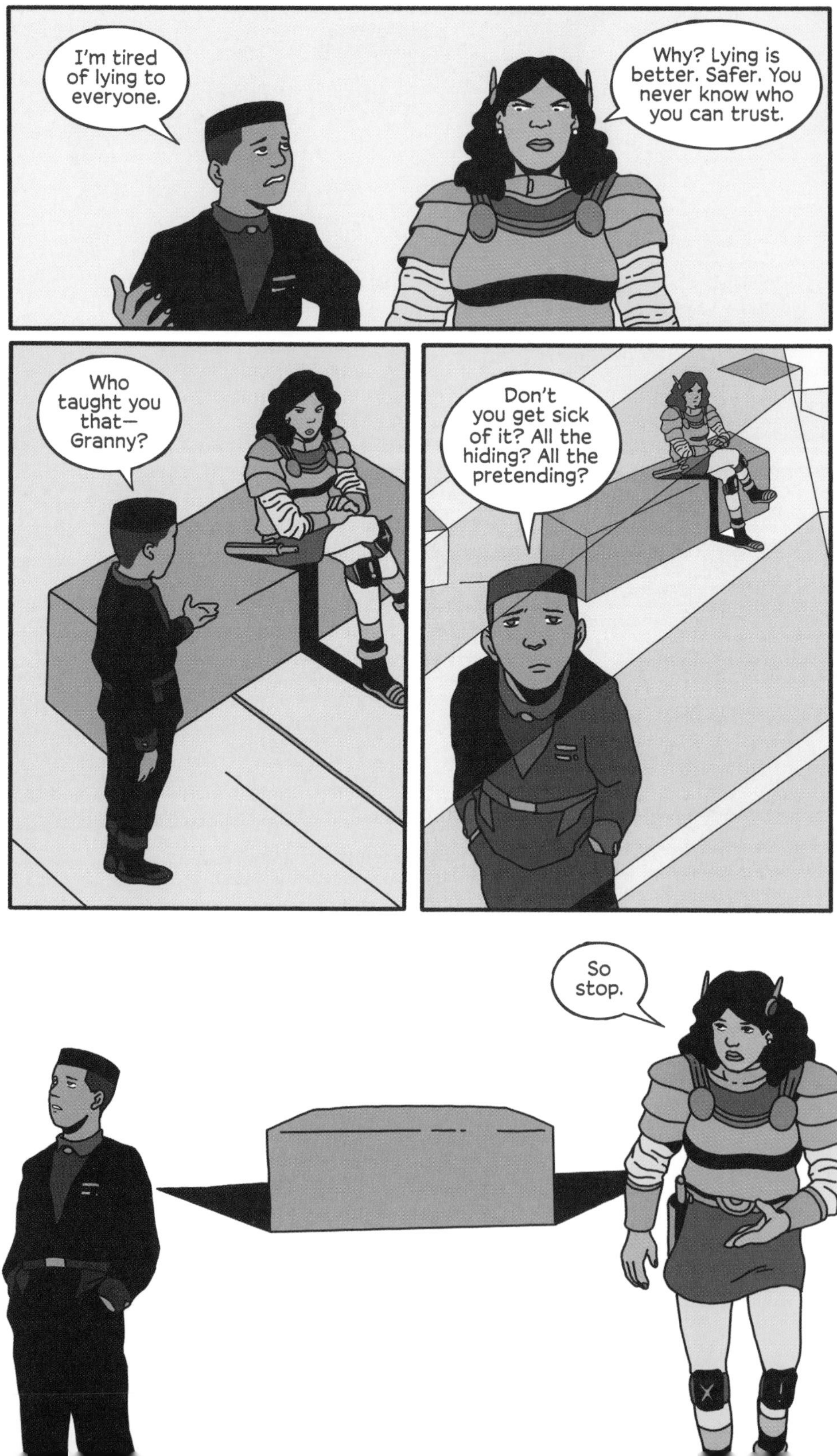
I'm tired of lying to everyone.
Why? Lying is better. Safer. You never know who you can trust.
Who taught you that— Granny?
Don't you get sick of it? All the hiding? All the pretending?
So stop.

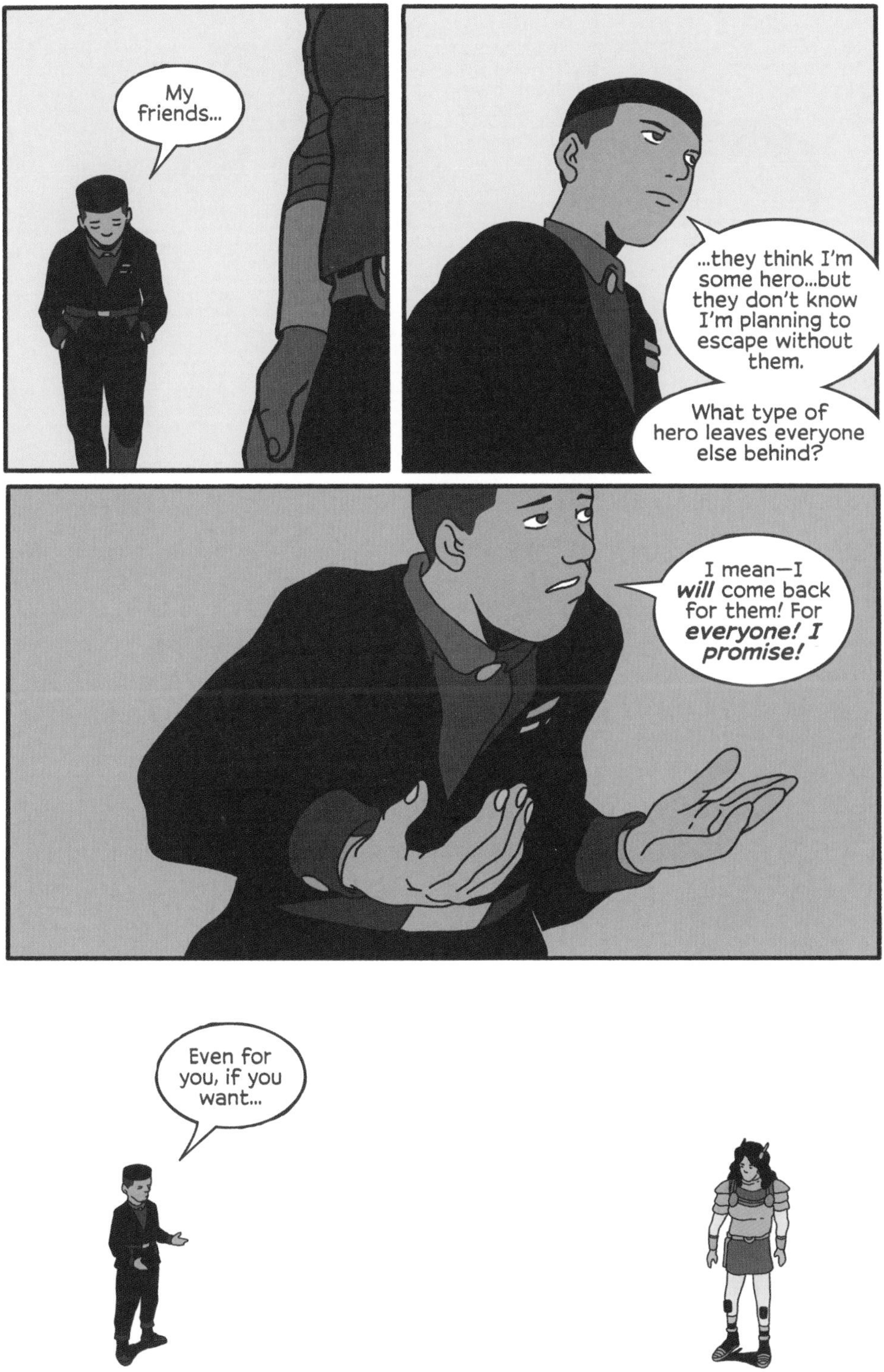
My friends...
...they think I'm some hero...but they don't know I'm planning to escape without them.
What type of hero leaves everyone else behind?
I mean—I ***will*** come back for them! For ***everyone! I promise!***
Even for you, if you want...

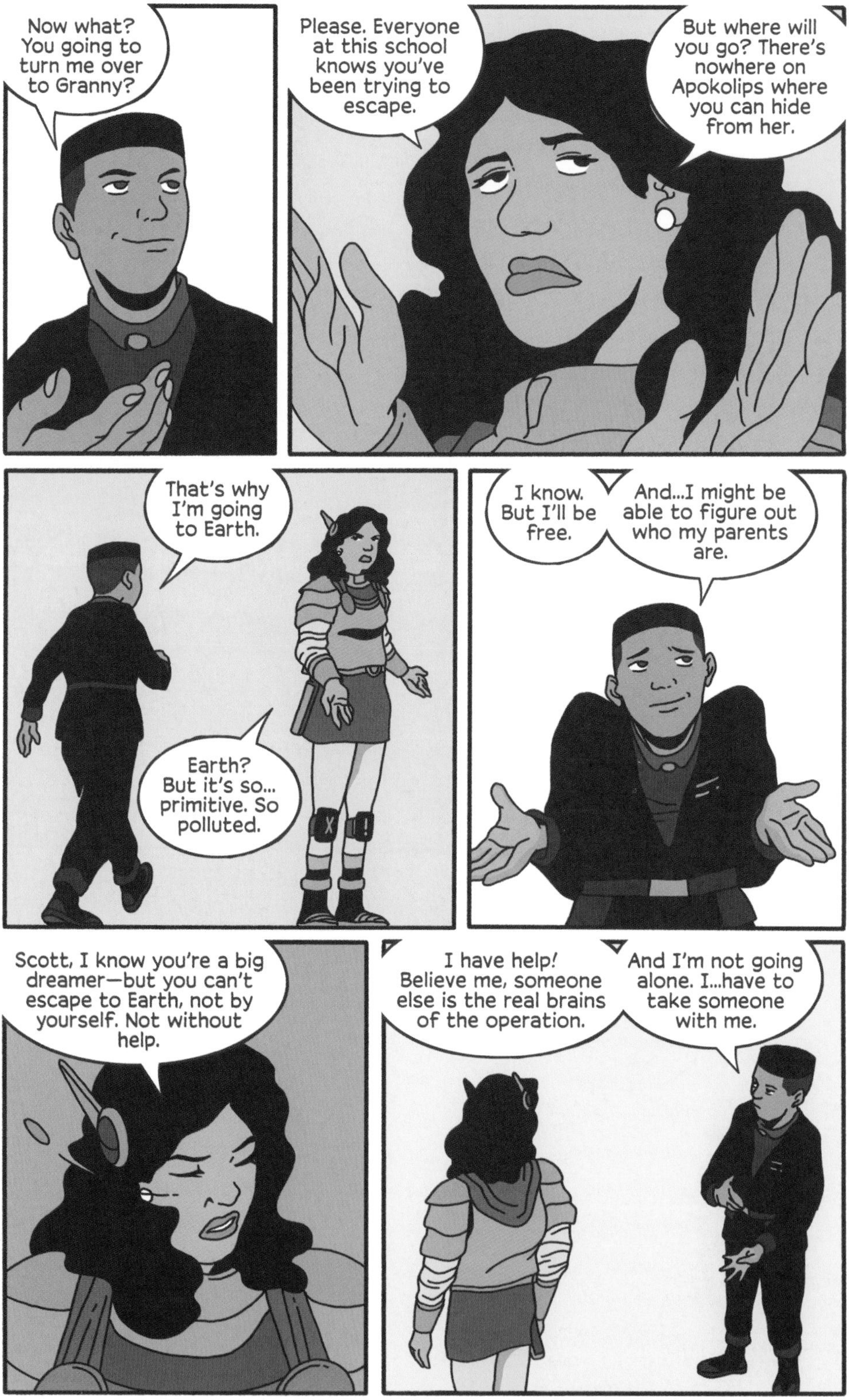
Now what? You going to turn me over to Granny?
Please. Everyone at this school knows you've been trying to escape.
But where will you go? There's nowhere on Apokolips where you can hide from her.
That's why I'm going to Earth.
Earth? But it's so... primitive. So polluted.
I know. But I'll be free.
And...I might be able to figure out who my parents are.
Scott, I know you're a big dreamer—but you can't escape to Earth, not by yourself. Not without help.
I have help! Believe me, someone else is the real brains of the operation.
And I'm not going alone. I...have to take someone with me.

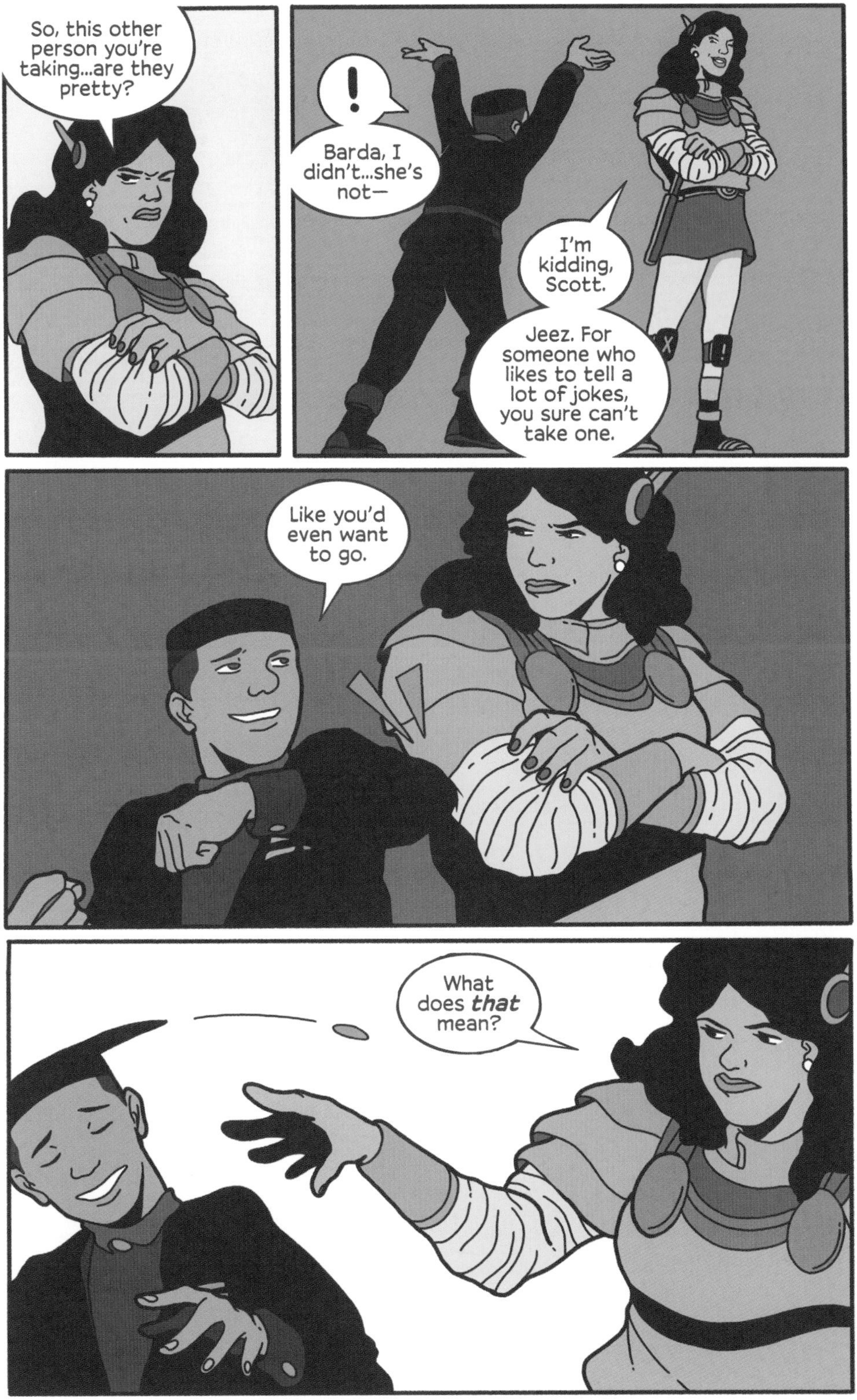
So, this other person you're taking...are they pretty?
!
Barda, I didn't...she's not—
I'm kidding, Scott.
Jeez. For someone who likes to tell a lot of jokes, you sure can't take one.
Like you'd even want to go.
What does ***that*** mean?

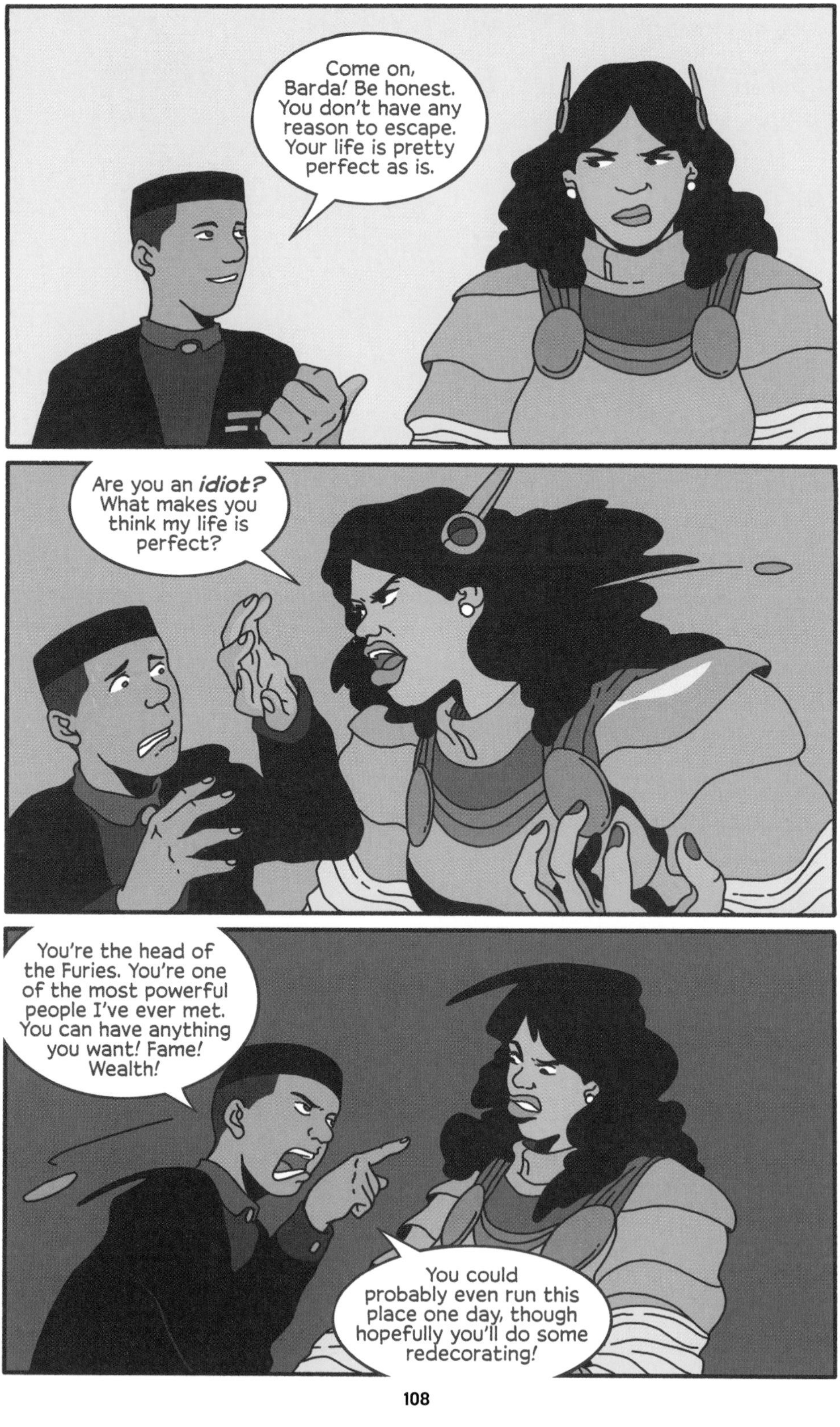
Come on, Barda! Be honest. You don't have any reason to escape. Your life is pretty perfect as is.
Are you an *idiot?* What makes you think my life is perfect?
You're the head of the Furies. You're one of the most powerful people I've ever met. You can have anything you want! Fame! Wealth!
You could probably even run this place one day, though hopefully you'll do some redecorating!

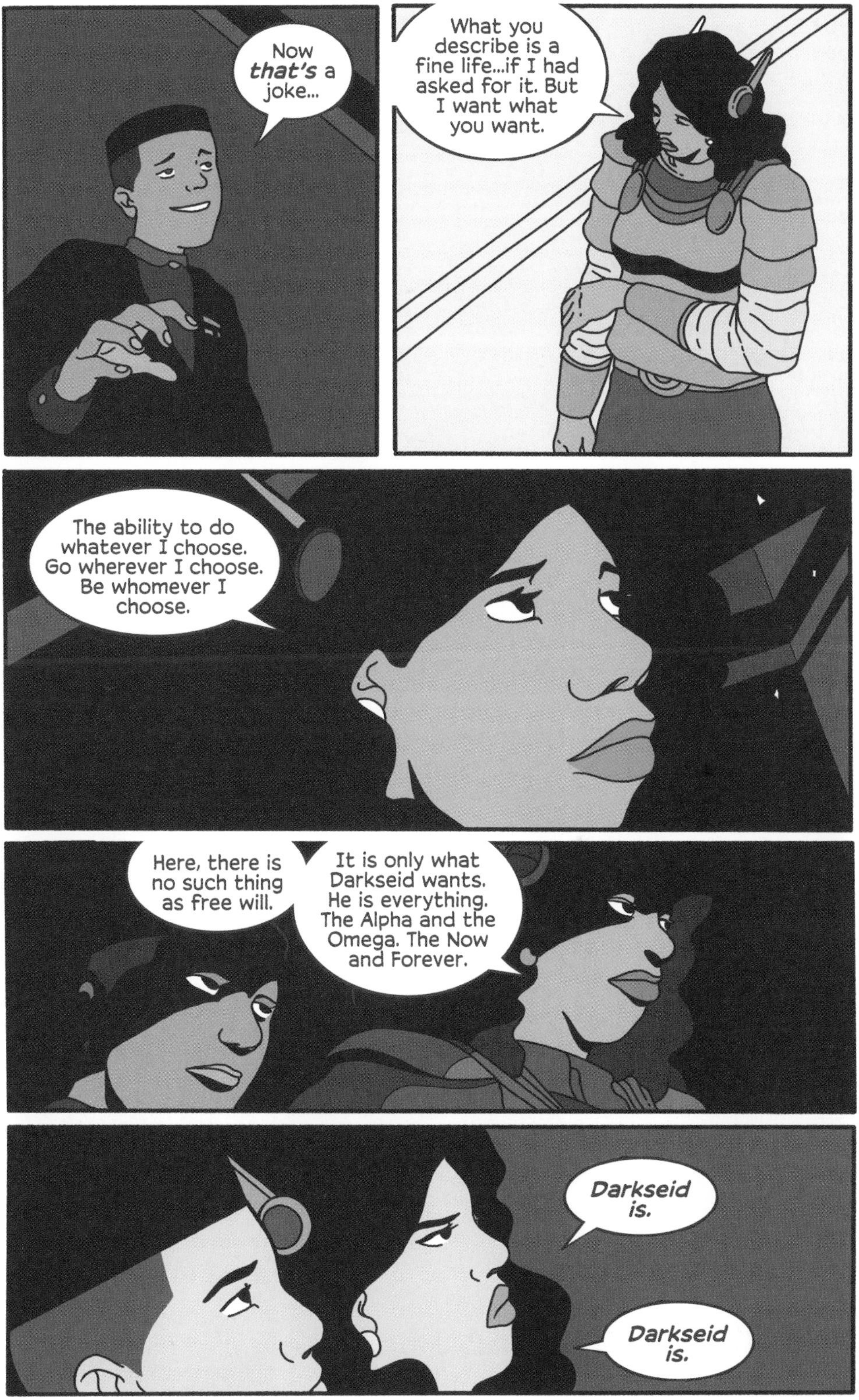
Now *that's* a joke...
What you describe is a fine life...if I had asked for it. But I want what you want.
The ability to do whatever I choose. Go wherever I choose. Be whomever I choose.
Here, there is no such thing as free will.
It is only what Darkseid wants. He is everything. The Alpha and the Omega. The Now and Forever.
Darkseid is.
Darkseid is.

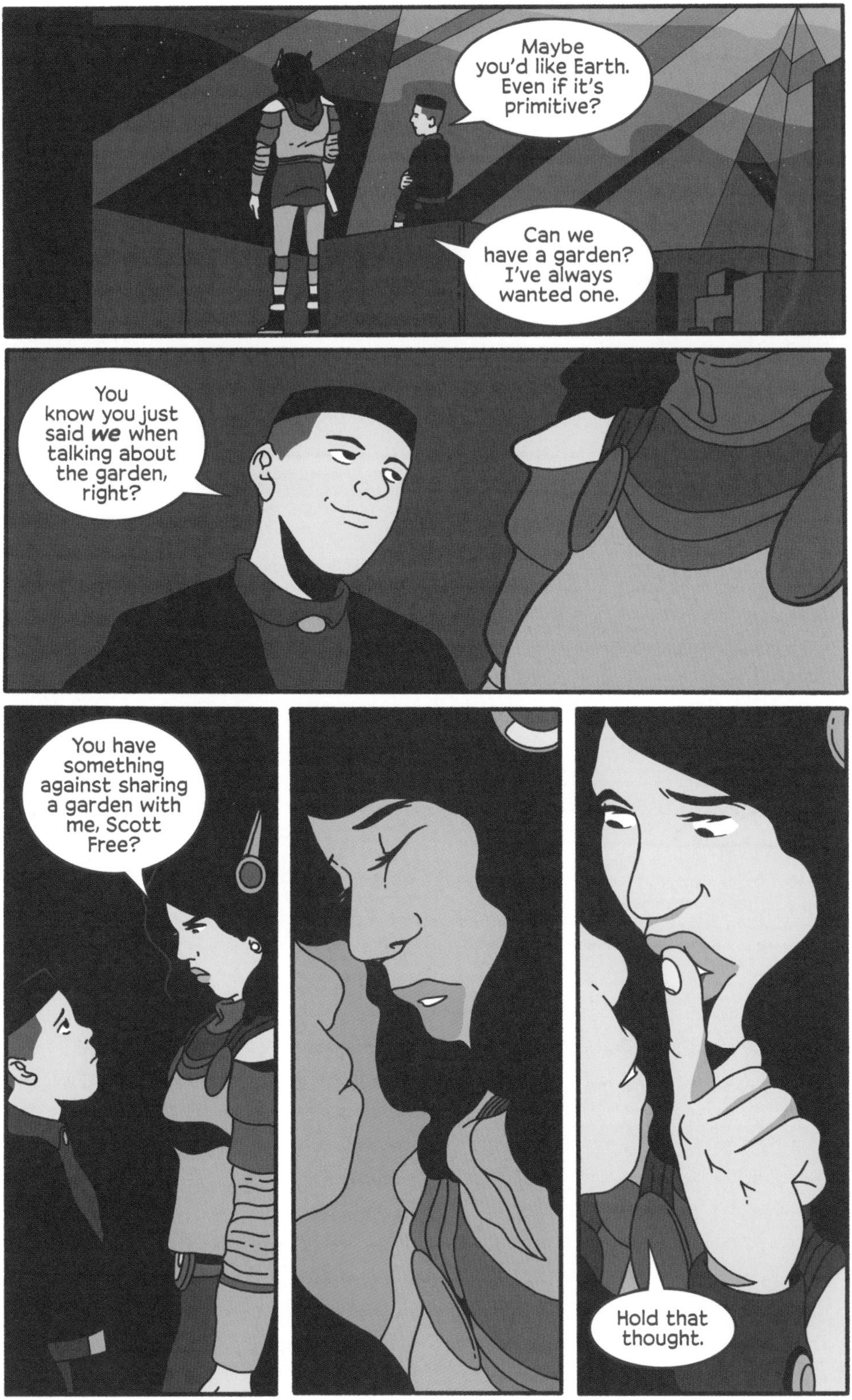
Maybe you'd like Earth. Even if it's primitive?
Can we have a garden? I've always wanted one.
You know you just said *we* when talking about the garden, right?
You have something against sharing a garden with me, Scott Free?
Hold that thought.

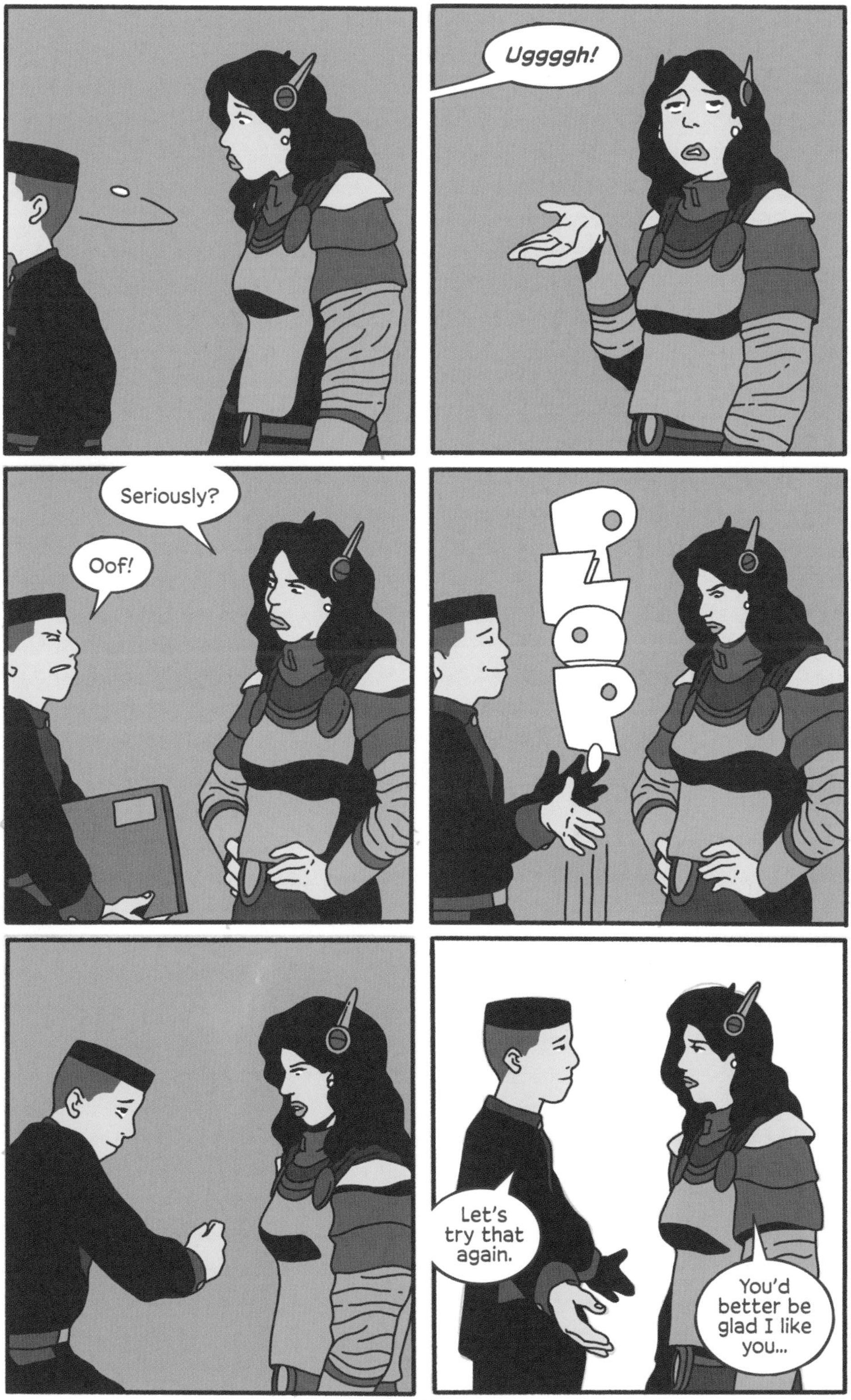
Uggggh!
Seriously?
Oof!
PLOOP
Let's try that again.
You'd better be glad I like you...

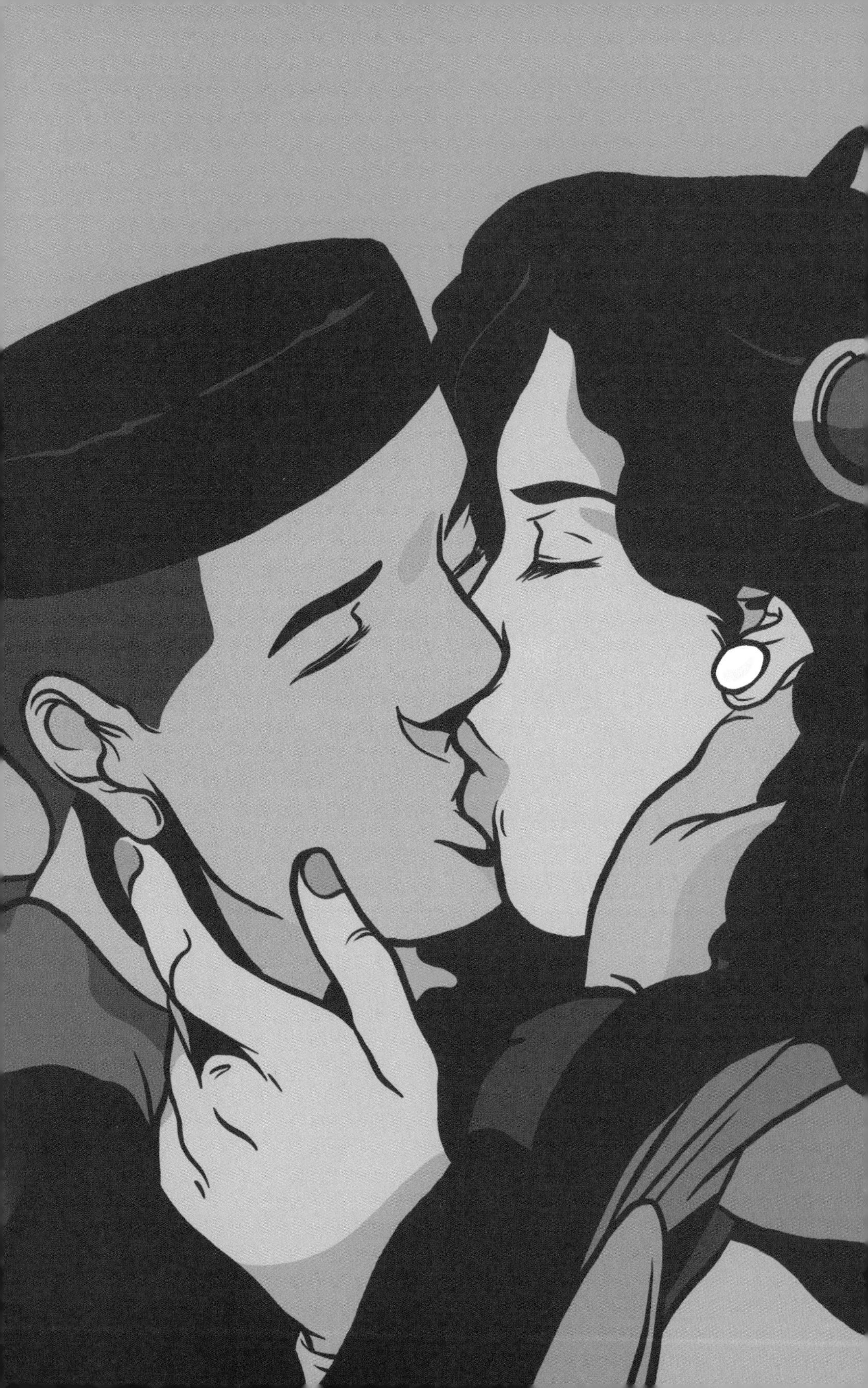

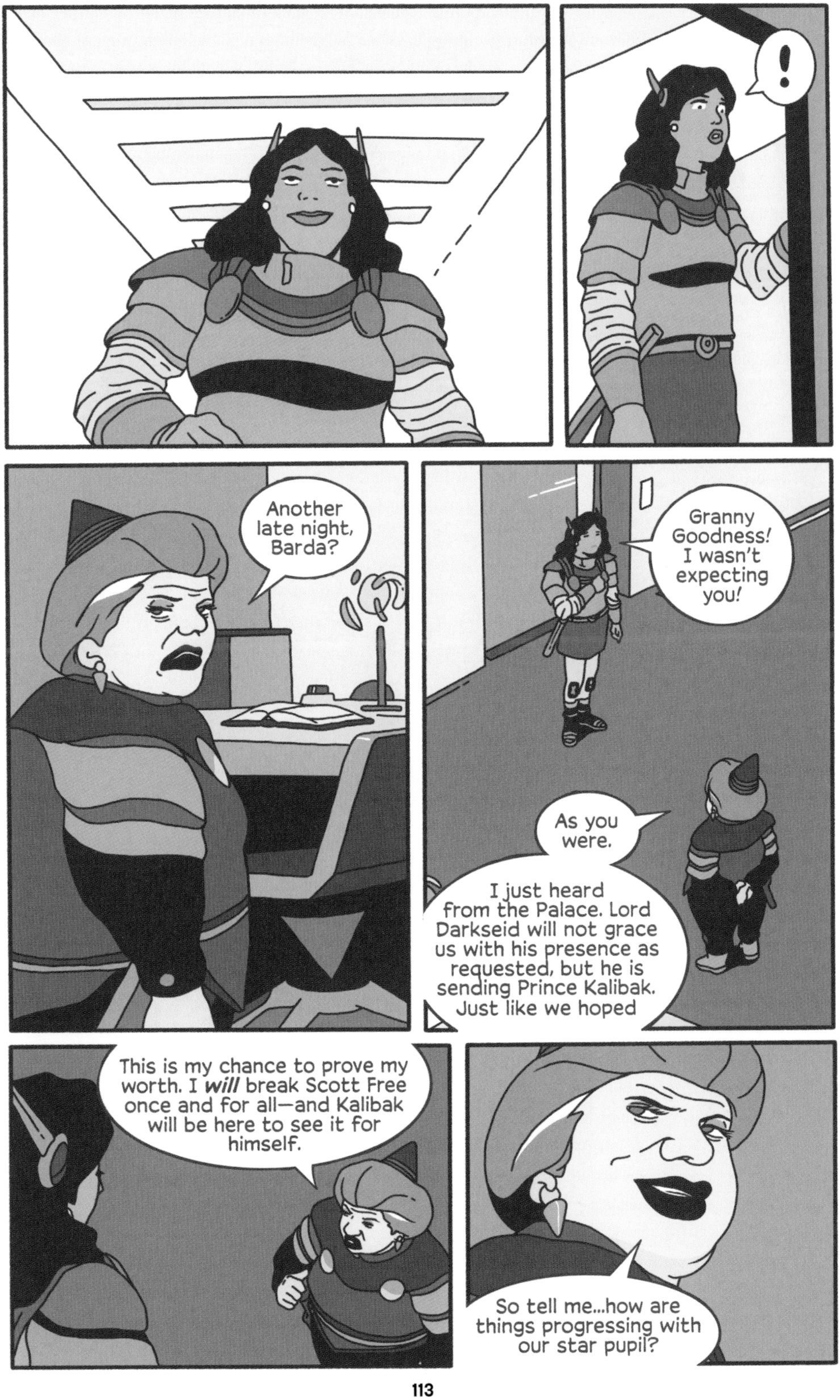
!
Another late night, Barda?
Granny Goodness! I wasn't expecting you!
As you were.
I just heard from the Palace. Lord Darkseid will not grace us with his presence as requested, but he is sending Prince Kalibak. Just like we hoped
This is my chance to prove my worth. I *will* break Scott Free once and for all—and Kalibak will be here to see it for himself.
So tell me...how are things progressing with our star pupil?

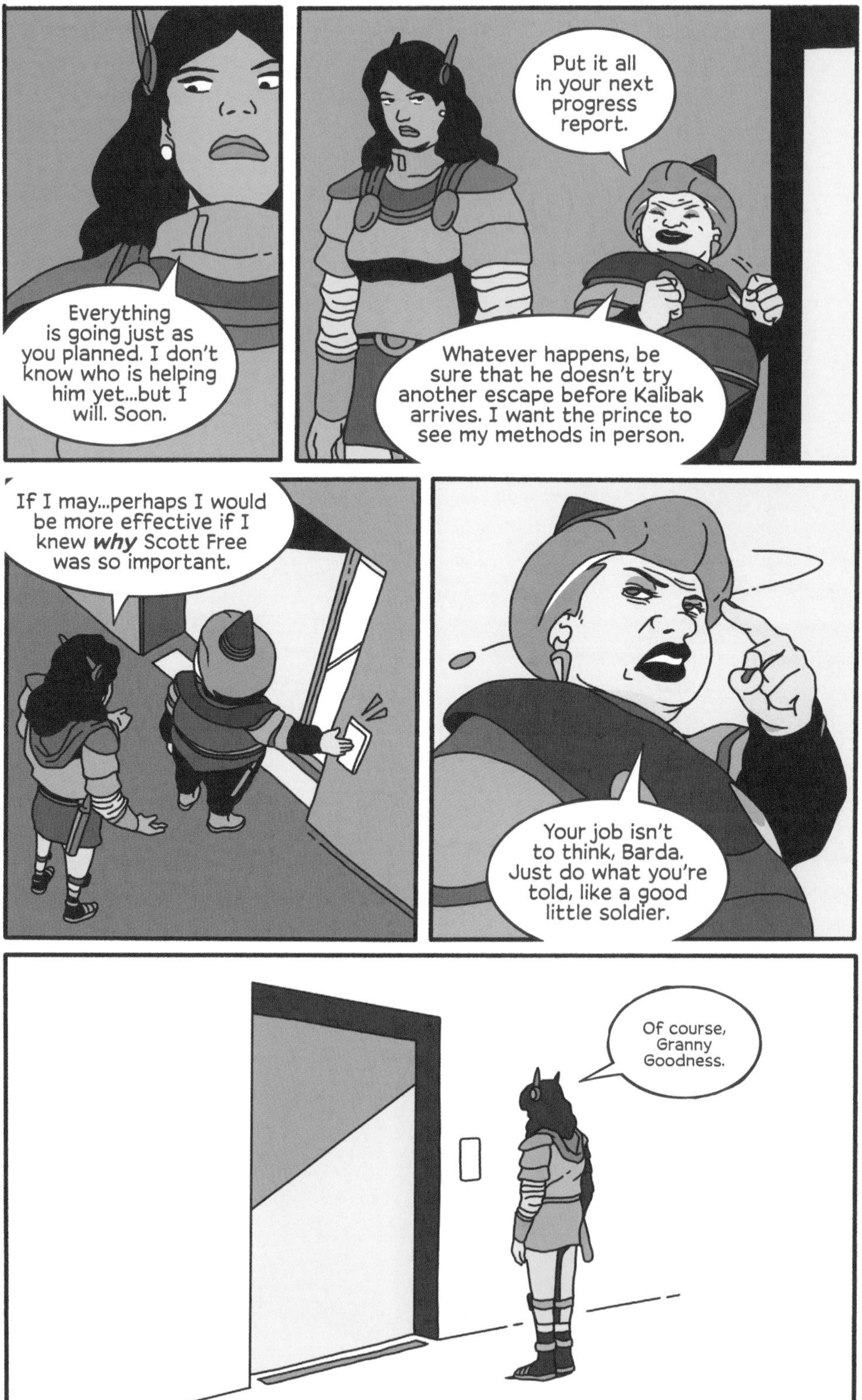
Everything is going just as you planned. I don't know who is helping him yet...but I will. Soon.
Put it all in your next progress report.
Whatever happens, be sure that he doesn't try another escape before Kalibak arrives. I want the prince to see my methods in person.
If I may...perhaps I would be more effective if I knew *why* Scott Free was so important.
Your job isn't to think, Barda. Just do what you're told, like a good little soldier.
Of course, Granny Goodness.

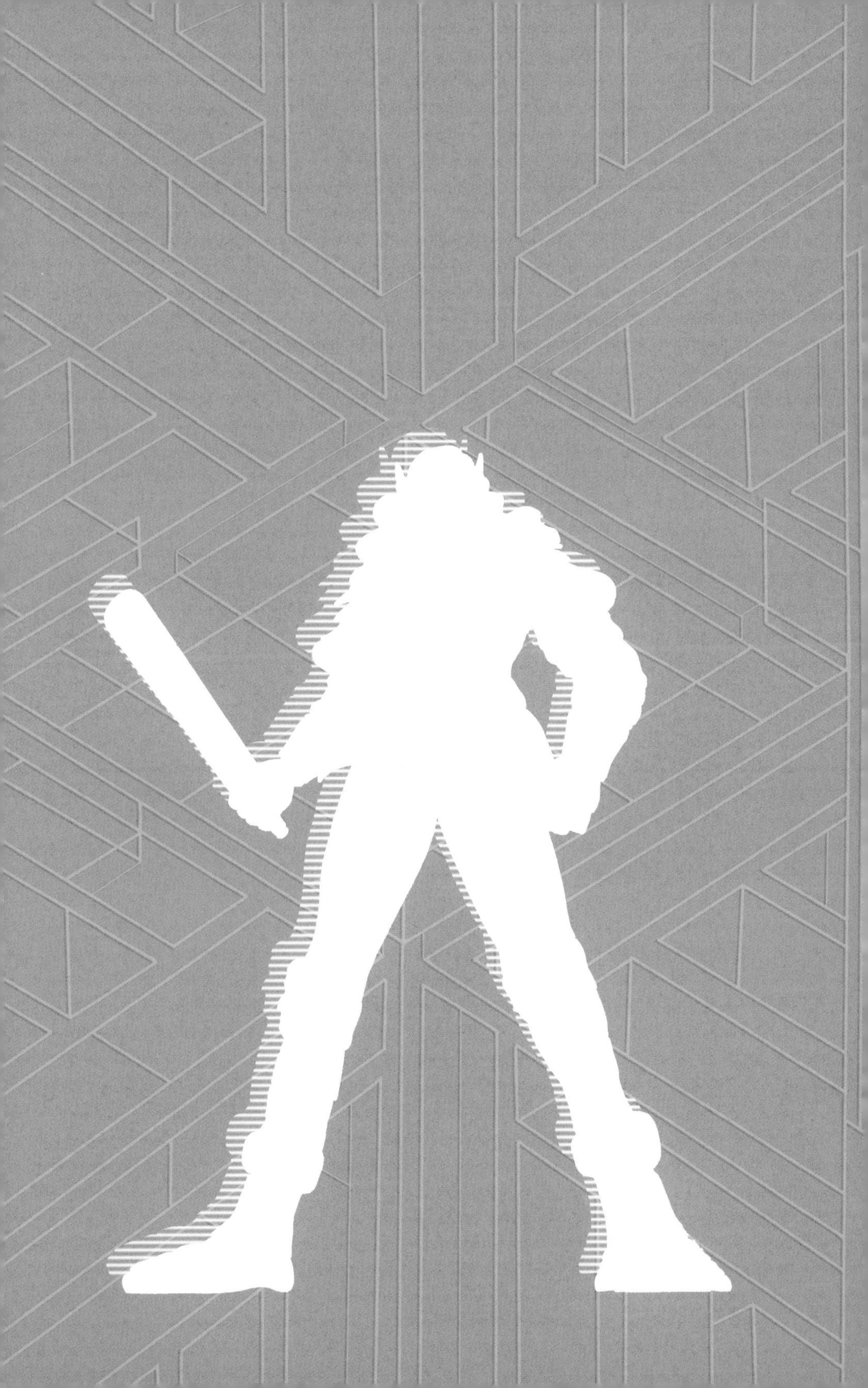

CHAPTER FOUR

I Heard It through the Grapevine

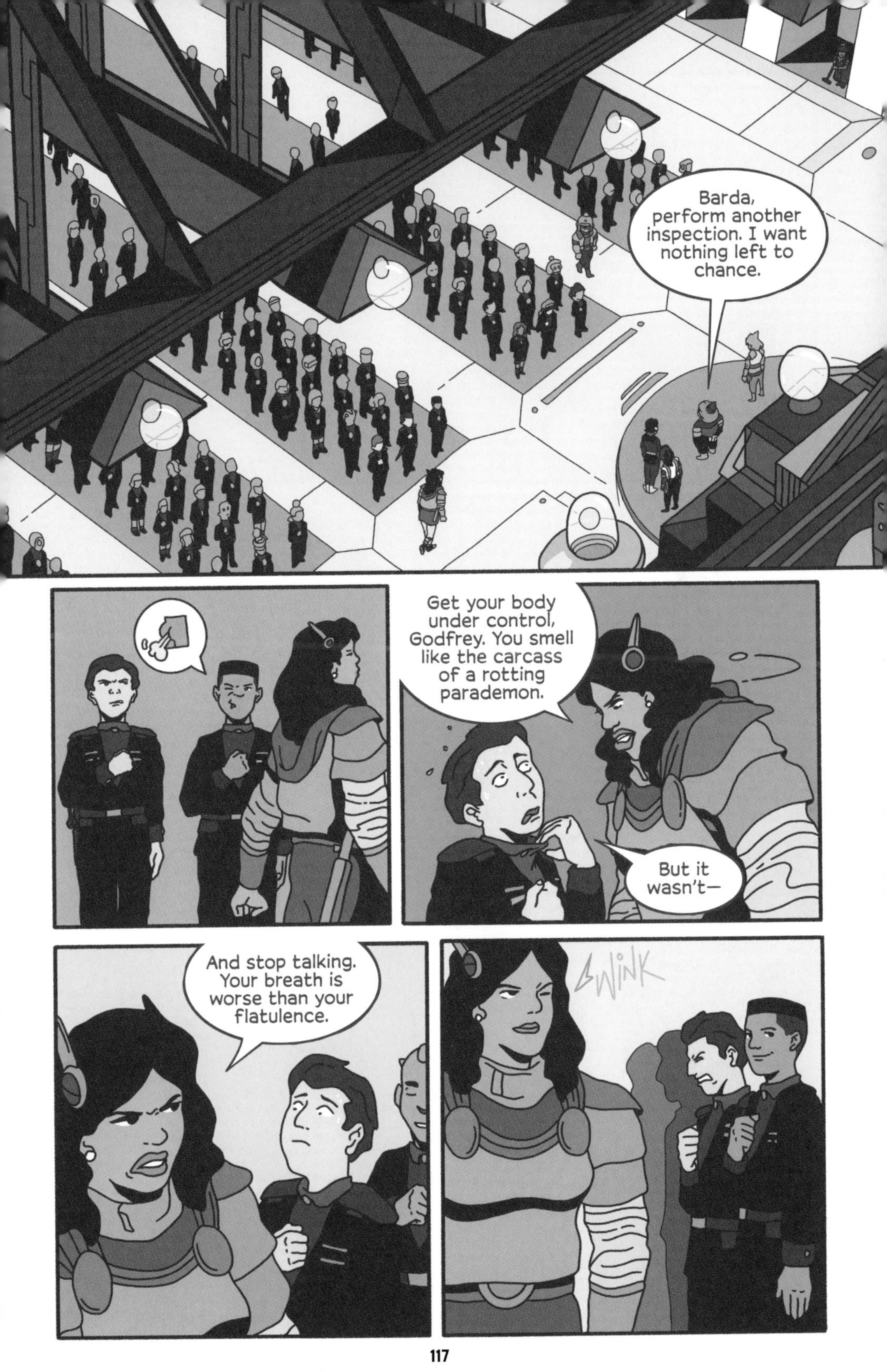
Barda, perform another inspection. I want nothing left to chance.
Get your body under control, Godfrey. You smell like the carcass of a rotting parademon.
But it wasn't—
And stop talking. Your breath is worse than your flatulence.
BWINK

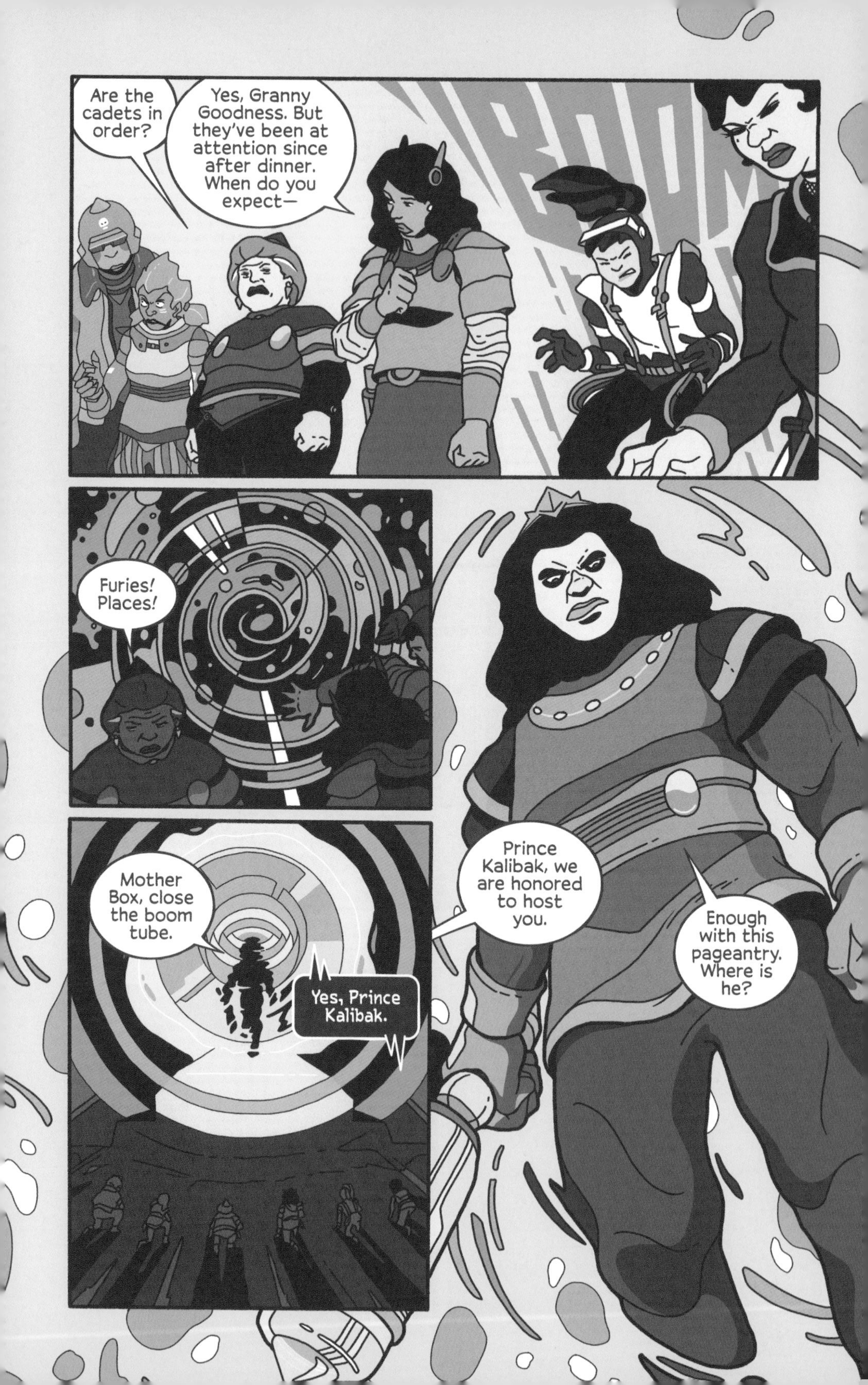
Are the cadets in order?
Yes, Granny Goodness. But they've been at attention since after dinner. When do you expect—
Furies! Places!
Mother Box, close the boom tube.
Yes, Prince Kalibak.
Prince Kalibak, we are honored to host you.
Enough with this pageantry. Where is he?

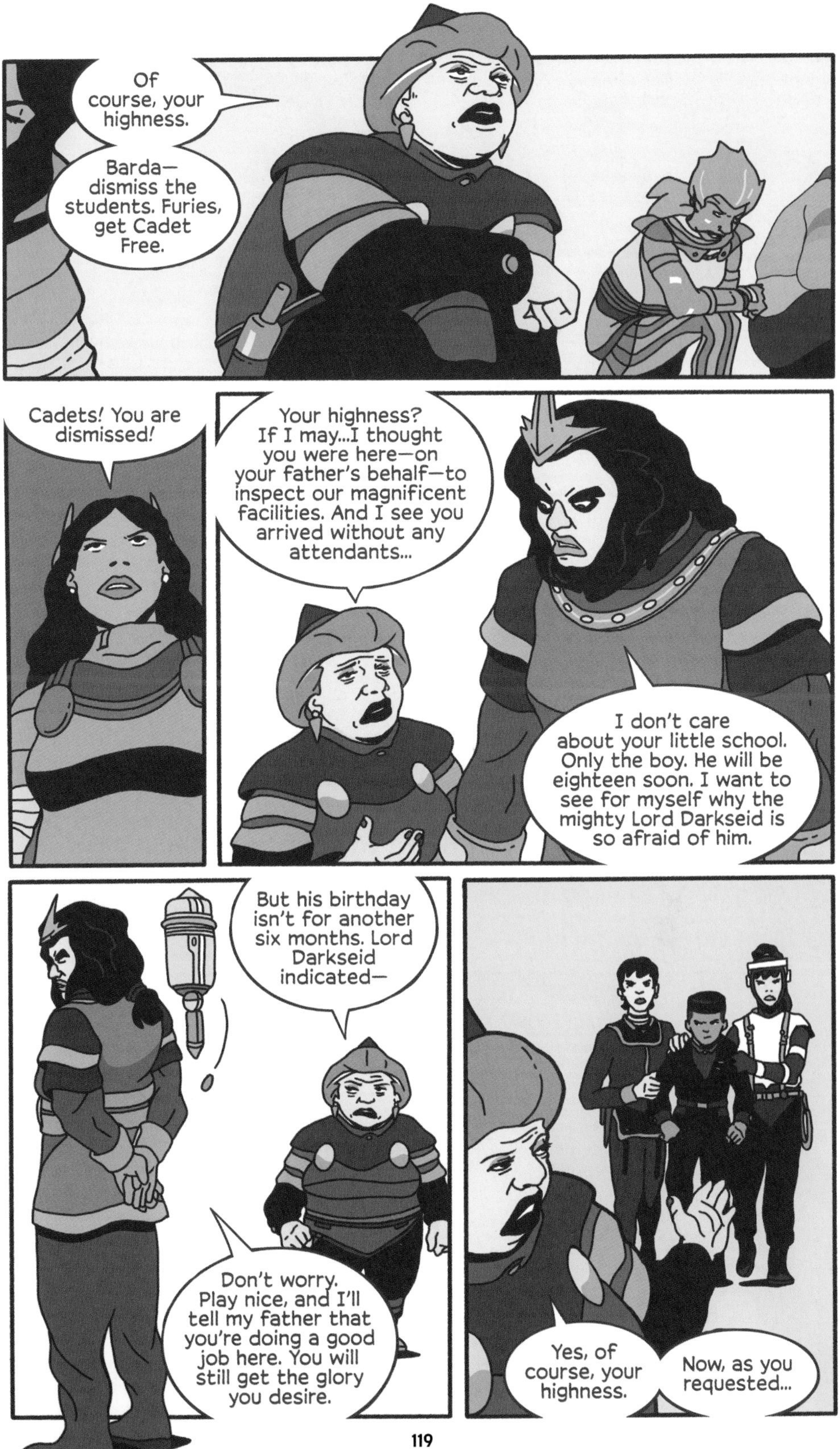

Of course, your highness.
Barda— dismiss the students. Furies, get Cadet Free.
Cadets! You are dismissed!
Your highness? If I may...I thought you were here—on your father's behalf—to inspect our magnificent facilities. And I see you arrived without any attendants...
I don't care about your little school. Only the boy. He will be eighteen soon. I want to see for myself why the mighty Lord Darkseid is so afraid of him.
But his birthday isn't for another six months. Lord Darkseid indicated—
Don't worry. Play nice, and I'll tell my father that you're doing a good job here. You will still get the glory you desire.
Yes, of course, your highness.
Now, as you requested...

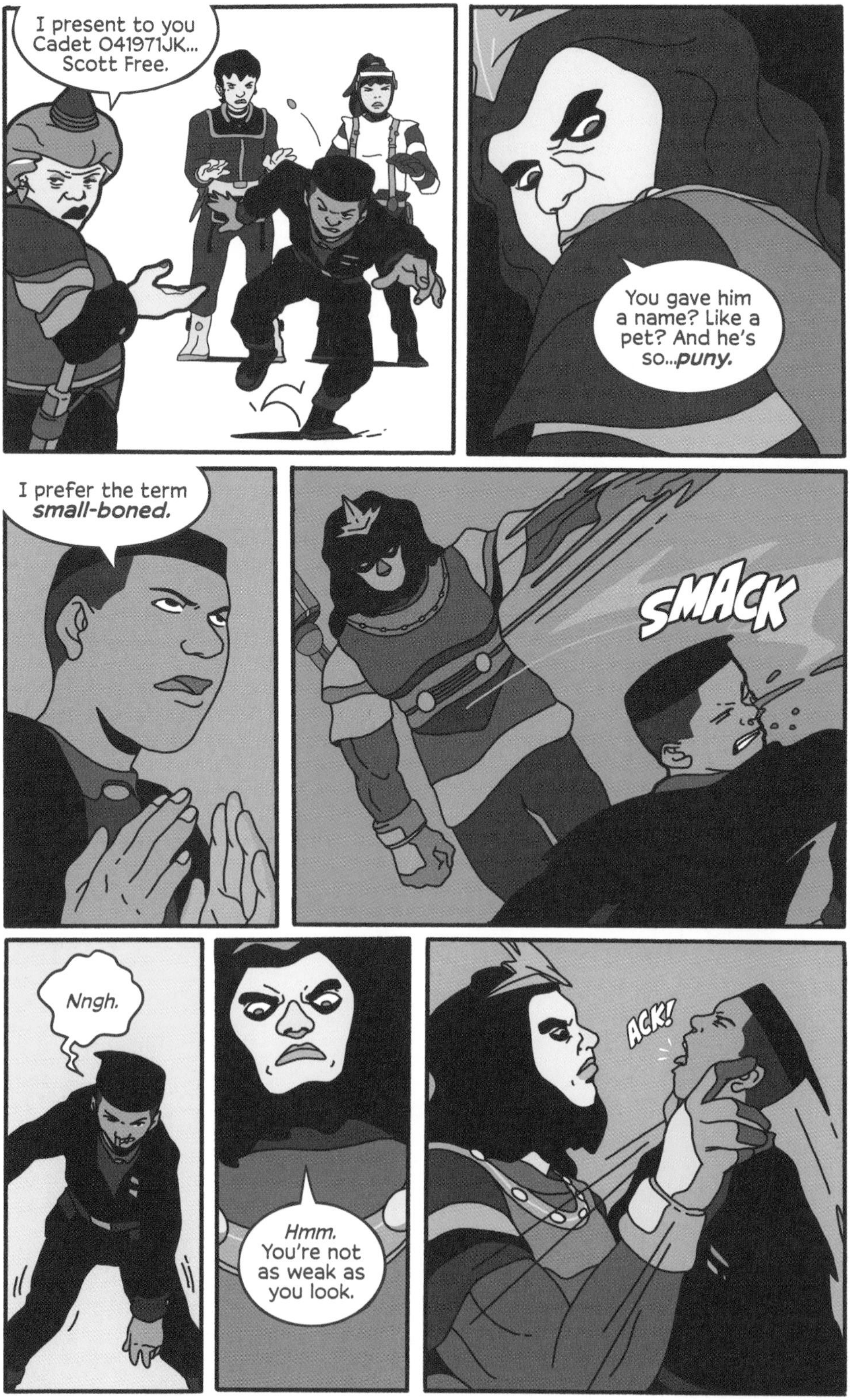
I present to you Cadet 041971JK... Scott Free.
You gave him a name? Like a pet? And he's so...*puny.*
I prefer the term *small-boned.*
SMACK
Nngh.
Hmm. You're not as weak as you look.
ACK!

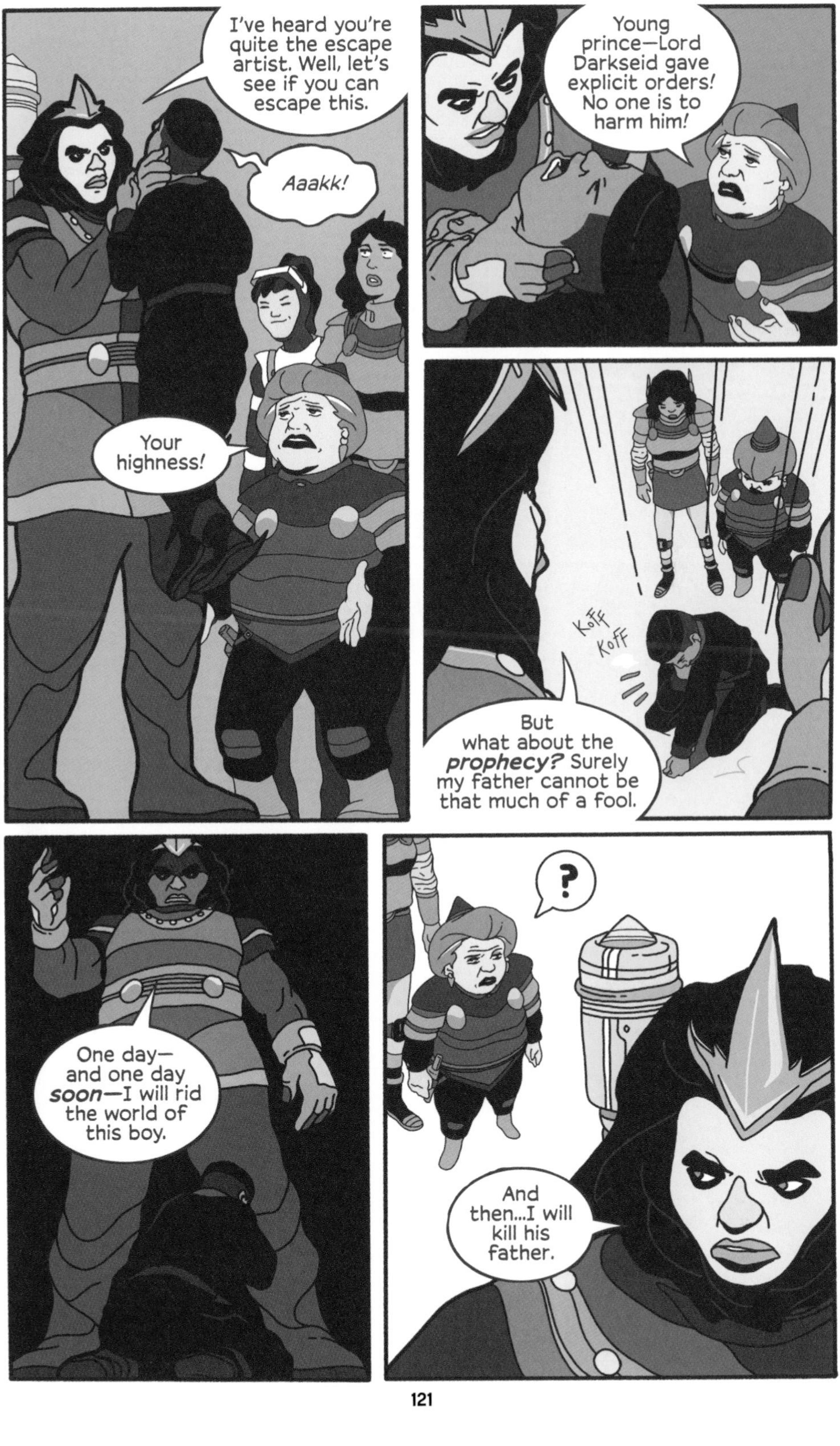
I've heard you're quite the escape artist. Well, let's see if you can escape this.
Aaakk!
Your highness!
Young prince—Lord Darkseid gave explicit orders! No one is to harm him!
KOFF KOFF
But what about the **prophecy?** Surely my father cannot be that much of a fool.
One day—and one day **soon**—I will rid the world of this boy.
?
And then...I will kill his father.

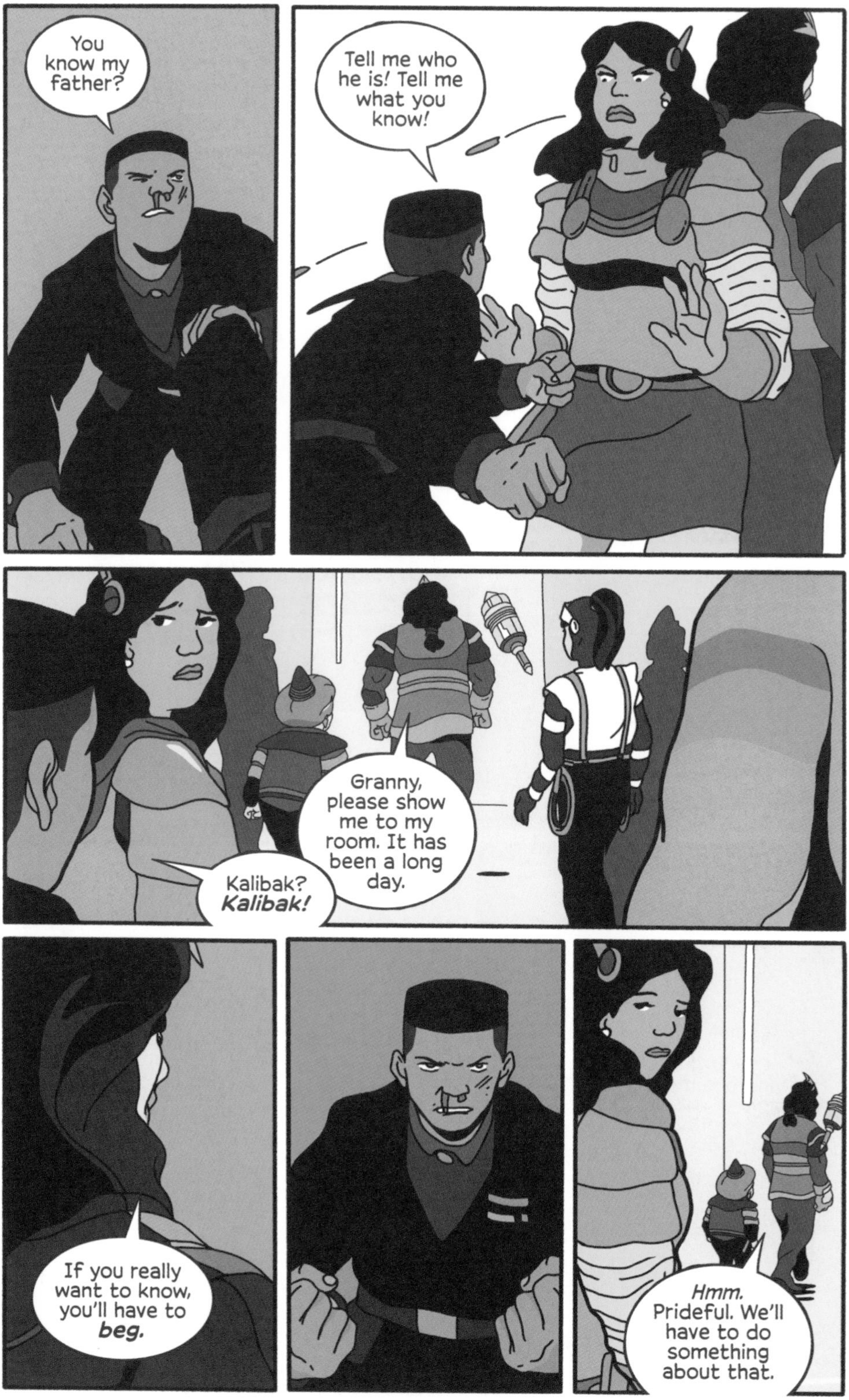
You know my father?
Tell me who he is! Tell me what you know!
Granny, please show me to my room. It has been a long day.
Kalibak? *Kalibak!*
If you really want to know, you'll have to *beg.*
Hmm. Prideful. We'll have to do something about that.

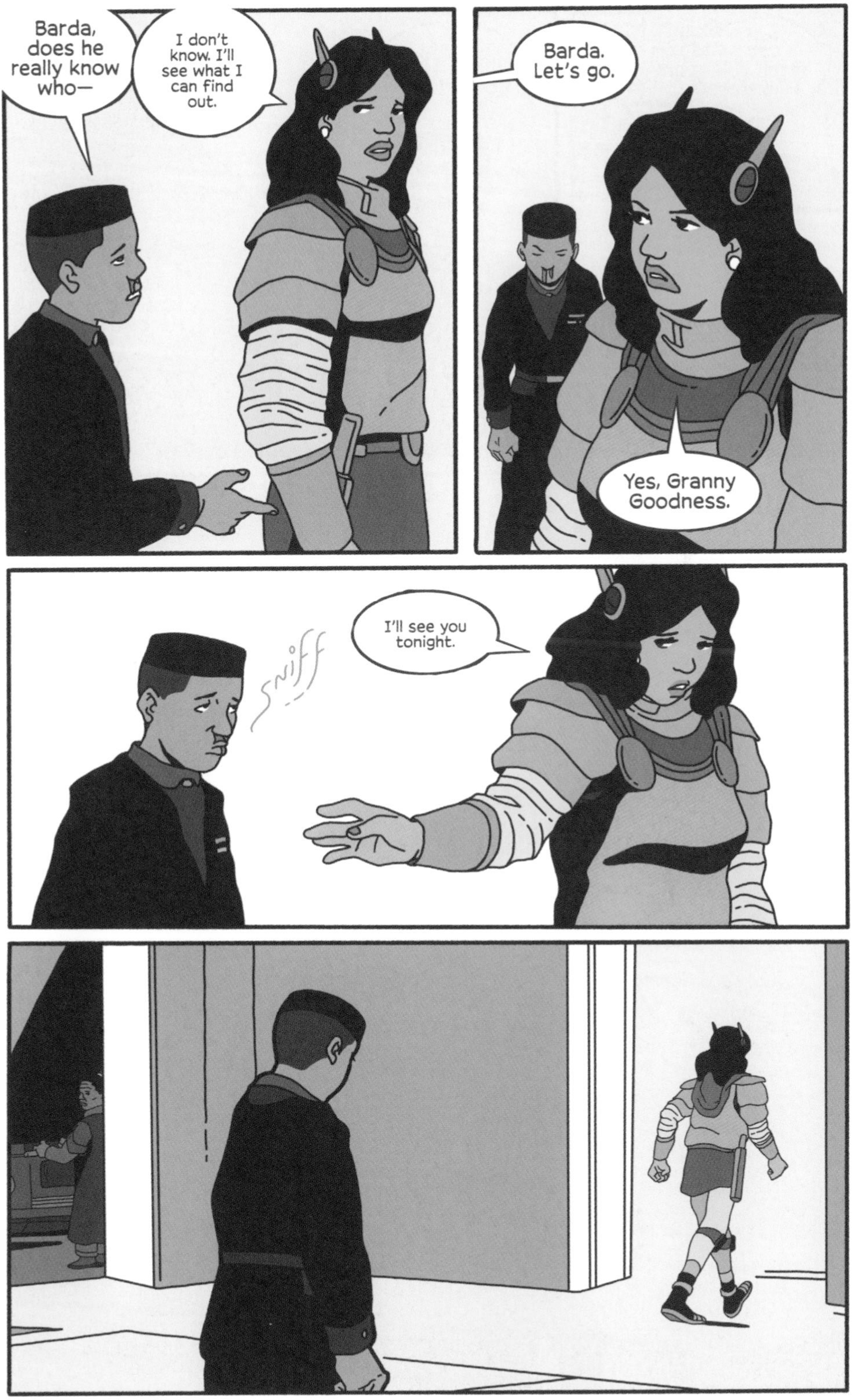
Barda, does he really know who—
I don't know. I'll see what I can find out.
Barda. Let's go.
Yes, Granny Goodness.
I'll see you tonight.
SNIFF

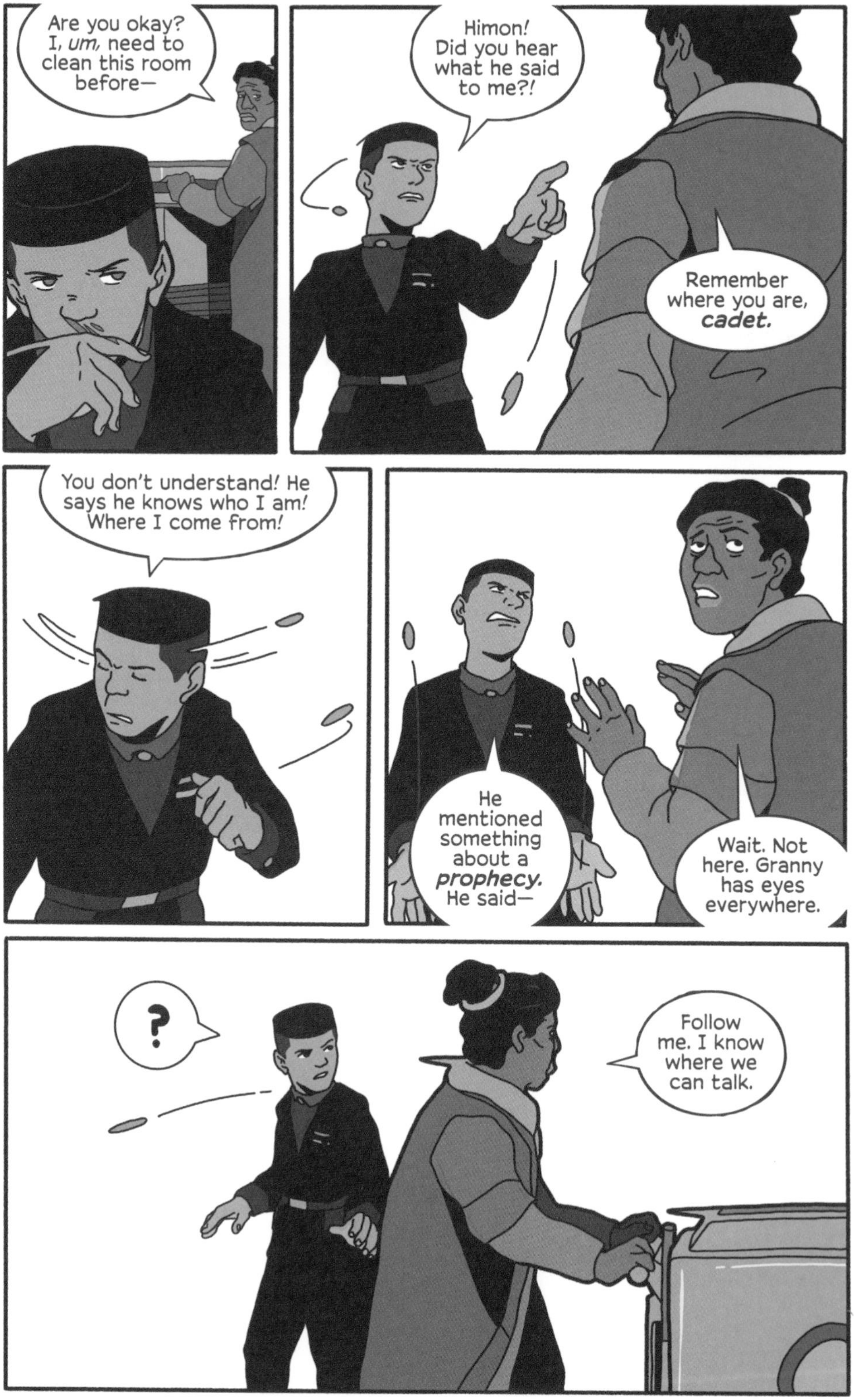
Are you okay? I, *um,* need to clean this room before—
Himon! Did you hear what he said to me?!
Remember where you are, ***cadet.***
You don't understand! He says he knows who I am! Where I come from!
He mentioned something about a ***prophecy.*** He said—
Wait. Not here. Granny has eyes everywhere.
?
Follow me. I know where we can talk.

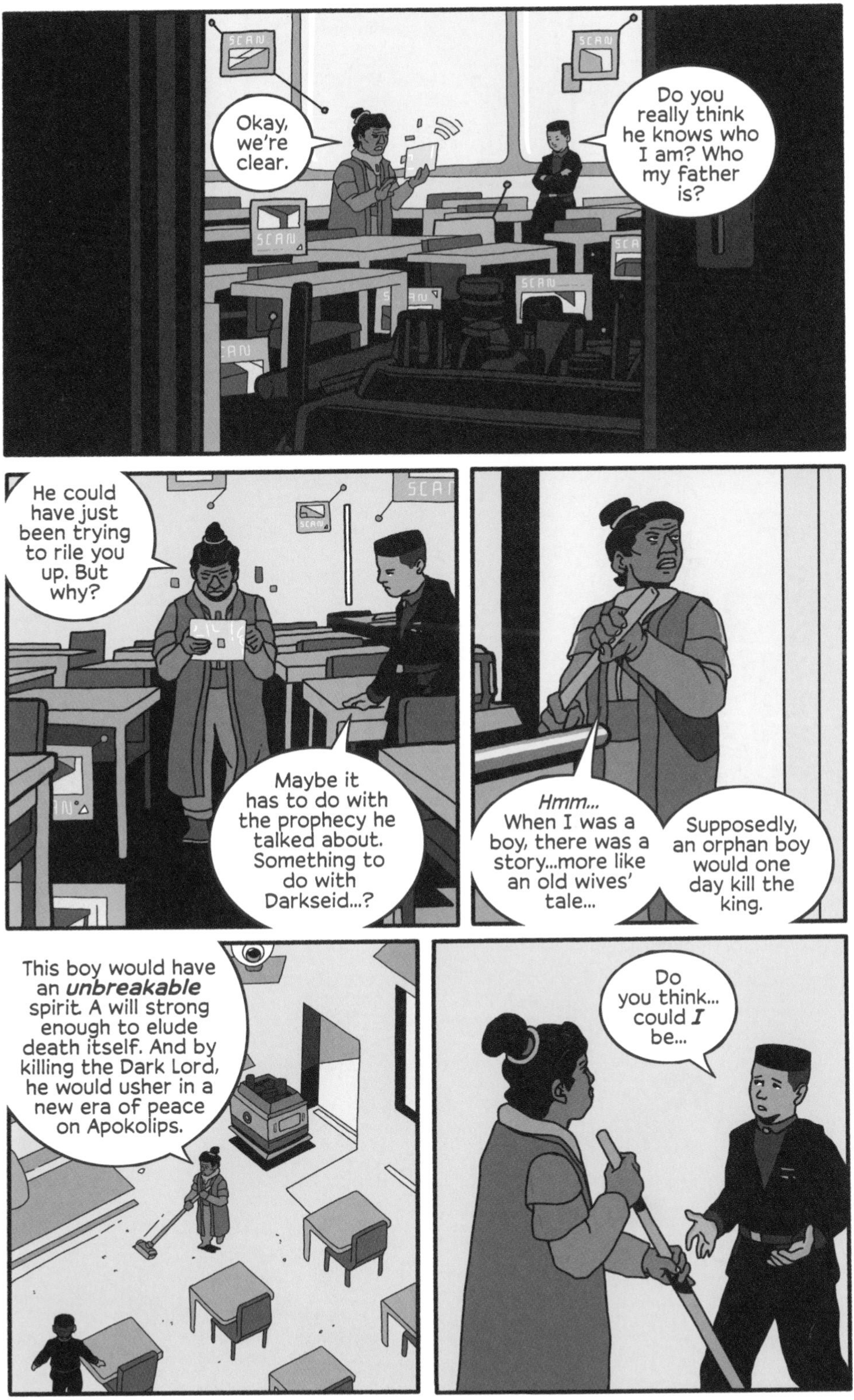
SCAN
Okay, we're clear.
Do you really think he knows who I am? Who my father is?
He could have just been trying to rile you up. But why?
Maybe it has to do with the prophecy he talked about. Something to do with Darkseid...?
Hmm... When I was a boy, there was a story...more like an old wives' tale...
Supposedly, an orphan boy would one day kill the king.
This boy would have an ***unbreakable*** spirit. A will strong enough to elude death itself. And by killing the Dark Lord, he would usher in a new era of peace on Apokolips.
Do you think... could ***I*** be...

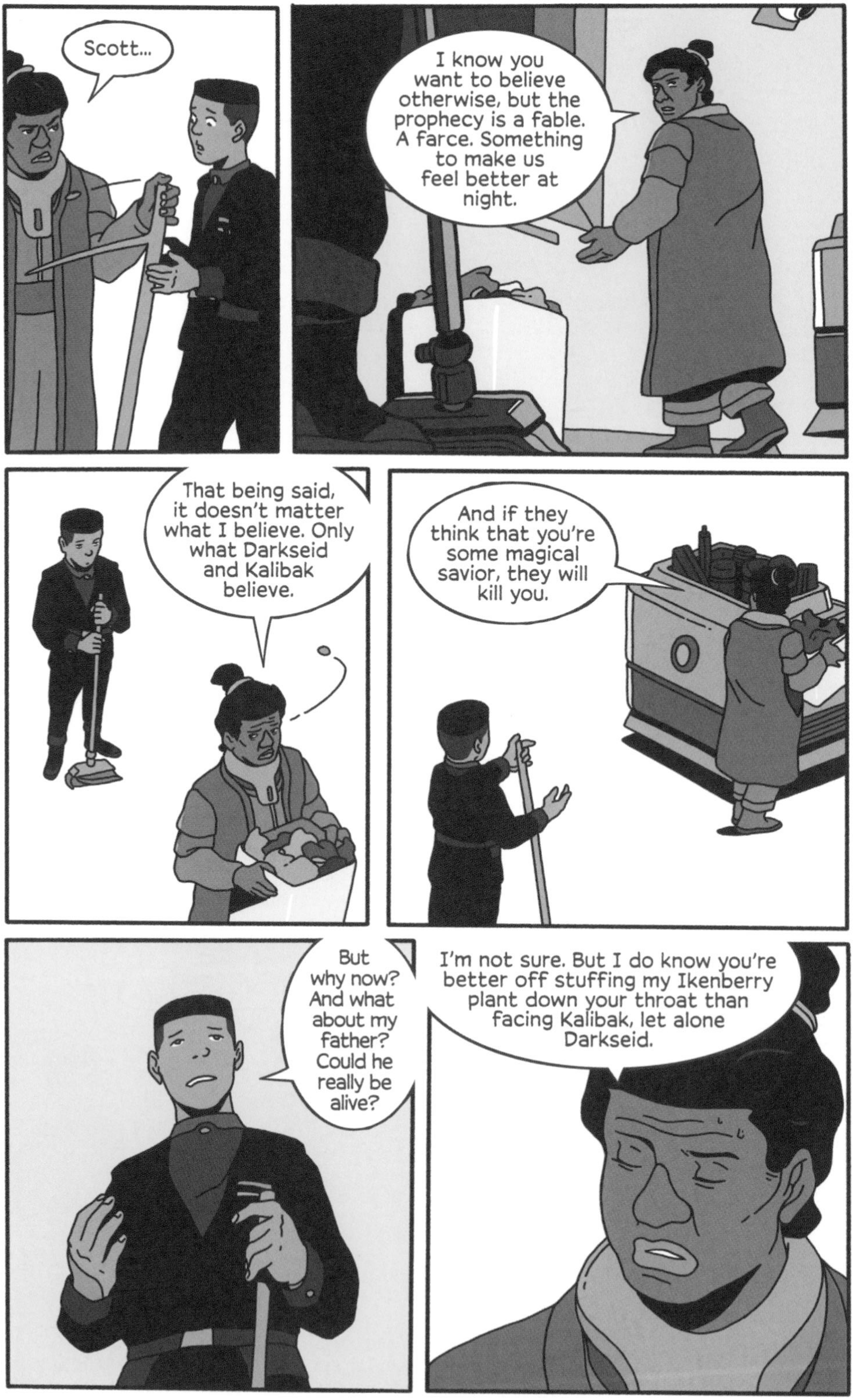
Scott...
I know you want to believe otherwise, but the prophecy is a fable. A farce. Something to make us feel better at night.
That being said, it doesn't matter what I believe. Only what Darkseid and Kalibak believe.
And if they think that you're some magical savior, they will kill you.
But why now? And what about my father? Could he really be alive?
I'm not sure. But I do know you're better off stuffing my Ikenberry plant down your throat than facing Kalibak, let alone Darkseid.

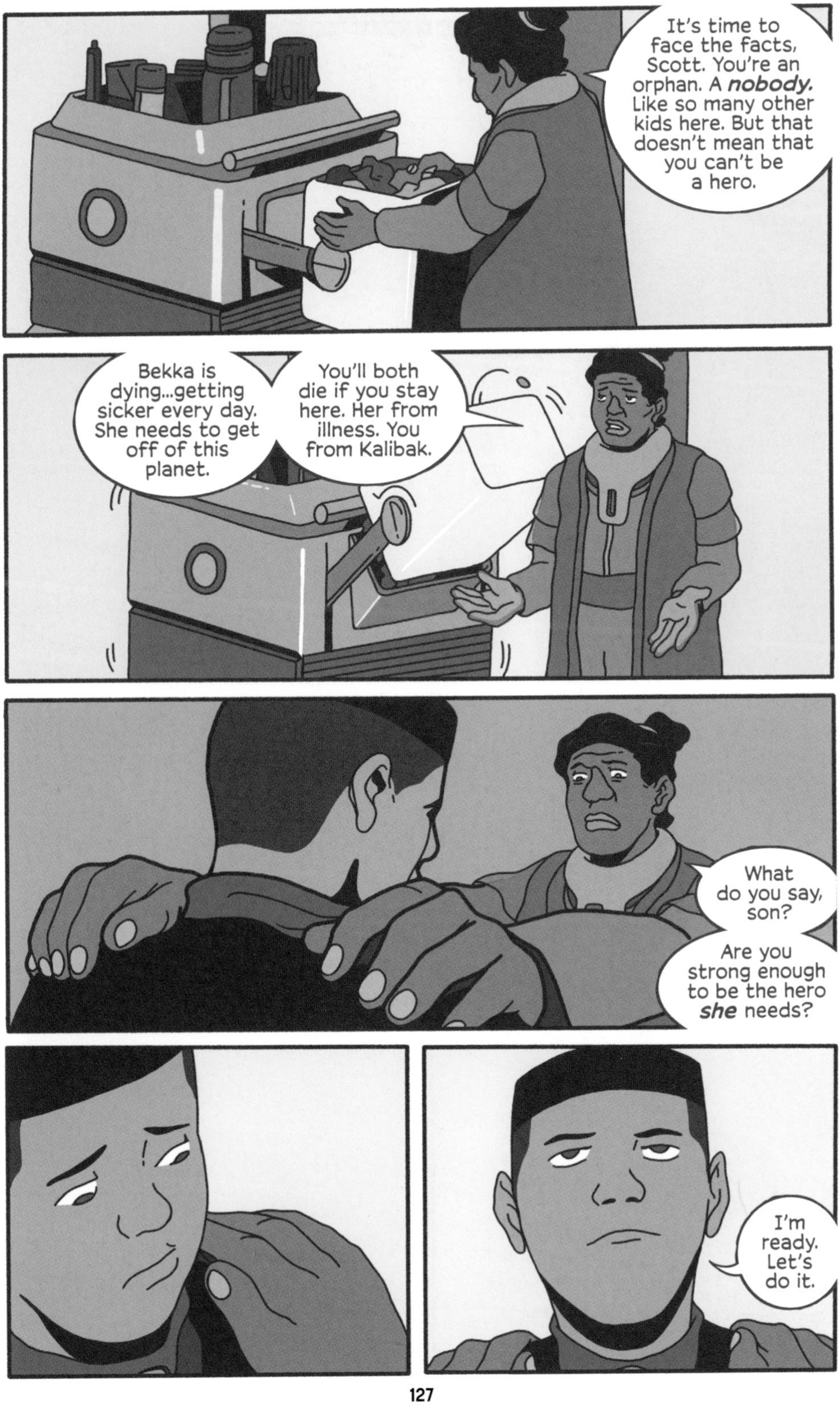
It's time to face the facts, Scott. You're an orphan. A ***nobody.*** Like so many other kids here. But that doesn't mean that you can't be a hero.
Bekka is dying...getting sicker every day. She needs to get off of this planet.
You'll both die if you stay here. Her from illness. You from Kalibak.
What do you say, son?
Are you strong enough to be the hero ***she*** needs?
I'm ready. Let's do it.

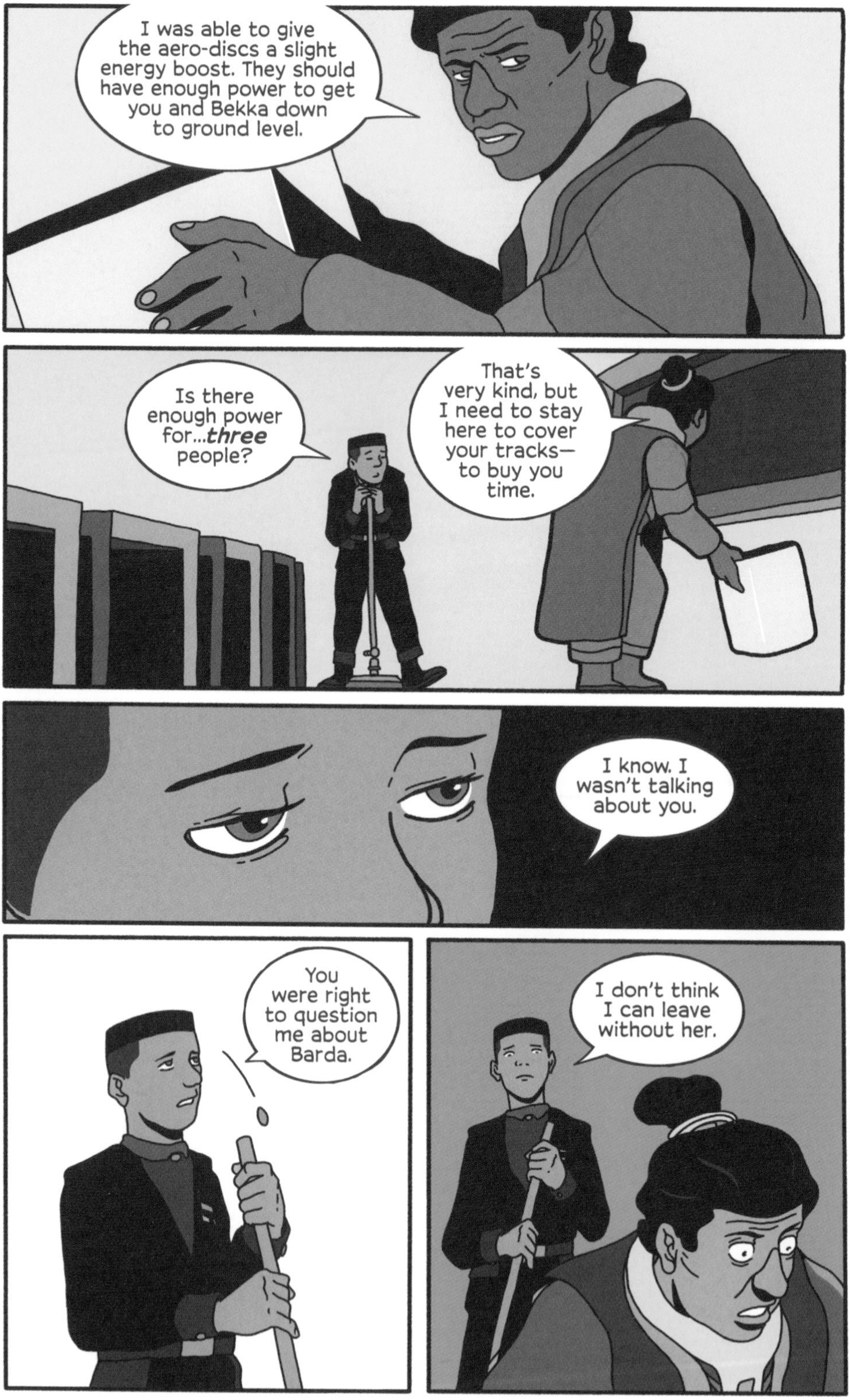
I was able to give the aero-discs a slight energy boost. They should have enough power to get you and Bekka down to ground level.
Is there enough power for...***three*** people?
That's very kind, but I need to stay here to cover your tracks— to buy you time.
I know. I wasn't talking about you.
You were right to question me about Barda.
I don't think I can leave without her.

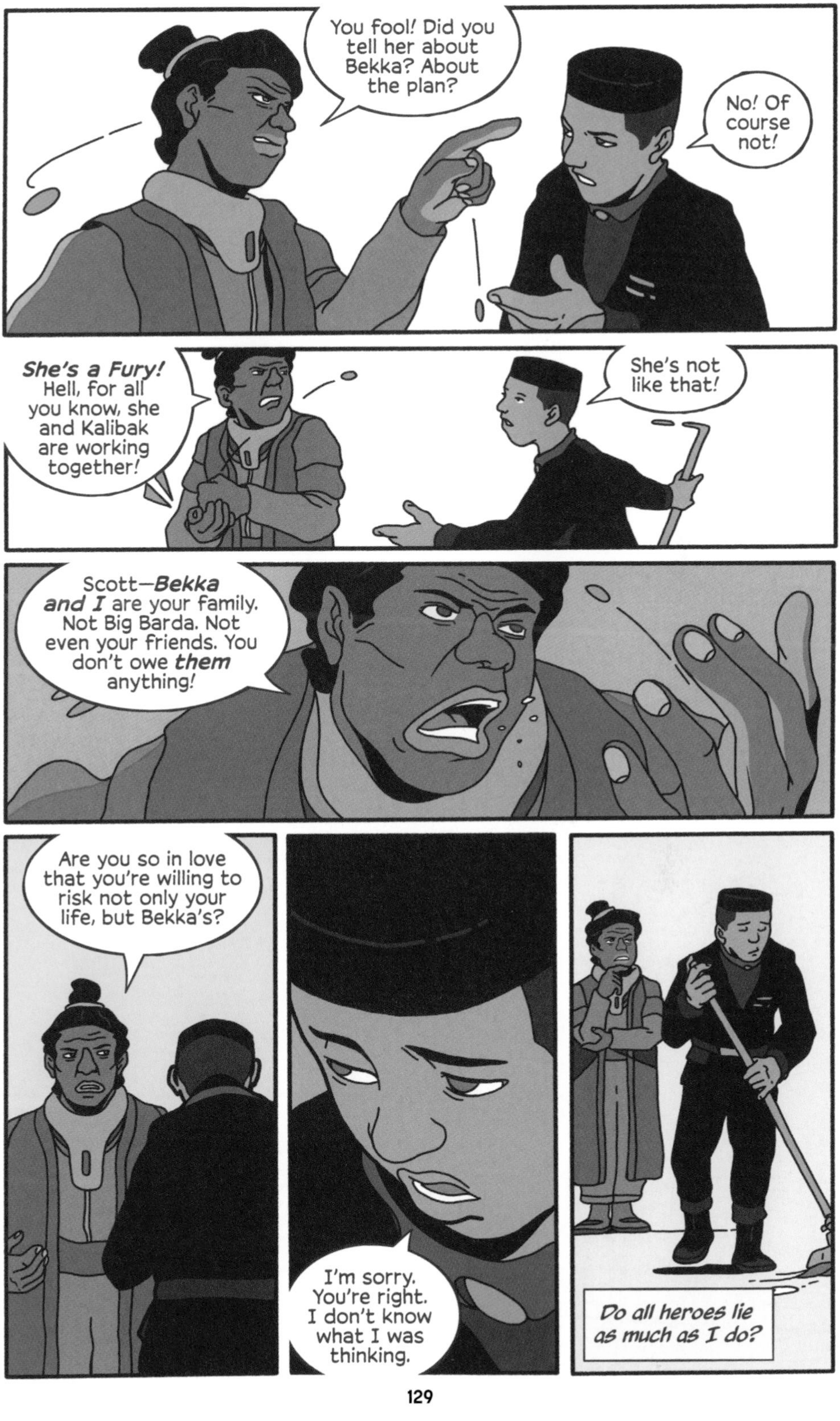
You fool! Did you tell her about Bekka? About the plan?
No! Of course not!
She's a Fury! Hell, for all you know, she and Kalibak are working together!
She's not like that!
Scott—*Bekka and I* are your family. Not Big Barda. Not even your friends. You don't owe *them* anything!
Are you so in love that you're willing to risk not only your life, but Bekka's?
I'm sorry. You're right. I don't know what I was thinking.
Do all heroes lie as much as I do?

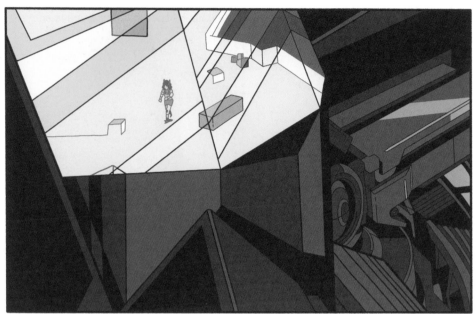

I tried to find out as much as I could about what Kalibak said about your father, but—

It's okay. I think he's lying. I mean—he *must* be.

You don't sound sure.

Just because you want something to be true doesn't mean that it is.

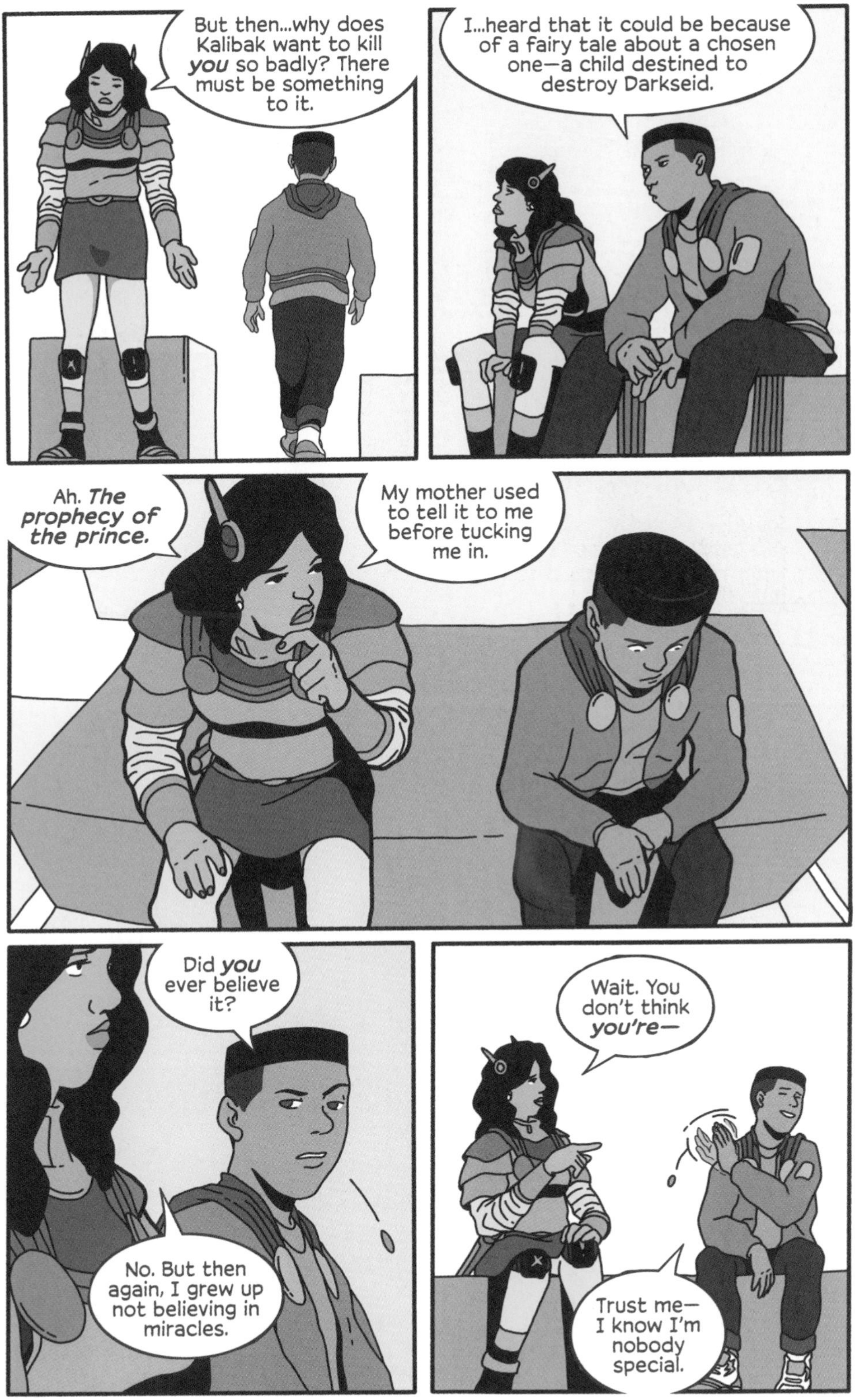

But then...why does Kalibak want to kill *you* so badly? There must be something to it.
I...heard that it could be because of a fairy tale about a chosen one—a child destined to destroy Darkseid.
Ah. *The prophecy of the prince.*
My mother used to tell it to me before tucking me in.
Did *you* ever believe it?
No. But then again, I grew up not believing in miracles.
Wait. You don't think *you're—*
Trust me— I know I'm nobody special.

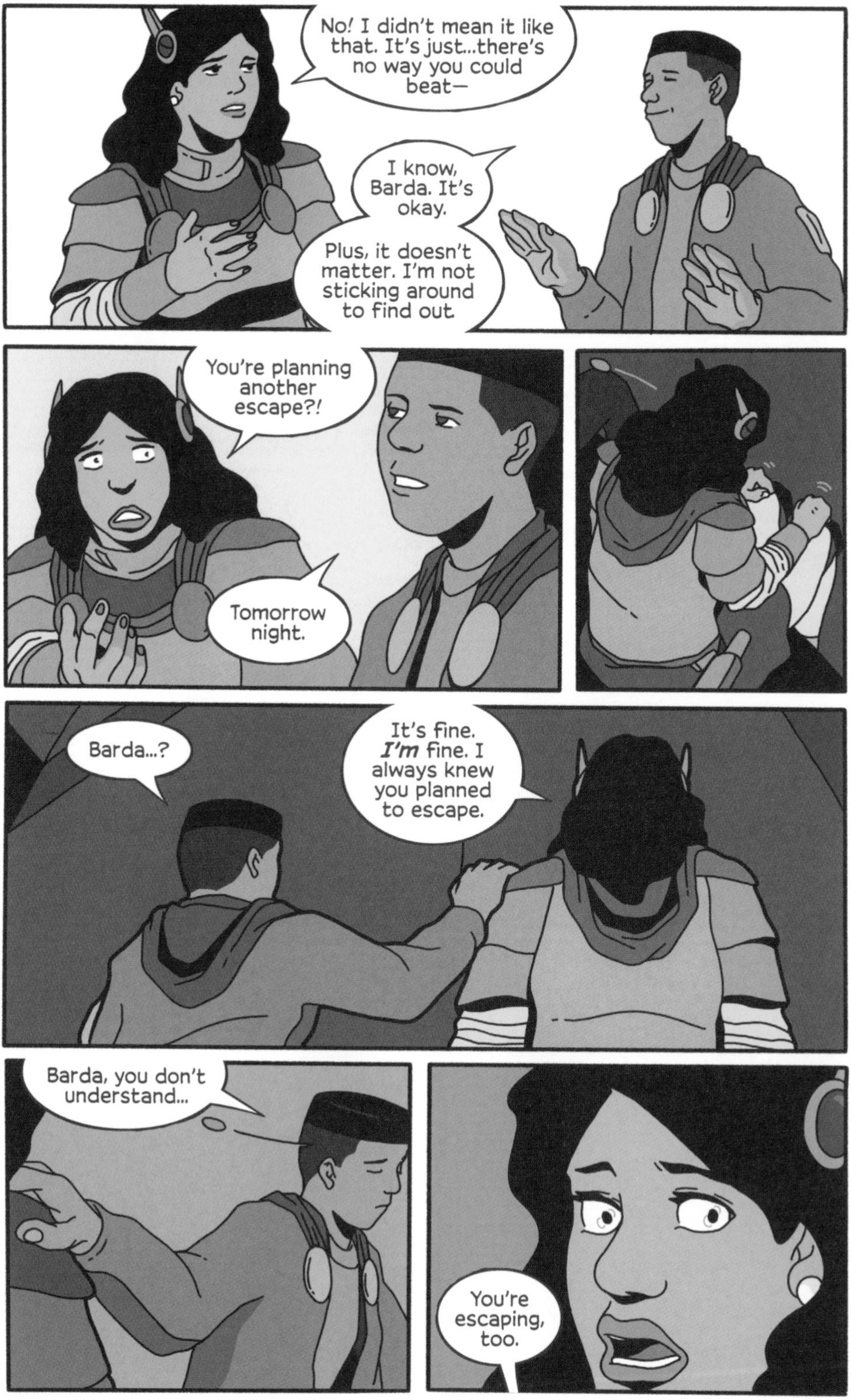

No! I didn't mean it like that. It's just...there's no way you could beat—
I know, Barda. It's okay.
Plus, it doesn't matter. I'm not sticking around to find out
You're planning another escape?!
Tomorrow night.
Barda...?
It's fine. *I'm* fine. I always knew you planned to escape.
Barda, you don't understand...
You're escaping, too.

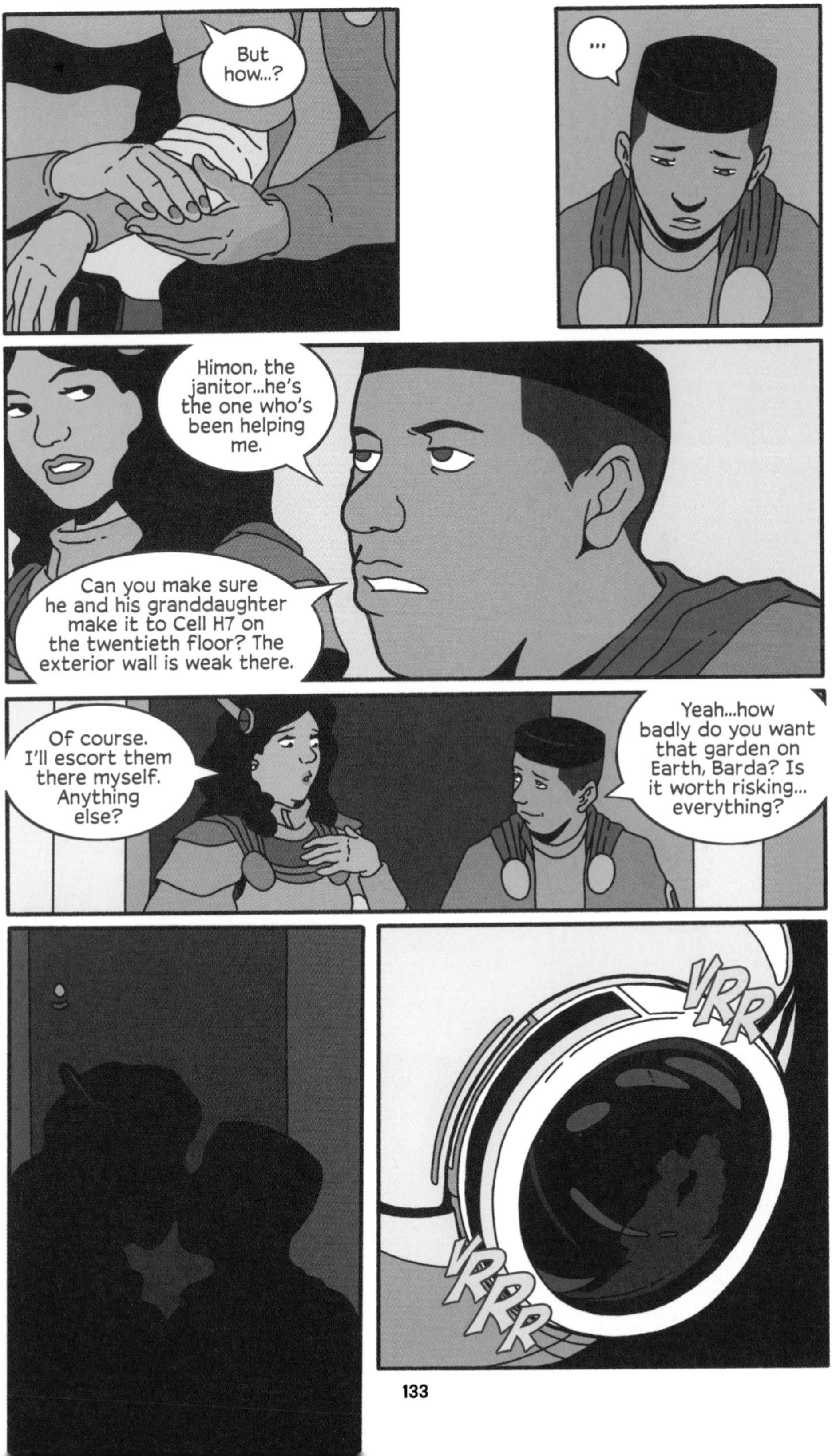
But how...?
...
Himon, the janitor...he's the one who's been helping me.
Can you make sure he and his granddaughter make it to Cell H7 on the twentieth floor? The exterior wall is weak there.
Of course. I'll escort them there myself. Anything else?
Yeah...how badly do you want that garden on Earth, Barda? Is it worth risking... everything?
VRR
VRRR

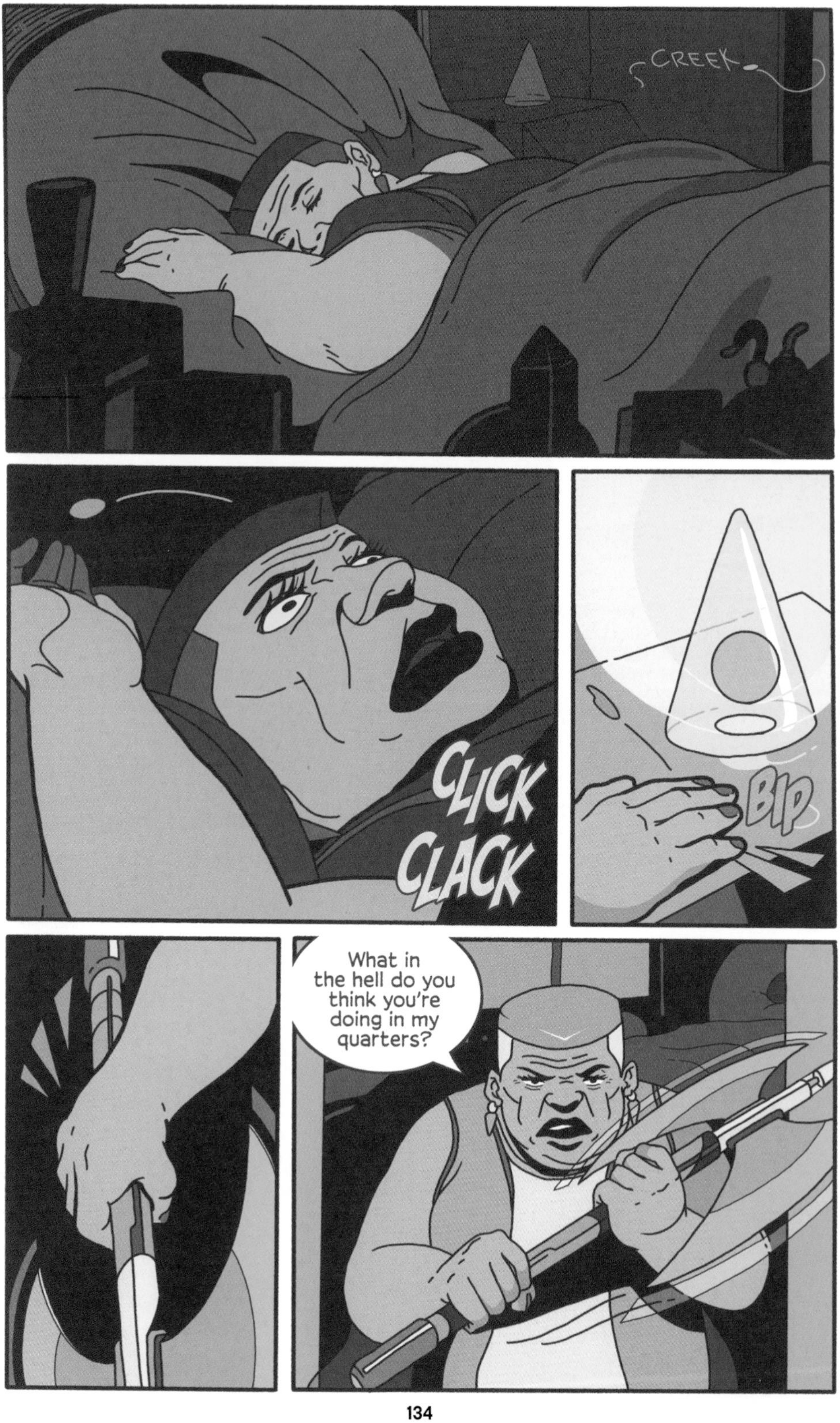
CREEK
CLICK
CLACK
BIP
What in the hell do you think you're doing in my quarters?

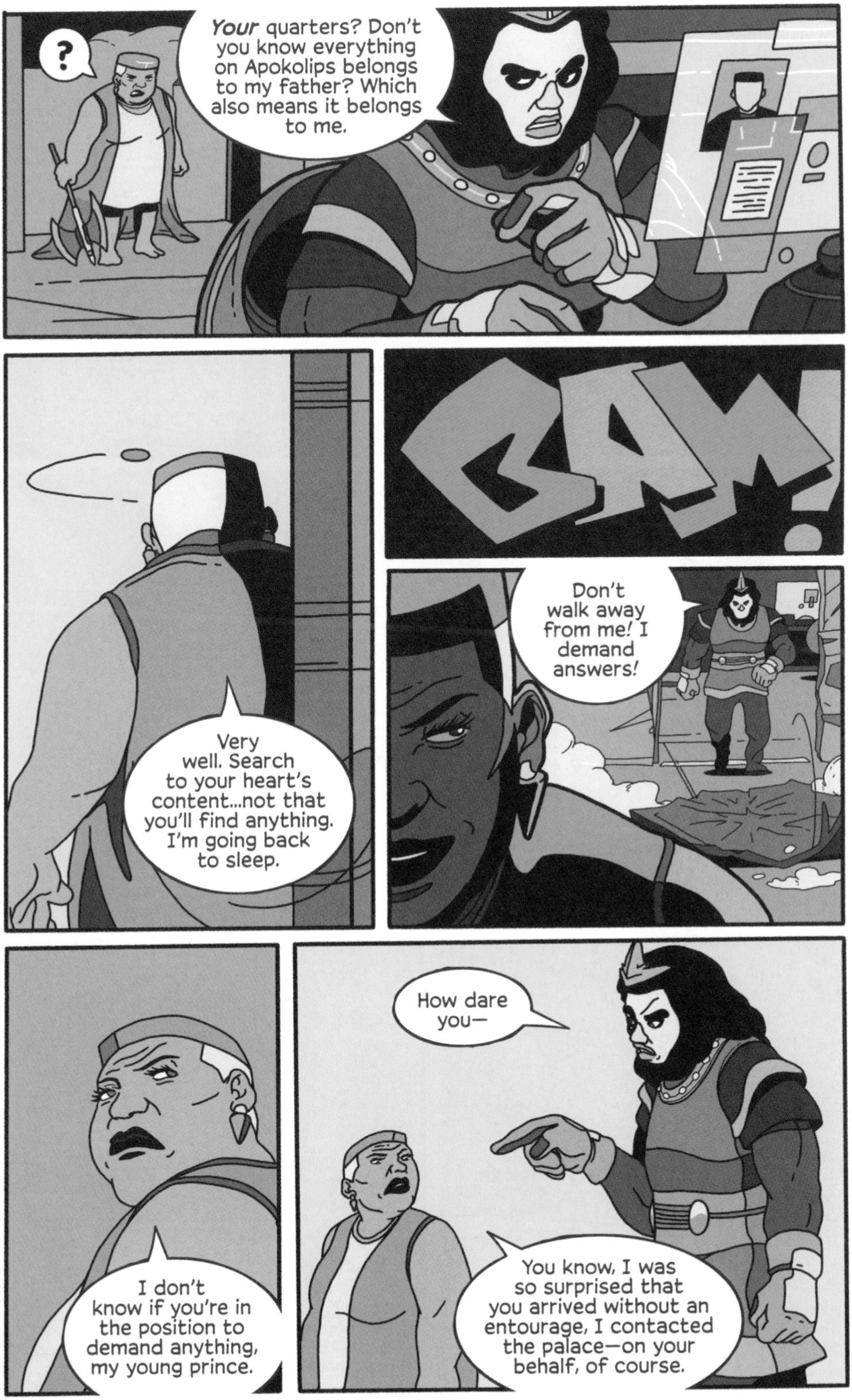
?
Your quarters? Don't you know everything on Apokolips belongs to my father? Which also means it belongs to me.
Very well. Search to your heart's content...not that you'll find anything. I'm going back to sleep.
BAM!
Don't walk away from me! I demand answers!
I don't know if you're in the position to demand anything, my young prince.
How dare you—
You know, I was so surprised that you arrived without an entourage, I contacted the palace—on your behalf, of course.

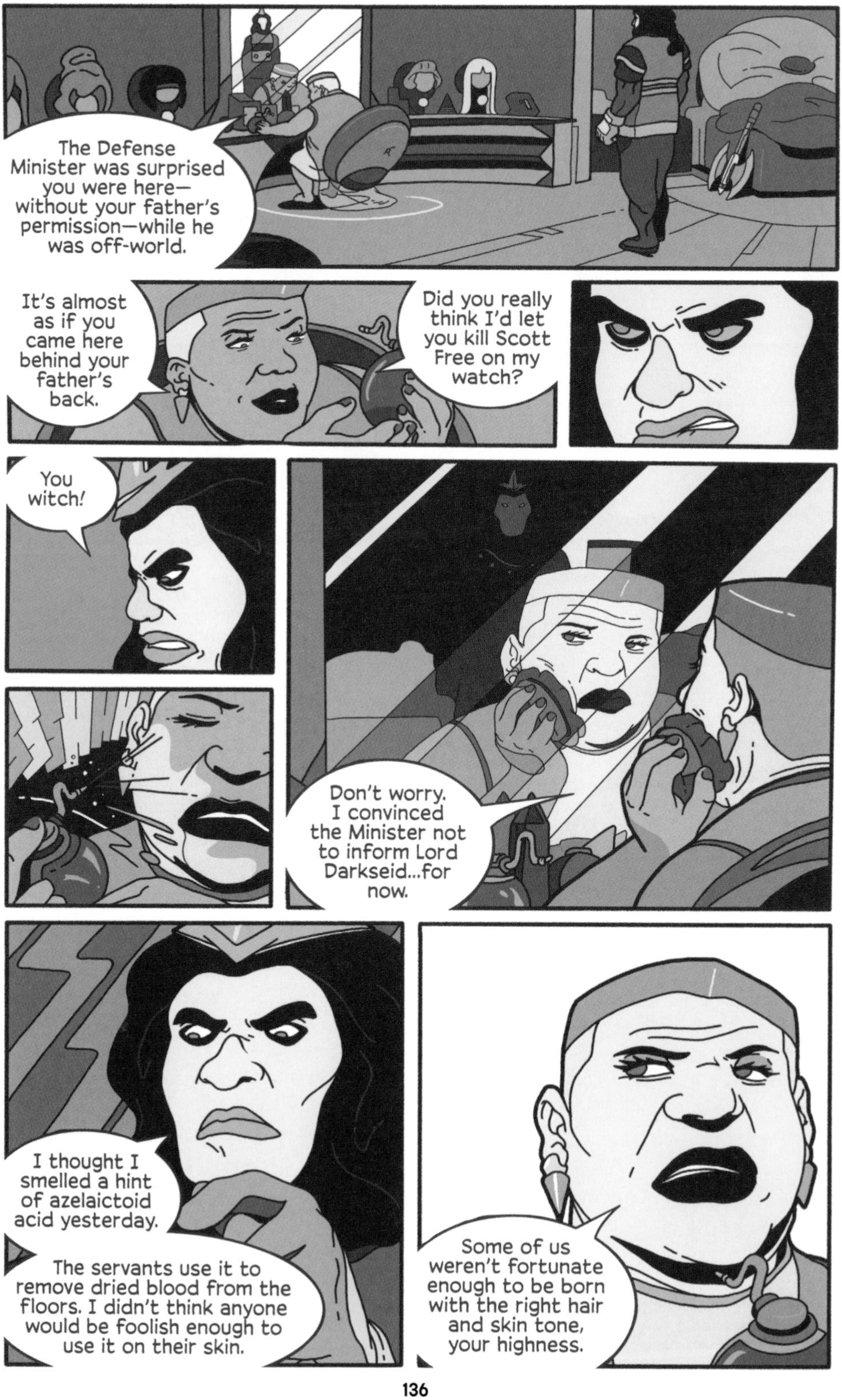
The Defense Minister was surprised you were here—without your father's permission—while he was off-world.
It's almost as if you came here behind your father's back.
Did you really think I'd let you kill Scott Free on my watch?
You witch!
Don't worry. I convinced the Minister not to inform Lord Darkseid...for now.
I thought I smelled a hint of azelaictoid acid yesterday.
The servants use it to remove dried blood from the floors. I didn't think anyone would be foolish enough to use it on their skin.
Some of us weren't fortunate enough to be born with the right hair and skin tone, your highness.

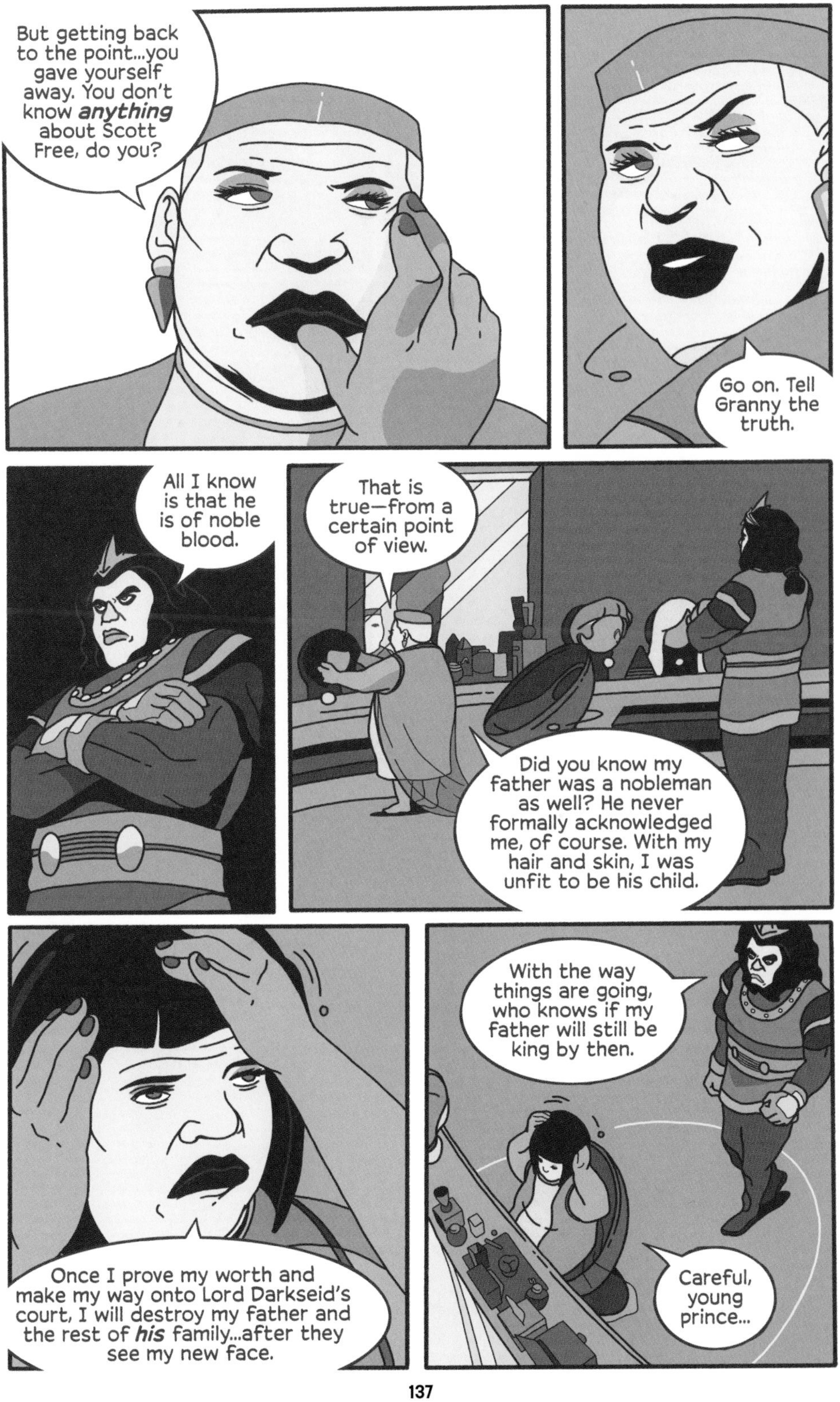
But getting back to the point...you gave yourself away. You don't know ***anything*** about Scott Free, do you?
Go on. Tell Granny the truth.
All I know is that he is of noble blood.
That is true—from a certain point of view.
Did you know my father was a nobleman as well? He never formally acknowledged me, of course. With my hair and skin, I was unfit to be his child.
Once I prove my worth and make my way onto Lord Darkseid's court, I will destroy my father and the rest of ***his*** family...after they see my new face.
With the way things are going, who knows if my father will still be king by then.
Careful, young prince...

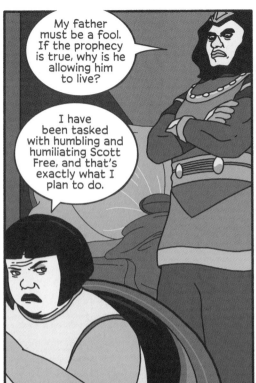

My father must be a fool. If the prophecy is true, why is he allowing him to live?

I have been tasked with humbling and humiliating Scott Free, and that's exactly what I plan to do.

But if you have other thoughts, I'd be happy to bring *all* of this to Lord Darkseid's attention...

That...will not be necessary.

"That will not be necessary..." *who?*

That will not be necessary... *Granny Goodness.*

That's a good boy.

Be patient, Kalibak. The prophecy ends tonight.

I will break Scott Free—once and for all.

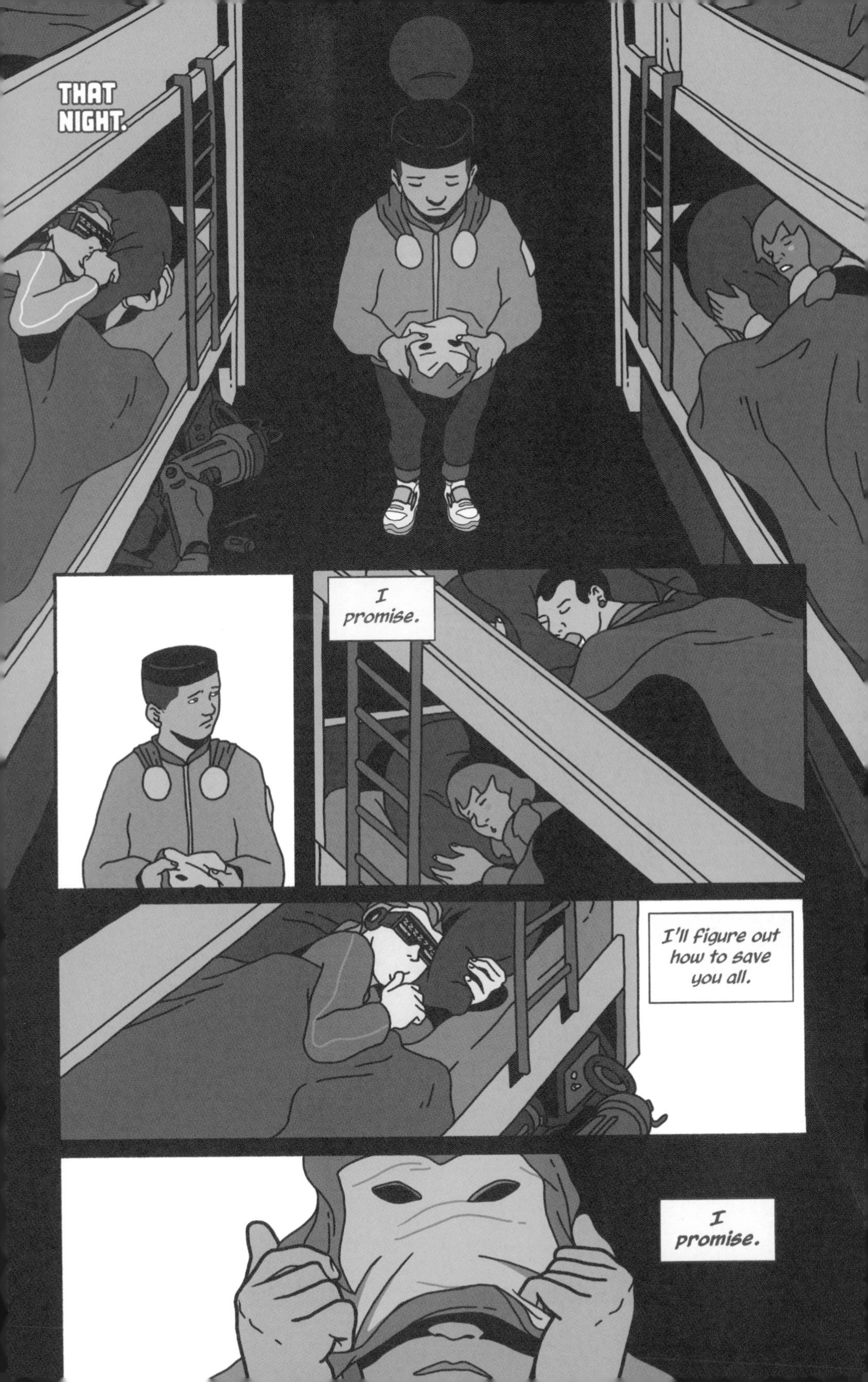
THAT NIGHT.
I promise.
I'll figure out how to save you all.
I promise.

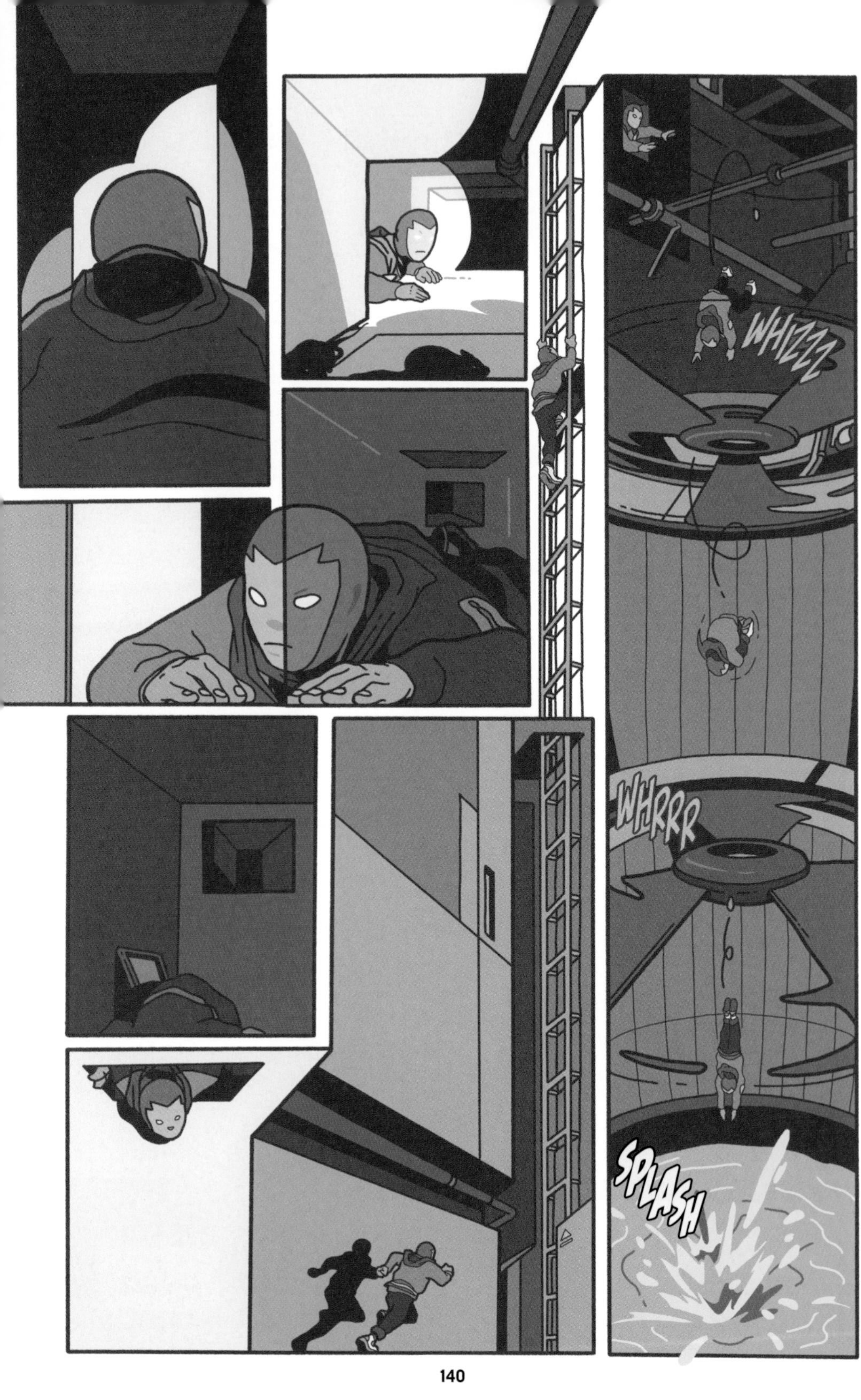
WHIZZZ
WHRRR
SPLASH

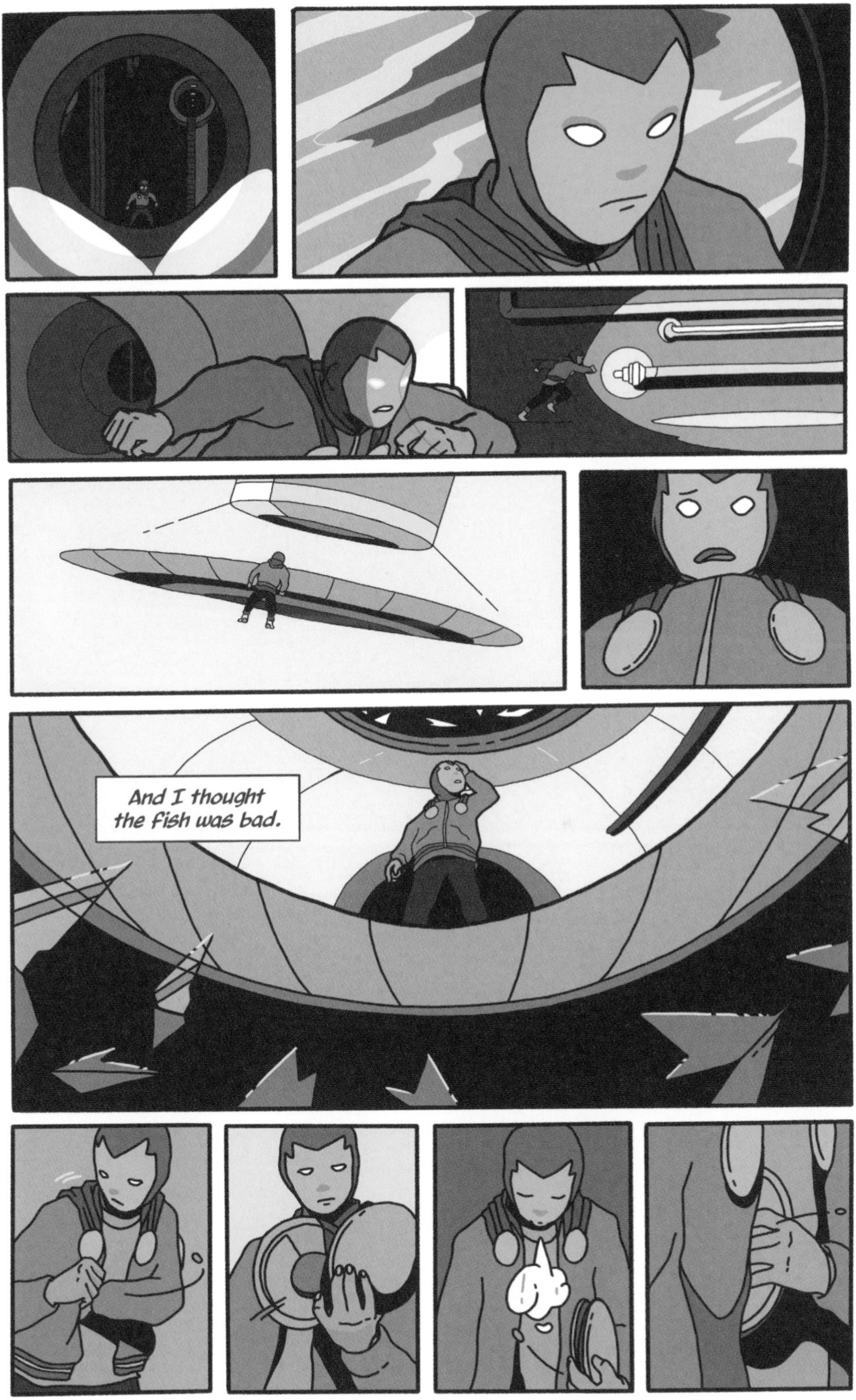
And I thought the fish was bad.

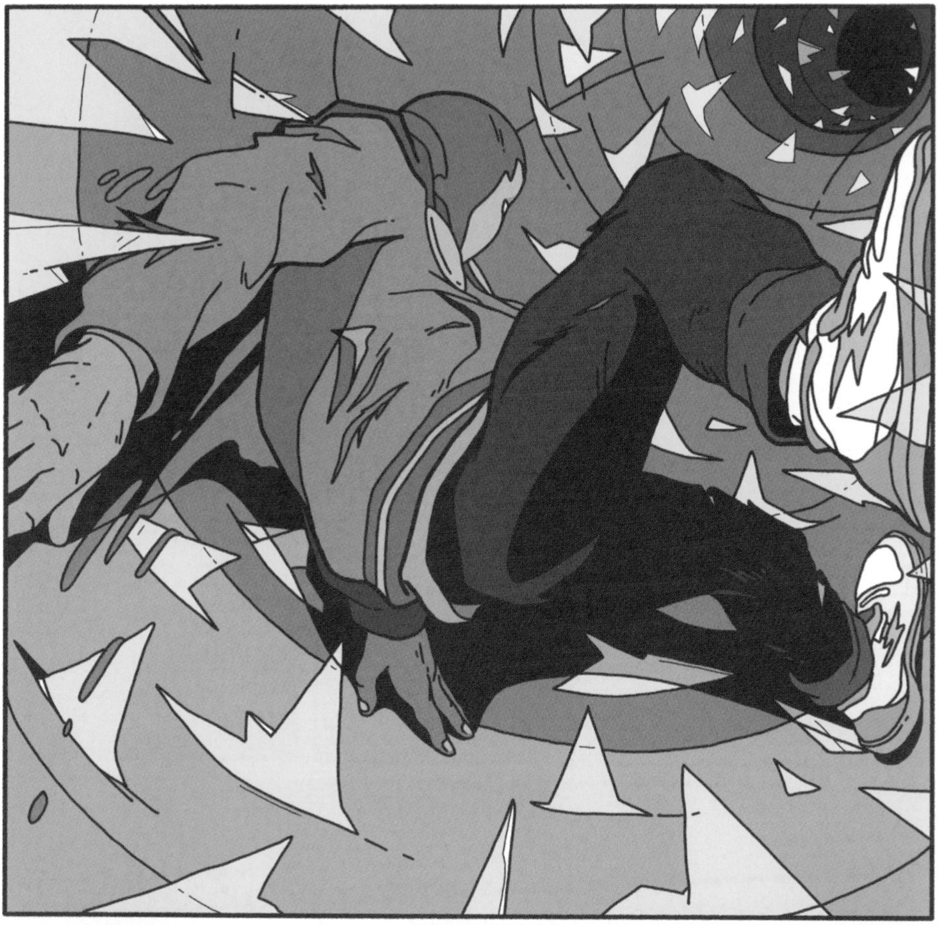

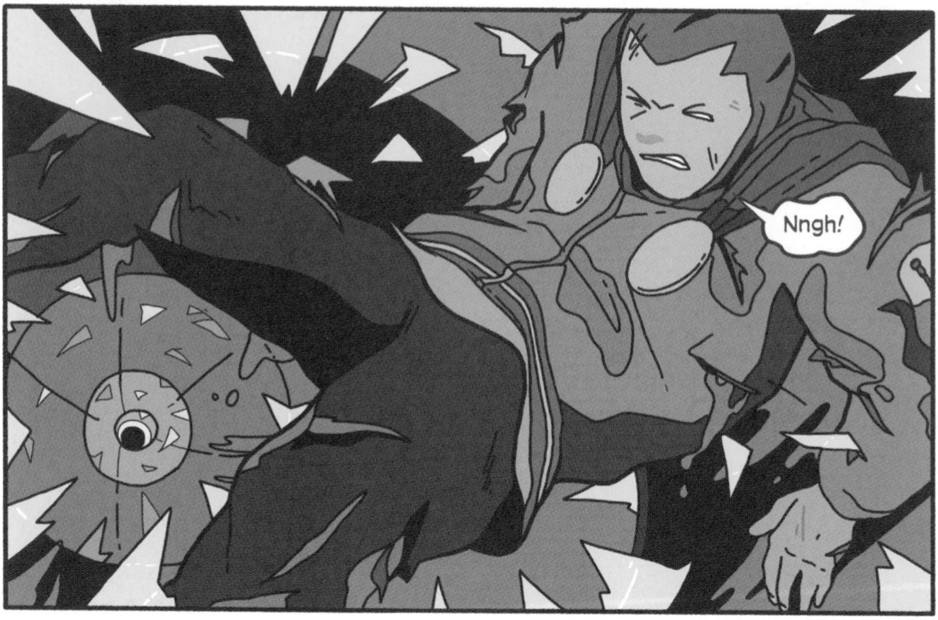
Nngh!

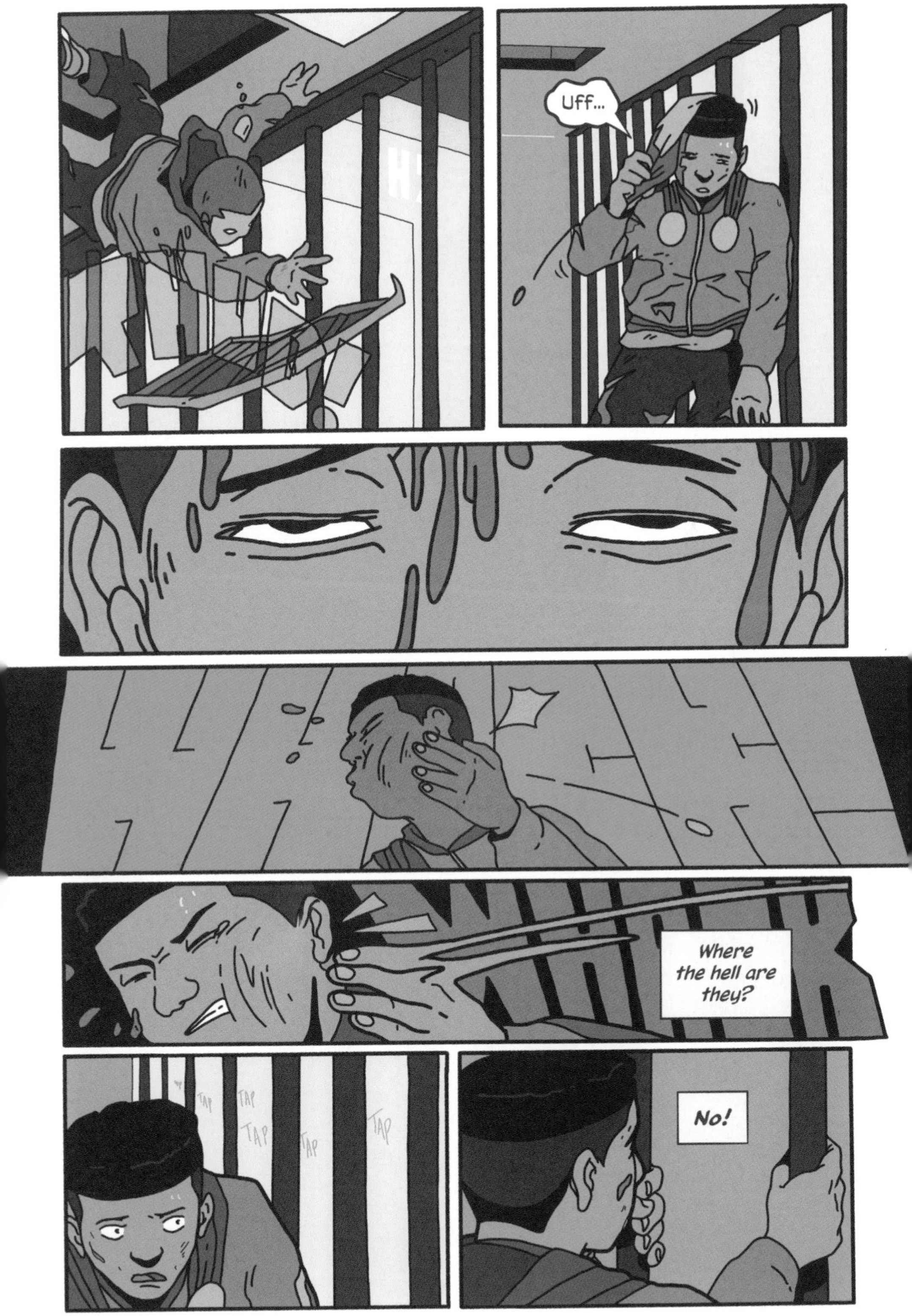
Uff...
Where the hell are they?
TAP
TAP
TAP
TAP
TAP
No!

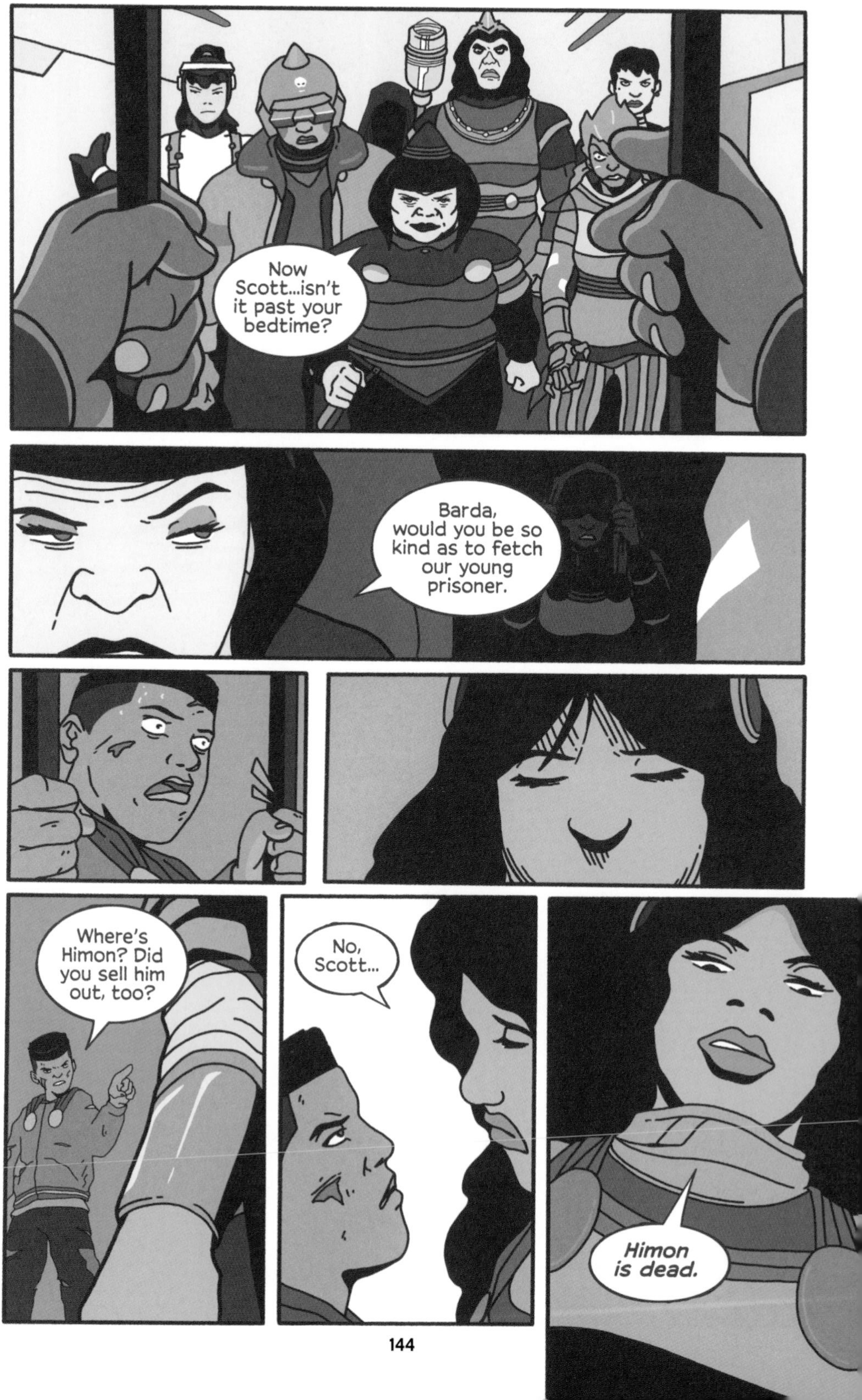

Now Scott...isn't it past your bedtime?
Barda, would you be so kind as to fetch our young prisoner.
Where's Himon? Did you sell him out, too?
No, Scott...
Himon is dead.

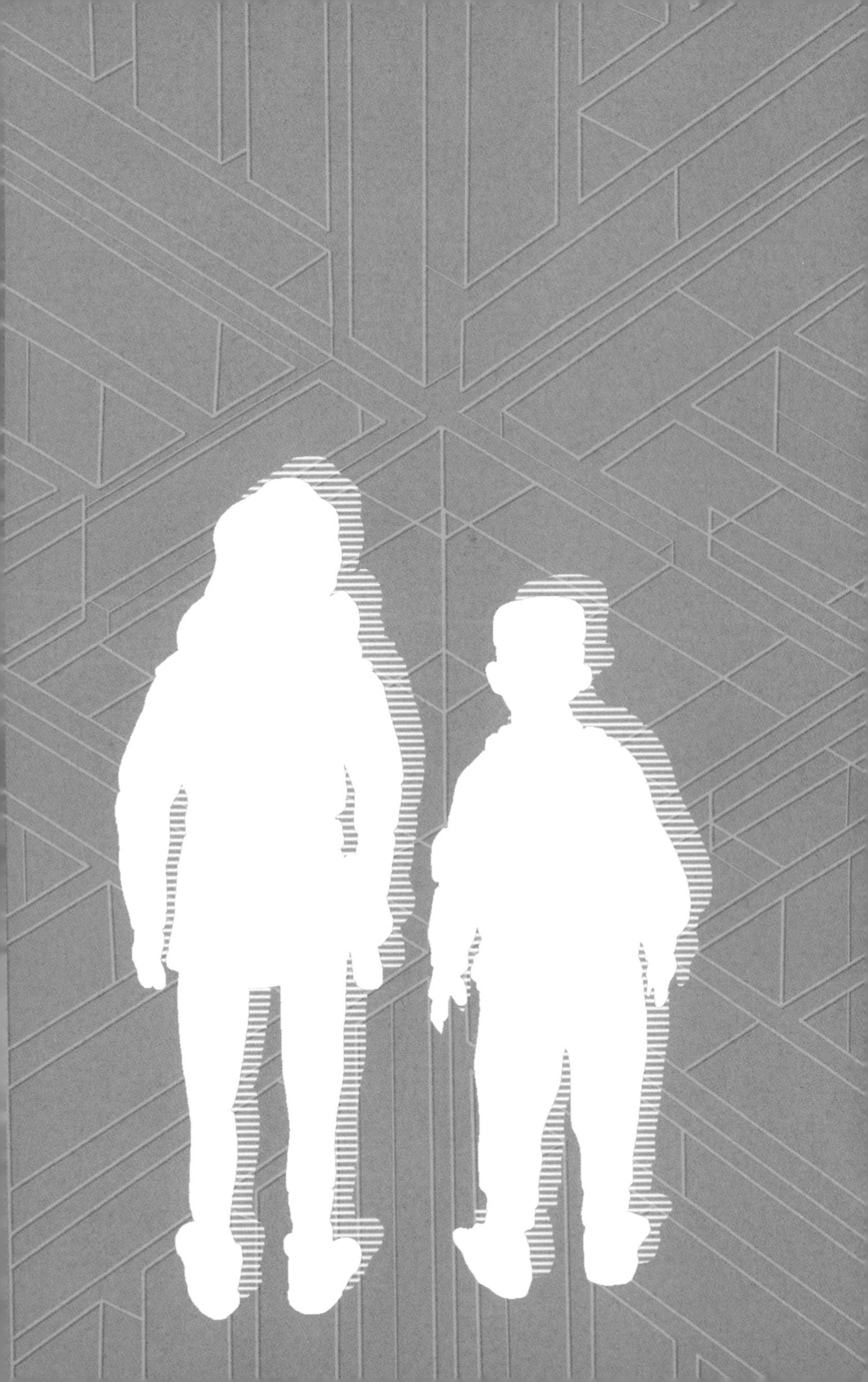

CHAPTER FIVE

Tears of a Clown

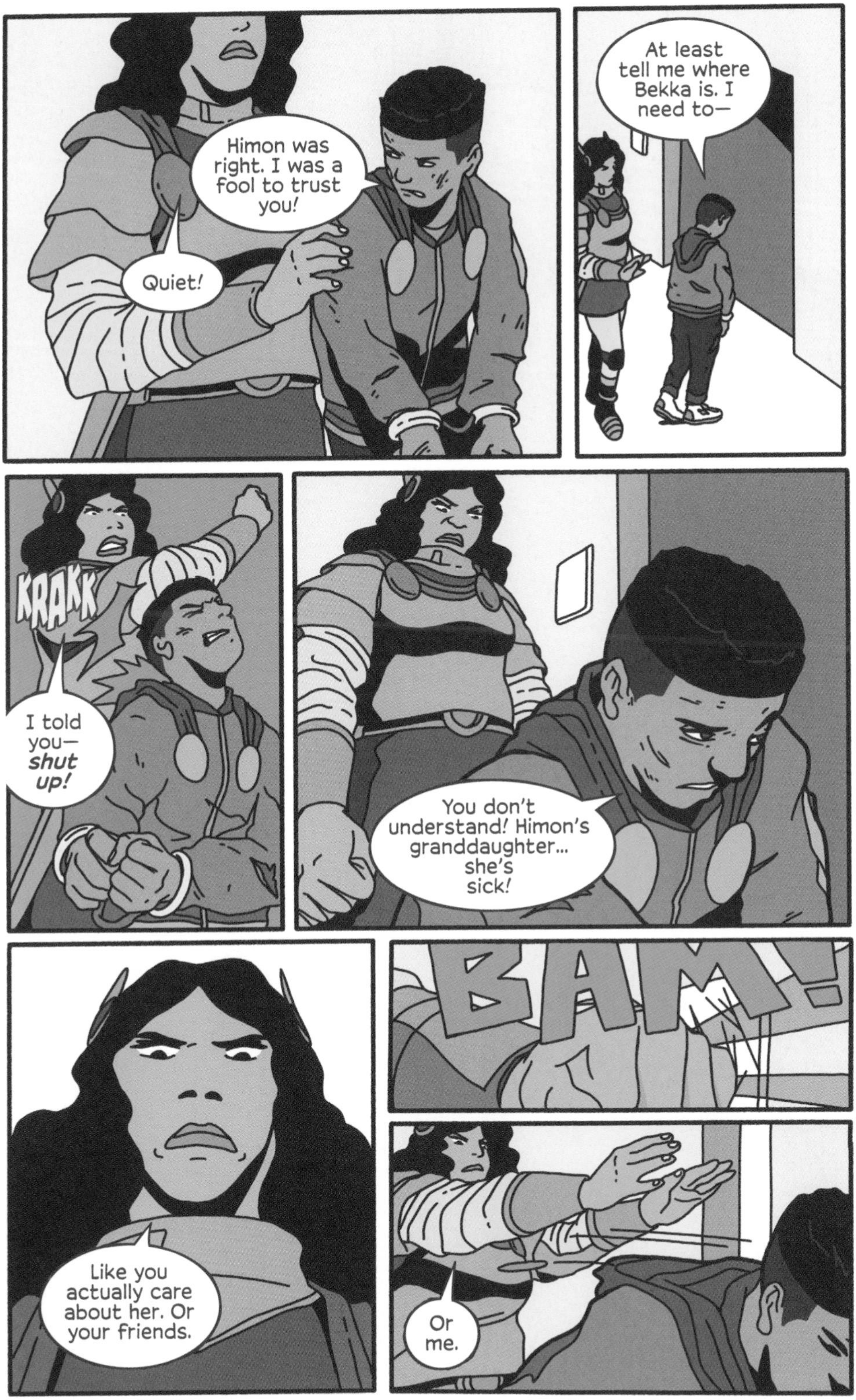
Himon was right. I was a fool to trust you!
Quiet!
At least tell me where Bekka is. I need to—
KRAKK
I told you— *shut up!*
You don't understand! Himon's granddaughter... she's sick!
Like you actually care about her. Or your friends.
BAM!
Or me.

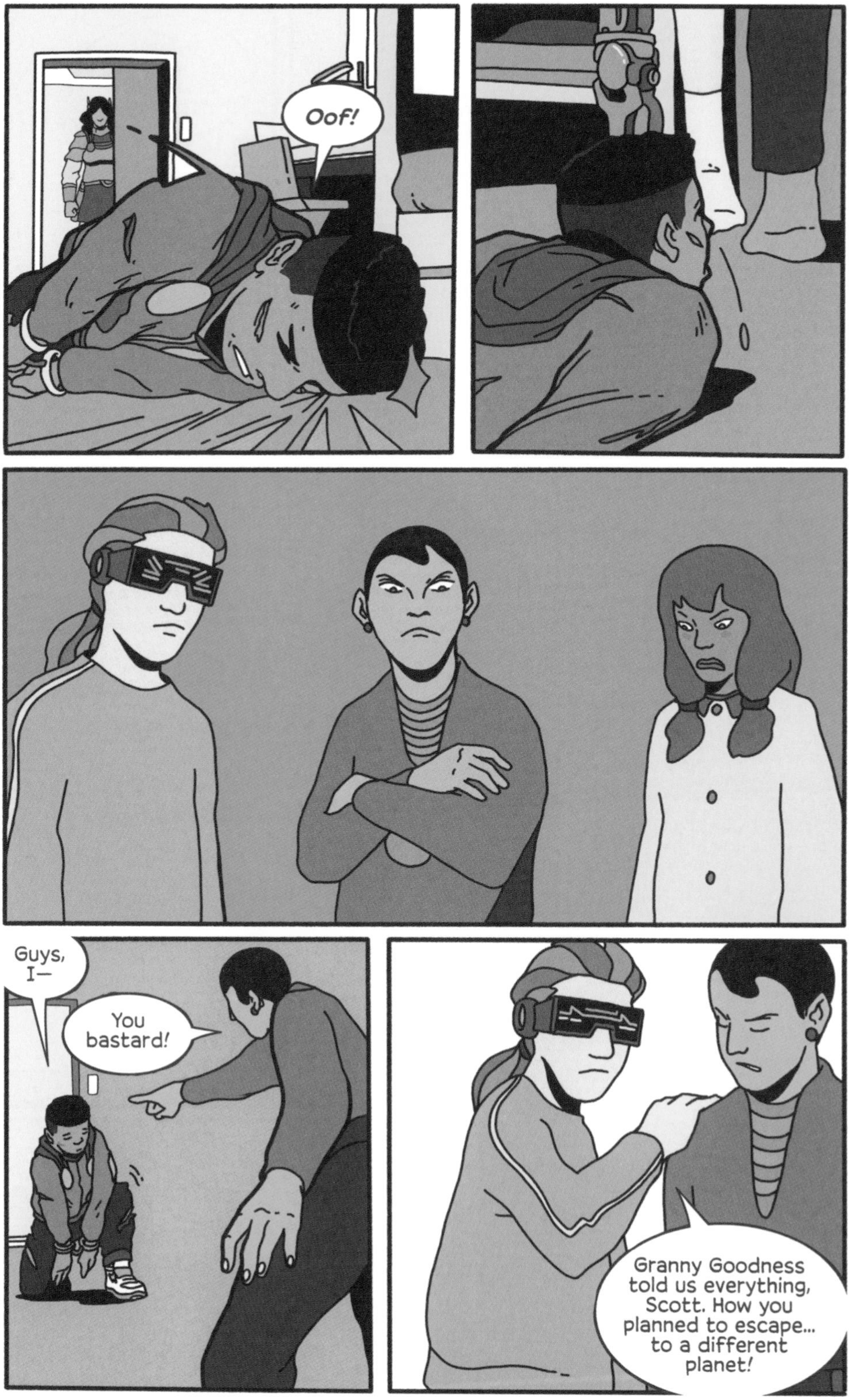
Oof!
Guys, I—
You bastard!
Granny Goodness told us everything, Scott. How you planned to escape... to a different planet!

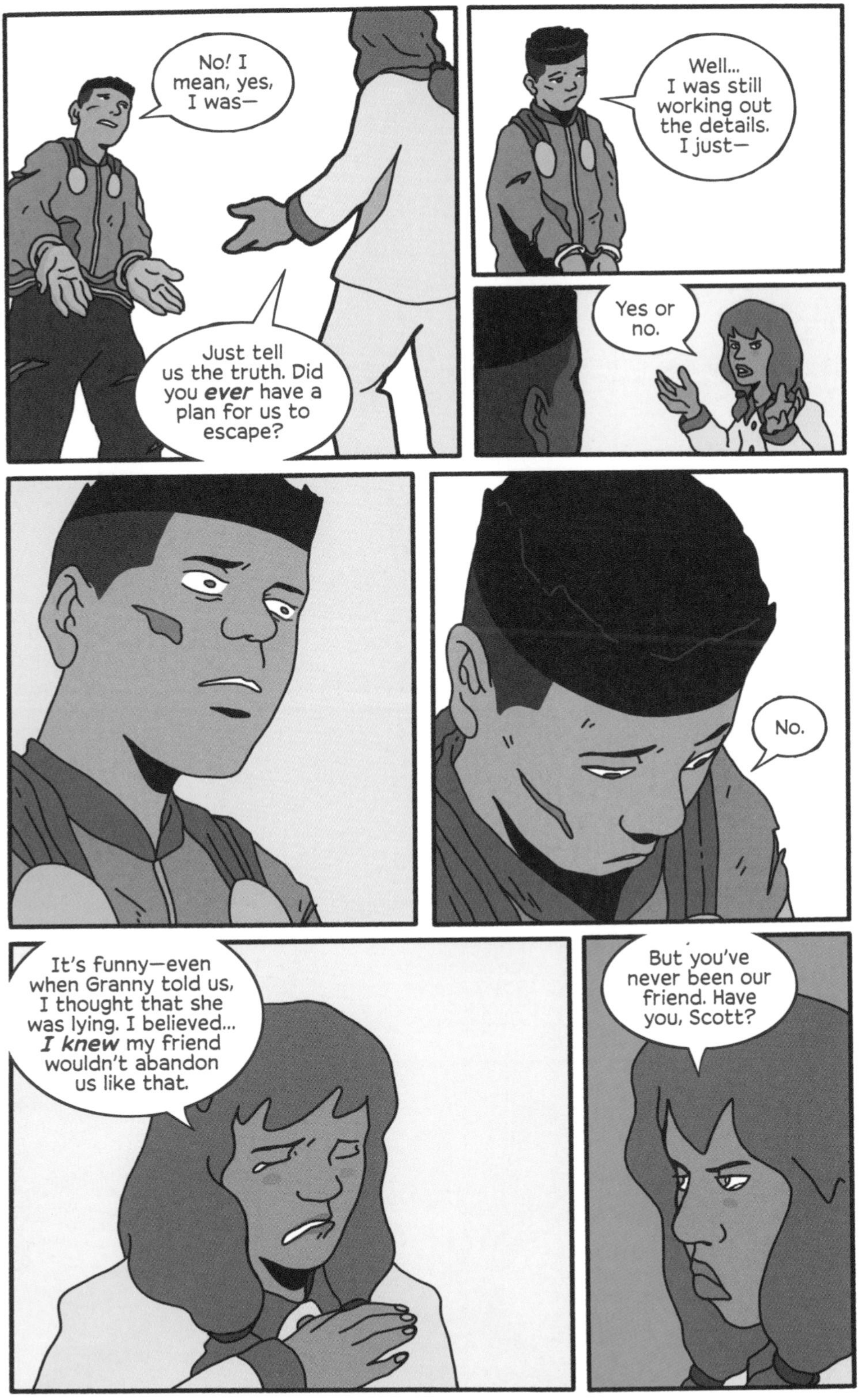
No! I mean, yes, I was—
Just tell us the truth. Did you ***ever*** have a plan for us to escape?
Well... I was still working out the details. I just—
Yes or no.
No.
It's funny—even when Granny told us, I thought that she was lying. I believed... ***I knew*** my friend wouldn't abandon us like that.
But you've never been our friend. Have you, Scott?

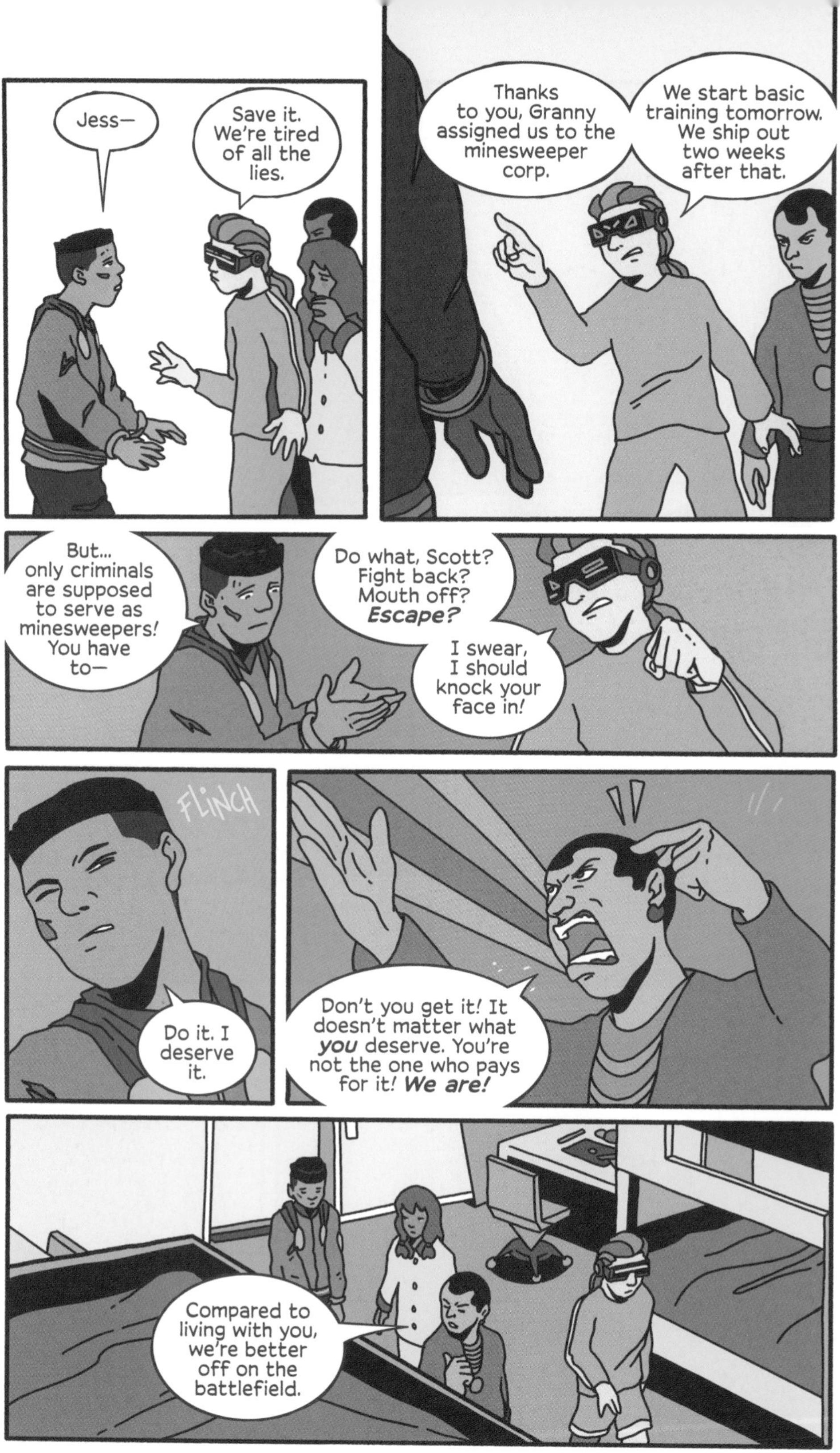
Jess—
Save it. We're tired of all the lies.
Thanks to you, Granny assigned us to the minesweeper corp.
We start basic training tomorrow. We ship out two weeks after that.
But... only criminals are supposed to serve as minesweepers! You have to—
Do what, Scott? Fight back? Mouth off? *Escape?*
I swear, I should knock your face in!
FLINCH
Do it. I deserve it.
Don't you get it! It doesn't matter what *you* deserve. You're not the one who pays for it! *We are!*
Compared to living with you, we're better off on the battlefield.

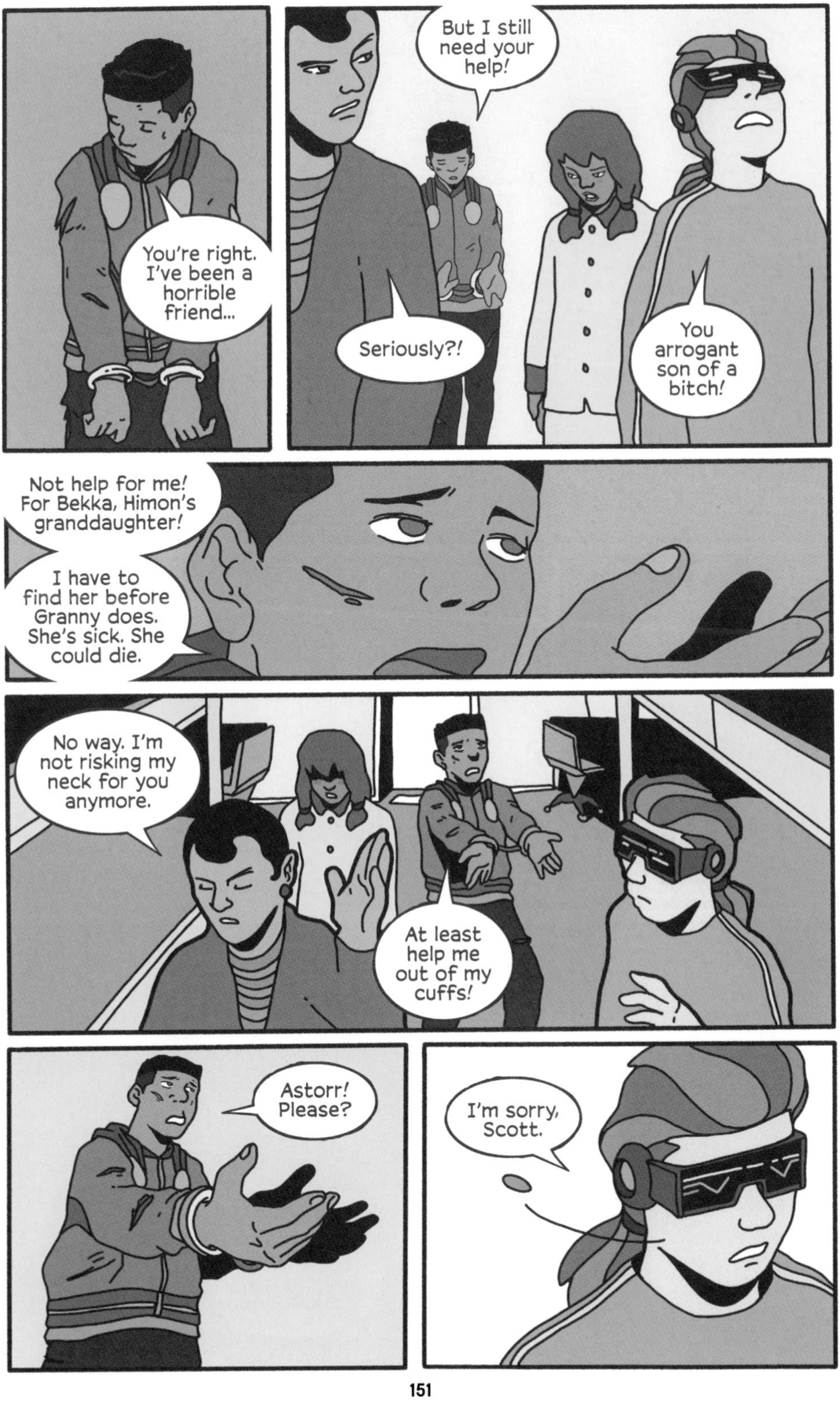
You're right. I've been a horrible friend...
But I still need your help!
Seriously?!
You arrogant son of a bitch!
Not help for me! For Bekka, Himon's granddaughter!
I have to find her before Granny does. She's sick. She could die.
No way. I'm not risking my neck for you anymore.
At least help me out of my cuffs!
Astorr! Please?
I'm sorry, Scott.

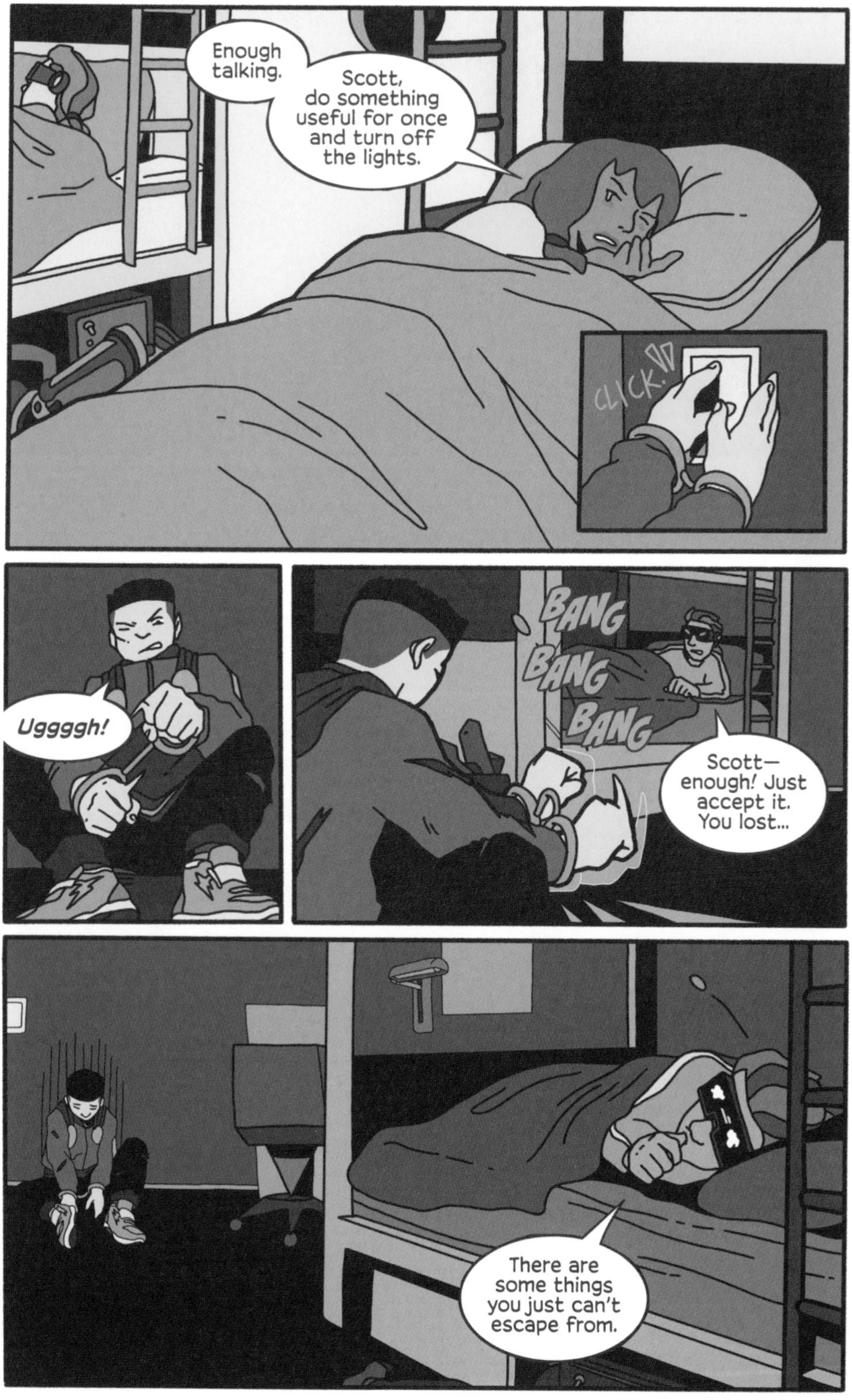
Enough talking.
Scott, do something useful for once and turn off the lights.
CLICK
Uggggh!
BANG
BANG
BANG
Scott—enough! Just accept it. You lost...
There are some things you just can't escape from.

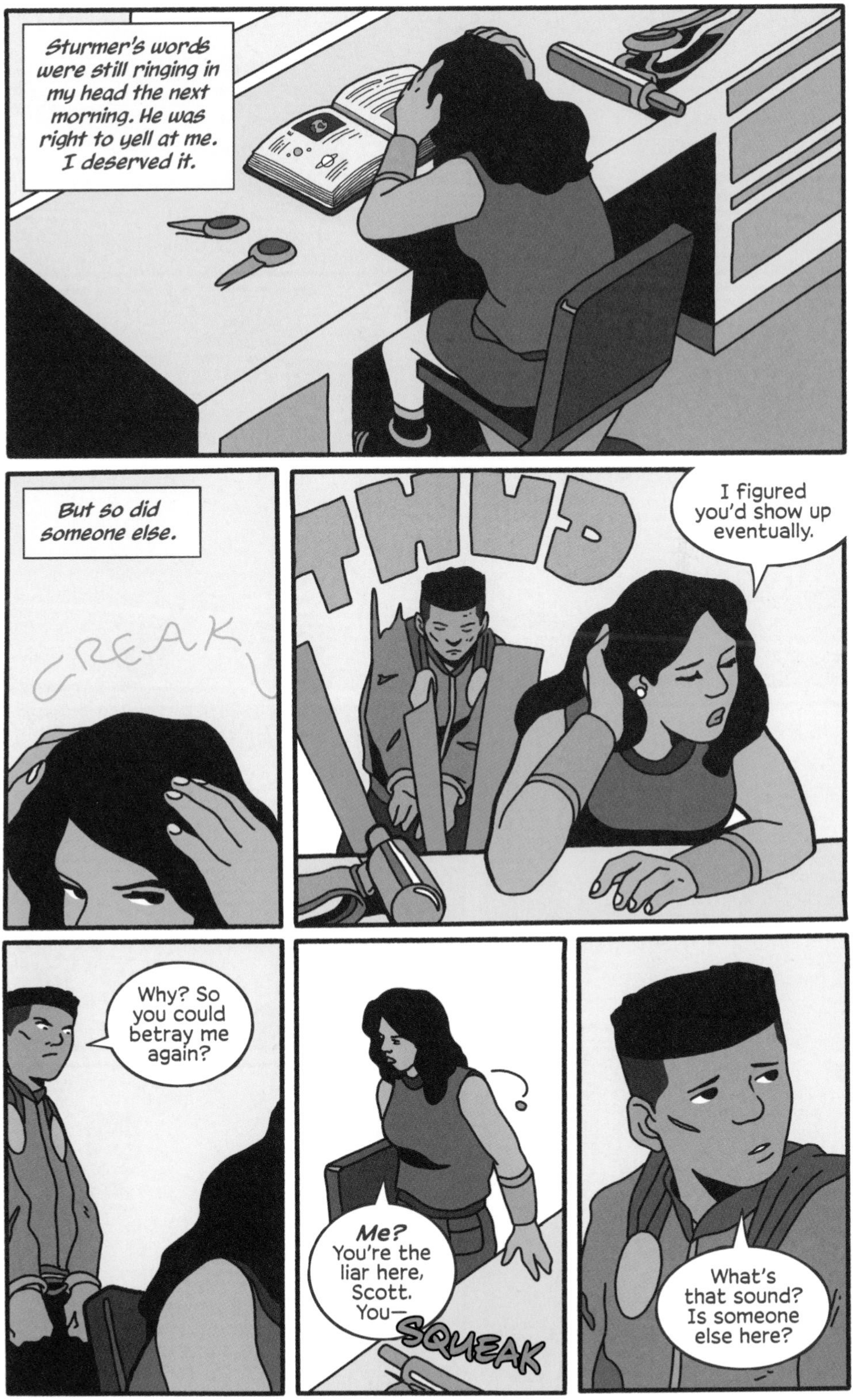
Sturmer's words were still ringing in my head the next morning. He was right to yell at me. I deserved it.
But so did someone else.
CREAK
THUD
I figured you'd show up eventually.
Why? So you could betray me again?
Me? You're the liar here, Scott. You—
SQUEAK
What's that sound? Is someone else here?

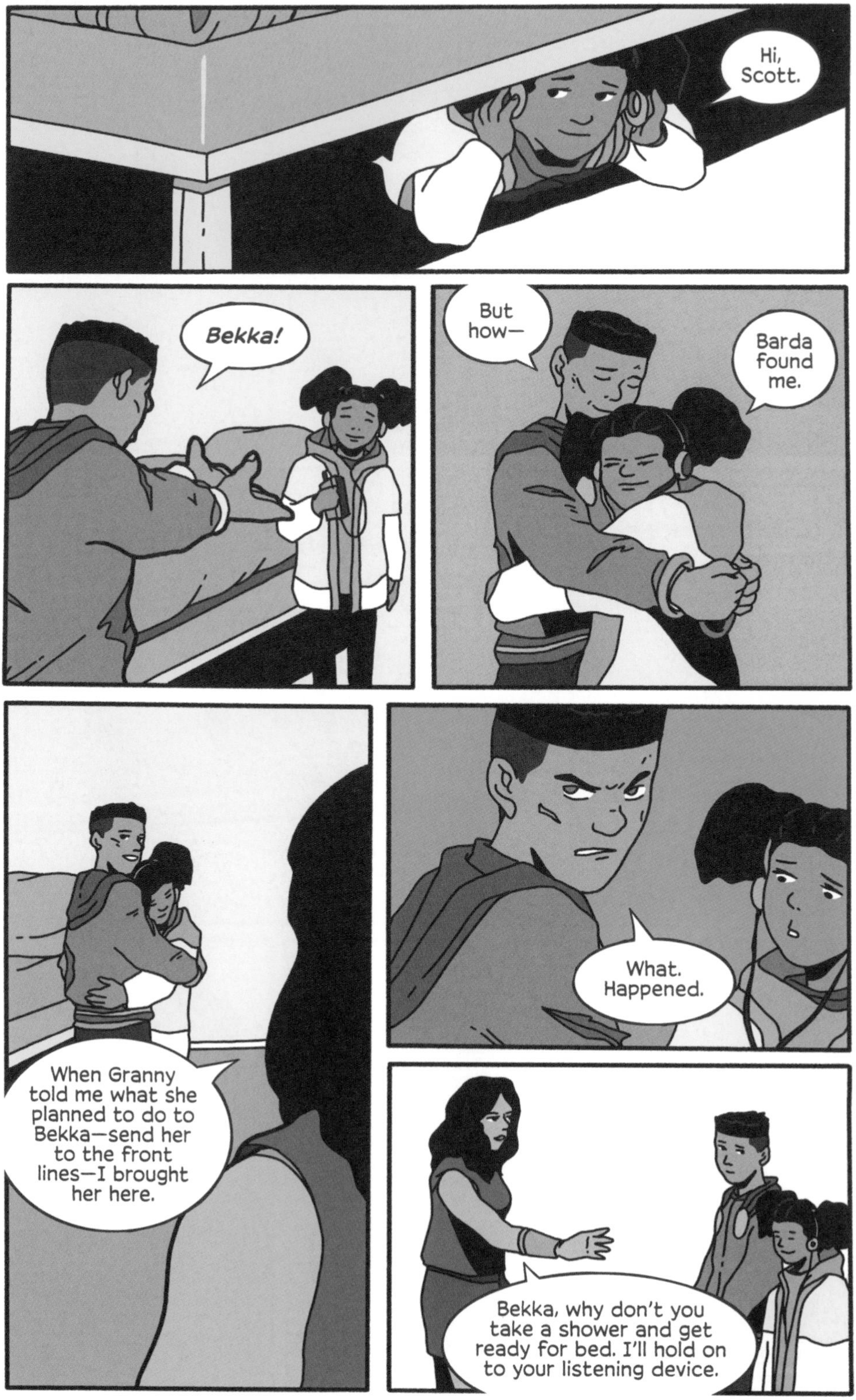
Hi, Scott.
Bekka!
But how—
Barda found me.
What. Happened.
When Granny told me what she planned to do to Bekka—send her to the front lines—I brought her here.
Bekka, why don't you take a shower and get ready for bed. I'll hold on to your listening device.

Okay! Thanks, Barda.

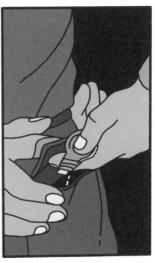

Maybe we should start at the beginning.

CLICK

You first.

Granny ordered me to spy on you. I was supposed to gain your confidence. Discover who was helping you.

But you were smart. You never revealed your accomplice. Until...

Until that last night in the tower.

Yes. And then I had everything I needed.

But I couldn't go through with it. Maybe I didn't want Granny to have the satisfaction.

155

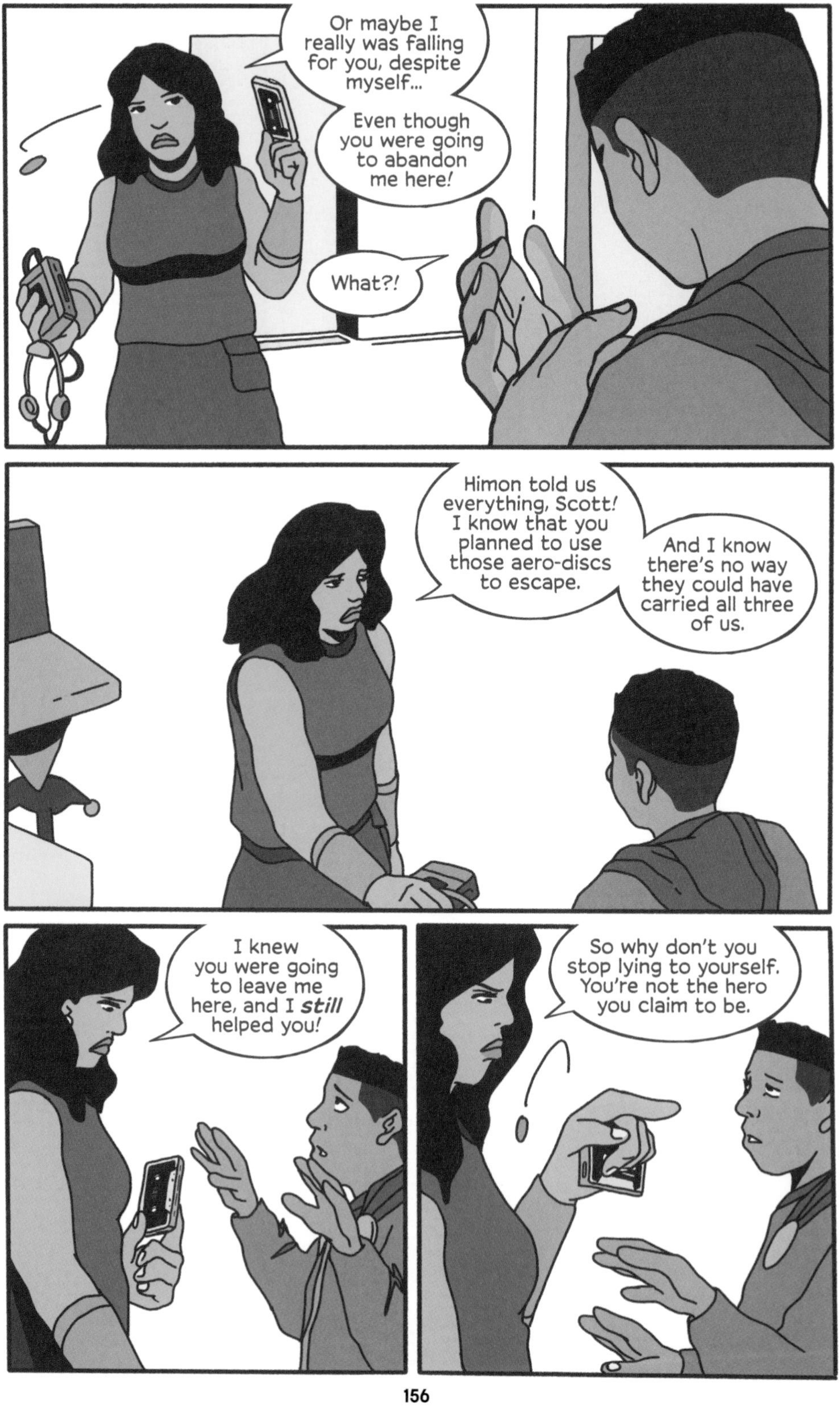
Or maybe I really was falling for you, despite myself...
Even though you were going to abandon me here!
What?!
Himon told us everything, Scott! I know that you planned to use those aero-discs to escape.
And I know there's no way they could have carried all three of us.
I knew you were going to leave me here, and I *still* helped you!
So why don't you stop lying to yourself. You're not the hero you claim to be.

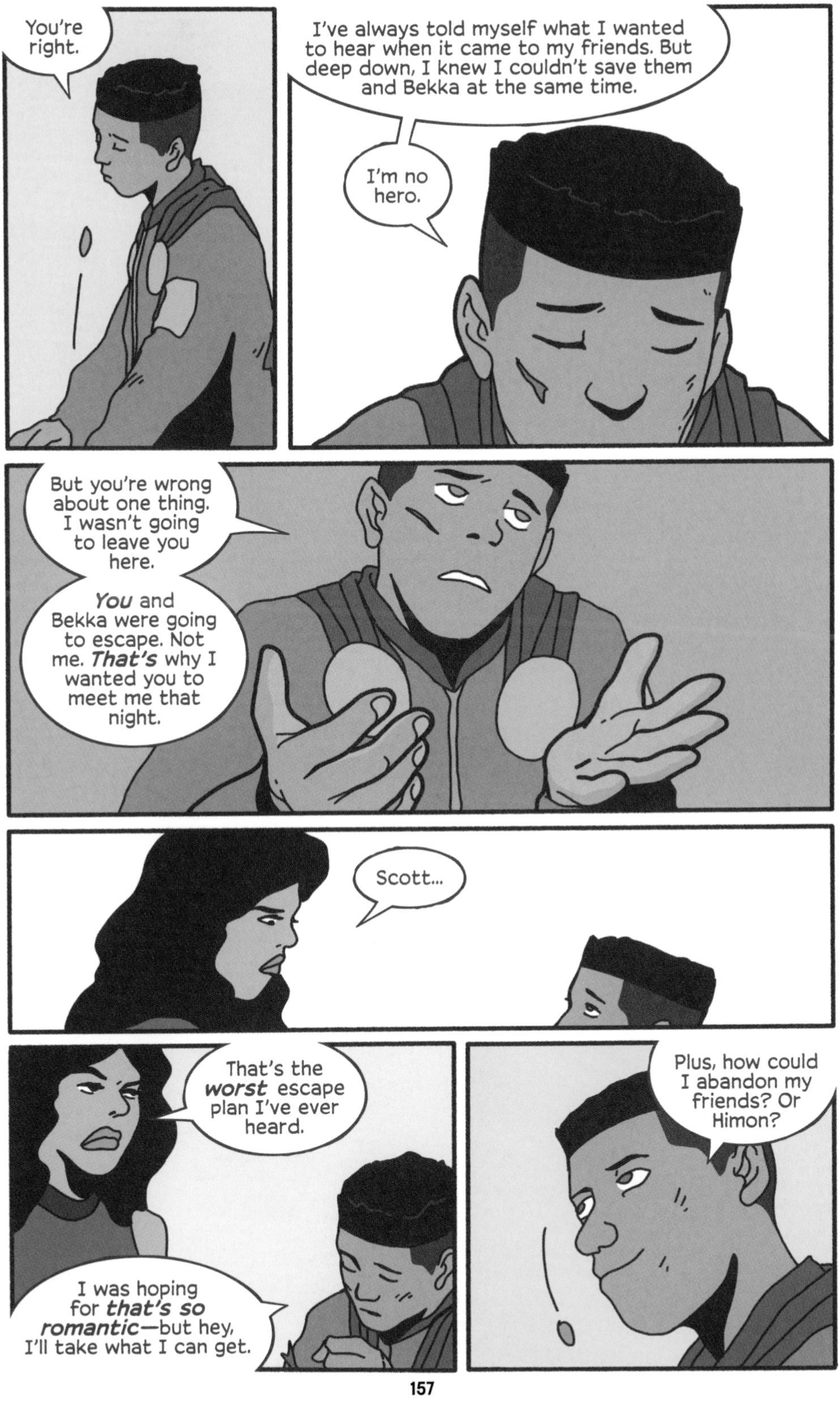
You're right.
I've always told myself what I wanted to hear when it came to my friends. But deep down, I knew I couldn't save them and Bekka at the same time.
I'm no hero.
But you're wrong about one thing. I wasn't going to leave you here.
You and Bekka were going to escape. Not me. ***That's*** why I wanted you to meet me that night.
Scott...
That's the ***worst*** escape plan I've ever heard.
I was hoping for ***that's so romantic***—but hey, I'll take what I can get.
Plus, how could I abandon my friends? Or Himon?

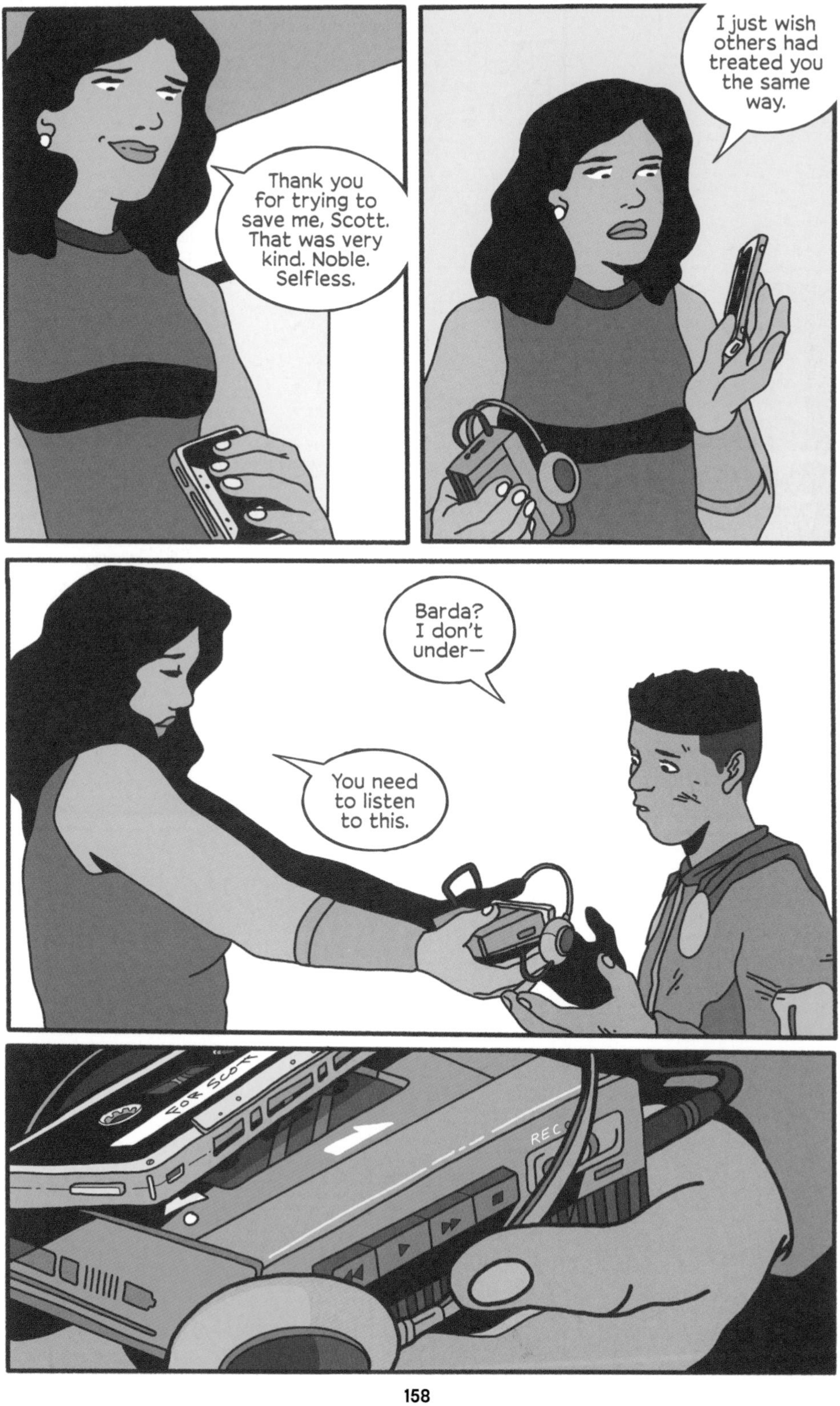
Thank you for trying to save me, Scott. That was very kind. Noble. Selfless.
I just wish others had treated you the same way.
Barda? I don't under—
You need to listen to this.
FOR SCOTT
REC

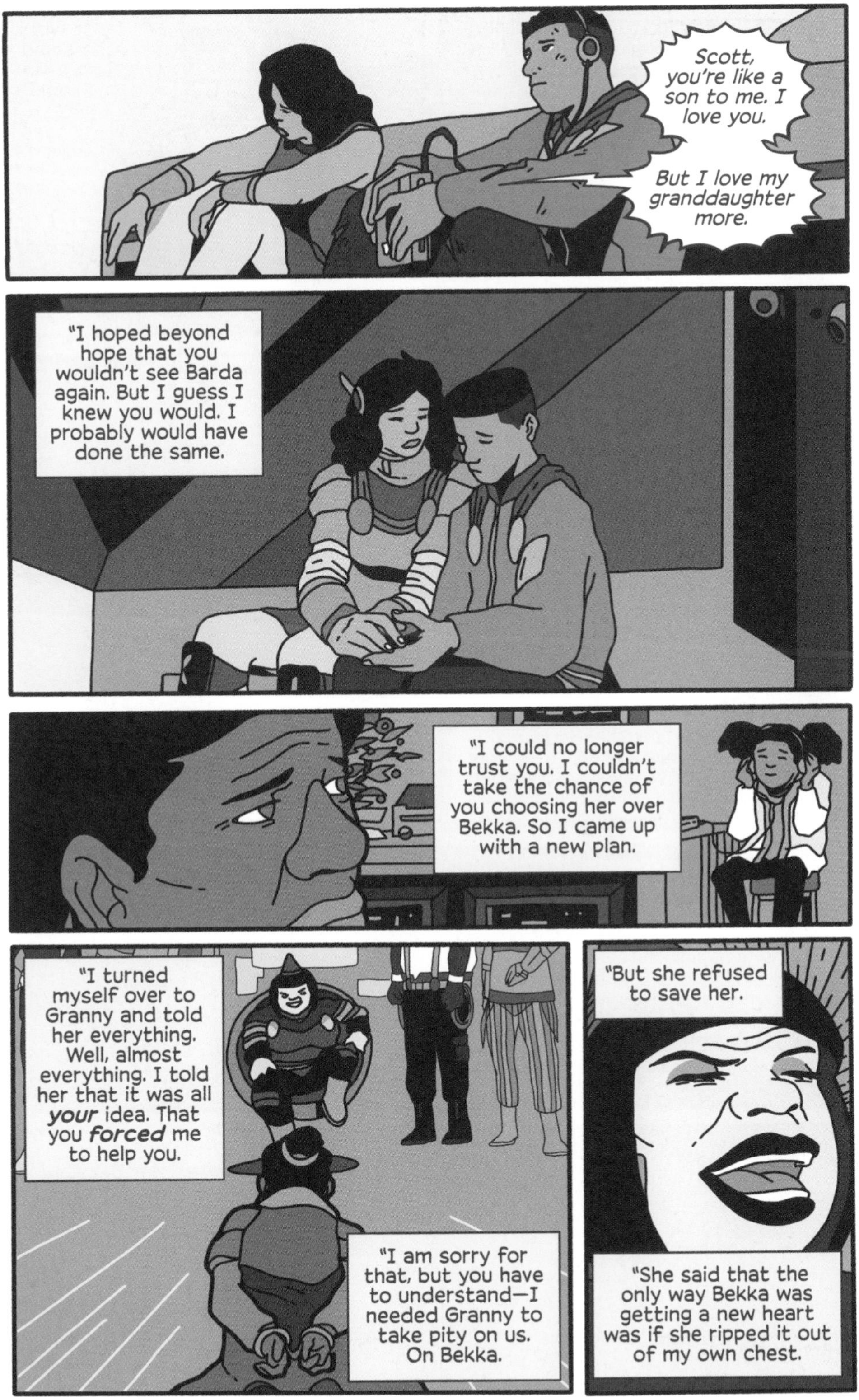
Scott, you're like a son to me. I love you.
But I love my granddaughter more.
"I hoped beyond hope that you wouldn't see Barda again. But I guess I knew you would. I probably would have done the same.
"I could no longer trust you. I couldn't take the chance of you choosing her over Bekka. So I came up with a new plan.
"I turned myself over to Granny and told her everything. Well, almost everything. I told her that it was all *your* idea. That you *forced* me to help you.
"I am sorry for that, but you have to understand—I needed Granny to take pity on us. On Bekka.
"But she refused to save her.
"She said that the only way Bekka was getting a new heart was if she ripped it out of my own chest.

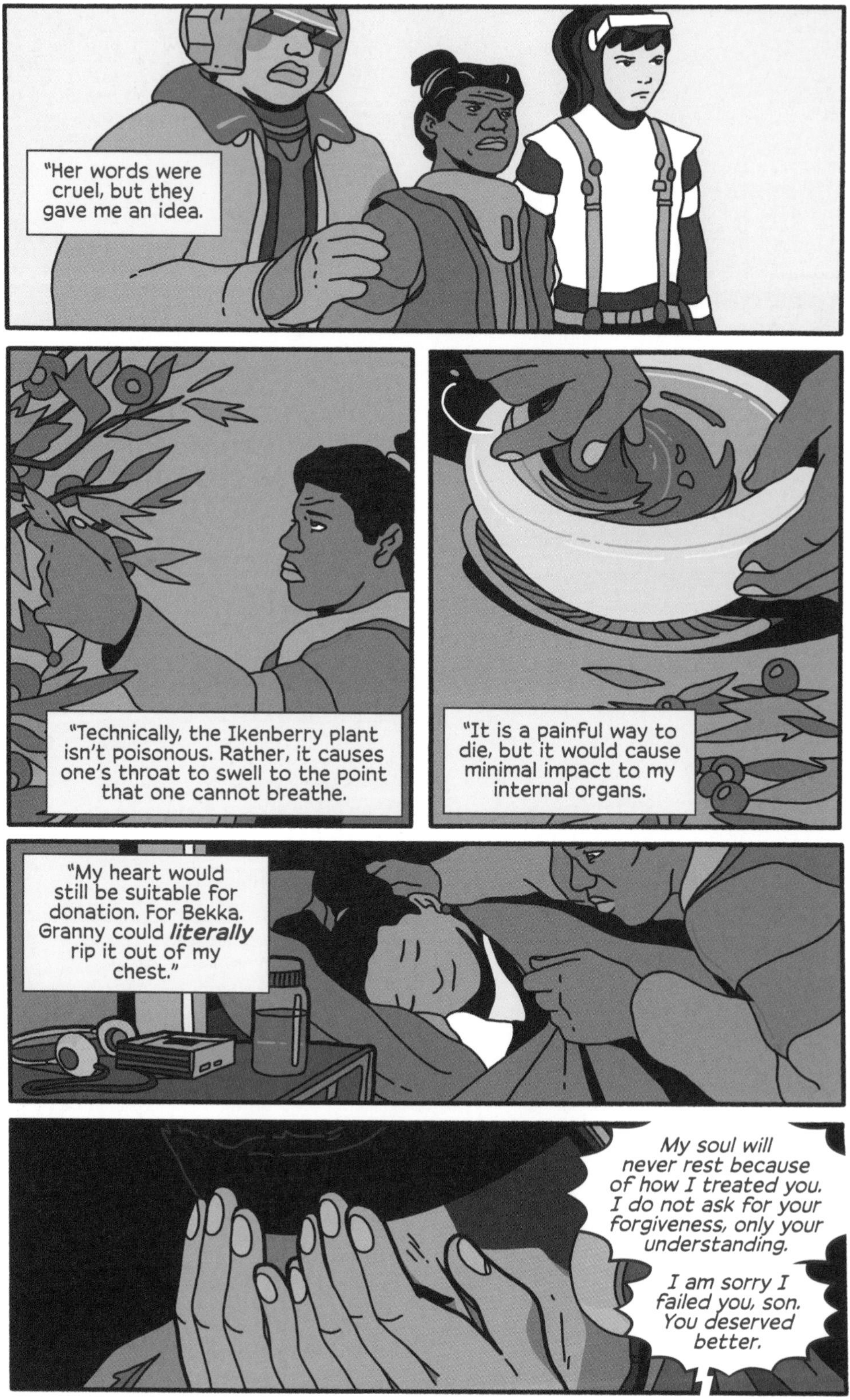
"Her words were cruel, but they gave me an idea.
"Technically, the Ikenberry plant isn't poisonous. Rather, it causes one's throat to swell to the point that one cannot breathe.
"It is a painful way to die, but it would cause minimal impact to my internal organs.
"My heart would still be suitable for donation. For Bekka. Granny could *literally* rip it out of my chest."
My soul will never rest because of how I treated you. I do not ask for your forgiveness, only your understanding.
I am sorry I failed you, son. You deserved better.

He's a bastard.

But...he wanted Bekka to have his heart. Maybe it's not too late. Maybe—

I'm sorry...

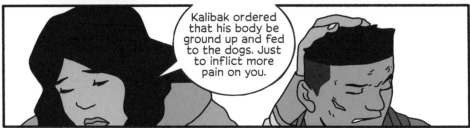

Kalibak ordered that his body be ground up and fed to the dogs. Just to inflict more pain on you.

I have to get Bekka off of this planet. She'll die if I don't. You and my friends, too.

Scott...

No. *Someone* must have escaped before.

Mother Box, has anyone ever escaped from the Goodness Academy?

No. Escape is impossible.

Barda, ask if there's a way for me to *earn* my freedom?

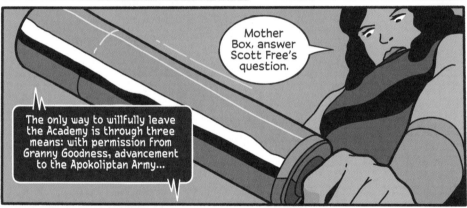

Mother Box, answer Scott Free's question.

The only way to willfully leave the Academy is through three means: with permission from Granny Goodness, advancement to the Apokoliptan Army...

Or victory through Trial by Combat.

And who would I have to challenge for my—*our*—independence?

No...

Ask the question, Barda. Or do you already know the answer?

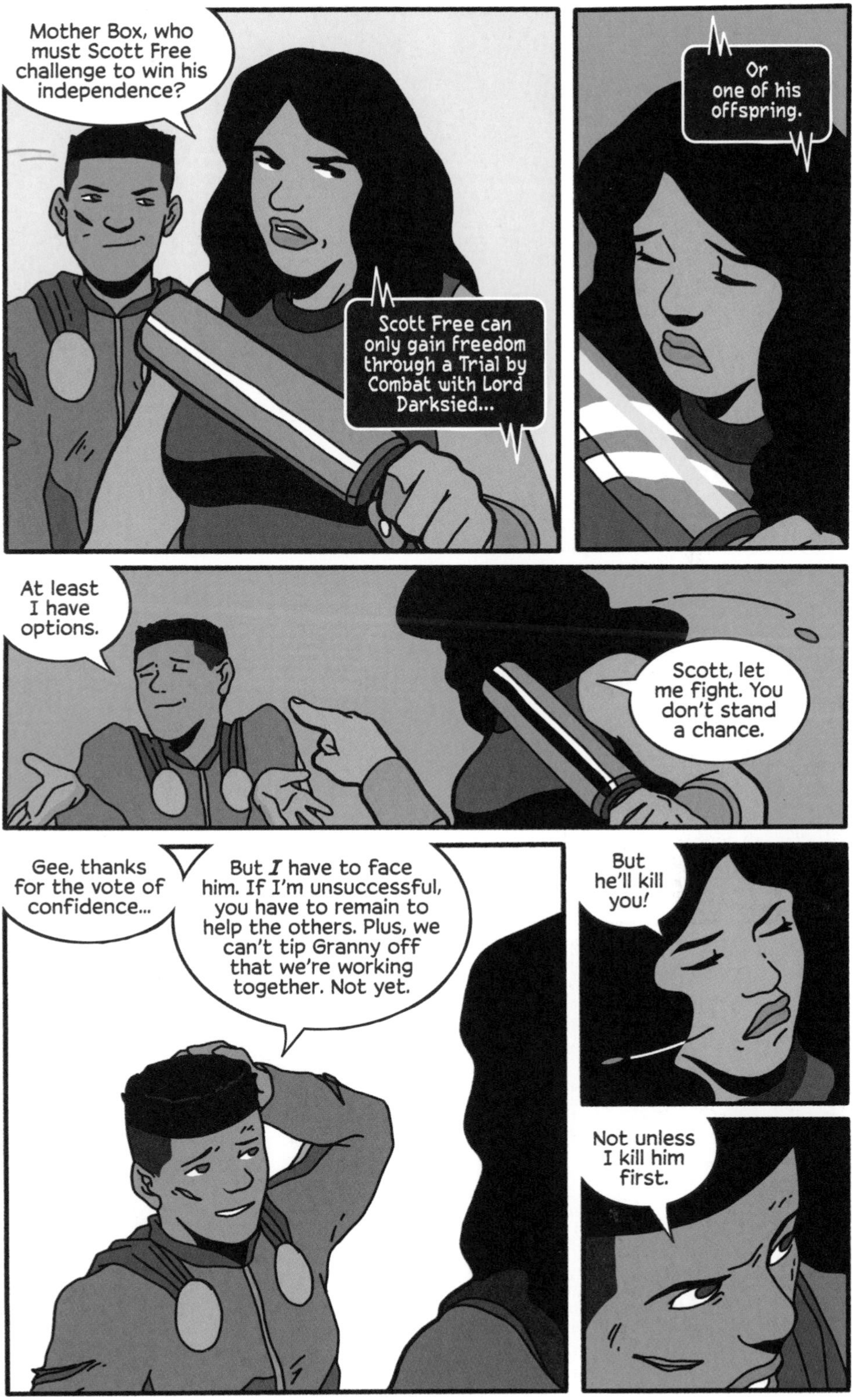

Mother Box, who must Scott Free challenge to win his independence?
Scott Free can only gain freedom through a Trial by Combat with Lord Darksied...
Or one of his offspring.
At least I have options.
Scott, let me fight. You don't stand a chance.
Gee, thanks for the vote of confidence...
But *I* have to face him. If I'm unsuccessful, you have to remain to help the others. Plus, we can't tip Granny off that we're working together. Not yet.
But he'll kill you!
Not unless I kill him first.

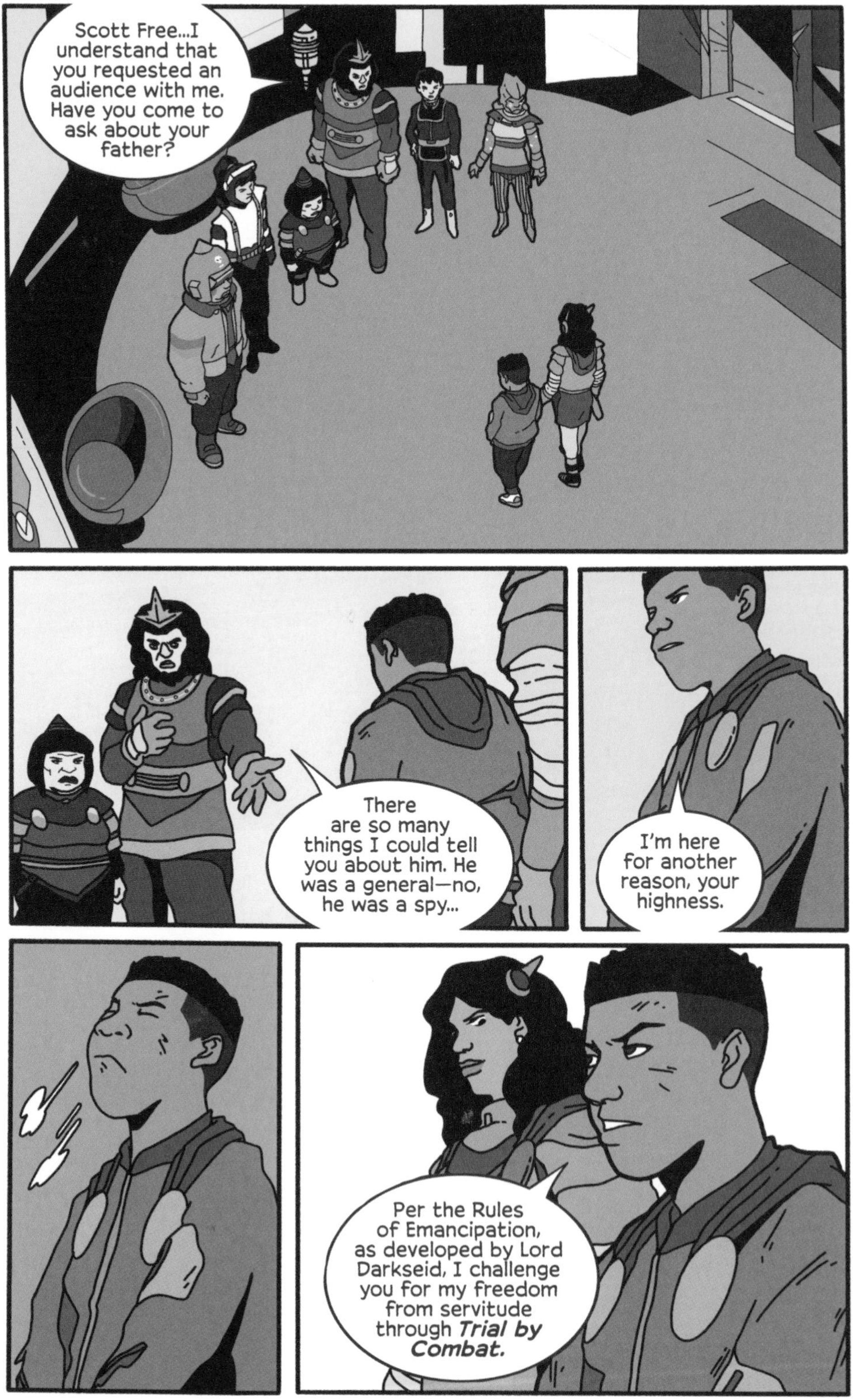
Scott Free...I understand that you requested an audience with me. Have you come to ask about your father?
There are so many things I could tell you about him. He was a general—no, he was a spy...
I'm here for another reason, your highness.
Per the Rules of Emancipation, as developed by Lord Darkseid, I challenge you for my freedom from servitude through *Trial by Combat.*

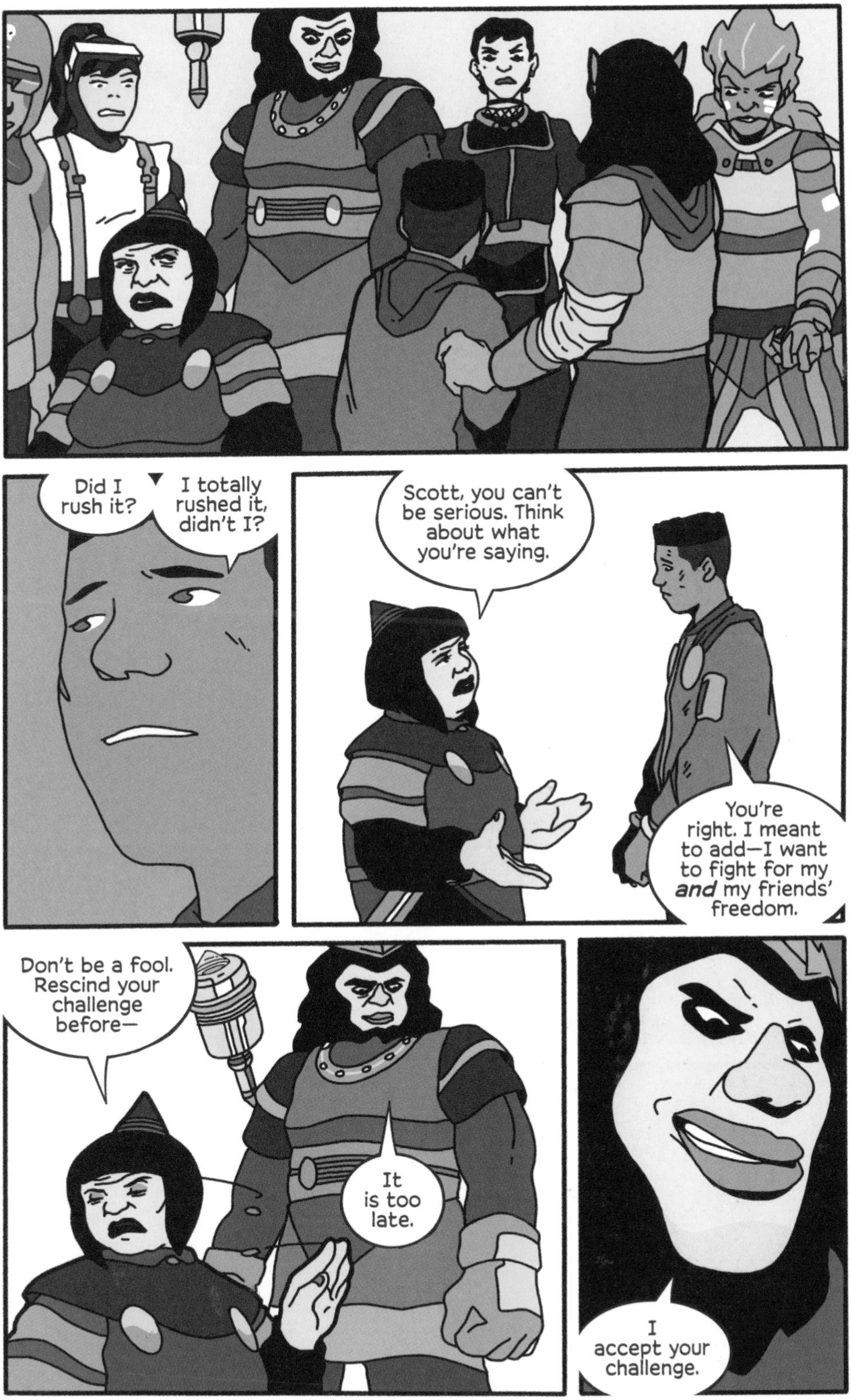
Did I rush it?
I totally rushed it, didn't I?
Scott, you can't be serious. Think about what you're saying.
You're right. I meant to add—I want to fight for my *and* my friends' freedom.
Don't be a fool. Rescind your challenge before—
It is too late.
I accept your challenge.

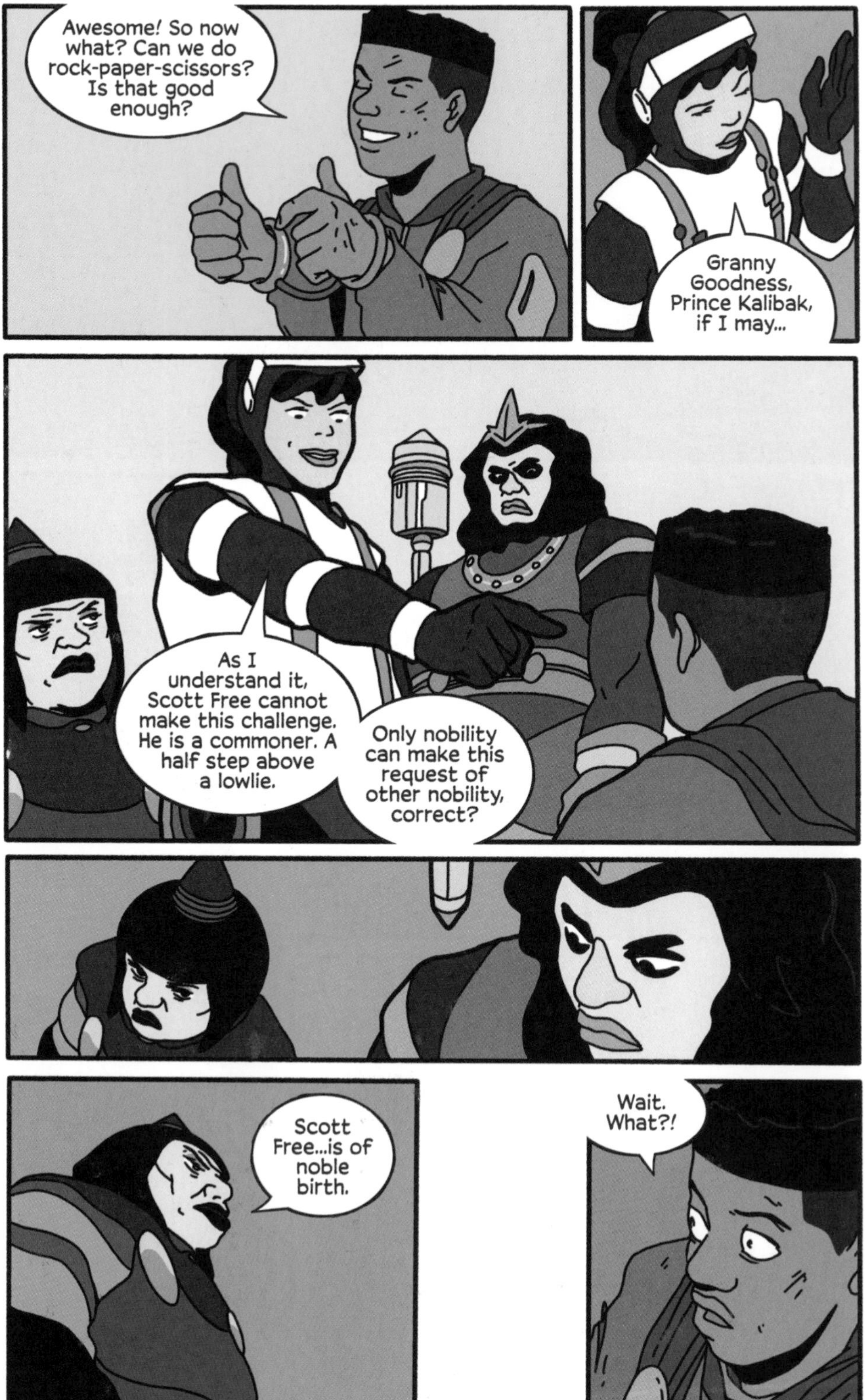
Awesome! So now what? Can we do rock-paper-scissors? Is that good enough?
Granny Goodness, Prince Kalibak, if I may...
As I understand it, Scott Free cannot make this challenge. He is a commoner. A half step above a lowlie.
Only nobility can make this request of other nobility, correct?
Scott Free...is of noble birth.
Wait. What?!

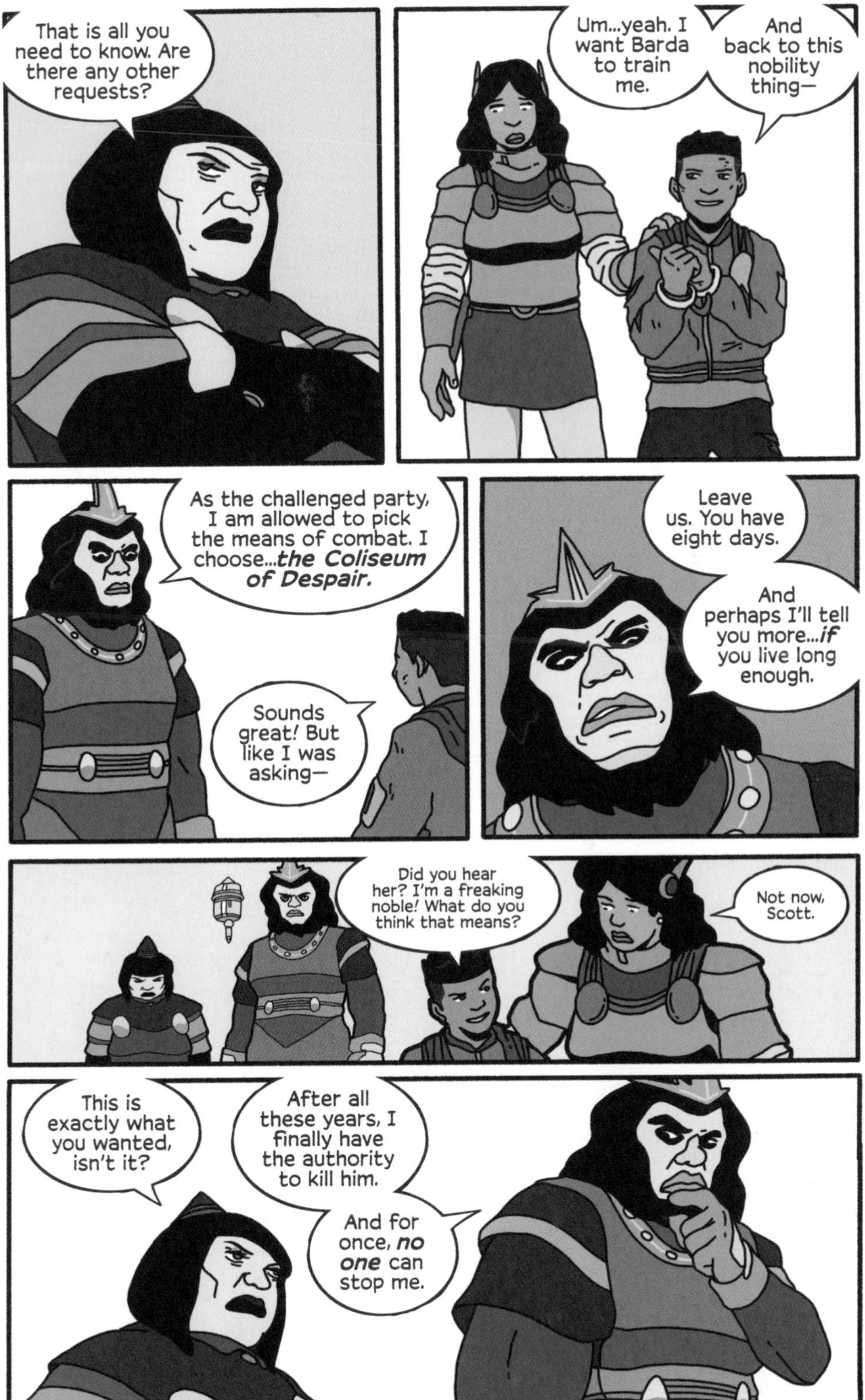

That is all you need to know. Are there any other requests?
Um...yeah. I want Barda to train me.
And back to this nobility thing—
As the challenged party, I am allowed to pick the means of combat. I choose...***the Coliseum of Despair.***
Sounds great! But like I was asking—
Leave us. You have eight days.
And perhaps I'll tell you more...***if*** you live long enough.
Did you hear her? I'm a freaking noble! What do you think that means?
Not now, Scott.
This is exactly what you wanted, isn't it?
After all these years, I finally have the authority to kill him.
And for once, ***no one*** can stop me.

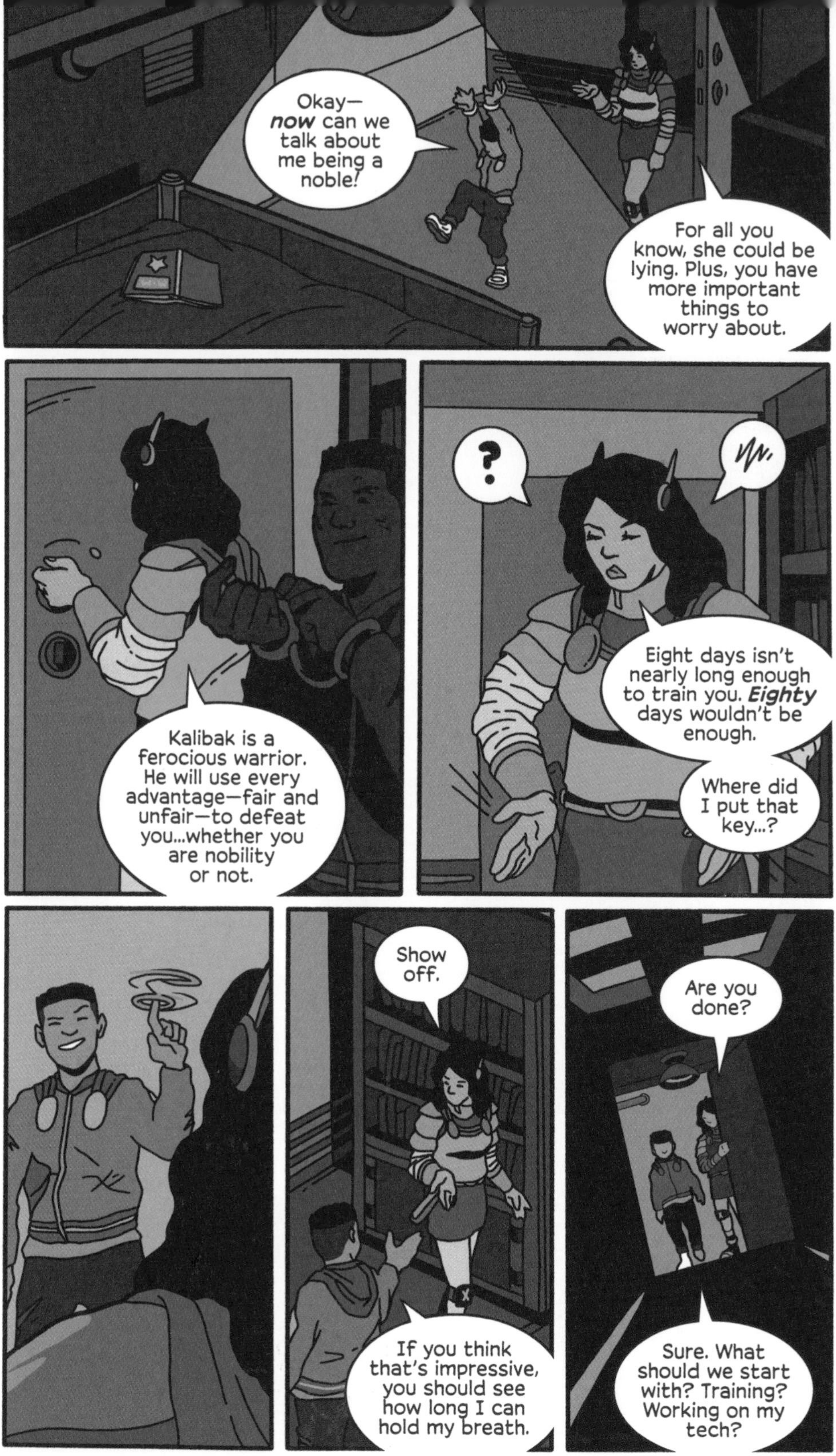
Okay—*now* can we talk about me being a noble!
For all you know, she could be lying. Plus, you have more important things to worry about.
Kalibak is a ferocious warrior. He will use every advantage—fair and unfair—to defeat you...whether you are nobility or not.
?
Eight days isn't nearly long enough to train you. *Eighty* days wouldn't be enough.
Where did I put that key...?
Show off.
If you think that's impressive, you should see how long I can hold my breath.
Are you done?
Sure. What should we start with? Training? Working on my tech?

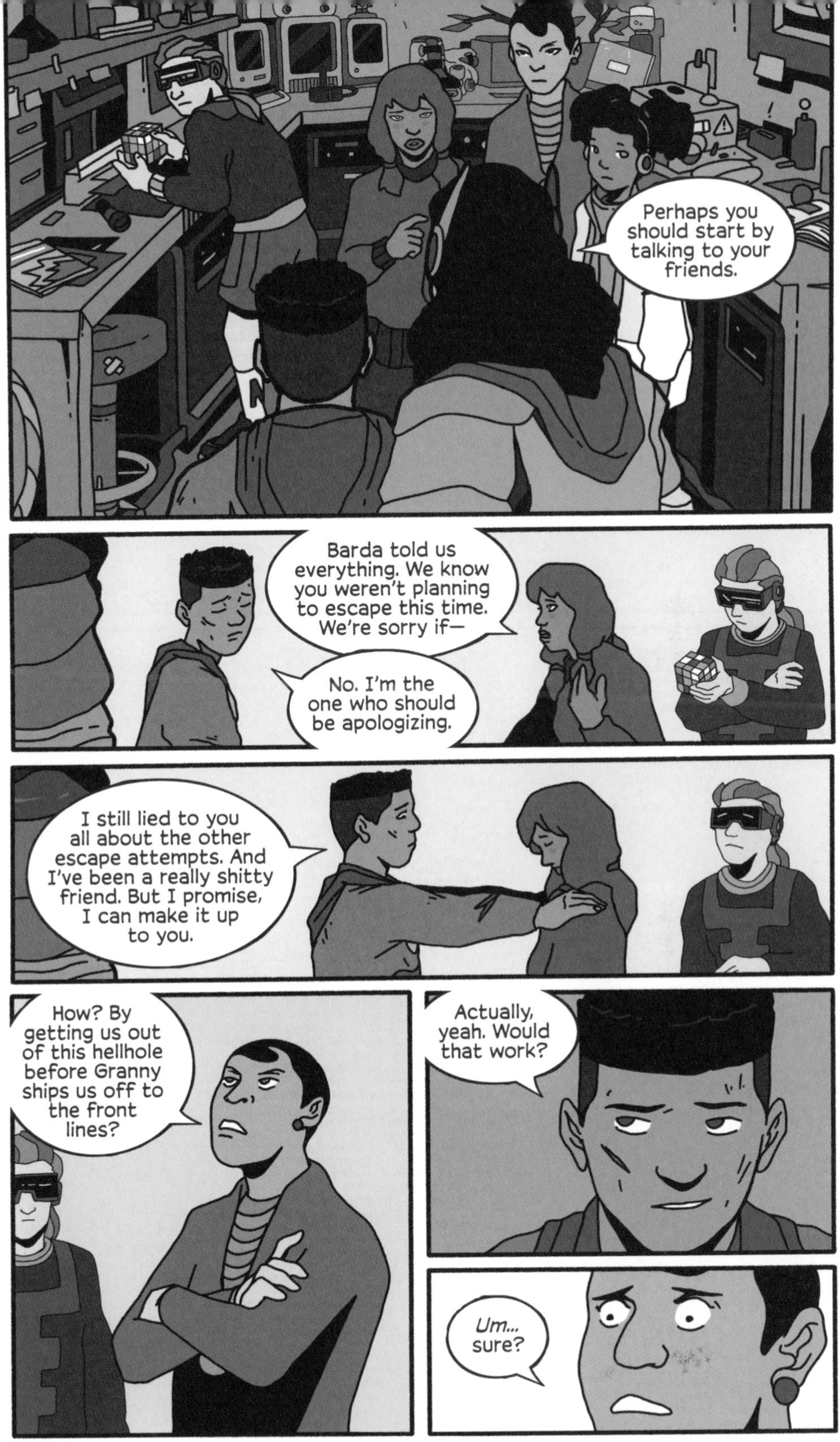
Perhaps you should start by talking to your friends.
Barda told us everything. We know you weren't planning to escape this time. We're sorry if—
No. I'm the one who should be apologizing.
I still lied to you all about the other escape attempts. And I've been a really shitty friend. But I promise, I can make it up to you.
How? By getting us out of this hellhole before Granny ships us off to the front lines?
Actually, yeah. Would that work?
Um... sure?

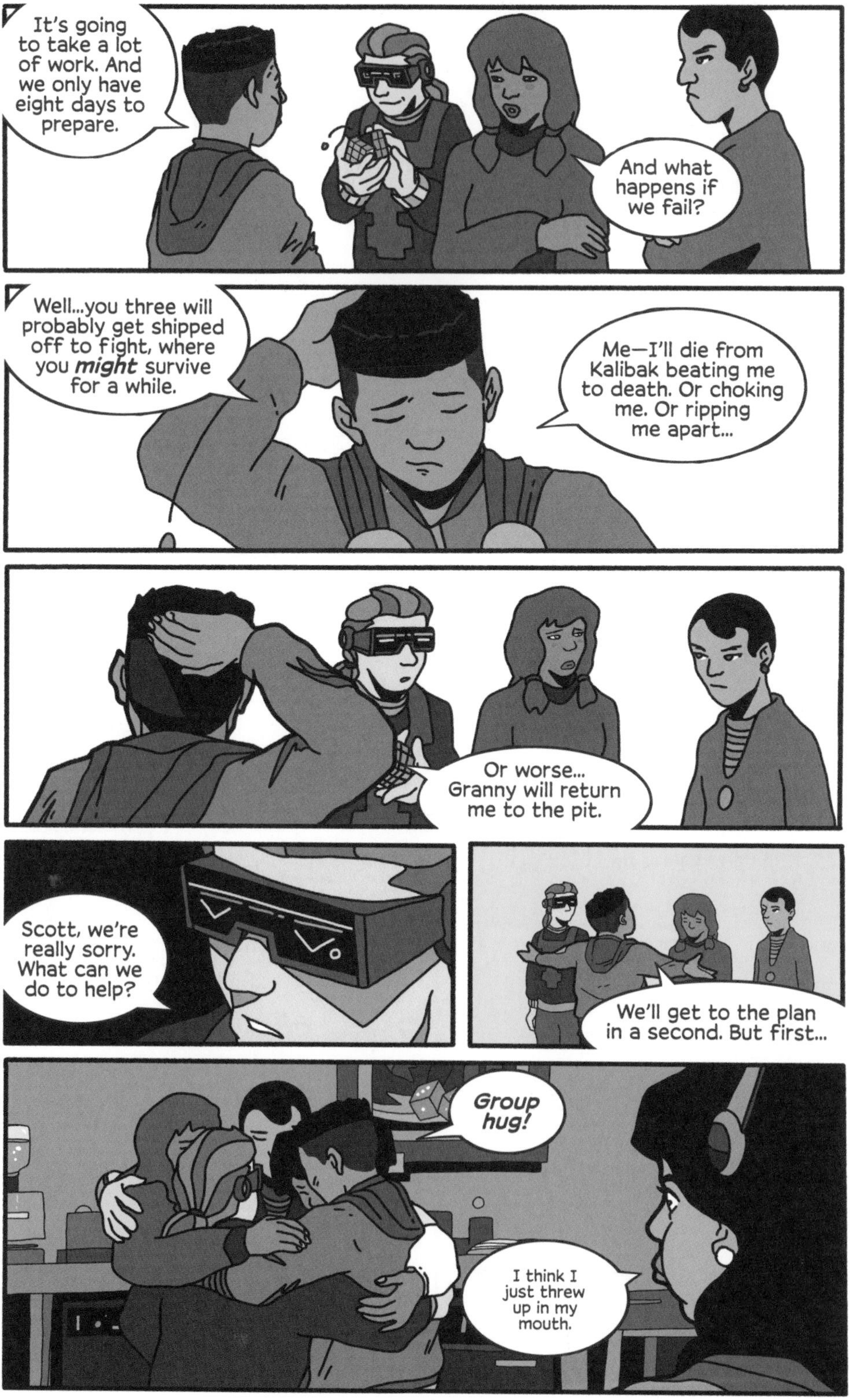
It's going to take a lot of work. And we only have eight days to prepare.
And what happens if we fail?
Well...you three will probably get shipped off to fight, where you *might* survive for a while.
Me—I'll die from Kalibak beating me to death. Or choking me. Or ripping me apart...
Or worse... Granny will return me to the pit.
Scott, we're really sorry. What can we do to help?
We'll get to the plan in a second. But first...
Group hug!
I think I just threw up in my mouth.

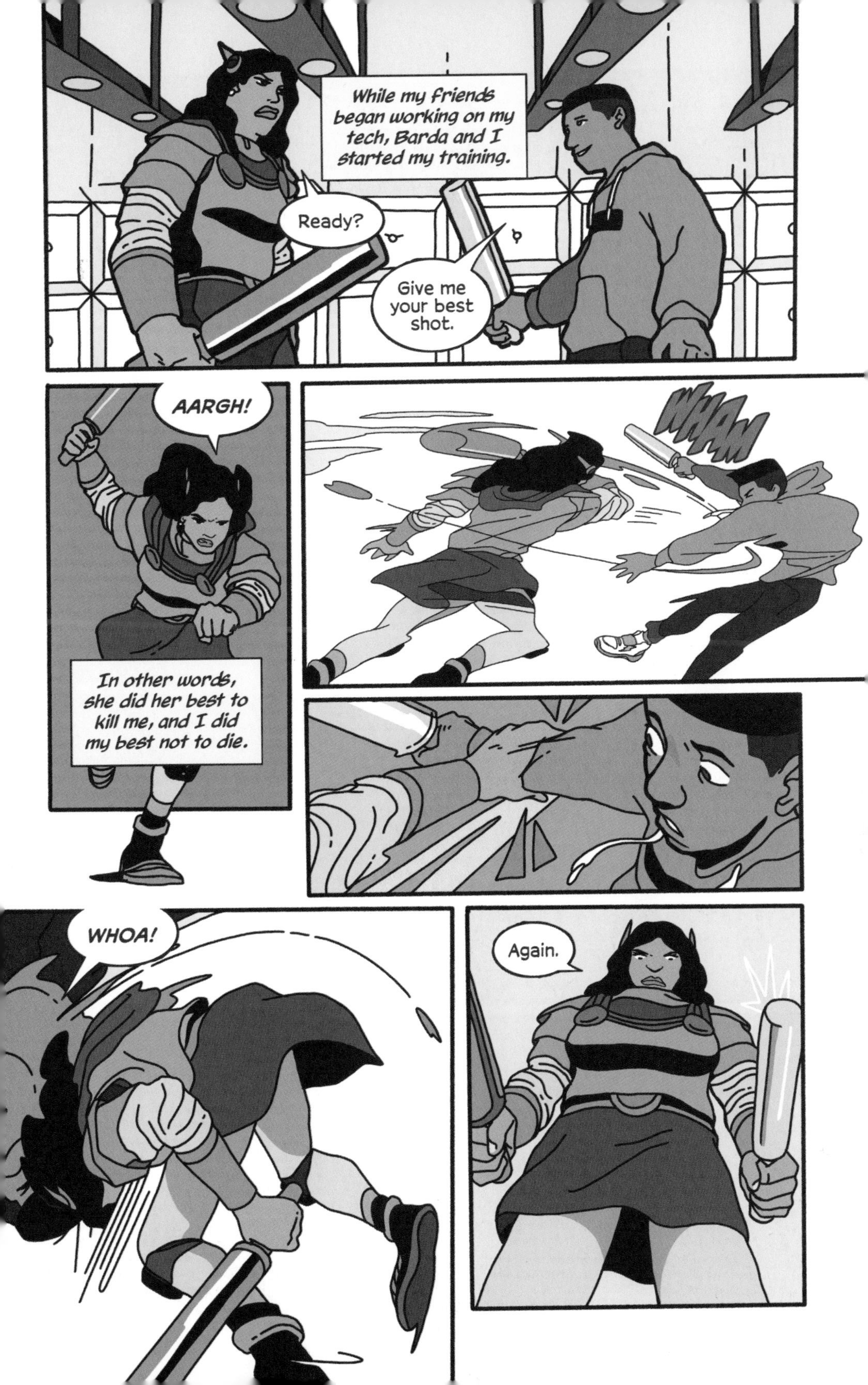
While my friends began working on my tech, Barda and I started my training.
Ready?
Give me your best shot.
AARGH!
In other words, she did her best to kill me, and I did my best not to die.
WHAM
WHOA!
Again.

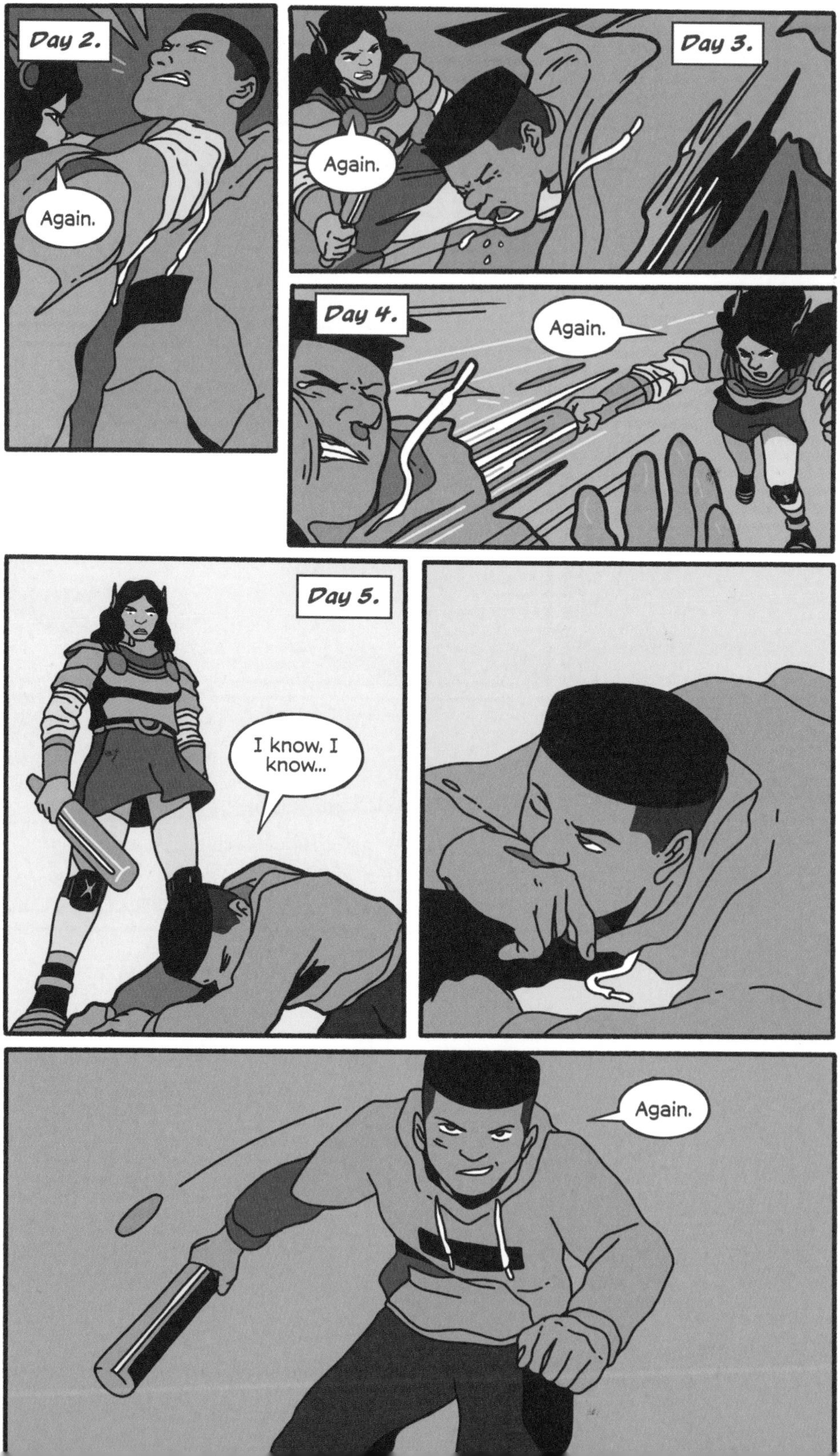
Day 2.
Again.
Day 3.
Again.
Day 4.
Again.
Day 5.
I know, I know...
Again.

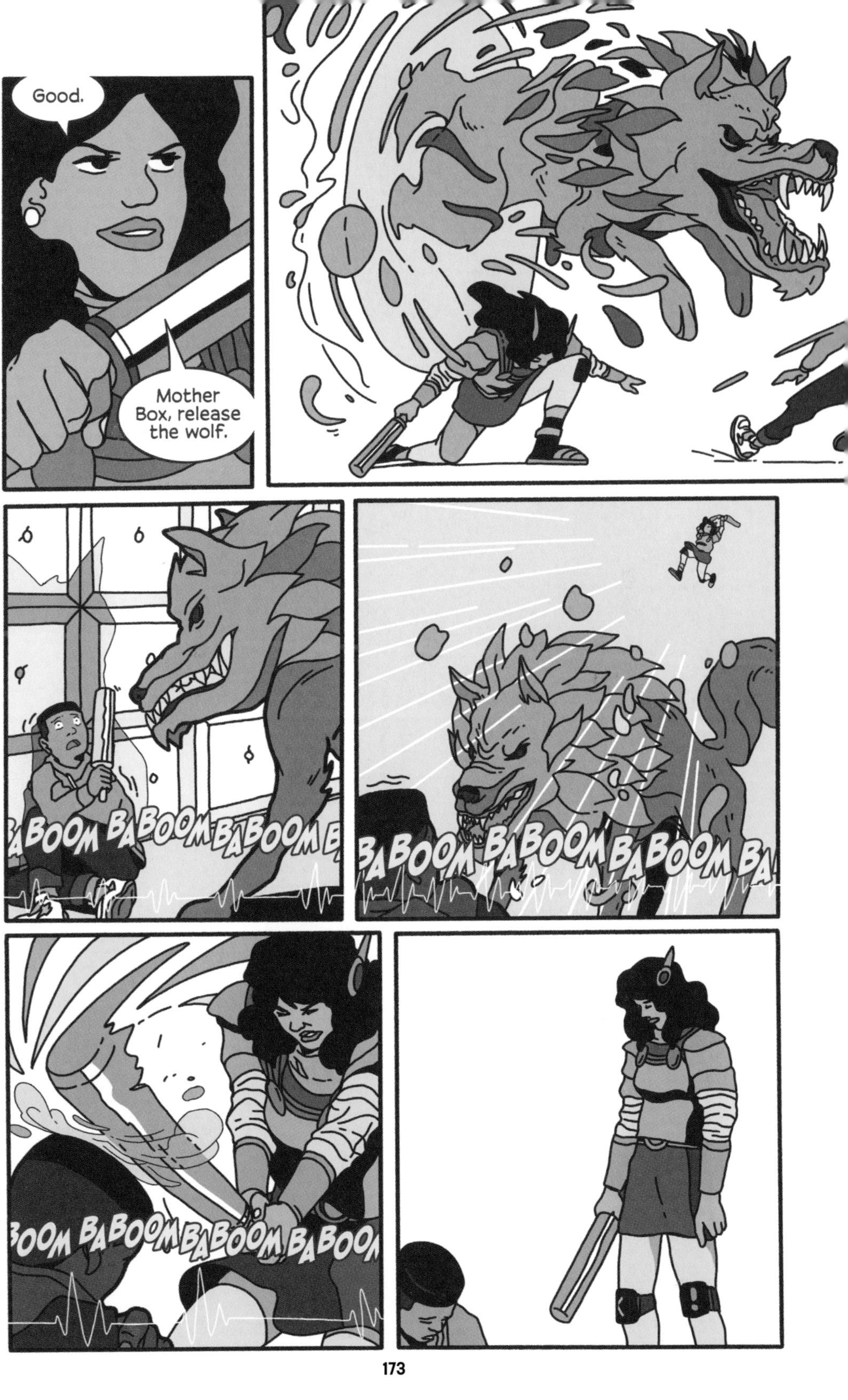
Good.
Mother Box, release the wolf.
BABOOM BABOOM BABOOM
BABOOM BABOOM BABOOM
BABOOM BABOOM BABOOM

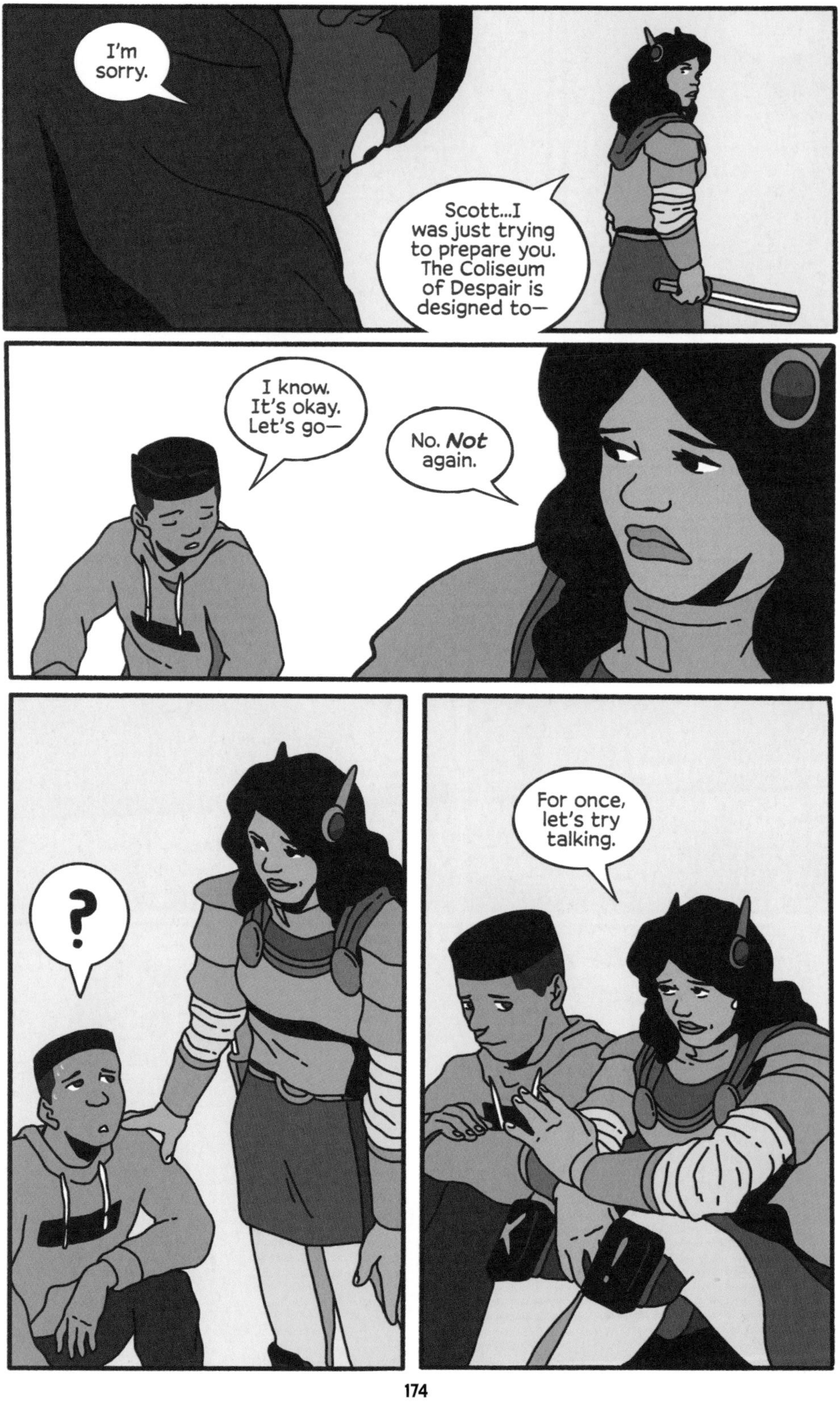
I'm sorry.
Scott...I was just trying to prepare you. The Coliseum of Despair is designed to—
I know. It's okay. Let's go—
No. ***Not*** again.
?
For once, let's try talking.

CHAPTER SIX

Don't You Worry 'bout a Thing

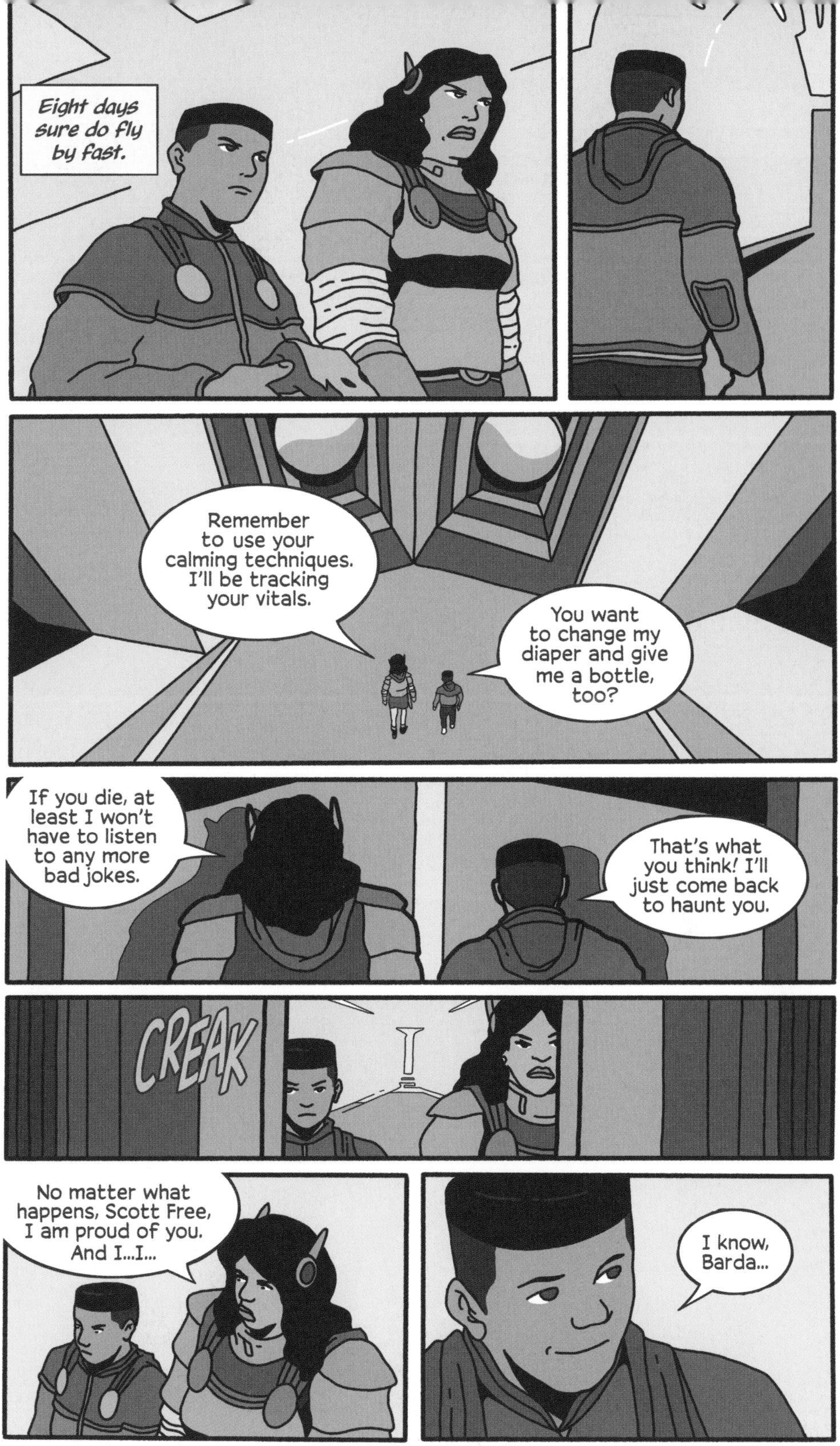
Eight days sure do fly by fast.
Remember to use your calming techniques. I'll be tracking your vitals.
You want to change my diaper and give me a bottle, too?
If you die, at least I won't have to listen to any more bad jokes.
That's what you think! I'll just come back to haunt you.
CREAK
No matter what happens, Scott Free, I am proud of you. And I...I...
I know, Barda...

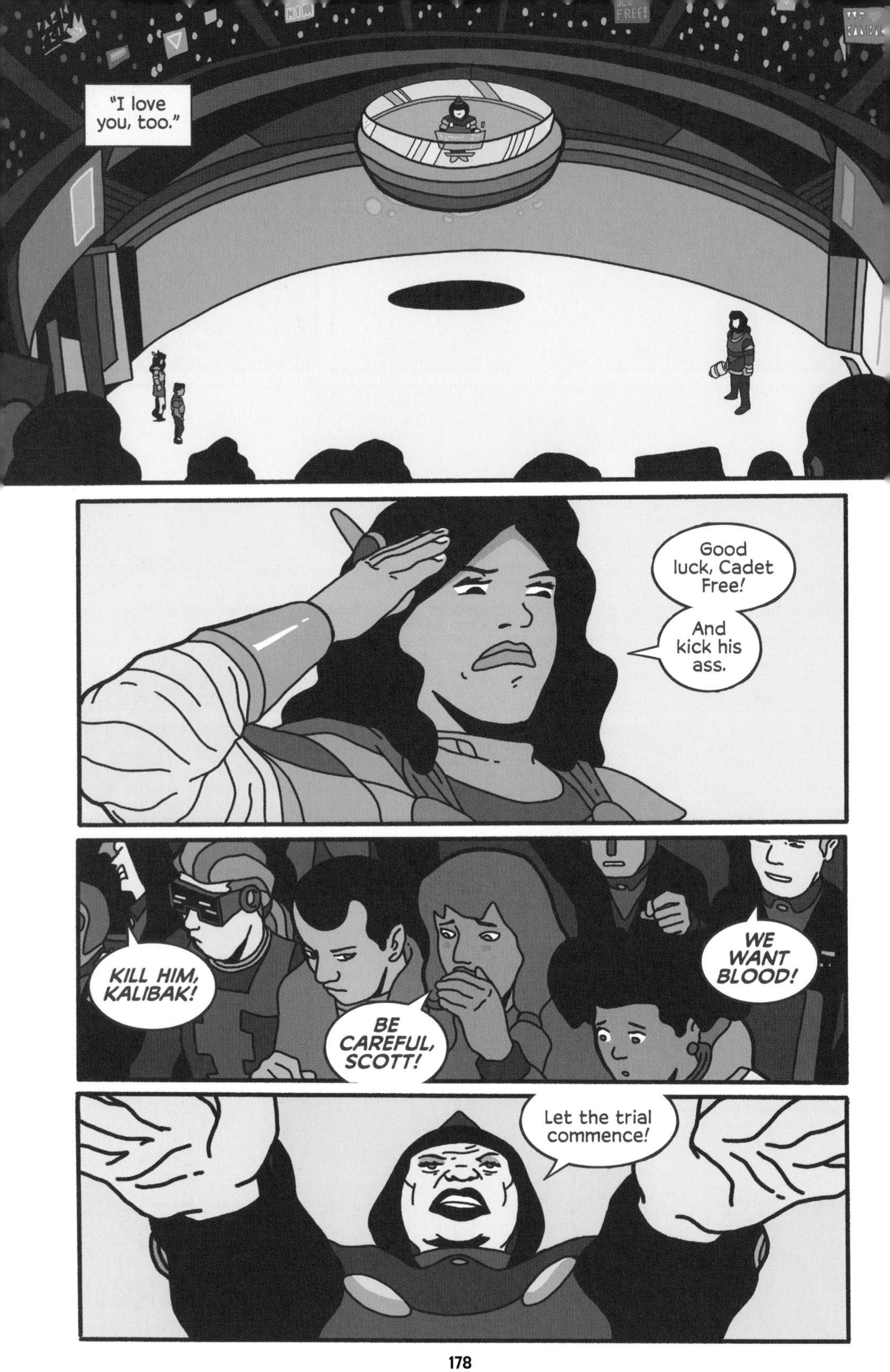
"I love you, too."
Good luck, Cadet Free!
And kick his ass.
KILL HIM, KALIBAK!
BE CAREFUL, SCOTT!
WE WANT BLOOD!
Let the trial commence!

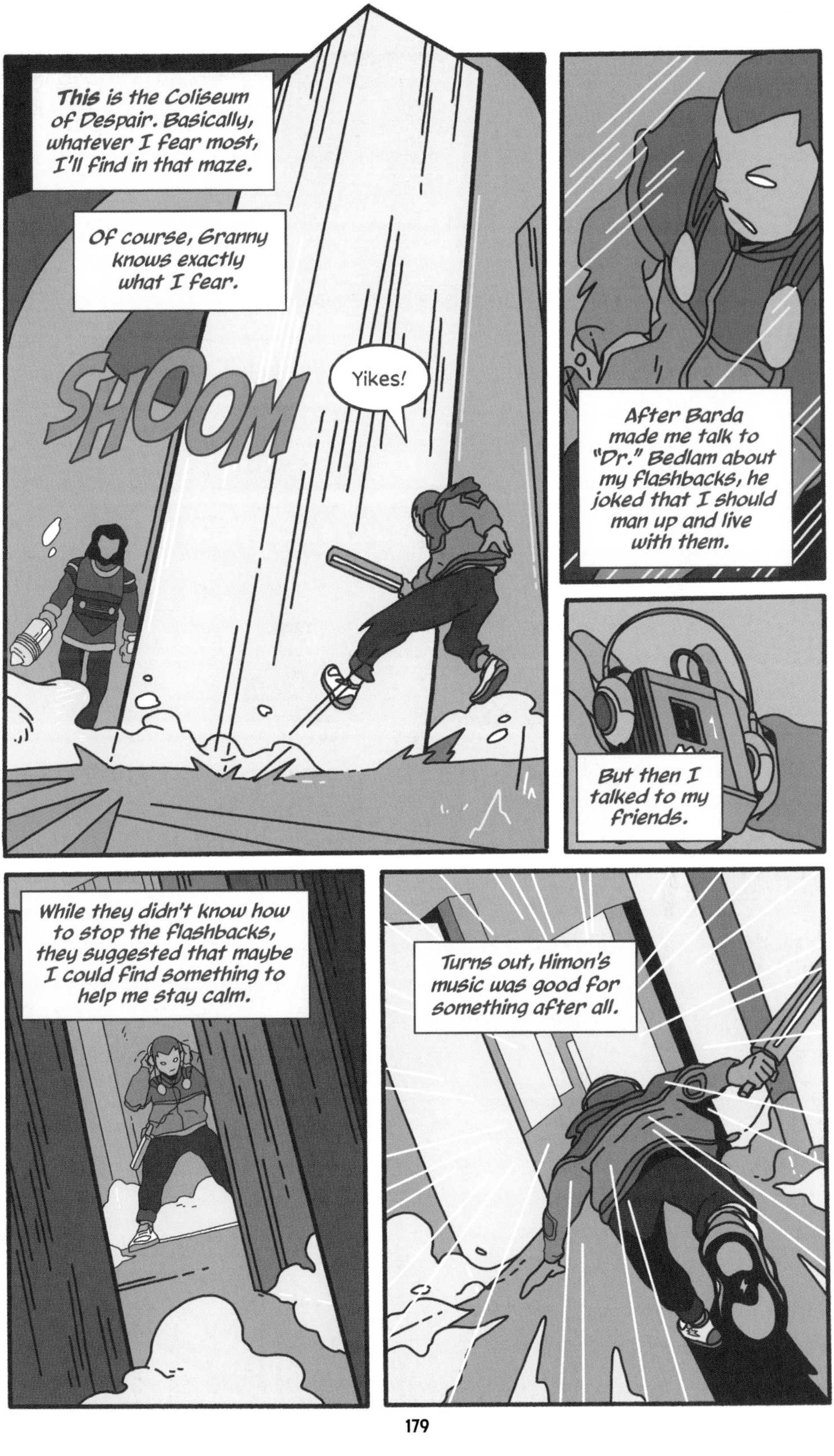
This is the Coliseum of Despair. Basically, whatever I fear most, I'll find in that maze.
Of course, Granny knows exactly what I fear.
SHOOM
Yikes!
After Barda made me talk to "Dr." Bedlam about my flashbacks, he joked that I should man up and live with them.
But then I talked to my friends.
While they didn't know how to stop the flashbacks, they suggested that maybe I could find something to help me stay calm.
Turns out, Himon's music was good for something after all.

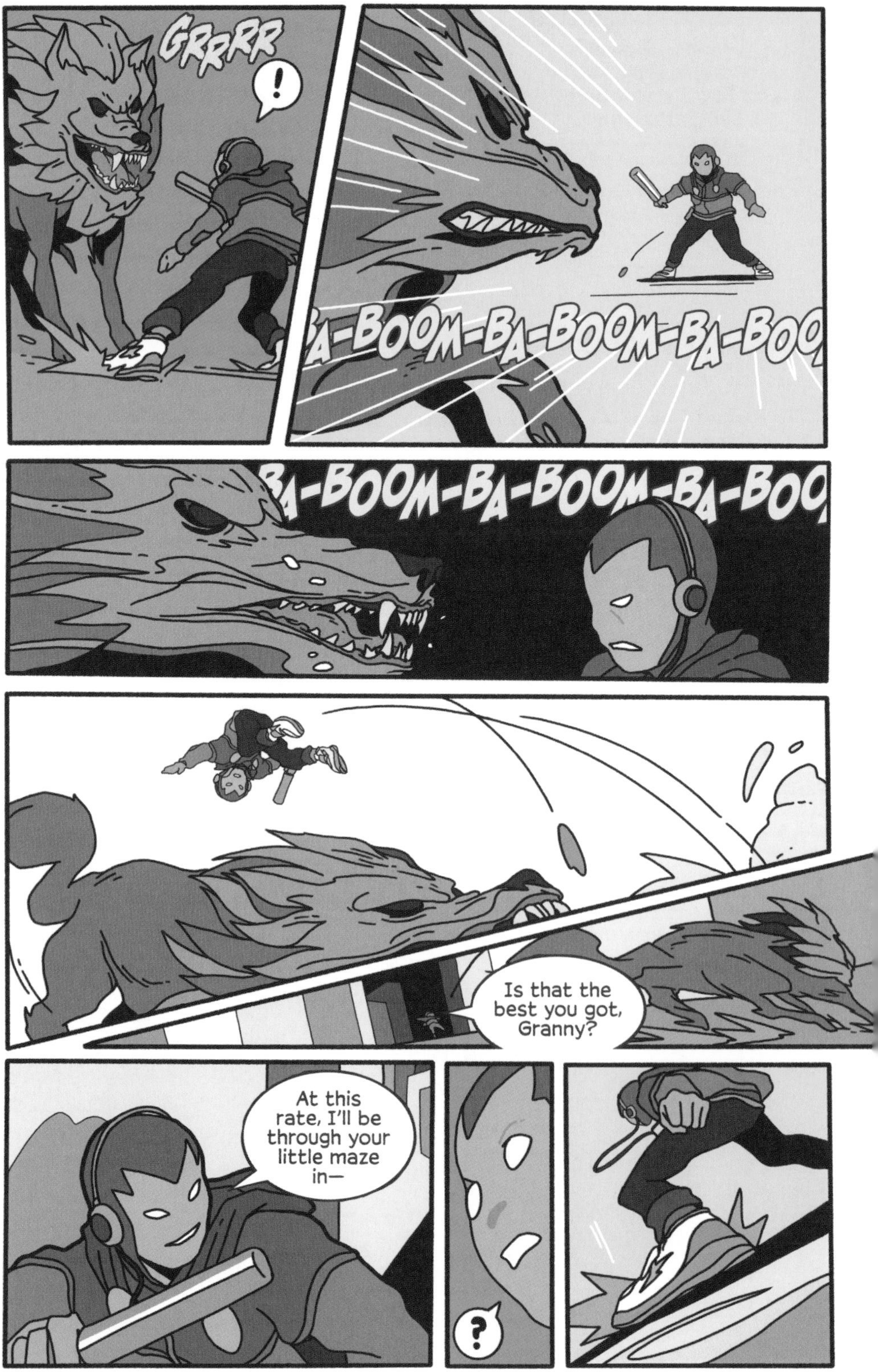
GRRRR
!
BA-BOOM-BA-BOOM-BA-BOO
BA-BOOM-BA-BOOM-BA-BOO
Is that the best you got, Granny?
At this rate, I'll be through your little maze in—
?

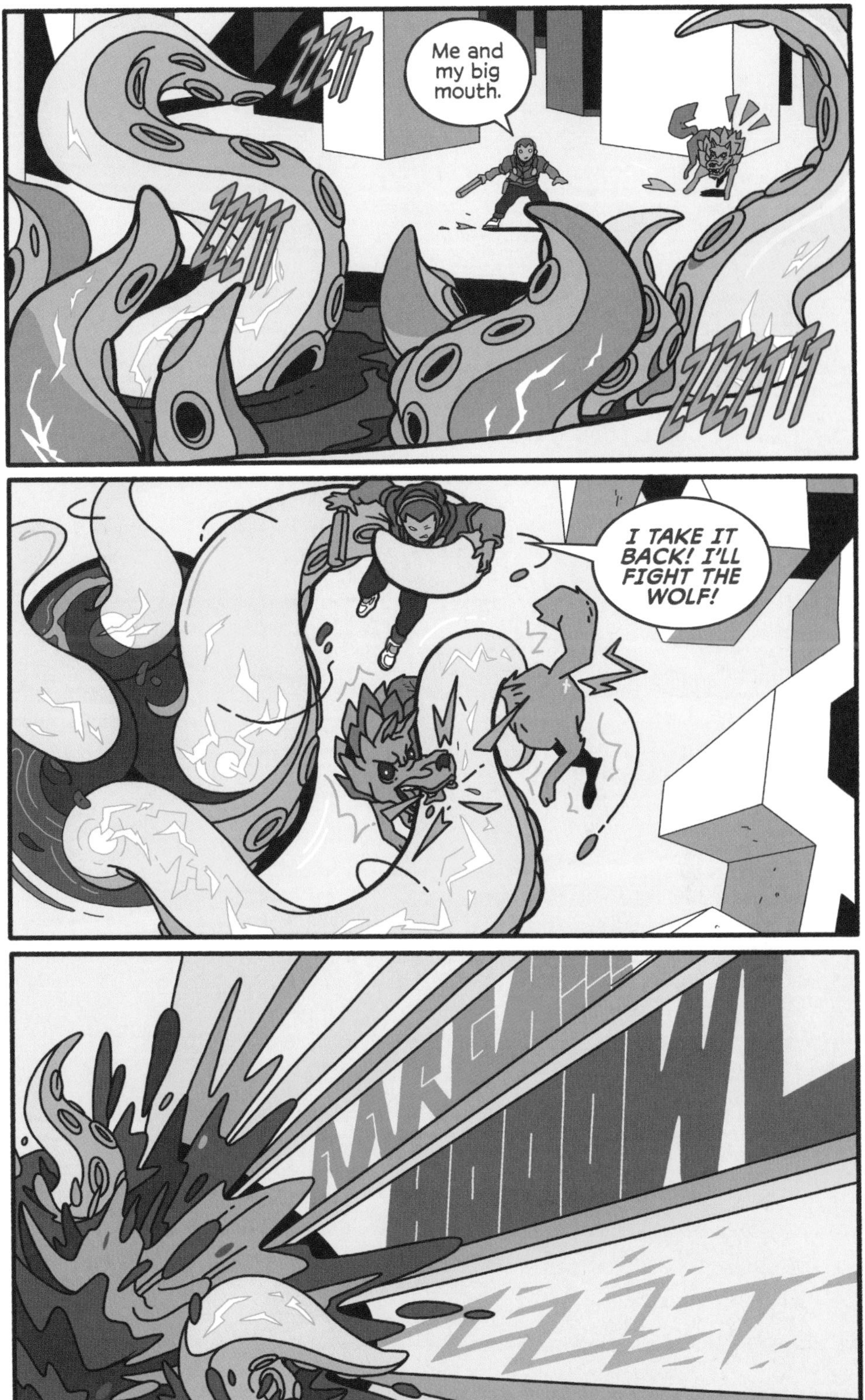
Me and my big mouth.
I TAKE IT BACK! I'LL FIGHT THE WOLF!

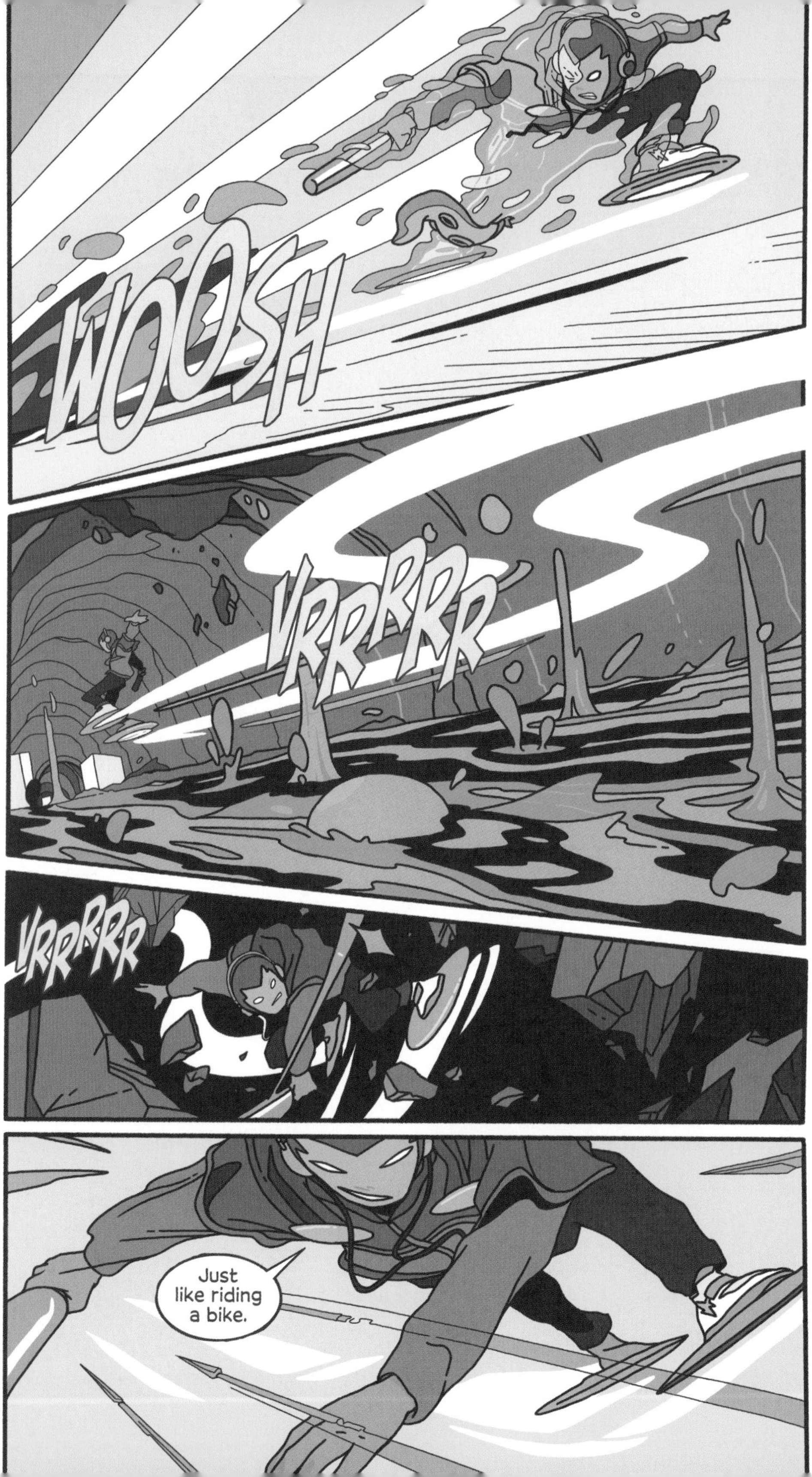
WOOSH
VRRRRR
VRRRRR
Just like riding a bike.

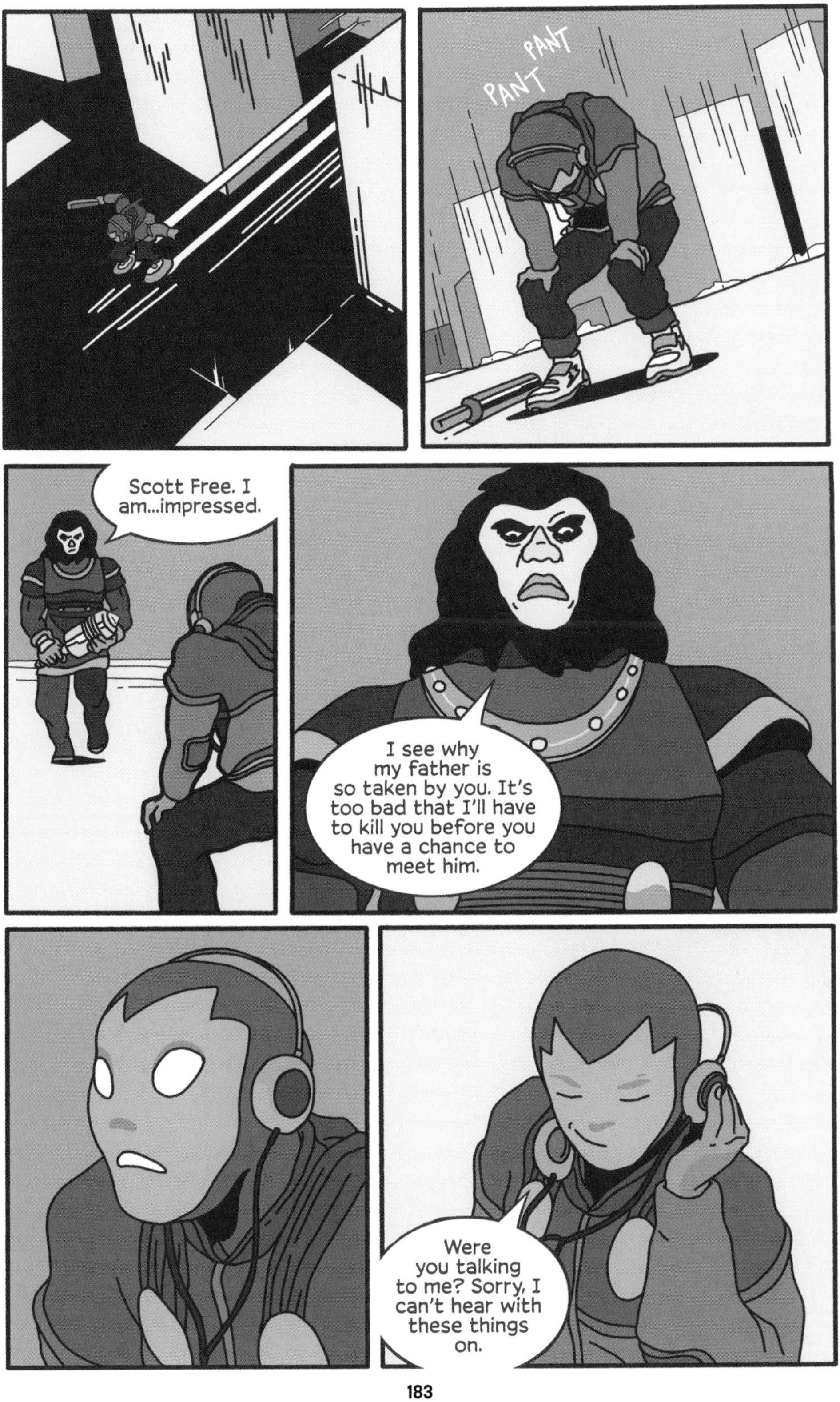
PANT
PANT
Scott Free. I am...impressed.
I see why my father is so taken by you. It's too bad that I'll have to kill you before you have a chance to meet him.
Were you talking to me? Sorry, I can't hear with these things on.

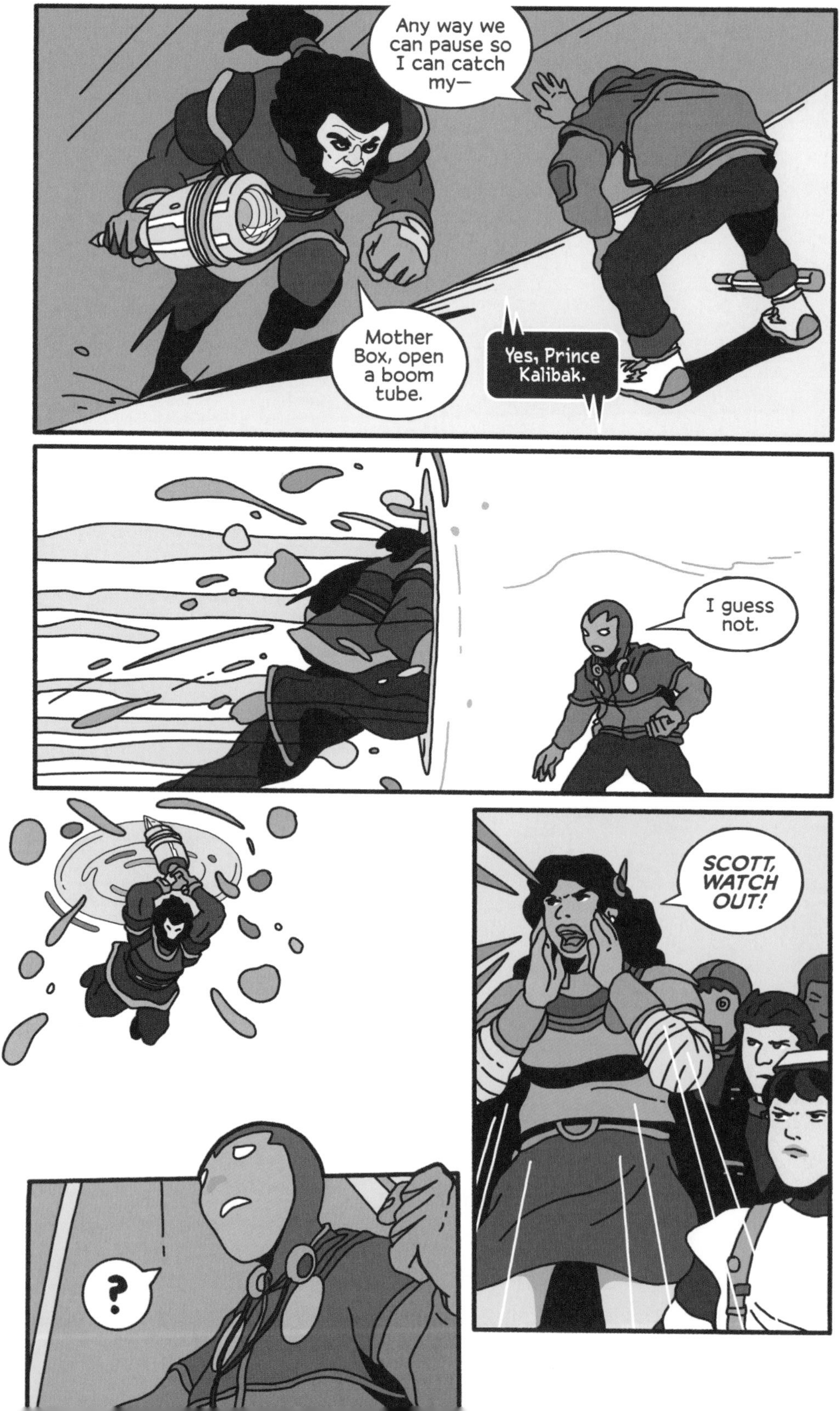
Any way we can pause so I can catch my—
Mother Box, open a boom tube.
Yes, Prince Kalibak.
I guess not.
SCOTT, WATCH OUT!
?

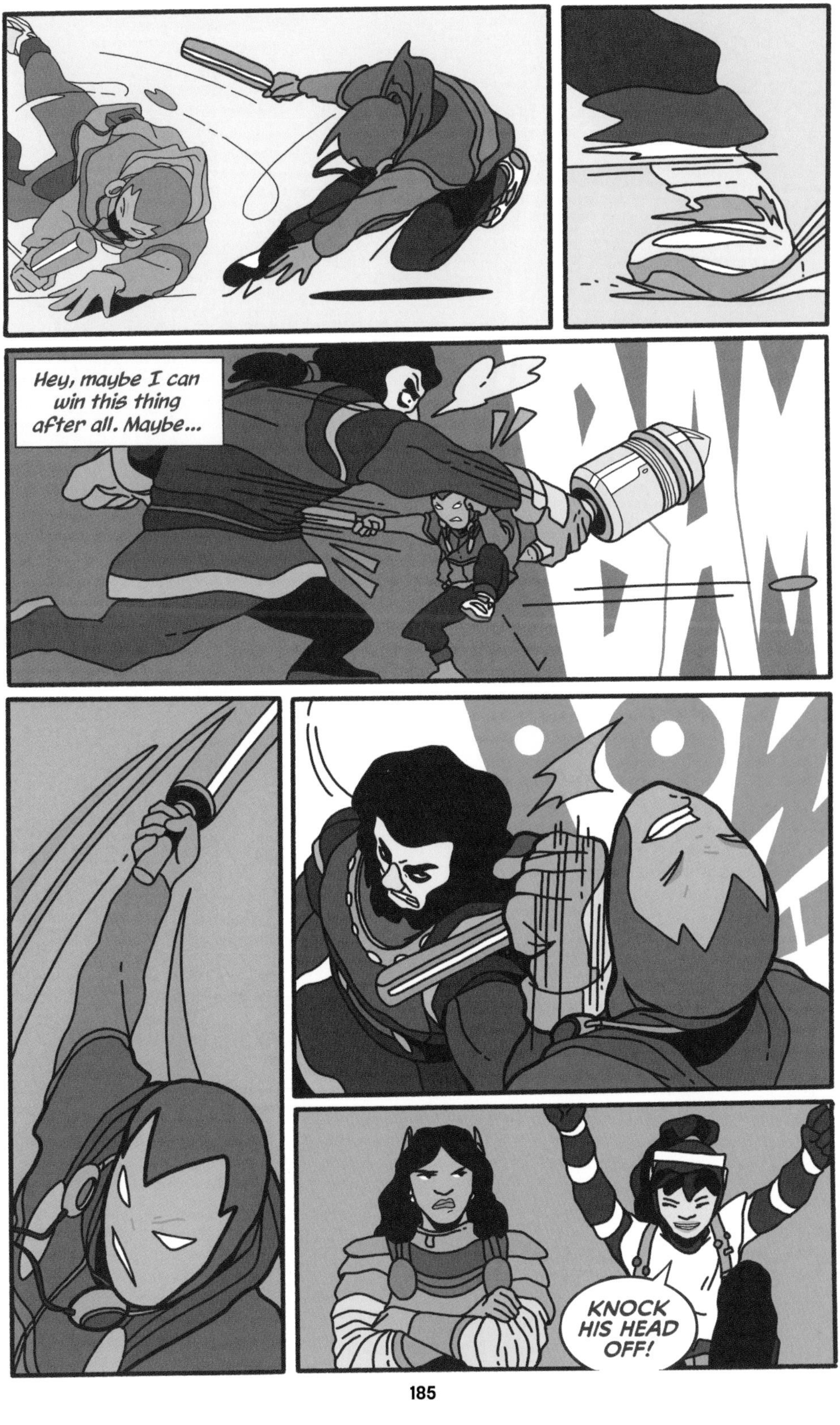
Hey, maybe I can win this thing after all. Maybe...
KNOCK HIS HEAD OFF!

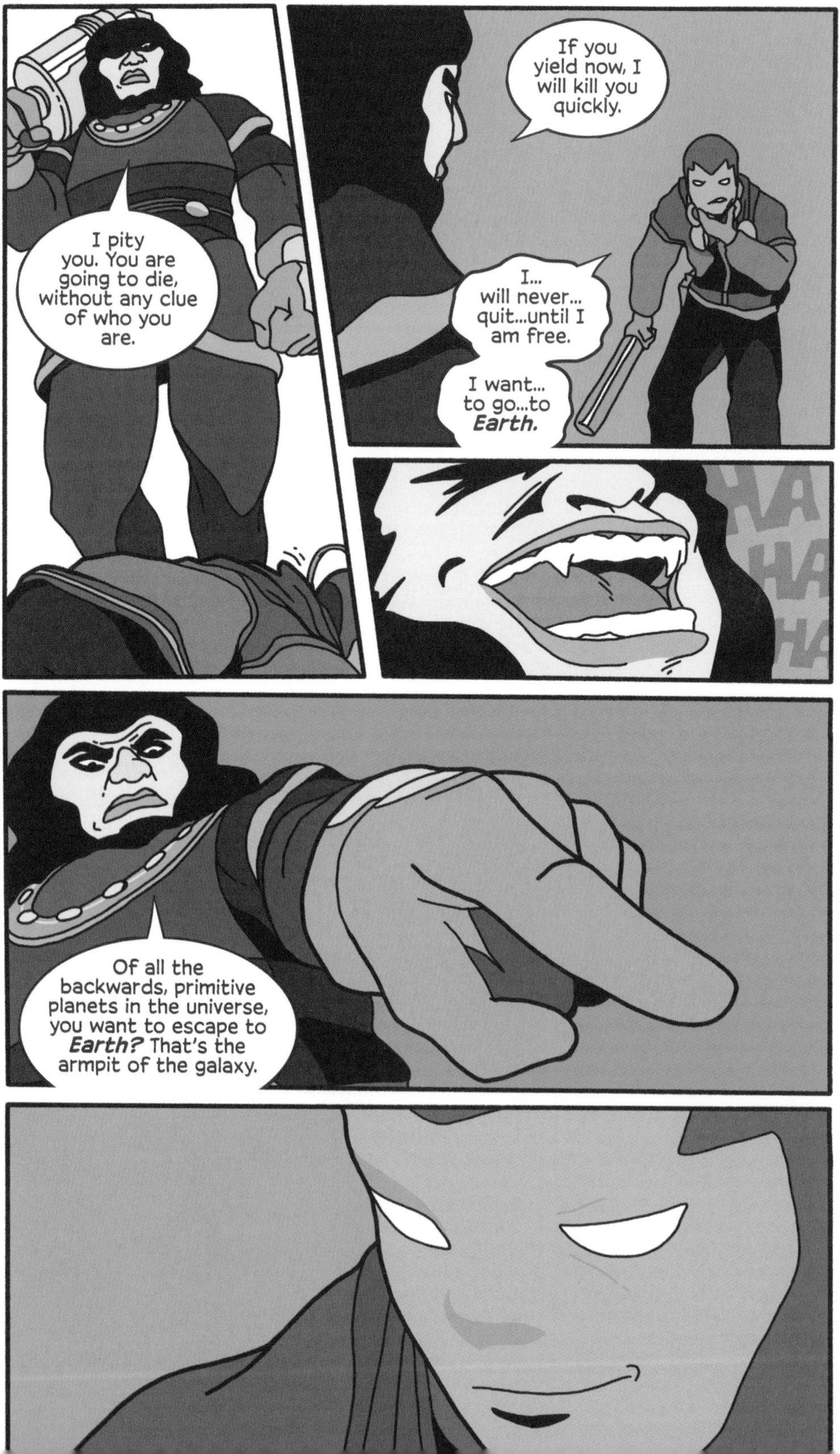
I pity you. You are going to die, without any clue of who you are.
If you yield now, I will kill you quickly.
I... will never... quit...until I am free.
I want... to go...to *Earth.*
HA HA HA
Of all the backwards, primitive planets in the universe, you want to escape to *Earth?* That's the armpit of the galaxy.

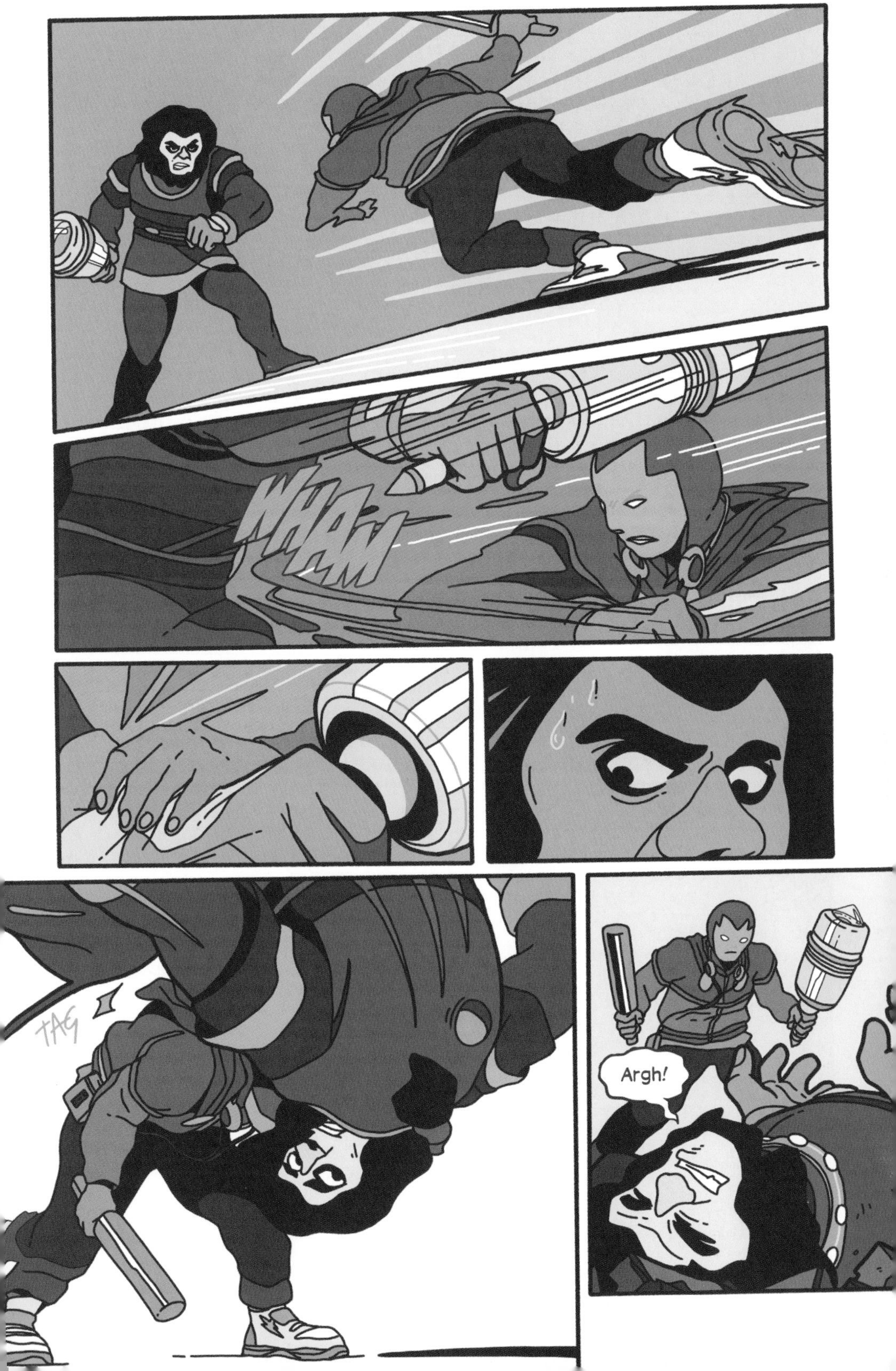
WHAM
TAG
Argh!

Well done, Scott Free. But you're only delaying the inevitable. You're only...

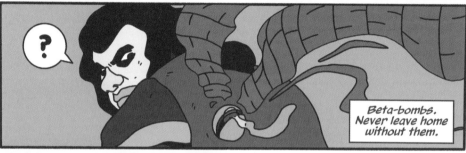

?

Beta-bombs. Never leave home without them.

Koff! Koff!

It's called Ikenberry. It swells your throat. Stops you from breathing.

My *friend* died after ingesting it. I hope you're ready to join him, you bastard!

Gasp!

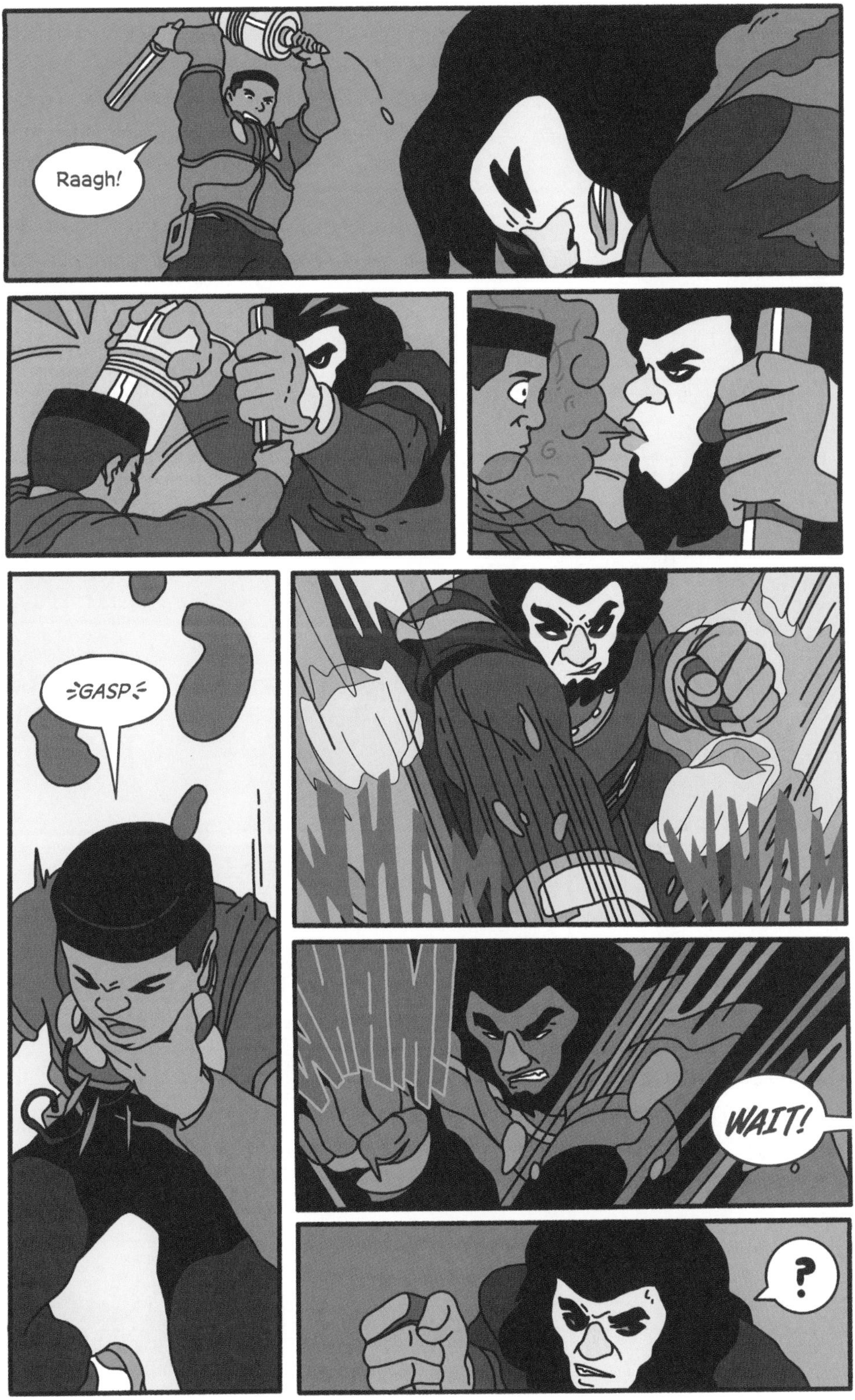
Raagh!
GASP
WHAM
WHAM
WHAM!
WAIT!
?

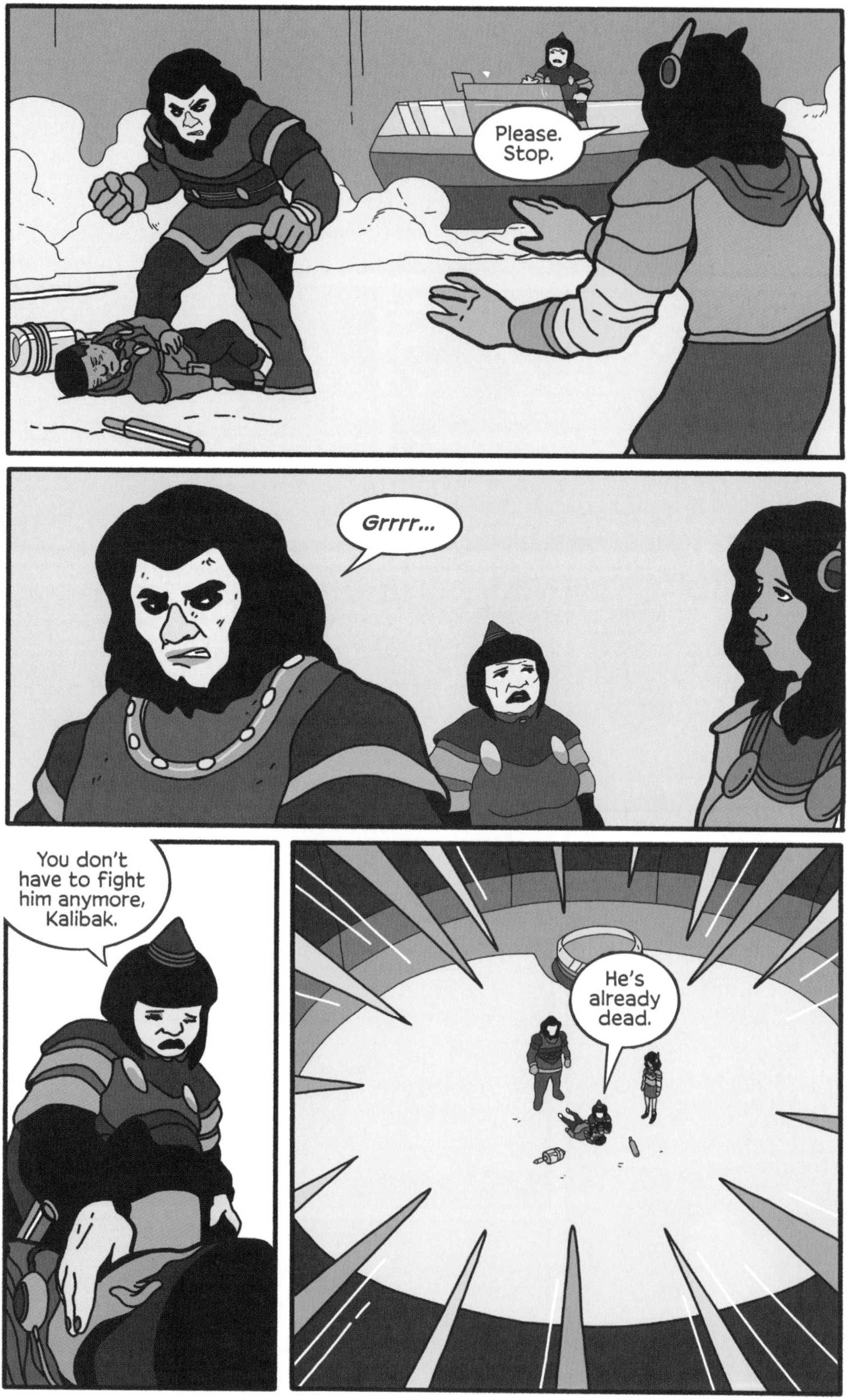
Please. Stop.
Grrrr...
You don't have to fight him anymore, Kalibak.
He's already dead.

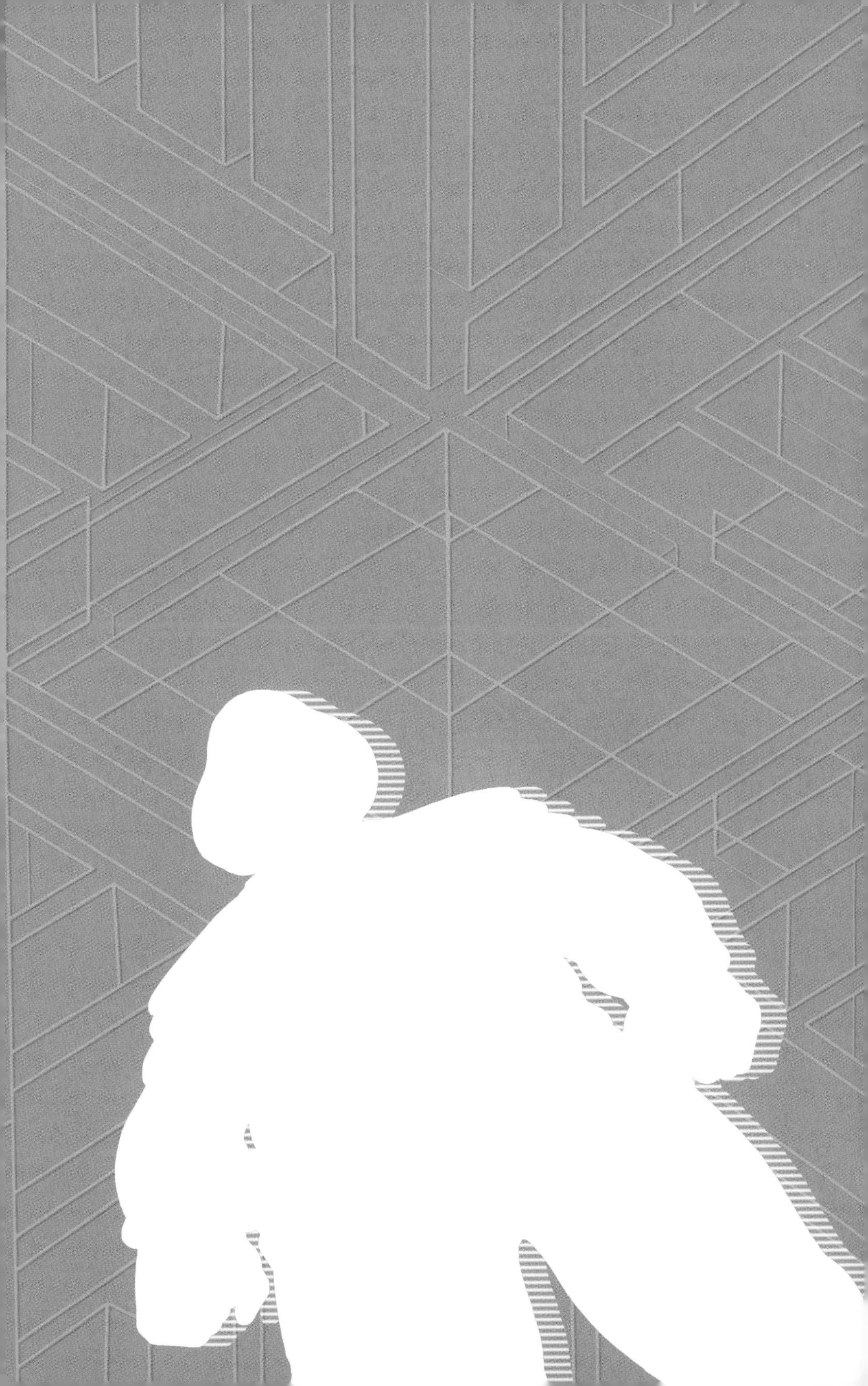

CHAPTER SEVEN

We Are Family

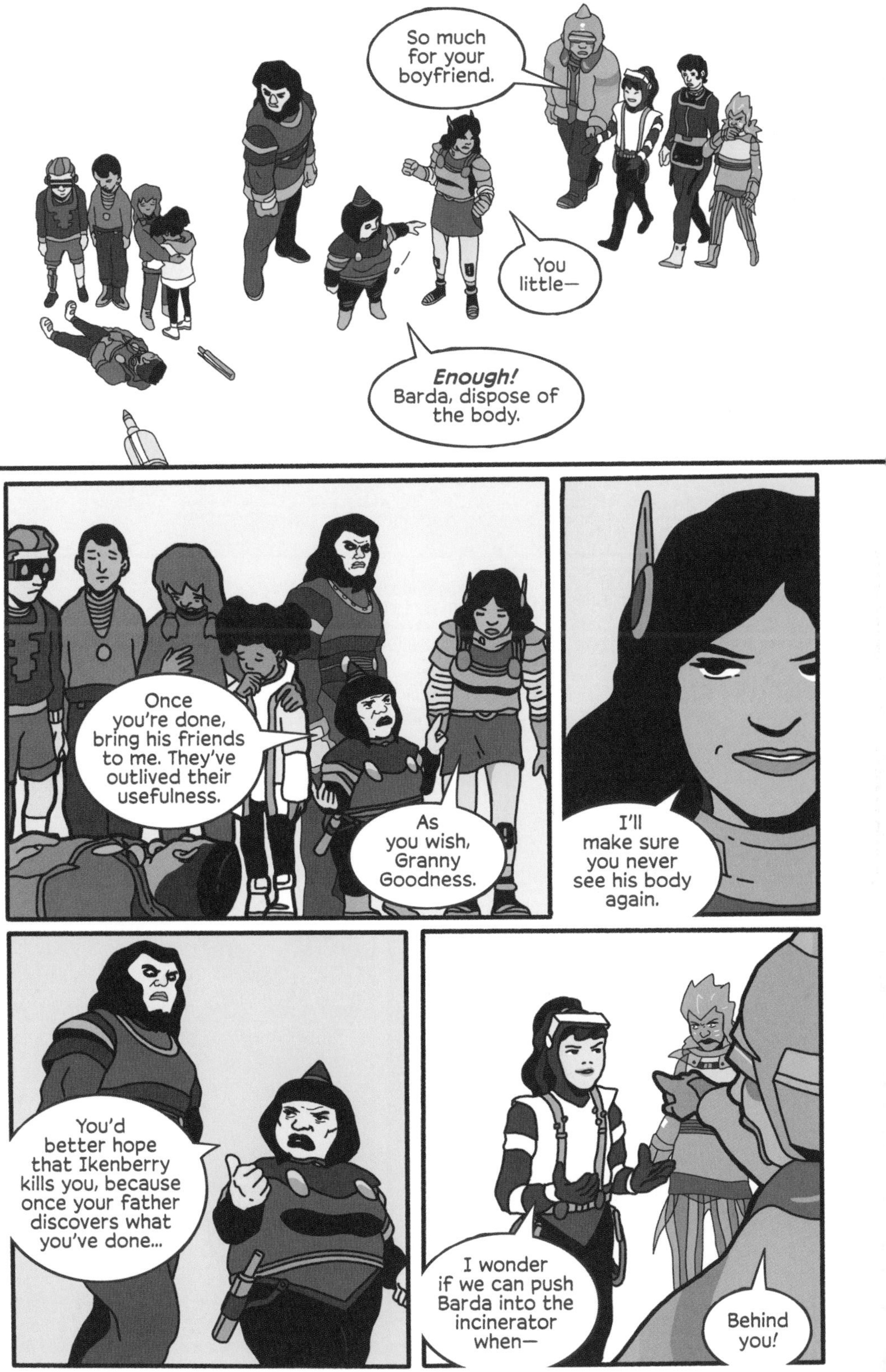
So much for your boyfriend.
You little—
Enough! Barda, dispose of the body.
Once you're done, bring his friends to me. They've outlived their usefulness.
As you wish, Granny Goodness.
I'll make sure you never see his body again.
You'd better hope that Ikenberry kills you, because once your father discovers what you've done...
I wonder if we can push Barda into the incinerator when—
Behind you!

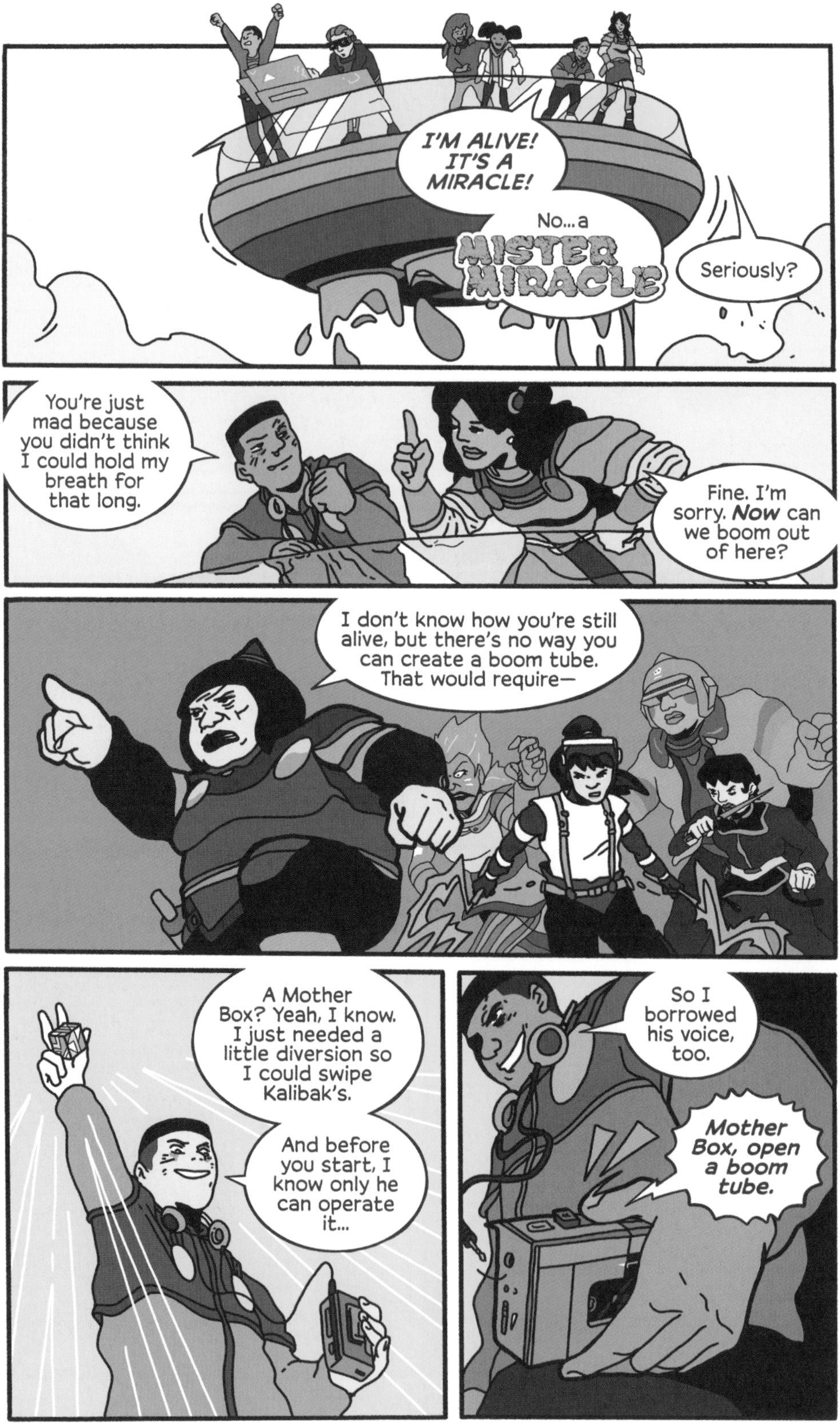
I'M ALIVE! IT'S A MIRACLE!
No...a MISTER MIRACLE
Seriously?
You're just mad because you didn't think I could hold my breath for that long.
Fine. I'm sorry. *Now* can we boom out of here?
I don't know how you're still alive, but there's no way you can create a boom tube. That would require—
A Mother Box? Yeah, I know. I just needed a little diversion so I could swipe Kalibak's.
And before you start, I know only he can operate it...
So I borrowed his voice, too.
Mother Box, open a boom tube.

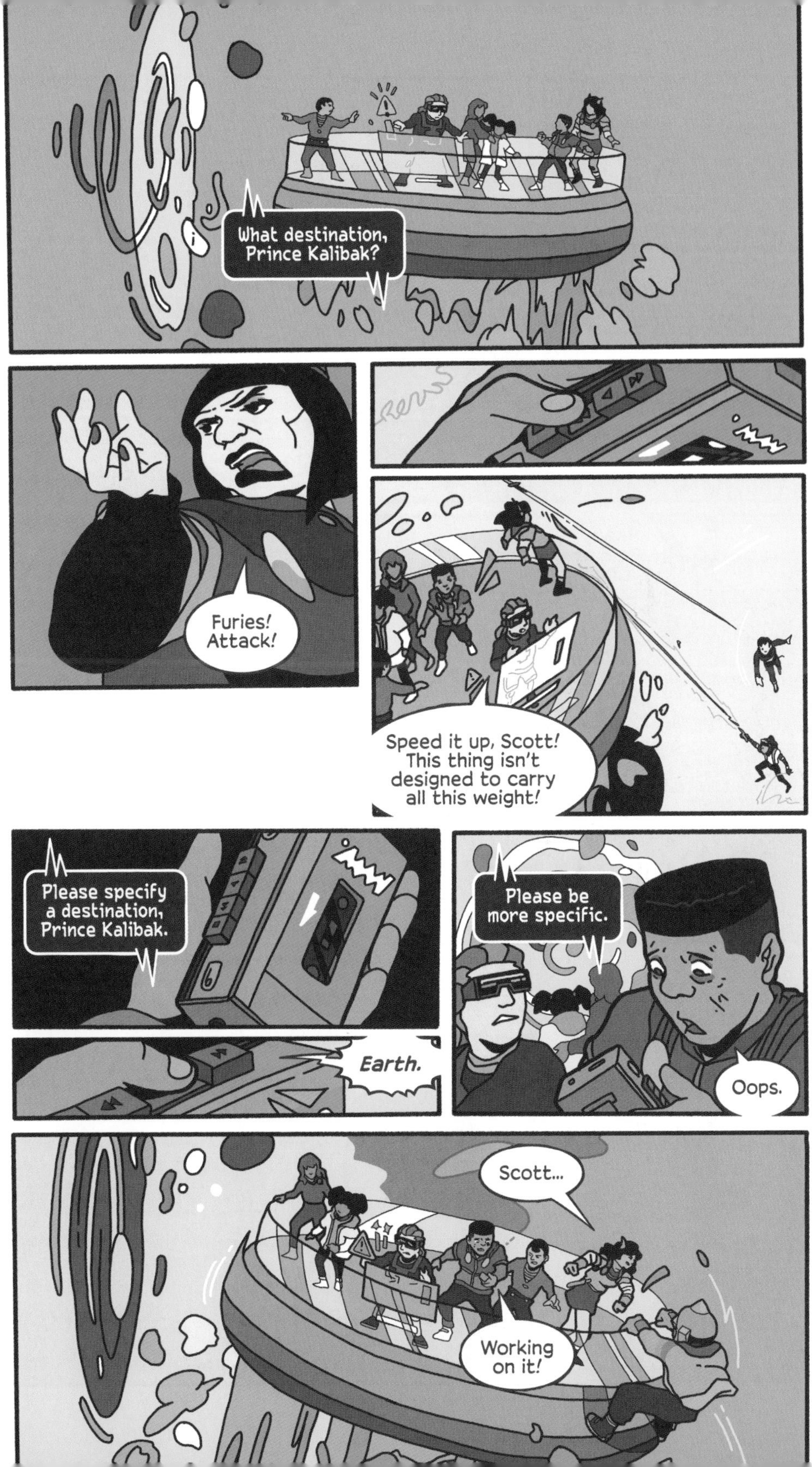
What destination, Prince Kalibak?
Furies! Attack!
Speed it up, Scott! This thing isn't designed to carry all this weight!
Please specify a destination, Prince Kalibak.
Earth.
Please be more specific.
Oops.
Scott...
Working on it!

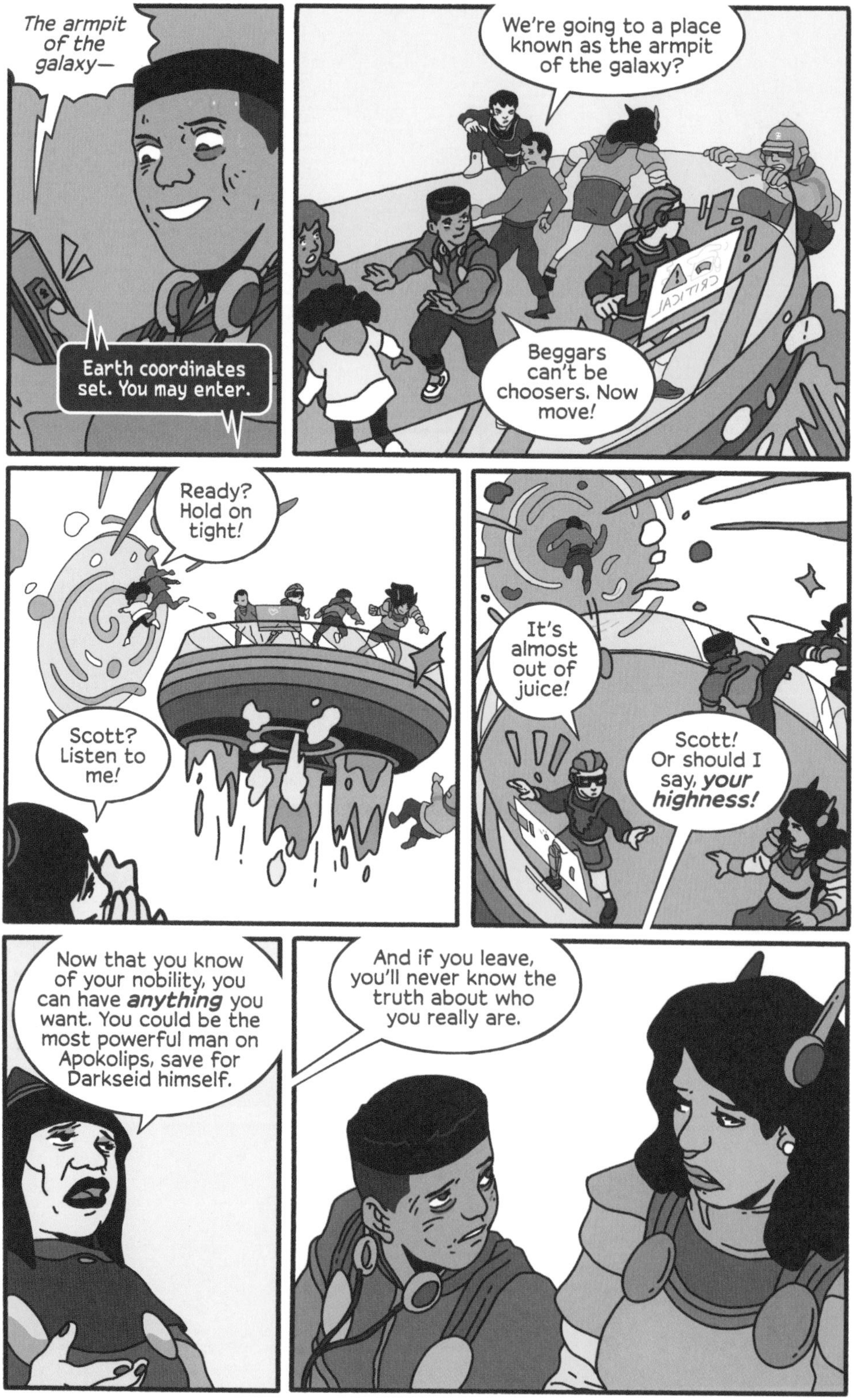

The armpit of the galaxy—
Earth coordinates set. You may enter.
We're going to a place known as the armpit of the galaxy?
CRITICAL
Beggars can't be choosers. Now move!
Ready? Hold on tight!
Scott? Listen to me!
It's almost out of juice!
Scott! Or should I say, ***your highness!***
Now that you know of your nobility, you can have ***anything*** you want. You could be the most powerful man on Apokolips, save for Darkseid himself.
And if you leave, you'll never know the truth about who you really are.

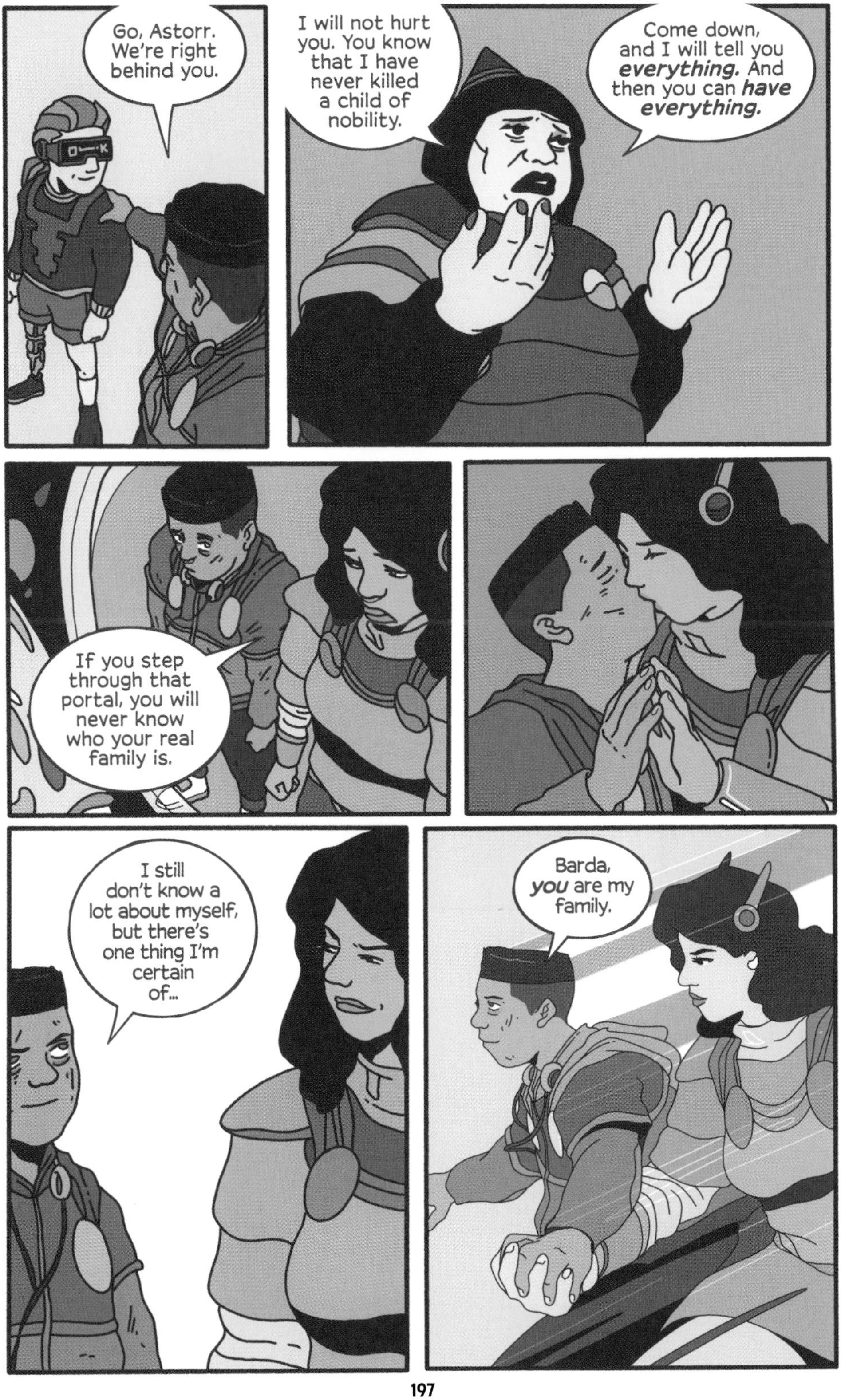

Go, Astorr. We're right behind you.
I will not hurt you. You know that I have never killed a child of nobility.
Come down, and I will tell you ***everything.*** And then you can ***have everything.***
If you step through that portal, you will never know who your real family is.
I still don't know a lot about myself, but there's one thing I'm certain of...
Barda, ***you*** are my family.

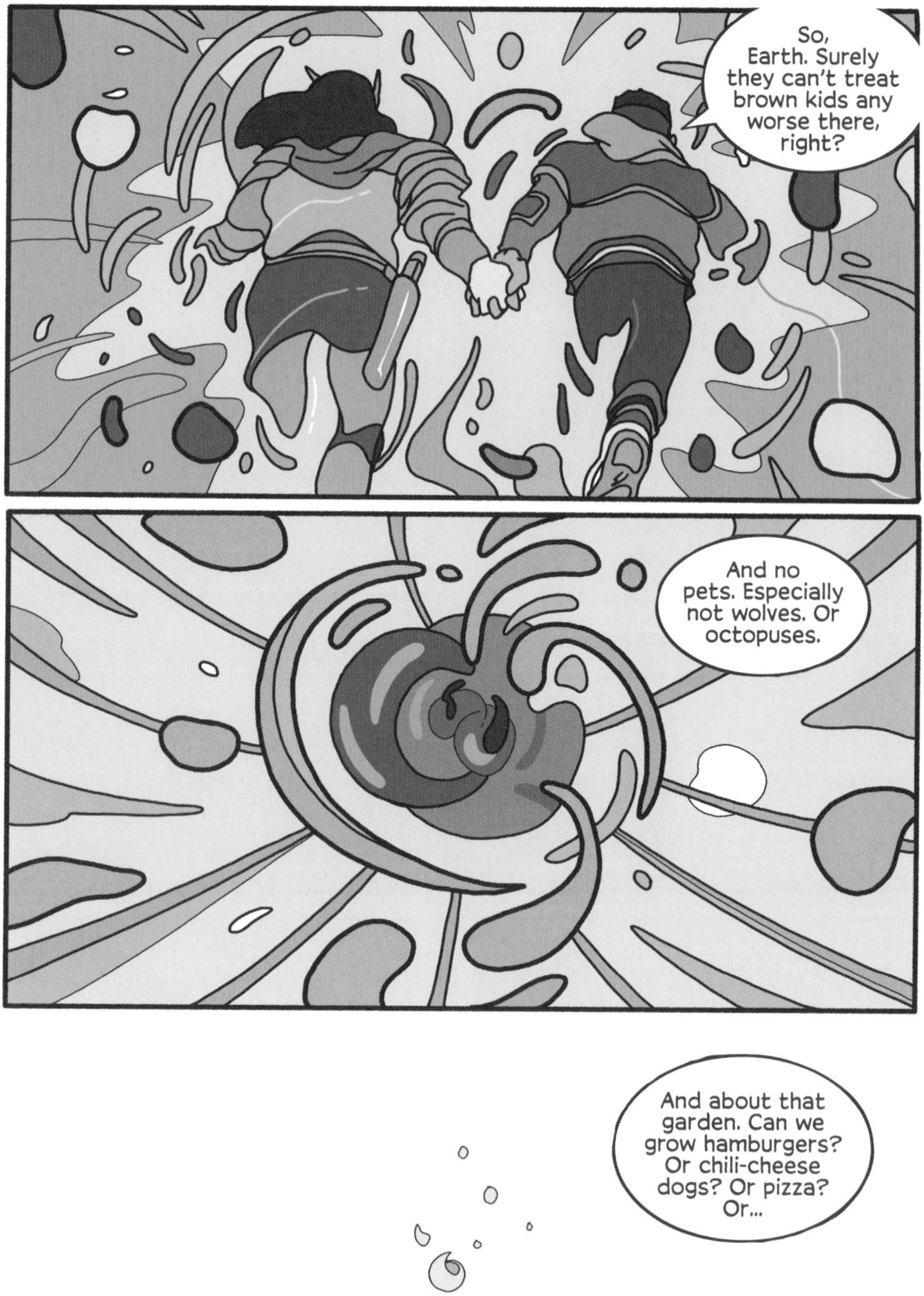
So, Earth. Surely they can't treat brown kids any worse there, right?
And no pets. Especially not wolves. Or octopuses.
And about that garden. Can we grow hamburgers? Or chili-cheese dogs? Or pizza? Or...

RESOURCES

If you, or a loved one, need help in any way, you do not need to act alone. Below is a list of resources that may be helpful to you. If you are in immediate danger, please call emergency services in your area (9-1-1 in the United States) or go to your nearest hospital emergency room.

The Jed Foundation
A nonprofit that exists to protect emotional health and prevent suicide for our nation's teens and young adults. Text "START" to 741-741 or call 1-800-273-TALK (8255). Website: jedfoundation.org.

NAMI: National Alliance on Mental Illness
Provides advocacy, education, support, and public awareness so that all individuals and families affected by mental illness can build better lives. Call the NAMI Helpline Monday through Friday, 10 a.m.-8 p.m. ET at 800-950-6264 or, in a crisis, text "NAMI" to 741-741 for 24/7 confidential, free crisis counseling. Website: www.nami.org

ADAA: Anxiety and Depression Association of America
ADAA's mission focuses on improving quality of life for those with anxiety, depression, OCD, PTSD, and co-occurring disorders through education, practice, and research. Visit their website at www.adaa.org or call them at 240-485-1001 (not a direct service line).

Safe Horizon
The largest provider of comprehensive services for domestic violence survivors and victims of all crime and abuse including rape and sexual assault, human trafficking, stalking, youth homelessness, and violent crimes committed against a family member or within communities. If you need help, call their 24-hour hotline at 1-800-621-HOPE (4673) or visit safehorizon.org.

Varian Johnson is the author of several novels for children and young adults, including *The Parker Inheritance*, which won both Coretta Scott King Author Honor and *Boston Globe/Horn Book* Honor awards; *The Great Greene Heist*, an ALA Notable Book for Children and *Kirkus Reviews* Best Book; and the Eisner-nomiated graphic novel *Twins*, illustrated by Shannon Wright, which won a BCALA Children & Youth Literary Award. Originally from Florence, South Carolina, he received an MFA in writing for children and young adults from Vermont College of Fine Arts and is honored to now be a member of the faculty. Varian currently lives outside of Austin, Texas, with his family.

PHOTO BY KENNETH B. GALL

ILLUSTRATION BY DANIEL ISLES

Daniel Isles is a professional artist committed to artistic practice, observation, themes, and expression to create entire worlds of his own. His unique illustration style has been used within many industries including fashion, music, authorship, and technology. He has worked and collaborated with Apple, DC Comics, Sega, Mighty Jaxx, Kidrobot, Timberland, and Owsla.

Welcome to a brand-new vision of one of comics' most famous tragedies, from *New York Times* bestselling author **Claudia Gray** and illustrator **Eric Zawadzki**.

In this second book of a graphic novel trilogy, two teenagers on opposite sides of the same extinction-level event get drawn deeper into conspiracies that could doom them—if the planet doesn't self-destruct first.

In stores now!

Keep reading for an exclusive sneak peek.

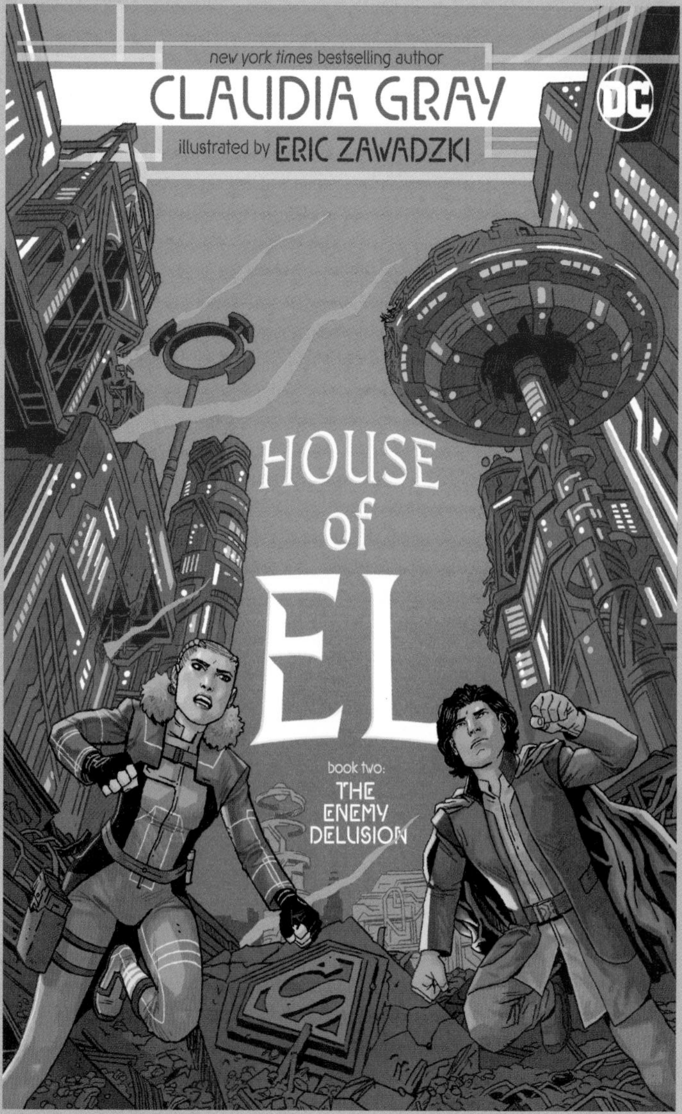

new york times bestselling author
CLAUDIA GRAY
DC
illustrated by ERIC ZAWADZKI
HOUSE of EL
book two:
THE ENEMY DELUSION

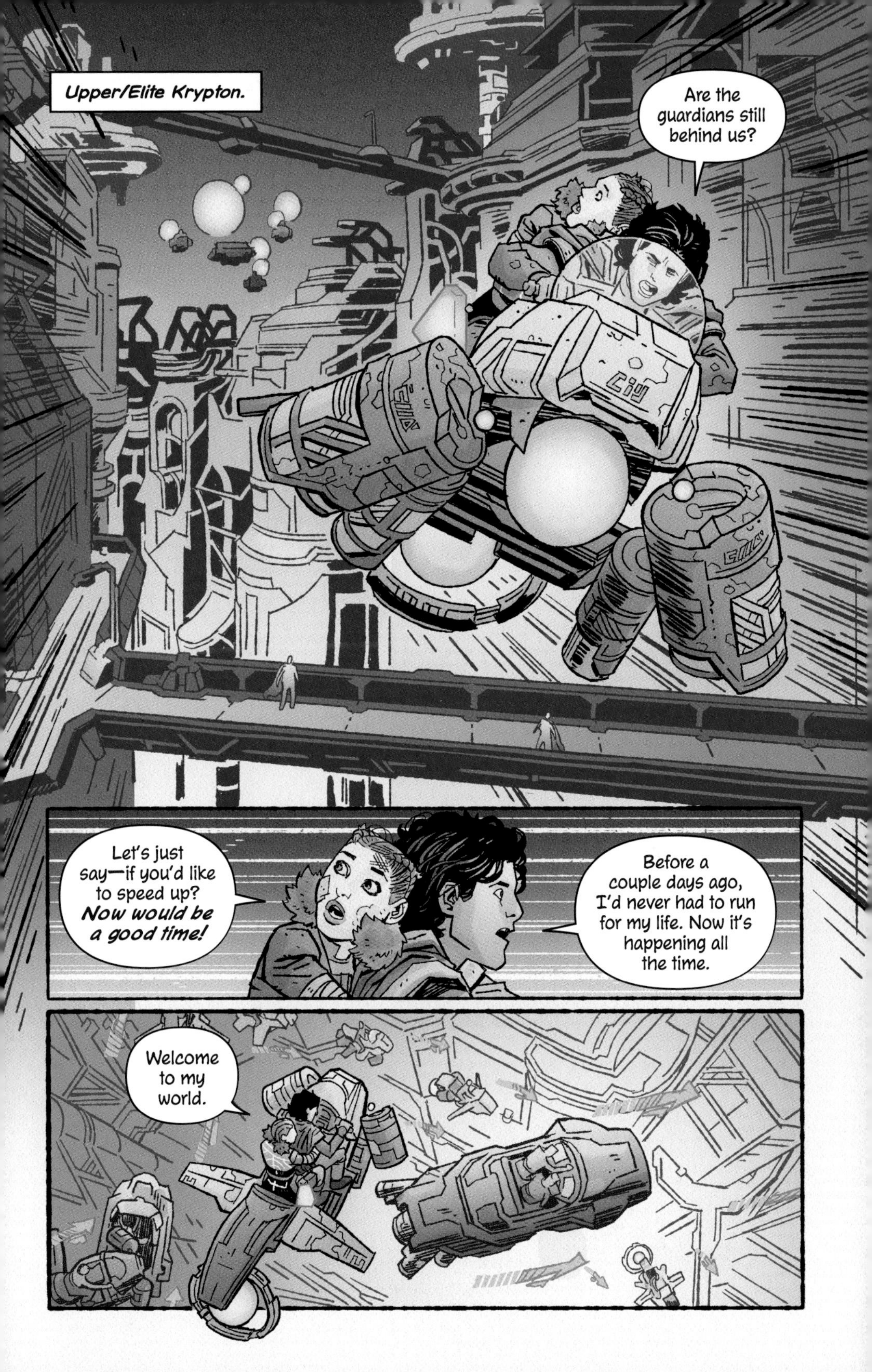
Upper/Elite Krypton.
Are the guardians still behind us?
Let's just say—if you'd like to speed up? *Now would be a good time!*
Before a couple days ago, I'd never had to run for my life. Now it's happening all the time.
Welcome to my world.

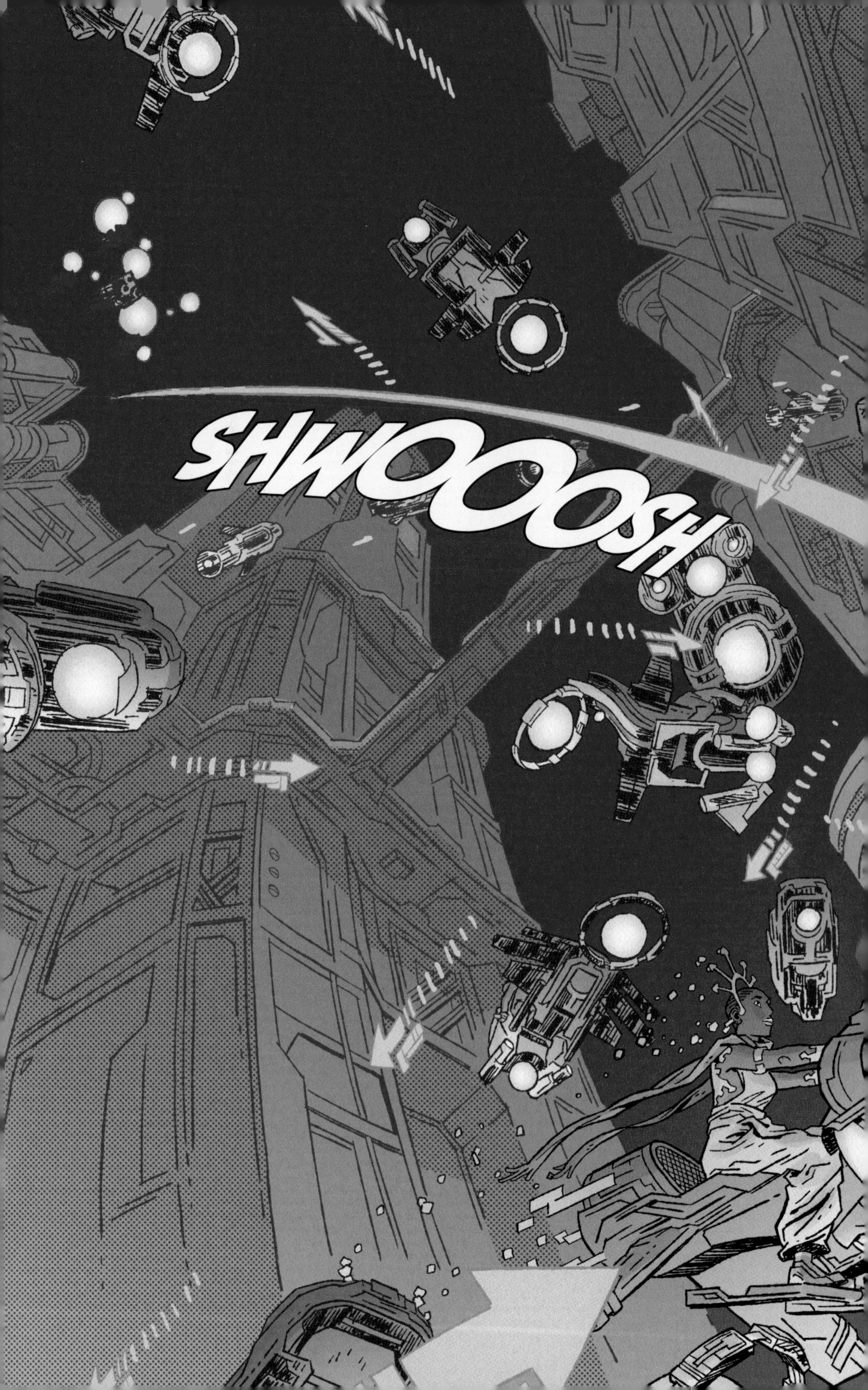
SHWOOOSH

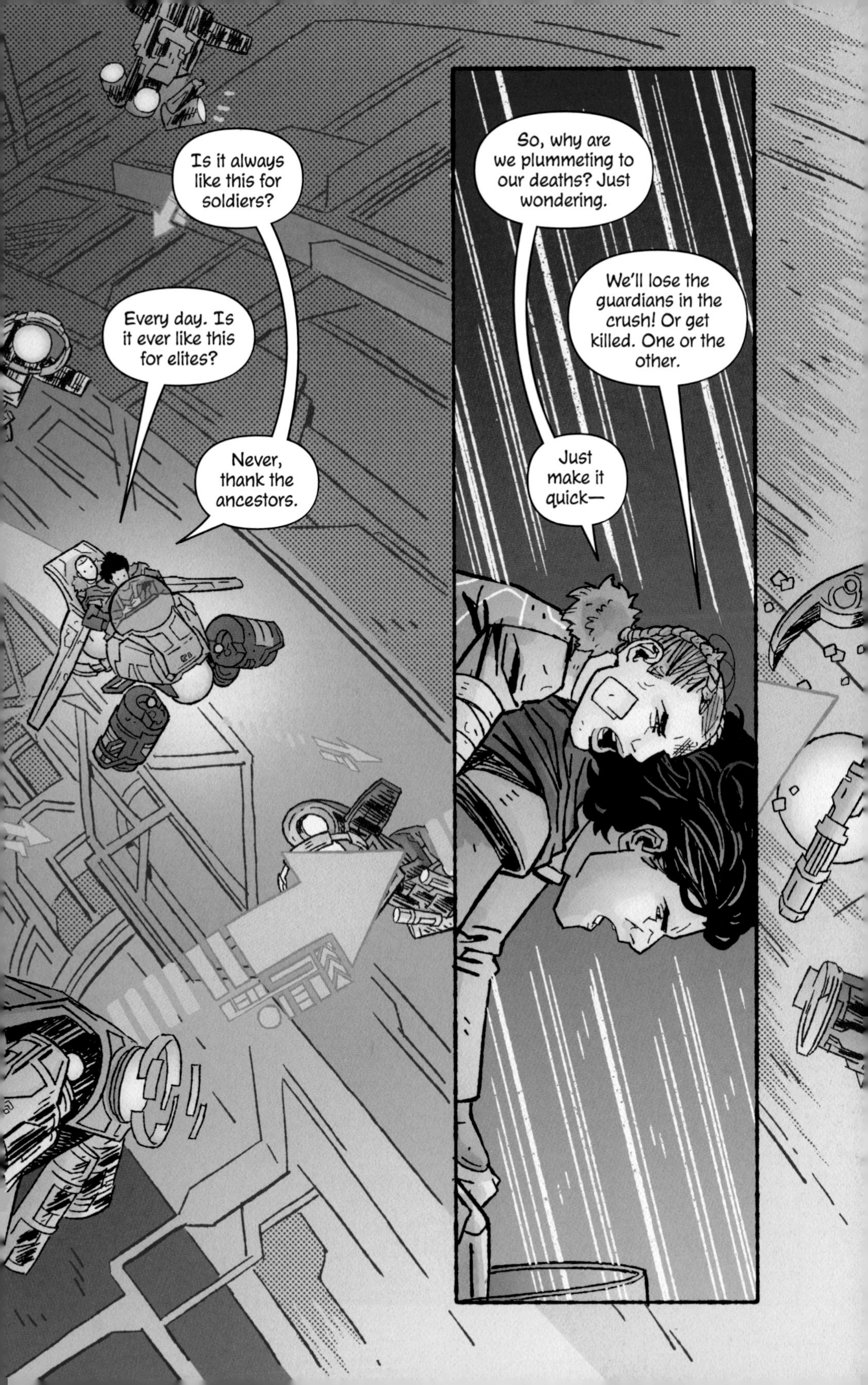
Is it always like this for soldiers?
Every day. Is it ever like this for elites?
Never, thank the ancestors.
So, why are we plummeting to our deaths? Just wondering.
We'll lose the guardians in the crush! Or get killed. One or the other.
Just make it quick—

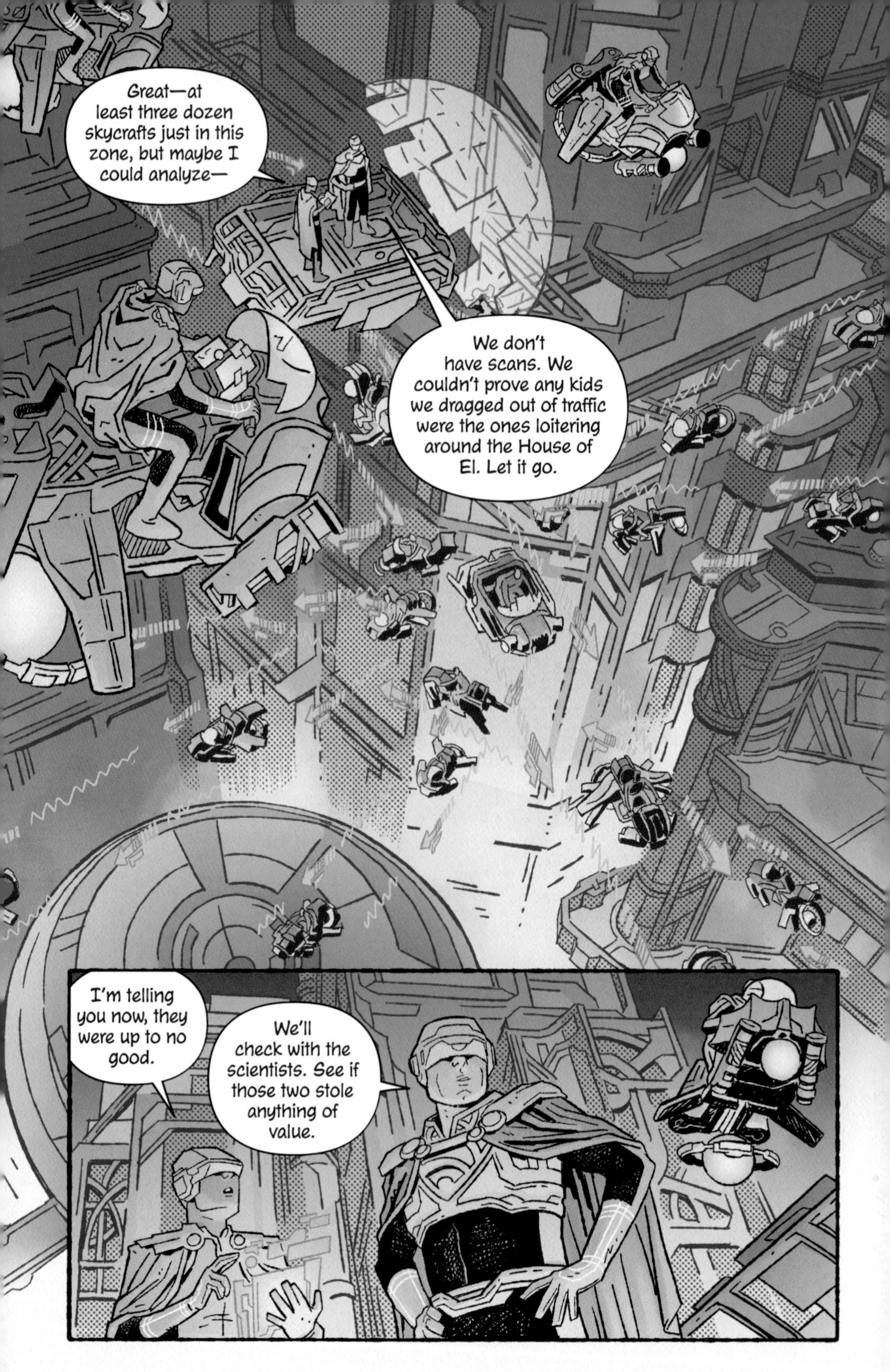
Great—at least three dozen skycrafts just in this zone, but maybe I could analyze—
We don't have scans. We couldn't prove any kids we dragged out of traffic were the ones loitering around the House of El. Let it go.
I'm telling you now, they were up to no good.
We'll check with the scientists. See if those two stole anything of value.

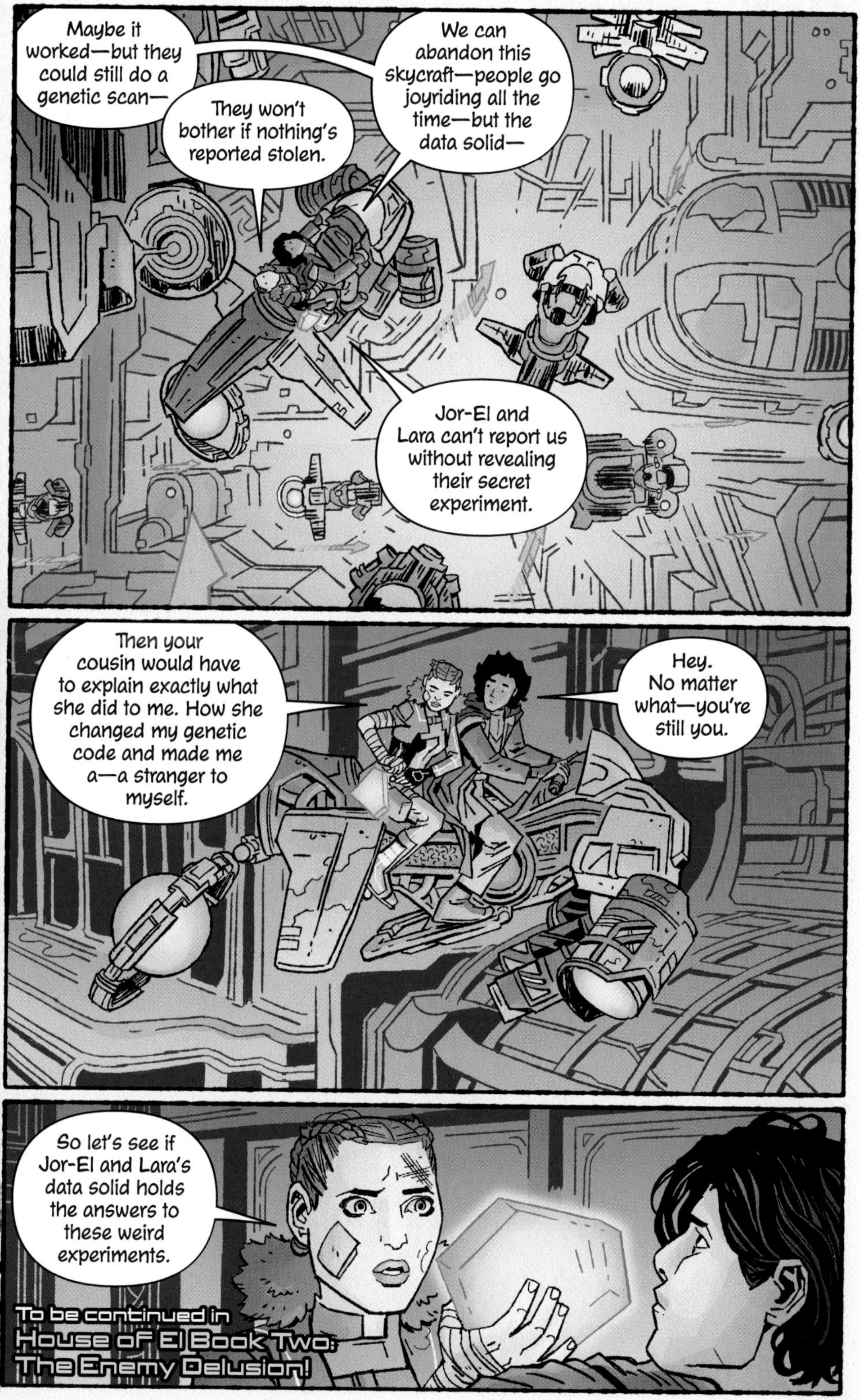
Maybe it worked—but they could still do a genetic scan—
We can abandon this skycraft—people go joyriding all the time—but the data solid—
They won't bother if nothing's reported stolen.
Jor-El and Lara can't report us without revealing their secret experiment.
Then your cousin would have to explain exactly what she did to me. How she changed my genetic code and made me a—a stranger to myself.
Hey. No matter what—you're still you.
So let's see if Jor-El and Lara's data solid holds the answers to these weird experiments.
To be continued in House of El Book Two: The Enemy Delusion!

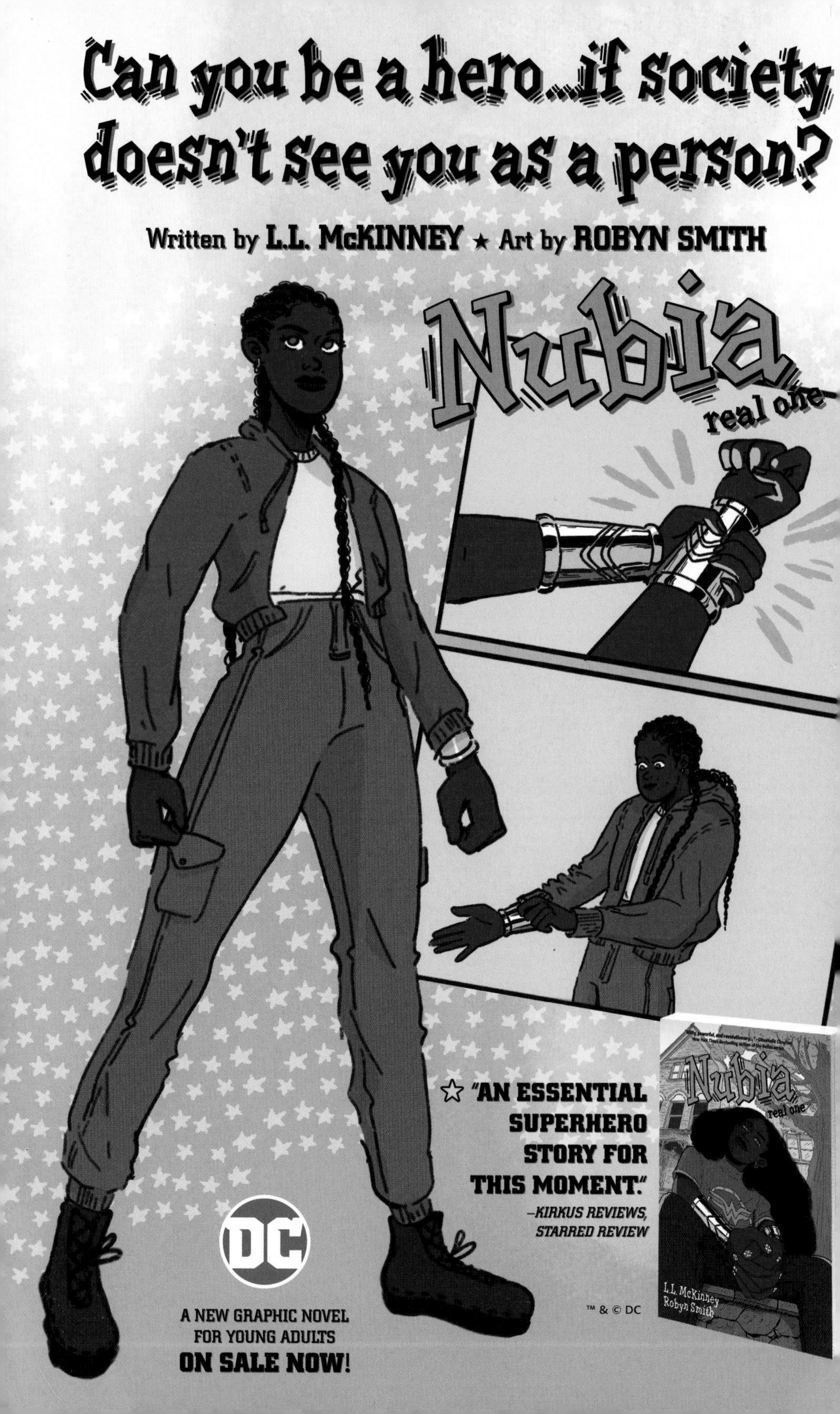
Can you be a hero...if society doesn't see you as a person?
Written by L.L. McKINNEY ★ Art by ROBYN SMITH
Nubia
real one
☆ "AN ESSENTIAL SUPERHERO STORY FOR THIS MOMENT."
–KIRKUS REVIEWS, STARRED REVIEW
DC
A NEW GRAPHIC NOVEL FOR YOUNG ADULTS
ON SALE NOW!
™ & © DC
Nubia
real one
L.L. McKinney
Robyn Smith